Pies

&

Prejudice

BY HEATHER VOGEL FREDERICK

THE MOTHER-DAUGHTER BOOK CLUB

Pies
&
Prejudice

Heather Vogel Frederick

Simon & Schuster Books for Young Readers
New York London Toronto Sydney

For my niece Jane, of course

SIMON & SCHUSTER BOOKS FOR YOUNG READERS
An imprint of Simon & Schuster Children's Publishing Division
1230 Avenue of the Americas, New York, New York 10020
This book is a work of fiction. Any references to historical events, real people, or real locales are used fictitiously. Other names, characters, places, and incidents are products of the author's imagination, and any resemblance to actual events or locales or persons, living or dead, is entirely coincidental.
Copyright © 2010 by Heather Vogel Frederick
All rights reserved, including the right of reproduction in whole or in part in any form.
SIMON & SCHUSTER BOOKS FOR YOUNG READERS is a trademark of Simon & Schuster, Inc.
For information about special discounts for bulk purchases, please contact Simon & Schuster Special Sales at 1-866-506-1949 or business@simonandschuster.com.
The Simon & Schuster Speakers Bureau can bring authors to your live event. For more information or to book an event, contact the Simon & Schuster Speakers Bureau at 1-866-248-3049 or visit our website at www.simonspeakers.com.
Also available in a Simon & Schuster Books for Young Readers hardcover edition
Book design by Tom Daly
The text for this book is set in Chapparral Pro.
Manufactured in the United States of America • 0316 OFF
First Simon & Schuster Books for Young Readers paperback edition September 2011
6 8 10 9 7
The Library of Congress has cataloged the hardcover edition as follows:
Frederick, Heather Vogel.
Pies & prejudice / Heather Vogel Frederick.
p. cm.—(Mother-Daughter Book Club)
Summary: Four girls, and their mothers, continue their mother-daughter book club via videoconference between Massachusetts and England, reading Jane Austen's *Pride and Prejudice*, and try to put friendship before romance.
ISBN 978-1-4169-7431-4 (hc)
[1. Interpersonal relations—Fiction. 2. Mothers and daughters—Fiction. 3. Clubs—Fiction. 4. Books and reading—Fiction. 5. Concord (Mass.)—Fiction. 6. England—Fiction. 7. Austen, Jane, 1775—1817—Fiction.] I. Title.
PZ7.F87217Pi2010
[Fic]—dc22
2010015921
ISBN 978-1-4424-2019-9 (pbk)
ISBN 978-1-4169-8259-3 (eBook)

AUTUMN

"I declare after all there is no enjoyment like reading! How much sooner one tires of anything than of a book!"

—*Pride and Prejudice*

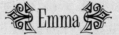

Emma

> "'I often think,' said she, 'that there is nothing
> so bad as parting with one's friends.
> One seems so forlorn without them.'"
>
> —*Pride and Prejudice*

Jess stares at me in disbelief. "What do you mean, you're moving to England?"

"It's just for a year."

Her blue eyes well up with tears. "Just for a year! It might as well be forever!"

I knew that breaking the news to my best friend would be hard, but I didn't know it was going to be *this* hard.

"Wouldn't you want to go, if you were me?" I ask softly.

The thing is, I really want Jess to be happy for me, the way I was for her last year when she got the scholarship to Colonial Academy. Of course I'll be sad to leave Concord, and all of my friends, especially her. But still—*England!*

I only found out about it myself an hour ago, at breakfast. My dad spilled the beans.

"Your mother and I have a surprise for you," he told my brother and me.

"Another one?" I asked. Two weeks ago, he got a call from a publisher in New York. They're going to publish his novel, the one he's been working on for years.

"Yes, another one," he replied. "Your mother and I have been talking, and we know we should probably put the money I'm getting into fixing a few things around the house, or replacing our rattletrap of a car, or beefing up your college funds."

"But . . ." my mother prodded.

He smiled at her. "But," he continued, "for once in our lives, we decided to throw caution to the wind and do something a little crazy."

My brother and I exchanged a wary glance.

"It's all your mother's fault," my father said, trying to look disapproving but failing miserably. "She's wanted to go back to England ever since she was a graduate student there."

"We're going to England?" I said eagerly.

"Actually," he replied. "We're moving there."

Our complete and utter shock must have showed on our faces because my mother started to laugh. "It's just for a year," she added.

"*A year?*" my brother repeated. I was too stunned to say anything at all.

I'm still stunned, but happy, too. I try and explain this to Jess. "I know, I know," I tell her. "You should have seen us when my parents told Darcy and me this morning."

Jess, who has been staring down at the floor, looks up at the mention of my brother's name. She's had a crush on him since elementary school.

"Is he excited about going?" she asks, wiping her nose on her sleeve.

I lift a shoulder. "We're both still getting used to the idea, you know?"

Which is kind of stretching the truth. Darcy was furious.

"What am I supposed to tell the football coach?" he'd demanded. "School is starting in a couple of weeks and there's a good chance he's going to pick me to be quarterback this year."

"Tell him the truth," my dad replied. "That an amazing opportunity came up for your family, and that you'll be back in time for your senior year. You can be quarterback then."

Darcy leaned back in his chair and whooshed out his breath. I could tell that moving out of the country was definitely not part of his plan. My brother is a total sports nut. He lives, breathes, eats, and sleeps football, hockey, and baseball. Did they even have those sports in England, I wondered?

"Where are we going to live?" I asked.

"I'm working on that," said my mother. "I found a website that arranges house swaps."

My brother frowned. "What's that?"

"Exactly what it sounds like," my father told him. "You live in someone else's home while they live in yours."

"You mean other people will be using our stuff?" I didn't like the sound of this idea at all. Someone else would be sleeping in my bunk bed, and using the rolltop desk that used to be my grandfather's? Someone else would be looking at the old-fashioned wallpaper with the yellow roses that my mother and I picked out for my room after reading *Anne of Green Gables*?

My mother reached over and patted my shoulder. "Don't worry, honey," she said. "Your dad and I have it all figured out. We'll rent a storage unit for the things we don't want anybody else using while we're gone."

"What about your job?" My mother works at the Concord Public Library.

"They're letting me take a leave of absence."

"A sabbatical," my dad explained.

My mother has not just one but two master's degrees—one in library science, and the other in English literature. Her specialty? Jane Austen. She's a complete Austen nut, which is why my name is Emma and my brother's is Darcy. We're named for a couple of characters in Jane Austen's novels.

"People have been swapping homes successfully for many years," she continued, swinging into full librarian "let me give you all the information" mode. "It's a very practical and economical arrangement. The service I've been working with has found someone they think would be perfect for us."

"Who?" I muttered.

"A professor who's coming here on a teaching exchange at Harvard.

Heather Vogel Frederick

He and his family had a house lined up in Cambridge, but it fell through at the last minute."

"He's a history professor, so Concord would be the perfect spot for him," added my father. "He wants to learn about the American Revolution from our perspective."

He was right about that. Concord, Massachusetts, is practically the birthplace of the American Revolution. One of the first major battles of the war was fought here, and just about every inch of our town oozes history.

"The family's name is Berkeley," my mother told us. "Professor Phillip Berkeley and his wife Sarah. They have two boys, Simon and Tristan."

They had names. They were real people. This was really happening.

It was more than just the thought of strangers living in our house and messing with our stuff that had my head spinning, though. It was the thought of missing out on my freshman year at Alcott High, and leaving Stewart Chadwick, my sort-of boyfriend, behind. If I went to England, the two of us wouldn't be able to work together on the school newspaper the way we'd planned. Plus, there were all my other friends, too, not to mention Pip, the golden retriever puppy I co-owned with my skating teacher. And what about—

"Book club!" I blurted. "What about our mother-daughter book club?"

My mother bit her lip. "That's one piece of the puzzle I haven't figured out yet. I'm sorry, sweetheart. Maybe you can write to them, the way you do with your Wyoming pen pal."

"So this is a done deal?" said my brother. "We don't have a say in it at all?"

My parents were looking worried by now. I guess they'd been expecting us to be all thrilled about their announcement.

"Come on, kids! Where is your sense of adventure?" my father coaxed. "This is a once-in-a-lifetime opportunity! We'll be back here in Concord before you know it."

"A whole year is hardly 'before you know it,'" Darcy said icily. "I vote no." And with that he got up from the table and stalked out of the room.

I sat there feeling uncertain and confused. Was my brother right? Should I boycott the idea too?

My mother slid a piece of paper across the table to me. "The agency e-mailed me a picture of the Berkeleys' house this morning. It's called Ivy Cottage."

Reluctantly, I glanced down at the picture, then drew in my breath sharply. Ivy Cottage looked like something out of a fairy tale. It was small and snug, like our house, but it was made of stone, not wood. The front door was nearly obscured by the thick ivy that clambered up the cottage's exterior, and the windows had little diamond crisscross patterns across them. There was something else, too. "It has a *thatched roof*?"

My father grinned. "How cool is that?"

Pretty cool, I thought. Trying not to show my excitement, I asked casually, "How old is it?"

Heather Vogel Frederick

"They're not exactly sure," my mother replied. "They think it was built sometime during the reign of Queen Elizabeth the First."

"Are you serious?" said Darcy, poking his head around the corner. He must have been listening from the hall. My brother is kind of a history buff.

Sensing they were winning us over, my parents pressed the point.

"The village where the Berkeleys live is supposed to be beautiful," said my mother. "It's on the outskirts of the city of Bath."

"Jane Austen territory," added my father with a wink. "Catnip to your mother."

He took her hand across the breakfast table. My parents hold hands a lot, which isn't so bad at home but can be really embarrassing in public. My dad always says he and Mom are as crazy about each other as they are about books.

He smiled at us. "You'll get to ride a double-decker bus to school, and we plan to do a lot of exploring on the weekends. England, Scotland, maybe a bit of Europe, too."

"What about Melville?" Darcy asked, reaching down to stroke our elderly marmalade-colored cat, who had finished his breakfast long ago and was hoping for some of ours.

"The Berkeleys are willing to look after him for us if we'll look after their parrot," my mother replied.

All of this replays in my head as I'm sitting here beside Jess. I slant a glance in her direction. She's still brooding. I give her blond braid a tug. "The Berkeleys have a parrot," I tell her, hoping this will pique her interest. Jess loves animals. "And check out their house." I take the picture my mother gave me out of my pocket and pass it to her. "It's called Ivy Cottage, and it's almost four hundred years old!"

"Half Moon Farm is nearly that old," Jess grumbles. "Why don't you just move in here with us?"

I sigh. Jess is being stubborn. I hate it when she gets like this.

I know why she's so upset, of course. It's not just because I'm going away. It's because Darcy's going away too. Jess almost didn't go back to Colonial Academy this year because she was so looking forward to being at Alcott High with him. Ultimately, she decided that she might as well continue at her private school, because she'd still get to see Darcy all the time anyway. She practically lives at my house, the way I practically live at hers.

Jess takes the picture from me and stares at it. "You're really going, aren't you?"

I nod. "Uh-huh."

A tear trickles down her cheek. "What am I going to do without you for a whole year?"

"You'll still have Cassidy and Megan and, well, Becca," I remind her. Becca Chadwick is in our book club, but she's not exactly our favorite person in the whole world. "And Frankie and Adele and all your other friends at Colonial. And we can e-mail and IM each other every day."

She gives me a sidelong glance. "Promise?"

"Promise." I bump her shoulder with mine. "What are best friends for?" I look at my watch. "I've got to go. I promised my mom I'd be back in time for lunch. She says we have a ton of stuff to do to get ready. We're leaving in two weeks."

"Have you told Stewart yet?"

"Nope. You were first on the list. Remember? BFBB?"

This earns me a halfhearted smile.

Best friends before boyfriends. Jess and I made a pact this summer. I almost broke it this morning, though. I had to ride right by Stewart's house on my way over here to Half Moon Farm and I was really tempted to stop and tell him first. But I didn't. And now here I am, holding up my end of the bargain, and Jess isn't excited for me at all. Not one bit. I feel like a deflated balloon.

I try not to show my disappointment, though. I know this is hard for her.

"When are you going to tell him?"

"Right now," I reply, strapping on my bike helmet.

"How about the rest of the book club?"

I grin. "They've probably already heard. My mom was on the phone with Cassidy's mom when I left, and you know the mother-daughter book club grapevine."

I give her a quick hug good-bye and head downstairs. Pedaling down Old Bedford Road a few minutes later, though, I start to worry. What if breaking the news to Stewart is even harder than telling Jess?

When I reach his house, I prop my bike against the wrought-iron fence that surrounds his front yard and head for the front door. Becca answers my knock. "Hey, Emma," she says, not sounding too thrilled to see me. But then, she never does. "What's up?"

"Um, is Stewart around?"

It still bugs Becca a little that her brother likes me. She jerks her thumb toward the hallway leading to the kitchen. "He's out in the backyard with Yo-Yo."

"Thanks," I reply. "I'll go around."

I skim back down the front steps and trot around the edge of the house, stopping abruptly when I almost collide with Mrs. Chadwick's bottom—smaller and less alarming than it used to be, thanks to a couple of years' worth of yoga classes, but still not something you'd want to meet in a dark alley, as my father would say. The bottom in question is sticking straight up in the air at the moment because Mrs. Chadwick is bent over, weeding. She spots me and straightens up.

"Hi, Emma!" She wipes her brow, and her gardening glove leaves a broad streak of dirt on her forehead.

I squelch a smile. "Hi, Mrs. Chadwick."

"Big news, huh?"

My heart sinks. She's heard about England, then, which means she's probably told Stewart. I'd hoped to get to him first. "Um—"

"Didn't Becca tell you? I'm going back to school." I must look surprised at this, because she adds, "I'm going to become a landscape designer."

Mrs. Chadwick has been going through a bit of a midlife crisis. At least that's what my parents call it. It started last year when she got a drastic new hairdo and started wearing all these outrageous clothes. Maybe it's over now, because compared to that, a degree in landscape design seems pretty tame.

"Sounds like fun," I tell her.

She nods enthusiastically. "I decided to get a head start, before classes begin. I need the practice, and my garden needs a makeover."

I glance around at the piles of mulch and clippings and dirt mounded everywhere, wondering if this is going to be another of Mrs. Chadwick's misadventures, just like her "whole new me" was last year. It looks like a giant mole has attacked her yard. The outside of the Chadwicks' house is just as formal as the inside, what with the wrought-iron fence and tall, stiff hedges that circle the property and the carefully placed shrubs patrolling the lawn at regular intervals. Not a daffodil is ever out of place; not a rosebush dares drop a petal on the perfectly mown grass. A row of small bushes severely clipped into ornamental shapes used to march around the house's foundation. What they were supposed to be, I'm not sure. I always thought they looked like chicken nuggets. Now, though, they've been uprooted and are lying on the ground like a row of sleeping soldiers.

"Do you know where Stewart is?" I ask.

"He and Yo-Yo are back there somewhere," she replies, waving her trowel vaguely toward the shed. "Would you like some lemonade? I think I'll take a break and make some."

"Thanks," I tell her. "Maybe in a while."

As I cross the lawn, I can hear Stewart talking to his dog. I flatten myself against the shed and peer around the corner, trying to sneak up on the two of them, but the second I poke my nose out Yo-Yo spots me. With a gleeful bark, he hurls himself through the air and a second later I'm lying flat on my back in the grass with his paws planted on my shoulders. I am one of Yo-Yo's favorite people.

"Hey, boy," I say, breathless, squirming to avoid his slobbery dog kisses. "Good to see you, too."

Yo-Yo is a Labradoodle, and the sweetest dog in the entire world next to Pip. He's not very well trained, though.

"Where are your manners?" scolds Stewart. He grabs Yo-Yo's collar and pulls him off me, then reaches out a hand and helps me to my feet.

"Hi," I say, a little breathless. We stand there holding hands, beaming at each other. I suddenly remember my parents at the breakfast table this morning doing the same thing, and that reminds me why I'm here. "I, uh, have something to tell you."

"You won the Nobel Prize for literature."

"Shut up! I'm serious."

"You were named the first teenage poet laureate of the United States."

"Stewart!"

"Sorry," he replies, grinning. Stewart loves to tease me. "What's up?"

"Um, I don't really know how to say this, so I'll just say it. We're moving to England."

Stewart's smile fades. He stares at me, openmouthed. *Uh-oh*, I think. Just like Jess.

"It's only for a year," I add hastily, and explain my parents' plan.

Stewart doesn't take his eyes off me as I talk. He has beautiful eyes, deep gray with a thick fringe of dark lashes. I love to look at them. Right now, though, I'm just relieved to see that he doesn't have the same deer-in-the-headlights look that Jess did when I broke the news to her.

"A whole year, huh?" he says when I'm done talking.

I nod.

"So you won't be going to Alcott High, obviously."

I shake my head.

"And we won't be working on the school newspaper together."

I shake my head again. "Not this year."

I can tell by the way he's chewing the inside of his cheek that he's thinking things over. That's another thing I really like about Stewart. He always thinks things through.

He lets go of my hand and leans down to grab the tennis ball by his feet, then throws it—hard. It soars across the yard and Yo-Yo tears off after it. Stewart turns back to me and before I realize what's happening, he puts his arms around me. And then, just like that, as if he's done it a million times before, he kisses me.

It's a real, proper kiss this time too, not a peck on the cheek or a forehead kiss like before. Maybe it's because he didn't give me any advance warning, but I don't feel awkward at all. All I feel is thrilled.

My heart is pounding like it's trying to leap out of my chest. Stewart's is too, I can feel it. I close my eyes and kiss him back, trying to memorize every single thing about this moment. I don't ever want to forget it as long as I live. I don't want to forget the warm sunlight filtering down on us through the branches of the apple tree overhead, or the distant buzz of a neighbor's lawnmower, or the sound of Yo-Yo's happy bark as he brings the ball back and drops it at our feet. And I especially don't want to forget the way Stewart's lips feel against mine.

It's a perfect first kiss.

There's only one problem.

I'm moving to England.

Heather Vogel Frederick

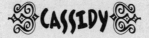

CASSIDY

"'My dear Mr. Bennet,' said his lady to him one day, 'have you heard that Netherfield Park is let at last?'"
—*Pride and Prejudice*

My stepfather wads up his napkin and chucks it at the TV in disgust. "Aw, come on!"

"You should have had that one!" I groan in agreement.

The camera zooms in for a close-up, and the outfielder in question looks away in embarrassment, as if he can hear us. Even though he's a moron for fumbling such an easy pop fly, I can't help feeling a little sorry for him. I know exactly what it feels like to mess up like that in public. I've had my fair share of mess-ups playing hockey. It must be worse, though, knowing you've done it in front of a gazillion disappointed fans.

The Red Sox are having a mixed season so far this year. They've been doing okay at home—one benefit of having a stepfather who's nuts about sports, and baseball in particular, is that he springs for tickets to Fenway Park as often as he can, so I've been to a ton of games this summer—but the minute they hit the road, it all falls apart. Like today, they're in Kansas City and the Royals are beating the pants off them. Our outfield has completely collapsed, plus nobody's batting worth beans. I could do a better job.

I heave a sigh and reach for another slice of pizza. A piece of pepperoni slides off and lands tomato sauce-side down on the couch. I shoot Stanley a guilty look, but he's not paying attention and even if he were, he probably wouldn't say anything. This is another benefit of having Stanley Kinkaid for a stepfather—he's really easygoing. Stuff that drives my mother nuts never seems to bug him. He doesn't pester me about my manners all the time, or bark at me when I forget and chew with my mouth open or accidentally spill something or let a burp slip out now and then.

I pick up the piece of pepperoni and pop it in my mouth, then wipe up as much tomato sauce as I can with the hem of my T-shirt. Mom would have a cow if she saw me, but she isn't here. She's out in California helping my older sister Courtney get settled at UCLA. We were supposed to go too, but it turned out that Courtney's freshman orientation was the same week as my hockey camp. Stanley offered to stay home with me, which was really nice of him. He hasn't complained once, even though I know he misses Mom and my baby sister, Chloe, and even though he's been spending an extra two hours in the car every day hauling me and my gear over to the rink in Acton in the mornings and home again in the afternoons.

Stanley's definitely growing on me.

Heather Vogel Frederick

"Like moss," he joked, when I told him so the other day after he let me order takeout from our favorite Chinese restaurant.

But it's true. He can be a pain sometimes, but we both like the same things—sports, fast food, TV, all that good stuff. This is the first time I've been with him all by myself for more than a few hours, and we've had a great time. All week long it's been eat, sleep, hockey, and Red Sox. What could be better? Plus, we've had almost all our meals in here watching the games, which I normally never get to do. Mom is all about families having dinner together at the dinner table, and that definitely doesn't include junk food or eating in front of the TV.

The other thing my mom is all about is cleaning. She keeps our house spotless. Partly that's because our old Victorian is the set of her TV show, *Cooking with Clementine*, and she's always saying she doesn't want to be disgraced on national television, and partly it's because she's a neat freak. So is my sister Courtney. I have no idea whether Chloe is too—she's not even walking yet, so vacuuming is out of the question— but I know for sure I missed out on that particular gene.

I think Stanley did too, because I noticed that since Mom's been away he's done pretty much squat in terms of cleaning. He ran the dishwasher through once three days ago, but that's about it. Right now there are empty soda cans stacked on the coffee table in front of me, and a pile of pizza boxes teetering on the edge. Our dog, Murphy, managed to snag one of them and drag it over into the corner behind Stanley's leather recliner, where he's busy gnawing it to death.

The Red Sox continue to make a mess of things through the last half of the eighth inning. When the game cuts to commercial, Stanley looks over at me and makes a face. Then he grins and pulls the lever on his recliner, catapulting himself into a standing position.

"Blitzkrieg!" he cries in this fake German accent that is incredibly stupid but makes me laugh anyway.

I hop up and salute, and we race each other out of the family room. I easily beat him to the doorway (my stepfather likes to watch sports but isn't much into playing them himself), then peel off toward the stairs while he heads for the kitchen.

Mom left us with a huge long list of chores to do while she was gone. Stanley and I checked it over that first night we were on our own, and I must have looked pretty grim because he laughed at me. Then he said, "I'll make you a deal, Cassidy. Let's put this list away for now, and just have a good time this week. But you've gotta promise to help me blitz this place before your mother gets home."

That was a no-brainer, and we clinched the deal with root beer floats.

Now, though, there's only an hour left until we leave for the airport. I still have to change the sheets on the beds, throw some laundry in, and dust and vacuum the upstairs. So far during the commercials I've managed to tidy up my room, which was a sty as usual, and scrub both bathrooms—Mom and Stanley's and Courtney's and mine, which is all mine now that Courtney's gone off to college. It doesn't feel real yet. The going-off-to-college part, I mean, not the bathroom-being-all-mine part. I know it will, though.

Heather Vogel Frederick

Grabbing fresh linens out of the linen closet, I jog into my mother's room. I definitely got the better deal when we divided the house up for cleaning. Stanley got stuck with the kitchen, which is pretty gross after being ignored all week.

I'm just stuffing the pillows into fresh pillowcases when I hear him holler, "Game's back on!" I grab all the dirty laundry and dump it into one of the big sheets that I stripped off the bed, then tie it up and throw it over my shoulder like Santa Claus's sack. Jogging back downstairs, I sling it onto the floor by the family room doorway, where it can wait until next commercial.

"C'mon, Sox!" I cry. "You can still turn it around!" Which is a complete lie. They are so going down in flames. It's important as a fan to try and encourage your team no matter what, though.

Giving myself a running start, I leap over the back of the sofa and land with my head on a pile of throw pillows at one end and my feet at the other. I pride myself on this talent, and I've gotten really good at it this past week without Mom around to yell at me. Jumping on the furniture is another thing she's definitely not all about.

Stanley checks his watch. "I hope they wrap up this miserable excuse of a game up soon," he says. "I want to leave plenty of time to get to Logan. You know what traffic is like."

Boston traffic is legendary. Even those of us who don't have our licenses yet know that.

Mom didn't want to miss the going-away party for Emma and her family, so she and Chloe are flying back home a day earlier than planned. There's a big potluck at Half Moon Farm tonight for the mother-daughter book club and our families.

Somehow, between hollering at the TV screen and finishing our pizza, Stanley and I manage to squeeze in the rest of our chores before it's time to leave. We spend most of the drive to the airport trash-talking the Red Sox and their pitiful performance and then arguing about whether there's even a chance, statistically, of a pennant run this year. After we manage to convince ourselves that maybe there's a glimmer of hope, our conversation turns to hockey.

"You had fun at camp this week, didn't you?" my stepfather asks, glancing over at me.

"Yeah."

I've been to hockey camps before, of course, but this one was different. It was for elite players, for one thing. And it was just for girls, for another. Ever since we moved here to Massachusetts from California a few years ago after my real father died, I've been playing hockey with boys. The schools here don't have girls' teams. It worked out fine and everything, but it's been totally sweet to play with other girls again. They came from all over New England for a chance to work with one of the former starting centers for the University of Wisconsin Badgers.

"You know," Stanley continues, "I was talking to the coach, and she says you're a gifted player. She told me you should be playing for a Division One club."

I make a face. "Mom said I can't, remember? Too much driving. It was the school team or nothing."

Heather Vogel Frederick

"Well, that was before she married me, back when she was the only one doing the driving," Stanley replies. "What if I were to take you to all the practices and games?"

"Really?" My heart gives a happy lurch. "Dude, that would be awesome!"

Stanley grins, and the top of his bald head turns pink the way it always does when he's pleased. "I had a feeling you'd think so. I've looked into it, and tryouts for the U16 team are this weekend. I haven't talked to your mother about it yet—"

I groan and he laughs. "I can be pretty persuasive, so don't give up all hope just yet, okay?"

"Okay," I reply glumly, and we drive along in silence for a while. I know what the schedule is like for select teams—practices three or four nights a week, games on the weekend, and all over New England too. Plus, there are tournaments just about every holiday, and Division 1 has a much longer hockey season than schools do. If I play for Alcott High on the boys team, the season goes from Thanksgiving through February, plus playoffs. Division 1 goes from September through March. I can't imagine Mom will go for the idea, no matter what Stanley says.

The airport is mobbed as usual, and it takes us a while to find Mom and Chloe.

"Hold your sister for me, would you, honey?" Mom asks, giving me a hug and a kiss as she hands her to me. Chloe makes happy-baby sounds and grabs my hair.

"Good to see you, too, monkey face," I tell her.

"Don't call her that," my mother says automatically, keeping one eye on the baggage carousel. She can't stand that nickname, but I think it fits. My little sister has the cutest little face, especially when she smiles and her nose scrunches up.

I press my lips against her ear. "Monkey face," I whisper, and she squeals with delight.

I can't believe how much Chloe has changed in just a week. She definitely feels a little heavier, and when she smiles I spot a new tooth poking through her bottom gum. I can't wait until she's old enough to walk. I figure once she can walk, she can skate. I plan to teach her the way Dad taught me, by having her push a chair around on the ice. I'm determined to make a jock out of her, because between my mom and Courtney our house has enough girly-girls.

"I need a shower," says my mother as we pull into our driveway a while later. "I smell like stuffy old airplane air." I grab her suitcase out of the van, and as I pass her to go into the house, she makes a face. "Phew! Maybe you should freshen up a little before the party too, sweetheart. At least put on a clean shirt."

I swear, my mother has a sense of smell like a basset hound. I glance down at my Red Sox T-shirt. Aside from the small pizza stain on the hem, it's pretty clean. I lift an arm and give a tentative sniff. I don't smell all that bad. It's not like I wore the shirt to hockey camp or something— I've only been wearing it to watch the Red Sox games this week. I figured it would be good luck not to wash it. Fat lot of good that did.

Heather Vogel Frederick

Arguing won't win me any points in her upcoming discussion with Stanley, though, so I dutifully go and change into a fresh T-shirt. My baby sister's room is right next to mine, and I can hear her giggling as Stanley changes her diaper. When she's bigger, Mom's planning to move her into Courtney's room unless I want it instead. But I don't want to think about that yet. I'm not even used to the idea of Courtney being away.

I pull out my cell phone—the new one Courtney managed to talk Mom into getting for me, since I don't have a very good track record with cell phones—and send her a text: HEY!

HEY BACK! comes her reply.

DID UR ROOMMATE SHOW UP?

YES! FAB!! LUV HER, LUV UCLA! HOW WAS UR LAST DAY OF CAMP?

SWEET. TWO GOALS AND A BUNCH OF ASSISTS.

YAY U! R MOM AND CHLOE HOME?

YUP. HEADING TO EMMA'S PARTY SOON.

GIVE HER A HUG 4 ME! GOTTA RUN. CIAO 4 NIAO!

Courtney's only been gone a week and I already miss her. Slipping the phone back into the pocket of my shorts, I head downstairs to wait for Mom and Stanley and Chloe.

"Too many things are changing around here," I tell Murphy, who is now innocently gnawing on a rawhide bone instead of a pizza box. Stanley destroyed all the evidence of our junk-food-a-thon, stuffing our trash way down deep into the recycling bin beneath a week's worth of newspapers.

Murphy looks up at me and cocks his head.

"Right, boy?" I scratch him behind the ears.

He doesn't reply but I'm sure he'd agree with me if he could. First my sister leaves, and now Emma's going away too. With Jess heading back to Colonial Academy, that leaves me starting Alcott High with only Megan Wong and Becca Chadwick for friends. Well, girlfriends. I have a bunch of guy friends from sports. Becca barely qualifies as a friend, though. She's okay, but we have absolutely nothing in common besides book club. Plus, she's the most boy-crazy girl I've ever met in my life, which can be really annoying.

I'm starving by the time we get to Half Moon Farm. Jess and her mom have looped crepe paper around everything and put flowers everywhere, and there's a big sign above the back porch door that says BON VOYAGE, HAWTHORNES! It looks great.

The food is good and there's plenty of it, which is always the case when the mother-daughter book club gets together. Mr. Delaney and Mr. Chadwick are in charge of the grill, and there are hot dogs and hamburgers and corn on the cob and baked beans and watermelon from the Delaneys' garden.

Megan's grandmother brought the same yummy Chinese dumplings that she made last Thanksgiving, which more than makes up for the bowl of mushy brownish something-or-other that Mrs. Wong plunks down beside them.

"It's my special Hummus Surprise," she says.

As far as I'm concerned, any food item with "surprise" in the

Heather Vogel Frederick

title is not a good thing, especially if Mrs. Wong is involved, and especially when it looks like something that might have come from Chloe's diaper.

Megan sees the look on my face and grins. "Don't worry," she whispers. "It's actually pretty good for once."

We grab our plates and line up, then find places to sit on the grass while our parents head for the picnic table and lawn chairs. I notice Jess drift over next to Darcy Hawthorne. Becca is hovering nearby too, but it's Jess I keep my eye on. She's got to be feeling pretty low right about now, losing her best friend and her crush. Jess doesn't think anybody but Emma knows, but anybody with half a brain cell can tell what's going on by the way she lights up whenever Darcy is around.

"Maybe you guys will come back with accents," I tell Emma and her brother.

This gets a grin from Darcy. "Jolly well right we will," he says in his best James Bond voice.

Jess's twin brothers, who are almost ten, think this is hilarious, and they leap up and chase each other around the yard, shouting "Jolly well right we will!" in fake British accents until their father tells them to pipe down.

I manage to stuff down two hamburgers, a hot dog, and a couple of ears of corn. "Oh, man, I'm stuffed," I groan happily, lying back on the grass and patting my stomach.

"Let's wait on dessert for a bit, then," says Mrs. Delaney.

"What is it?" I ask, because even though I couldn't possibly eat another bite, there's always room for dessert.

She smiles. "Kimball Farm, of course." Going out for ice cream after our first meeting of the year is a mother-daughter book club tradition. Except as it turns out, this time Kimball Farm has come to us. "There are three gallons in the freezer, courtesy of the Chadwicks."

"Gentlemen—how about a nice civilized game of croquet while the ladies conduct their business?" asks Mr. Delaney.

Darcy and Stewart Chadwick and our dads shoulder their mallets and head for the course that's set up in the field behind the barn. I'd follow them if I could move.

Our mothers bring their chairs over to where we're lolling in the grass.

"Gather round, everybody," says Mrs. Wong.

I manage to crawl over to my mother and flop down on my back again beside her. Chloe thinks this is a game and squirms her way out of my mother's lap, then flings herself onto my stomach.

"Oof," I groan. "Careful, monkey face."

"Cassidy!" my mother protests.

I grin. "Sorry."

"Phoebe," Jess's mother says, smiling at Mrs. Hawthorne, "you've been the captain of this ship for three years now, and with you at the helm our book club has been safely steered through waters both serene and, uh, stormy." She flicks a glance at the Chadwicks. Things haven't always been easy with Becca and her mother as part of our

Heather Vogel Frederick

group. "Our gratitude knows no bounds, and when Lily and Calliope and Clementine and I got together to plan this party, we all decided that you deserve a well-earned break. And so, we have taken matters into our own hands."

She reaches into a bag behind her chair and pulls out a present. I know what's in it, just like I know what's in Emma's, but we've all been sworn to secrecy. I sit up. My left knee starts bouncing up and down in excited anticipation.

Mrs. Hawthorne tears off the wrapping paper. "Oh," she says politely, "how nice."

It's a paperback copy of *Pride and Prejudice*. Everybody in Concord knows that Jane Austen is Mrs. Hawthorne's favorite writer, and that *P&P*, as she calls it, is her favorite book. She has a gazillion copies of it on her bookshelf at home, but there's something special about this one.

"Look inside," I urge.

She opens the book, and her eyes widen as she gets to the end of the inscription, which we all signed. "Really?" she asks, scanning our little circle hopefully.

"Yep," says Mrs. Wong, grabbing a bag from behind her chair and tossing identical paperback copies of the book to the rest of us. "Absolutely. It's time. We all agreed."

"Even me," I tell her cheerfully, even though personally I'd like a change from all these classics we've been reading over the past few years. Something with a little more action, maybe. "What's one more musty, dusty old book?"

My mother leans down and kisses the top of my head. "And what better year for us all to finally learn about your beloved Jane, Phoebe, than the year you and Emma head to her home turf?"

Mrs. Hawthorne's face falls. "Oh. But how will we—"

"Wait!" cries Mrs. Delaney. "It gets better!" She reaches into the bag again and emerges with a slim rectangle, brightly wrapped in pink polka-dot paper. She passes it to Emma. "This was Megan's idea."

My knee is going like a jackhammer by now. I can't wait to see Emma's face when she finds out what's inside. The Wongs just wanted to go ahead and pay for it, but Jess thought it would be nice if we all chipped in, so that it really would be from all of us. It wasn't that expensive, and we all have jobs. Not like Megan's job, of course. Her grandmother wangled this deal for her with a French clothing company called Bébé Soleil, and she has her own line of baby clothes. Still, we all earn a little money of our own. I teach private skating lessons, and Jess and Becca babysit. Although I can't imagine anyone asking Becca Chadwick to watch their kids. That would be like letting a shark loose in a tank of goldfish.

Emma removes the wrapping paper and opens the box, then pulls out a flat white object not much bigger than the copy of the book that's lying on the grass beside her. Megan leans over and flips up the lid.

Emma's mouth drops open. "You guys got me a *laptop*?!"

"A mini one," explains Mrs. Wong. "Jerry has one for when he travels, and Megan thought it would be perfect for you. She organized the whole thing."

Emma's gaze darts uneasily over to her mother. "I hope it wasn't too expensive."

"That's the beauty of it—netbooks aren't expensive at all! Everybody chipped in. And look, this is the best part." Mrs. Wong points to a tiny round hole centered above the computer's small screen. "It has a webcam! And Wi-Fi, too. You and your mom can still be part of our book club this year. We can videoconference with you."

Emma's face lights up. So does her mother's. We all crowd around as Megan and her mother point out the computer's features. Mrs. Hawthorne keeps shaking her head. "Such a simple solution. I should have thought of it."

"It's a wonder you've had time to think of anything at all, Phoebe," says Mrs. Delaney. "I still can't believe that you managed to pull off this house swap in such a short time."

"So are you all packed?" asks Mrs. Chadwick.

Mrs. Hawthorne nods. "I'm just finishing up a list of information for the Berkeleys."

"When do they arrive?" my mother asks her.

"The day after tomorrow, right after we leave. I'm sorry we won't be able to meet them—our planes will practically pass in midair."

"How old are their boys again?" asks Mrs. Wong.

"Simon will be a freshman, just like you girls, and Tristan is a junior like Darcy and Stewart."

"We'll be sure to stop by and say hello," my mother promises.

I can see the wheels spinning in her head already. She's probably already figured out what she's going to put in their welcome basket.

"I was counting on that," says Mrs. Hawthorne. "I've left them a list of local contact names and numbers, and yours are all right at the top."

We talk for a while longer. The light fades, and a few fireflies flicker at the far edge of the yard. Out of the corner of my ear I hear the crack of croquet mallets behind the barn. I'm itching to go join the game, but Chloe's dozing in my lap and I don't want to wake her up.

Dylan and Ryan appear around the corner of the barn. "Is it time for dessert yet?" one of them calls. I still have a hard time telling Jess's brothers apart.

"Absolutely," says Mrs. Delaney, hopping up from her chair. "Calliope? Do you want to help do the honors?"

We all crowd into line at the picnic table and a few minutes later I'm holding a cone piled high with a scoop of vanilla, strawberry, and black raspberry. "It's as close as I could get to the colors of the Union Jack," Becca's mother explains.

"The union what?" I ask.

"Duh," says Becca. "Everybody knows what the Union Jack is. It's the British flag."

"Well, la-de-dah," I tell her, stung. She didn't have to make me feel stupid. I decide to get even. "Mmm, this black raspberry smells delicious," I say, inching my nose close to my ice cream. "Really amazing. How about yours?"

Becca falls for it hook, line, and sinker. She lifts her cone to take a sniff and as she does, I jam it into her face, smearing ice cream all over.

"Cassidy!" she hollers.

I spring back out of reach, laughing. Emma and Jess and Megan start laughing too, which just makes her madder.

"That's the oldest trick in the book!" I crow. "I can't believe you fell for it!"

"Why don't you just grow up?" Becca sputters, wiping her face with her napkin.

"Never!" I climb onto the top rail of the pasture fence and perch there, licking my ice-cream cone. Looking down at my friends, I really mean it too. I wish we could stop time, right here and now. I wish Courtney didn't have to go to college, and I wish Emma didn't have to move, and I wish we didn't have to go to high school. I wish everything could stay the same.

But of course it can't.

I'm not very good at gooshy stuff, so I keep it short and sweet when it's finally time to say our good-byes. "Have fun in England, Emma," I tell her, giving her a hug.

The ride home is quiet, partly because Chloe is asleep in her car seat and partly because my mother and I are already lonely for our friends.

Two days later, my mother picks me up at the rink where I've been scrimmaging with Stewart Chadwick and Kyle Anderson and a few of my buddies from the middle school team. Tryouts for the Alcott High team aren't for a few more weeks, and I haven't decided yet what I'm going to do. I don't mind playing on a boys' team again, but I'm kind of waiting to hear the outcome of Stanley's discussion with my mother.

"I thought we'd swing by the Hawthornes with a welcome basket for the Berkeley family," she tells me as I throw my hockey stick and skating bag into the back of our van.

I suppress a smirk.

"What?"

"Nothing," I reply. I knew she wouldn't be able to resist. My mother loves giving people baskets filled with homemade food.

"I made some chili and picked up a loaf of sourdough bread from Nashoba Bakery, plus I stopped at Half Moon Farm for some of Shannon's wonderful strawberry jam. Oh, and a log of their goat cheese too."

"Not Blue Moon, I hope." Blue Moon is a particularly stinky variety that got me into a whole lot of trouble last year.

My mother laughs. "No, not Blue Moon. We'll wait until we know them better to spring that on them."

I'm dying to know if she and my stepfather have talked yet. I'm just about to fish around to see if I can find out when she brings it up.

"So, I hear you're interested in trying out for a Division One team this year." Her tone is neutral, and I look over to see if her expression reveals a little more about what she thinks of the idea. Nope, not a trace.

"Yeah," I reply cautiously.

"You don't sound too thrilled."

"No, it's not that—I am—I just, well, I didn't think . . ." My voice trails off.

Heather Vogel Frederick

My mother reaches over and pats me on the knee, then grins. "It's okay, you can say it. You didn't think I'd let you, did you?"

"You mean I can?"

She nods and I let out a whoop.

"Stan swears he's happy to drive you, and I just figure this will give you two more bonding time."

I'm still smiling a few minutes later when we pull into the Hawthornes' driveway. The lights are on inside, so the Berkeleys must have arrived.

"Isn't it weird to think that somebody else is going to be living in Emma's house this year?"

"A bit," my mother replies. "But just think what an adventure they're all going to have. Plus, you'll probably make two new friends. Maybe Simon and Tristan play hockey."

Encouraged by this thought, I grab the welcome basket and follow her to the front door. We knock, and after a minute it flies open.

"Hello," says a polite voice belonging to a boy who looks about my age. He's average height, which means shorter than me, because I'm nearly six feet tall, and he has curly blond hair and brown eyes and a friendly smile.

"Hello," says my mother. "I'm Clementine Sloane-Kinkaid, and this is my daughter Cassidy. We're friends of the Hawthornes and we just wanted to welcome you to Concord."

The door opens wider and the boy steps back to let us in. "Mum!" he calls. "Visitors!"

A moment later his mother appears. She has the same open, friendly face as her son, and the same hair and eyes. She's wearing jeans and a T-shirt with MANCHESTER UNITED on it. That's one of England's most famous soccer teams. I wonder if the T-shirt is hers, or if she borrowed it from one of her sons. If it's hers, I like her already.

We introduce ourselves, and I pass her the welcome basket.

"How lovely!" she says. "This is very thoughtful of you. Would you like to come in for a cup of tea?"

"I wish we could," my mother replies. "But I have a baby in the car and it's her dinnertime. You know how that is."

Mrs. Berkeley laughs. "Indeed I do. Doesn't change really, does it? They just get taller and hungrier." She puts her arm around her son. "Simon, go and see what your father's up to, would you, darling? I'd like him to at least say hello. Oh, and give your brother a shout as well."

"How was your flight?" my mother asks politely.

"Fine, thank you," says Mrs. Berkeley. "I still can't believe we're actually here!" She looks at me. "It must seem very odd to you, us living in your friend Emma's home."

Startled, I wonder for a moment if Mrs. Berkeley is a mind reader. "Uh, yeah, I guess."

"Well, I promise you we'll take very good care of everything—and of Melville, too."

As if conjured from thin air, the Hawthorne's big orange tiger cat appears. He makes a beeline for my mother and me, probably relieved to see familiar faces.

Heather Vogel Frederick

"Hey, Mel!" I squat down and scratch him under the chin. "He loves cheese," I tell Mrs. Berkeley. "He'll go nuts if you give him some of that stuff in the basket."

"Good to know," she says with a wink. "I do so want us to be friends. Oh, there you are, darling. Phillip, this is Clementine Sloane-Kinkaid and her daughter Cassidy. They're friends of the Hawthornes."

Professor Berkeley is tall and skinny, with thinning dark hair flecked with gray, dark blue eyes, and a wide smile like Simon's. "So pleased to meet you." He peers a little more closely at my mother as they shake hands. "I say, you aren't, well, *the* Clementine, are you?"

My mother laughs. "Let's just say I used to be."

My mother was a model a long time ago, a really famous one. It was back before she had me and Courtney, and before my father died and we moved to Concord, but people still recognize her.

"And this is Tristan." Mrs. Berkeley propels her other son forward. "Say hello, Tris."

"Hello," he says, without enthusiasm.

Tristan Berkeley is tall, like his father, with the same dark coloring. He's got one of those jawlines that looks like it was chiseled out of granite, and a long, straight nose. He's working really hard right now to look down it at me, which is pretty much impossible since we're the same height. As we shake hands he recoils slightly, flicking a glance at my hockey shirt. When he looks up again our eyes lock for a moment and I know exactly what he's thinking, just as clearly as if he'd said it aloud. *You stink.*

That would be because I just came from the rink, you moron, I want to tell him, but for once I mind my manners and don't.

My mother is the one who speaks up. "Cassidy's just been at the rink," she says coolly, a hint of Queen Clementine in her voice. That's what I call it when she means business. She must have noticed his reaction too. "She plays hockey. On an elite girls' team. The Lady Shawmuts." This last bit is stretching the truth since I haven't even been to tryouts yet, but I know she said it because she wants to defend me and that makes me feel really good.

Mrs. Berkeley laughs. "We know all about sports, don't we, boys?" she says. "Simon plays football—I mean soccer. That's what you call it here in America, right? And Tristan is into ice dancing."

Ice dancing? I choke back a laugh. That's going to go over big at Alcott High. Tristan spots the expression on my face and glowers at me.

Ignoring him, I point to Mrs. Berkeley's T-shirt and ask, "So is Manchester United your favorite team?"

"Absolutely," she replies. "We're all huge fans."

"I watched them win the World Cup last summer," I tell her.

"Isn't this splendid, boys?" says their father. "Cassidy likes sports too. When you get to school tomorrow, you'll already have a friend."

Simon looks so pleased at this thought that I can't help smiling back at him. My smile fades as Tristan shoots me another glance, though. *As if,* says this one.

"Nice to meet you," he says tonelessly, then stalks back down the hall toward the kitchen.

Heather Vogel Frederick

"Well, then," harrumphs Professor Berkeley, blinking at us awkwardly.

"Jet lag," Mrs. Berkeley says. "So sorry."

Jet lag my eye, I think.

My mother waves her hand and smiles. "Not to worry," she replies. "I have plenty of experience with teenagers. How about I call you in a few days after you're settled in, and we'll find a time to have you all over for dinner?"

She and Mrs. Berkeley exchange phone numbers, and we head to the car.

"Lucky us," I mutter. "Dinner with Tristan Jerkeley."

"First impressions aren't always accurate," my mother says lightly as we pull out of the driveway onto Lowell Road. "It was probably just jet lag, like his mother said."

"Yeah, right." I glance over my shoulder at Emma's house. Simon seemed okay, but I'd be happy if I never saw his brother again in my life.

Final score: Tristan Berkeley: 1; and a big fat zero for Cassidy Sloane.

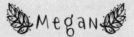

Megan

"Bingley was sure of being liked wherever he appeared;
Darcy was continually giving offence."
—*Pride and Prejudice*

"Pardon me, but I believe you dropped this."

I hear the voice before I see its owner. It's a nice voice, husky and a bit on the quiet side. If it were fabric, it would be corduroy. Soft, wide wale corduroy. I know exactly who it belongs to as well. The British accent is a dead giveaway.

I turn around to see Simon Berkeley holding out a black notebook bristling with magazine clippings and photographs.

"Oh, my gosh!" I grab it from him and hug it to my chest. "Thank you so much!"

I would die if I ever lost my sketchbook. Shrugging off my backpack, I lean over to stuff it back inside. It's a struggle to keep my footing in the stream of passing students. I thought the hallways at Walden Middle School were crowded, but Alcott High is ridiculous. A pair of football players who must be nearly seven feet tall brush past me, and

I stagger slightly. Simon places a hand on my shoulder, steadying me.

"Thank you," I repeat, straightening up. We stand there smiling at each other. I try and think of something to say. I'm not usually so tongue-tied and I feel really stupid all of a sudden.

"See you in Biology class then, Megan."

"Uh, yeah, right—see you!"

He knows my name. For some reason, this makes me really happy. I had no idea Simon Berkeley even knew who I was. Biology is the only class we have together, and it's huge. There are, like, nearly forty kids in it. I always sit with Becca, who's my lab partner, and our table is on the other side of the room from Simon and Zach Norton.

Zach has been my secret crush since kindergarten and the main subject of nearly all of my conversations with Becca Chadwick since fourth grade. But as I watch Simon Berkeley disappear down the hall, it occurs to me that Zach could have some serious competition this year.

Shouldering my backpack, I set off upstream in the opposite direction toward the math classrooms. At least I think the math classrooms are this way. High school is so different than I expected. Better in some ways, worse in others. I like the fact that we get to pick our own classes, especially the electives. I'm taking ceramics this semester, which is really fun. On the downside, though, Alcott is at least twice as big as Walden. I've been here every day now for a month, and I still get lost half the time.

The other thing I don't like is that I don't quite feel like I fit in yet.

I was comfortable at Walden. People knew who I was. I had friends to sit with at lunchtime. Here at Alcott, I feel awkward and invisible and out of place.

My parents keep telling me I should get involved in something, but what? Roots and Shoots, the environmental club that my mother is all hot for me to join, just isn't my thing. Becca tried to talk me into trying out for the cheerleading squad with her, but that's not me, either. Team sports are out of the question since I'm not particularly athletic. I don't play an instrument, so that knocks band and orchestra off the list, and I have no interest in any of the foreign language clubs or in working for the school newspaper or the yearbook or running for student government. That leaves Mathletes—a big joke, since I still struggle with long division—or the Chess Club, where I could totally ruin my chances at a social life by becoming BFFs with Kevin Mullins.

Poor Kevin. By the end of last year he'd finally managed to fit in at Walden Middle School, more or less, and now he's a small fish in a big pond again. A very small, very odd fish. Kevin's probably the tiniest boy at Alcott High. He's at least three years younger than any of the other freshmen because he skipped a bunch of grades back in elementary school. Plus, he's a genius. Cassidy calls him the Boy Wizard.

I spot him up ahead at the end of the hall, fiddling with the combination to his locker. A couple of upperclassmen hover nearby, which is not a good sign. From the very first day of high school, Kevin's destiny was clear—he'll be spending the next four years being stuffed into trash cans and lockers.

The two upperclassmen swoop in, lifting Kevin off his feet. He kicks wildly as they start to wedge him into his now-open locker. Someone streaks past me. It's Cassidy.

"Hey!" she calls. "Leave him alone!"

Cassidy Sloane has been here at Alcott exactly as long as I have, but while I'm still mostly invisible, somehow she's managed to make it onto the school radar screen. Partly that's because she's tall—at five foot eleven, she tends to stick out in a crowd. Partly it's because of her flaming red hair. But mostly it's because, well, she's Cassidy.

"What's the big deal?" mutters one of them.

"Is he your shrimp boyfriend?" taunts the other.

"I'll tell you what he is," Cassidy retorts. "He's off-limits. Out of bounds. Get it?" She's right in their faces, hands on her hips and glaring. "Leave him alone."

"Whatever." They let go of Kevin and swagger away.

"You okay?" Cassidy asks.

Kevin nods, but behind his glasses I can see that his eyes are filled with tears. It's just not fair, letting someone like Kevin loose at a big place like Alcott. Aren't there special schools around for miniature geniuses where they don't get trampled and picked on?

Cassidy grabs him by his backpack and hauls him to his feet. "Next time pick on somebody your own size," she tells him with a wink.

Kevin swipes at his eyes and nods, then scuttles off. He's probably heading to Super Advanced Honors Physics for Brainiacs or something.

"He's a twerp," says Becca, coming up behind us. She and Cassidy and I are in the same math class. It's not a class for geniuses, that's for sure.

"Yeah, but he's our twerp," says Cassidy.

"Think of it as having a mascot," I add. "Or a pet."

Becca shrugs. Taking out her lip gloss, she dabs at her mouth. It's a nice color, sort of a pinkish plum. Before I can ask its name, though, her brother Stewart pokes his head around the corner.

"Hey, Cassidy, are you planning on taking pictures for the school newspaper again this year?" he asks. "Our first editorial meeting is this afternoon."

She shakes her head. "I don't think I'll be able to fit it in, dude."

Cassidy made it onto this select hockey team for girls and hardly has time to tie her shoes these days. She practically sleeps at the rink.

"Oh, yeah, right." Stewart looks disappointed. "I forgot." He droops off. He's been looking pretty droopy in general since Emma left for England.

Math is boring as usual. The minute the final bell rings, the three of us bolt out the door and head for the cafeteria.

Lunch is another thing I'm not so sure I like about high school. It's only twenty minutes long, for one thing, which is barely enough time to scarf down a sandwich, let alone hang out with my friends. And hanging out with friends is pretty much the main reason for going to school, if you ask me. For another thing, Tuesday and Friday are the only days I even have friends to eat with. All the other days I have late

Heather Vogel Frederick

lunch because of ceramics, and the only person I know who's on that schedule is Kevin. Yesterday I went ahead and ate with him, because he was the only person in the entire cafeteria I recognized and because I figured I'd look like a complete loser sitting at a table all by myself. Although now that I think about it, I probably looked like even more of a loser eating with Kevin.

Becca and I plop our trays down across from Cassidy. As usual, she's digging into an amazing lunch, courtesy of her mother's TV show. Some sort of pasta salad with shrimp and artichokes and sun-dried tomatoes, which beats the pants off an Alcott High grilled cheese.

"Here," says Cassidy, shoving a plastic container filled with brownies toward us. "I'm not supposed to eat sugar."

"Says who?" I ask, surprised. Sugar has always topped Cassidy Sloane's list of major food groups.

"Says my hockey coach. She wants us in peak physical condition this season. Dessert is for weekends only."

"How's it going, anyway?" asks Becca.

Cassidy's face lights up. "Awesome."

"Yeah, I love cheerleading, too."

As they jabber on about how much fun they're having and how cool high school is, I stare down at my grilled cheese. All my friends are involved in something they love except me.

"Hi, you guys."

We look up. It's Zach Norton. He plunks himself down next to

Cassidy. "You all know Simon, right?" He jerks his thumb toward Simon Berkeley. We nod, and Simon sits down too.

In a flash Zach and Simon and Cassidy are off and running about sports. I try to follow along, but honestly, I'm just not that interested. Plus I have no idea who or what Manchester United is.

I sneak peeks at Simon over my sandwich, admiring the way his hair curls behind his ears and at the base of his neck. He has really nice hands, too, with long fingers that look like they'd be good at playing the piano or something. And that accent!

Cassidy shouts with laughter at something he says, and I turn my gaze on her. We've been friends for three years now, but she's still a bit of a mystery to me. I mean, she's actually really cute, with that fabulous hair and spattering of freckles on her slightly upturned nose. There's something about her face that always looks like she's on the verge of laughing, too, which is mostly true except when she's ticked-off about something. She could be incredibly pretty if she took an interest in her looks and maybe brushed her hair once in a while, but she comes to school every day looking like she got dressed with her eyes closed. And still the boys all like her.

Does that include Simon Berkeley? I wonder, watching him. Zach Norton does—or did last year. He and Cassidy have always been good friends and everything—they played baseball together in middle school and joked around in classes and stuff. But she had absolutely no romantic interest in him whatsoever. Nada. Zip. And then last spring he went and kissed her, which made her so mad she

Heather Vogel Frederick

barely talked to him all summer. They must have straightened things out finally, though, because now they're obviously friends again.

I turn to Becca. "Can I see that lip gloss you have on today?"

"Sure." As she's reaching into her backpack to fish it out, Simon smiles at me. I smile back, then feel really stupid when I realize he's looking over my shoulder at someone else.

"Tristan!" he says. "Come join us!"

We turn around to see Simon's older brother standing there. He is drop-dead handsome. I try not to stare, but it's pretty hard. He looks from Becca and me to Cassidy and back again, sizing us up like he's measuring fabric. He shakes his head. "No, thanks. Catch you later, Si."

"Was it something we said?" says Becca, watching him walk away.

"Don't mind Tristan," says Simon. "He's just a little shy." He smiles again, and this time he's not looking over my shoulder. He's looking straight at me. I smile back.

A few minutes later, as we're clearing our trays, Cassidy leans over to me. "Just a little shy?" she whispers. "Just a little lame is more like it."

"Maybe, but he's still gorgeous," Becca murmurs back, tapping away on her cell phone. She's probably texting Ashley. "Talk about tall, dark, and handsome."

Cassidy snorts. "How about tall, dark, and loser?"

"Simon's cuter anyway, in my opinion." I'm itching to sketch his hands, but I'll have to wait until after school. Right now, I've got Spanish class to find.

When I finally get home, the house is empty. There's a note

propped on the kitchen table that says "Gone apple picking." After my grandmother came to live with us last year, things got a little rocky. She and my mother are as different as burlap and velvet, and everything came to a head when we went to Wyoming over summer vacation. They worked most of the stuff out, though, and one of the things they decided was that they needed to find more things to do together.

Apple picking fits the bill. Fresh air, supporting an organic farm— that'll make Mom happy. And Gigi loves food and loves to cook, so apples will make her happy.

I fix myself a snack and head for the deck instead of my room since it's such a nice afternoon. I love having the house to myself. Cutting through the living room, I pop in a CD and crank up the volume. I hardly ever get to blast my music, and it's fun. I dance my way across the floor to the sliding doors.

We're hosting the first book club videoconference with Emma and her mother this weekend, and my dad already has a pair of giant speakers set up, along with a fancy microphone and webcam. Somehow he's hooked his laptop to our big-screen TV too. My dad's a technology whiz and totally gets into this kind of project.

Because of all the state-of-the-art equipment at our house, my mother offered to host book club meetings for the whole year. The other moms discussed it, and said the only way they'd agree is if they could take turns bringing the food. Cassidy says letting my mom off the hook with cooking was just self-preservation, not generosity, and she's got a point because my mother is the world's worst cook and every-body knows it.

It's a warm day for October, and the sun feels really good. Much better than being cooped up inside. I buzz through my homework, not because I'm dying to do it but because I don't want to have to listen to my mother nag me about it all weekend. Plus, I'd just as soon get it out of the way and have the rest of the weekend to do what I want. Afterward, I mess around with my sketchbook for a while, seeing if I can draw Simon Berkeley's hands from memory. I think I get pretty close.

Then I go back to my room, where I hop online and check out my favorite fashion websites, including Flashlite.com. I see a few outfits and designs that I like, and I send them to the printer to add to my sketchbook later.

As I'm doing that, I hear the rumble of the garage door opener, so I shut my laptop and head for the kitchen. Mom and Gigi come in carrying boxes full of apples.

"We had a wonderful time!" says my grandmother, giving me a kiss. She's wearing a tailored lilac jogging suit—designer, of course—with a white silk scoop-neck T-shirt and the diamond earrings she's let me borrow a couple of times. Even for something as casual as apple picking, Gigi can be counted on to accessorize. I adore her sense of style.

"We drove out to Carlisle to that orchard on Acton Road," says my mother, who's dressed in jeans and one of her oldest, rattiest hoodies. A little more suitable for knocking around a farm, but still, I can't help wishing she had just a smidge of Gigi's style.

"I think we should make pies for book club this weekend, don't you?" my grandmother asks.

"Clementine offered to bring the food this time," my mother reminds her. "And I'm pretty sure she said something about pie."

"You can never have too many pies," Gigi says firmly.

The following afternoon she sets me to work peeling and slicing apples while she whips up a pair of crusts. In no time at all the pies are in the oven and kitchen smells deliciously of cinnamon. The scent lures my father out of his office.

"I smell something wonderful!" he says, sniffing the air and rubbing his hands together. Dad's gotten a little chubby since Gigi moved in. He doesn't seem too upset about it, though.

She pinches his cheek. "Apple pies. One for the book club, and one for my favorite son-in-law."

He laughs. "You mean your *only* son-in-law."

"You're still my favorite."

After dinner, my father takes me into the living room and shows me how to run all the videoconferencing equipment.

"I'll be around to help if you run into any problems," he assures me. "But I'll probably be hiding in my office. I don't want to get in the way of all your girl fun."

Most of our dads go into hiding whenever our book club gets together.

Finding a time to schedule our meetings is getting harder this year. Everyone's so busy. We have to work around Cassidy's hockey

Heather Vogel Frederick

schedule and Becca's cheerleading practices, plus Jess is on the equestrian team at Colonial Academy and she's in MadriGals, too, her school's special a cappella chorus. I'm more flexible, but still, there's homework and all that, plus England is five hours ahead of us so we have to take that into account too. Sunday afternoons seem to be the only time that works for everybody.

After lunch the next day, Cassidy arrives straight from practice. While she heads down the hall to my bathroom to shower and change, Jess and Becca and I hang out in the living room with our moms and Gigi and Mrs. Bergson, waiting for her. Mrs. Bergson is Emma's skating teacher, but she's more than that. She's like Emma's surrogate grandmother. She and Gigi call themselves the book club's wise old owls. Mrs. Chadwick and my mother get into a discussion about something called vermiculture, which I am totally grossed out to find means raising worms.

"Eeeew," I say, and Mrs. Chadwick laughs. She's like my mother's new best friend now that she's all into this gardening program.

"It's a wonderful way to improve your soil," she tells me.

I glance over at Becca, who makes a face. "She keeps them in a bucket on our kitchen counter."

"Gross," I reply. "Please don't get any ideas, Mom."

"Somehow I don't think your grandmother would go for that," she says, smiling.

"Lily, you read my mind!" says Gigi. "In fact, let's change the subject." She turns to Jess. "How are things at Colonial this year?"

"Great!" Jess replies. "I like it a lot better than last year."

"The only problem with that is we hardly ever see her on the weekends anymore," says Mrs. Delaney. "Not that I'm complaining."

"Are you rooming with Savannah again?" asks Becca.

"No. She's with Peyton Winslow this year. I'm in a triple with Adele and Frankie."

"I remember them from last year," says Becca. "They're fun."

"Yeah," Jess agrees.

Cassidy finally reappears, wearing clean sweatpants and a long-sleeve T-shirt and toweling her hair.

"Everybody ready?" I ask, and my friends all nod. I click on the icon onscreen, and we hear a phone ringing. Then Emma says hello and we all squeal with excitement. A few seconds later, the video feed kicks in and she and her mother appear on the TV screen.

"Hi, you guys!" Emma shouts at us, waving madly. "This is so cool!"

We wave back.

"What the heck are you wearing?" I ask her.

She laughs. "I knew you'd notice!" She stands up and twirls around. "Ta-da! It's my new school uniform. What do you think?"

It's far, far worse than what we had to wear at Walden Middle School last year.

Cassidy peers more closely at the screen. "Is that a *tie*?"

Emma nods. "Yup. I had to learn to tie it and everything. Can you believe it?"

In addition to the red necktie, she's wearing a navy skirt, a blue-and-white-striped shirt, and a navy blazer. The words KNIGHTLEY-

Heather Vogel Frederick

MARTIN SCHOOL are embroidered above the fancy crest on its chest pocket.

"My goodness, it looks like the uniform I had to wear to school back in the 1940s," says Mrs. Bergson

Gigi nods. "Mine too."

"Pretty sad, Emma," I tell her.

"I know!" she agrees. "The only good thing is, everybody else is stuck wearing it too."

As if on cue, her brother Darcy springs onto the screen next to her. He's wearing his uniform as well, and we all scream with laughter.

"Darcy! Shoo!" says Mrs. Hawthorne, and he grins and waves to us, then disappears. "So," his mother continues, "now that we've covered British school fashion, would you like a tour of Ivy Cottage?"

We all chorus "yes" and the picture on the screen tilts wildly as Mrs. Hawthorne picks up Emma's laptop. "Come with me, then."

She slowly pans the camera lens around the living room. It has white walls and a low ceiling with dark wooden beams stretching across it. "We spend most of our time here and in the kitchen."

There's a big stone fireplace at one end flanked by two plump armchairs, and a long sofa under a bank of windows overlooking a garden. The windows have those same diamond crisscross patterns as the windows in the turret at Cassidy's house, and the sofa and armchairs are upholstered in fabric covered with bright flowers.

"English chintz," Mrs. Sloane-Kinkaid says with a sigh. "Perfect."

The coffee table and other small end tables scattered around the room are made of heavy dark wood, and so are the dining table and chairs at the far end of the room, the matching sideboard, and the bench in the front hall.

"It's Jacobean," Mrs. Hawthorne explains, zooming in for a closer look at the bench, which is intricately carved with fruit and flowers. "The Berkeleys are collectors. Look at this detail, Clementine."

"Gorgeous," Cassidy's mother murmurs.

"It looks like a throne or something," says Cassidy.

"Jacobean means it was made in the early seventeenth century, during the reign of King James the first," says Emma, who as usual is a fountain of information.

Becca nudges me and rolls her eyes.

"You've gotta admit it's cool, though," I whisper, and she gives a grudging nod.

"There are just three rooms downstairs," says Mrs. Hawthorne. "I'll save the kitchen for last, but take a look at Nick's office." She sticks the laptop through the door of the adjoining room, which is filled with the same style furniture as the living room. Emma's dad looks up from his desk and waves.

"Hello, Concord!"

"Hi, Mr. Hawthorne!" we chorus back.

We tour the upstairs next, following the laptop camera's bumpy procession up a steep, narrow staircase. Emma's bedroom is tucked in a corner, with a sloped ceiling and windows on two sides. It reminds

Heather Vogel Frederick

me a little of Cassidy's room, because the shelves are covered with trophies.

"They're all Tristan's," says Emma, and Cassidy smirks at us. She told us he's an ice dancer.

Mrs. Hawthorne pans the camera over to the bed, which has a cheerful yellow-and-white striped comforter on it and a stack of books piled on the pillow.

"Now, that looks more like you, Emma," says Mrs. Bergson.

"Yes," says Mrs. Hawthorne. "The Manchester United bedspread was a bit much."

Emma waves her hand in front of the lens. "Mom, we've got to show them the hat!" she begs.

"But my bed's not made!" her mother protests.

"They don't care."

"My bed's never made," says Cassidy.

Her mother sighs. "What can I say? I try." She smiles. "Emma's right, though, Phoebe—we don't care. Show us this mysterious hat."

"Okay," says Mrs. Hawthorne. "But don't say I didn't warn you."

Curious, we all stare at the screen as Mrs. Hawthorne carries the laptop back down the hall. She opens another door, revealing a large room with a four-poster bed—unmade—and a big window.

"I don't see a hat," says Becca.

"Wait for it," says Mrs. Hawthorne, and the camera slowly pans up the front of a wardrobe standing against the far wall. Perched on top is a bowler hat.

"Check it out!" crows Emma, pointing to a spiral of green leaves encircling it.

The camera follows the trail of ivy from the hat across the top of the wardrobe, down the wall, and out through a small crack in the window frame.

"You've got to be kidding me," says Cassidy. "You mean that's real? It grew that way?"

"Isn't it funny?" Emma agrees.

"Ivy Cottage is well named, I'd say," notes Mrs. Bergson.

"I know." Emma sighs. "I love this house."

"We've saved the best for last," says Mrs. Hawthorne, taking us back downstairs. "It's not pink like ours is at home, but we like it anyway."

The kitchen is big and sunny, with a stone floor and an open hutch at one end with blue and white dishes displayed on its shelves. Unlike the rest of the furniture in the house, the hutch is made of pale wood.

"A Welsh cupboard!" cries Mrs. Sloane-Kinkaid in delight. "I've always wanted one."

"Look at the windowsill." Emma crosses the room to a broad table made of the same pale wood as the dish cupboard. Beyond it is a window with a deep, whitewashed sill lined with pots of bright red geraniums and more pieces of blue and white china. My fingers itch for my sketchbook.

"The walls are nearly two feet thick," boasts Emma. "All the windows are like window seats. I sit in the one in my room upstairs all the time."

Heather Vogel Frederick

"DARCY ROCKS!" screams someone offscreen, and we all jump.

Out of the corner of my eye, I notice Jess's face flush. She doesn't know that I know she likes Emma's brother. I'm pretty sure we all know, actually.

"Oh, and this is Toby," says Mrs. Hawthorne, zooming in on a parrot in a cage in the corner. "Toby, say hello to our friends."

"GO RED SOX!" Toby squawks.

Mrs. Hawthorne laughs. "I guess you can tell who's been spending the most time with Toby."

"He wouldn't shut up about Manchester United," Emma tells us. "Darcy and I figured we had to do something."

"Can we see the garden?" begs Mrs. Chadwick, and the camera bumps its way out the back door and down a gravel path.

Our mothers ooh and aah over all the flowers and shrubs. Becca's mother whips out her notebook and starts barking questions at Mrs. Hawthorne.

"I'm afraid I'm not much help," Emma's mother apologizes. "I have no idea what all the plants are—I'm just trying to keep up with the weeding and watering."

She offers to take pictures of everything and send them along in an e-mail, which makes Mrs. Chadwick happy, then finishes our tour by taking us around to the front of the house. It looks even better in real life than in the picture Emma showed us at her going-away party.

"You certainly landed in a beautiful spot, Phoebe," says Jess's mother.

Mrs. Hawthorne turns the laptop around and points it at herself. Her face looms large on the TV screen. "Didn't we, though?" she replies, smiling broadly. "I wish Emma and I could take you for a walk through the village and down by the canal, too, but I don't think our Wi-Fi would reach that far. Here, maybe you can at least take a peek at the view." She turns the laptop around again and aims it over the hedge, revealing a cluster of tidy homes similar to Ivy Cottage.

"Idyllic," murmurs Mrs. Bergson. "Just the way an English village should look."

"Well, I suppose we should get our meeting started," Mrs. Hawthorne says. "Enough of this dawdling."

"Dawdling is the best part of life," says my grandmother.

"This wise old owl thinks so, too," says Mrs. Bergson, and they both laugh.

Back in the kitchen, Emma's mother sets the computer on the table and puts a cover over Toby's cage. "I think we've heard enough from you for the time being."

"What do you do with him when you're off exploring?" asks Jess.

"The Berkeleys arranged for a neighbor boy to take care of him for us."

"Roooooo-pert!" moos Emma in the background.

"Emma!" her mother scolds. "Rupert Loomis is a very nice boy."

Emma leans in toward the webcam. There's a glint in her eye and her lips are quirked up in a little grin. "He's a nincompoop," she says in a stage whisper, and Becca and Cassidy and Jess and I all giggle.

Heather Vogel Frederick

"So," says Mrs. Hawthorne, ignoring her, "what do you all think of *Pride and Prejudice* so far?"

"Can we eat before we talk about it?" asks Cassidy. "I'm starving."

"Why not," says Mrs. Hawthorne. "I'll put the kettle on."

"And I'll do the same," says my mother, jumping up off the sofa. She and Gigi disappear into the kitchen, emerging a few minutes later with trays loaded with teacups, plates, sandwiches, and pies—Mrs. Sloane-Kinkaid's, and the ones my grandmother and I made last night.

"It's a bake-off!" says Cassidy's mother, catching sight of our pies.

"Hey, we're having apple pie too," says Emma.

"Courtesy of Nicholas, of course," adds her mother. My mother might be a terrible cook, but Mrs. Hawthorne doesn't cook at all. She says she's dangerous in the kitchen, and besides, Emma's dad loves to cook.

"You know, Jane Austen loved pie," says Mrs. Hawthorne, who always manages to steer our conversations back to book club stuff. "Why don't we get to know her a little bit better while we're eating, and then we can discuss *Pride and Prejudice*. Lily, did you receive the e-mail attachments I sent you?"

My mother grabs a folder off the mantel, then passes out its contents.

FUN FACTS ABOUT JANE

1) Jane Austen was born on December 16, 1775, in Steventon, England. She was the seventh of eight Austen children,

and one of two girls. The other was her sister, Cassandra.

2) The Austens were a close-knit, lively, loving family of bookworms. In a letter to her sister, Jane once said that her family were "great novel-readers, and not ashamed of being so." The young Austens also enjoyed putting on plays for their parents, and sometimes turned their barn into a private stage.

3) Jane loved to play the piano and sing, and she was an excellent dancer, attending numerous balls as a young woman.

4) Reading was a large part of Jane's education. Her formal education ended at age eleven, and after that she was largely homeschooled. She had free rein over her father's library of some 500 books.

5) Jane began writing at age ten or eleven, and at sixteen copied out her early works to date, which included comical sketches, short stories, plays, a novel, and a spoof entitled *The History of England*.

6) There's only one portrait of Jane in existence—a drawing done by her sister—but she was said to have been a pretty girl with chestnut hair, hazel eyes, and a round face.

Heather Vogel Frederick

"She only went to school until she was eleven?" cries Cassidy. "Lucky!"

"I can't believe she wrote all that stuff by the time she was sixteen," says Emma. "Talk about making me feel like a loser."

Emma wants to be a writer when she grows up, just like her father.

"I think it's interesting that she was born in 1775," says Jess. "Right before the American Revolution. It's almost like she has a Concord connection."

Onscreen, Mrs. Hawthorne holds up her copy of *Pride and Prejudice*. "Shall we turn our attention to the book at hand?" she says. "Have you all read or listened to the first five chapters?"

We all nod. Mom and Gigi and I have been listening to the book together every night after supper, while we clean up the kitchen. Mom thought that an audio book was wimping out at first, but Gigi explained that it's a big help to her, so she eventually gave in. My grandmother's English is amazing—she went to a British school in Hong Kong when she was my age—but Jane Austen writes in kind of an old-fashioned style, and reading it is challenging for her. Heck, it's challenging for *me*, and English is my native language.

Anyway, the three of us are really enjoying listening to the story. The actress who reads it is great, and so far I understand everything.

"Mrs. Bennet is *hilarious*," I say. "I think she's my favorite character so far. I love the way she's always flying around having fits about everything."

"I love her too," says Emma. "She's such a flibbertigibbet."

"What's a flibbertigibbet?" asks Becca.

"Someone who's scatterbrained," says her mother.

"Flighty," adds Mrs. Delaney.

"Ditsy," notes my mother.

"Silly," says Mrs. Sloane-Kinkaid.

The Hawthornes made up this stupid thing called the synonym game back when Emma and Darcy were little. They have the whole book club addicted to it now.

Mrs. Bergson takes a sip of tea. "We used to call people like her 'Nervous Nellies' when I was growing up."

She smiles at us, and I smile back. I haven't felt this happy and relaxed for a long time. This is what I've been missing so far at high school. I love spending time with people I'm really comfortable around, and can just say whatever I want to without worrying about sounding stupid, or not fitting in. I love our little rituals—even something as dumb as the synonym game. It's familiar and comforting, and feels like, well, home.

"Don't you love the way the book starts, too?" Mrs. Bergson continues, and suddenly she and all the other grown-ups—and Emma, too, of course—chant: "'It is a truth universally acknowledged, that a single man in possession of a good fortune must be in want of a wife.'"

The rest of us listen, openmouthed.

"What's up with that?" asks Cassidy.

"It's one of the literature's greatest opening lines," Mrs. Hawthorne tells her.

"If you say so."

Heather Vogel Frederick

"Cassidy!" her mother protests. "Don't be rude."

"Seriously, Mom, I don't get it. I mean, okay, so the Bennets have five daughters. I understand that part. They don't have a lot of money and they're worried that some relative of Mr. Bennet's is going to snatch their house away from them if he dies. But why is Mrs. Bennet so totally obsessed with getting everybody married off? Can't she just send her daughters to college or help them find jobs or something? I mean, she's ready to pounce on this poor Bingley guy the minute he moves into the neighborhood."

Mrs. Hawthorne laughs. "The thing is, Cassidy, back in Jane's day, women didn't go to college, and respectable women didn't have jobs."

"Except a few, who were governesses," says Mrs. Delaney. "Remember *Jane Eyre*?"

The moms—and Emma, who's read every book in the universe—all nod. "Of course," says Mrs. Hawthorne. "But for most young women, marriage was virtually the only career choice. Especially for those with no money of their own. It was the only way a girl would ever be assured of having a home of her own, or achieving any sense of independence and financial security."

"That's lame," says Cassidy.

"No kidding," Becca agrees.

Mrs. Hawthorne shrugs. "Lame or not, it's simply the way it was. And understanding that will help you understand the book better."

"I can't believe what a snob Mr. Darcy is," I say, changing the subject. "It's a good thing nobody likes him."

My mother and Gigi exchange a glance. "Mmm," says my mother. "Wait and see."

My dad wanders in. "Any pie left?" he asks hopefully, waving to Emma and her mother onscreen.

Gigi hops up and serves him a couple of slices. "This one's mine, and this one's Clementine's," she tells him, watching as he takes a bite of each.

"So what's the verdict?" she asks.

"They're both amazing," my father replies diplomatically. "I'd say it's a tie."

Cassidy holds out her plate. "I need to try some more before I'm ready to vote."

That's another thing that puzzles me about Cassidy. She eats like a horse. I can't believe she eats as much as she does and stays so slim. It must be all that hockey.

"Why don't you girls visit with Emma a bit more while we clear up the dishes," says my mother, and she and the other grown-ups take their plates out to the kitchen.

"Tell us about school," prompts Jess. "Have you made any new friends?"

Emma shrugs. "A few. There's a nice girl across the street named Lucy. We ride the bus together to school. A red double-decker bus."

"Cool!" says Cassidy, her mouth still full of pie.

"Yeah, actually, it is."

Heather Vogel Frederick

"Do you ride up top?" asks Becca.

"Duh," Emma replies. "Of course. Wouldn't you?"

"So what's school like?" I ask.

"Uh, sort of the same, but different. Like for instance they call math 'maths' over here, which is weird, and in history class, instead of studying U.S. Government I'm learning about Parliament, and instead of learning U.S. History I'm learning about the kings and queens of England and all that. But you know, school is school."

"Is there a newspaper for you to work on?"

Emma shakes her head. "No. Knightley-Martin has a literary magazine, though—it's called a magazine but it's not all that fancy—and I want to write something for that."

"So who is this Rupert guy?" Becca asks.

Emma starts to snicker. "He's like Kevin Mullins's bigger, dimmer older brother," she tells us. "He lives in this huge house with his great-aunt, and he's got a really weird, formal way of talking. He's super serious all the time too. Darcy calls him Eeyore."

Now it's our turn to laugh.

"Oh, and I forgot to tell you about Annabelle," she continues.

"Who's she?" Cassidy asks.

"Simon and Tristan's cousin. Well, distant cousin. She's a junior, like Darcy, only over here it's called Lower Sixth. She and Tristan are ice-dancing partners. I see her at the rink sometimes, but she never talks to me. I think she's mad that I'm living in their house, like it's my fault they moved away or something. Anyway, you know the type," she continues, with a quick glance at Becca. "She and her posse rule the school."

Becca and her clique used to make life miserable for Emma and Jess back in middle school. I guess I didn't help much either, since I was part of it for a while. Things are completely different now, though, and we're all friends more or less.

"By the way, Stewart says hi," Becca tells her, and Emma's face goes as red as the geraniums on the windowsill behind her. "He's pining away for you."

"Uh, tell him hi back," mumbles Emma, then looks over at me. "How about you, Megan? You seem kind of quiet today."

I shrug. "It's okay, I guess. I don't quite . . . I'm not—"

"She doesn't feel like she fits in yet at school," says Cassidy, and I make a face. It's true, though.

"I tried to get her to go out for cheerleading," adds Becca. "You've got to get involved to really feel part of things."

"Becca's right," says Jess. "I didn't feel like part of Colonial Academy until I joined the equestrian team and tried out for MadriGals. It really helps."

"So what am I supposed to do?" I ask my friends. "There's nothing that really interests me. I mean, I suppose I could start a fashion club or something."

"Right, and do what?" scoffs Cassidy. "Admire each other's shoes?"

"Cassidy!" says Emma, scolding her from three thousand miles away.

"You're kind of a one-woman fashion club already anyway," adds

Heather Vogel Frederick

Becca. "I mean, what with Bébé Soleil and everything."

"Maybe you could design costumes for the drama department," Jess suggests.

I shrug. "Maybe."

"Or how about starting a blog about fashion?" says Emma.

"I don't know," I reply doubtfully. "You're the writer, not me."

"That's the cool thing with blogs, you don't have to write if you don't want to. You could post some of your sketches, and pictures and stuff, and talk about anything you want to. Kind of like your sketch-book, only online."

"Hey, that could be fun," says Becca, warming to the idea. "You could talk about fashion trends, and what it's like to be a high school fashion designer, and stuff like that. I'll bet a ton of people would read it."

"My sister has a blog," says Cassidy, serving herself up yet another piece of pie. Honestly, if I ate as much as she does, I'd burst out of my clothes. "She had to make one for her mass communications class at UCLA. She told me how it works—they're not hard to set up." Pointing her fork at me, she narrows her eyes. "Just one thing, though, Wong. If you ever, *ever* post a picture of me on yours, you are so dead."

We all laugh, and the subject changes after that. Later, though, after they all go home, I get to thinking about the idea. Back in my room, I flip open my laptop and I find the website Cassidy told me about. She's right—setting up a blog is easy.

With a growing sense of excitement, I follow the directions and begin the design process. Mom would flip out if I put pictures of myself on there—she's way into privacy, and I know she's got a point—so I hunt around online and find the portrait that Cassandra Austen did of Jane instead. It's not very flattering, but there's another one that she did, not a portrait exactly, but a watercolor that shows Jane from the back, seated on the ground and wearing a bonnet. I decide to go with that one. It fits better anyway, since I'm thinking I should keep my blog anonymous.

Now I need a title.

I stare out the window, resting my chin in one hand and drumming the fingers of my other against the desk. I sit up. Got it! I start to type.

FASHIONISTA JANE. I smile as the words appear on the screen. Perfect. I take a deep breath and continue:

It is a truth universally acknowledged, that a single girl in possession of a passion for fashion must be in want of an audience.

This is going to be fun!

Heather Vogel Frederick

Jess

I love this time of year.

I love everything about late fall—the way the sky goes all flat and gray, the way the air smells clean and cold, the way the trees look after all the leaves have fallen, their bare branches stark as bones. I love to listen to the wind whistling through the crack in my bedroom window at night, especially after my mother and I have taken the flannel sheets and down comforters out of the old cedar chest and put them on the beds. I love trading T-shirts and shorts for sweaters and scarves, and knowing that Thanksgiving is just around the corner and after that, winter. Winter is the only quiet season at Half Moon Farm, and even then it's not all that quiet. There are still animals to feed and chores to do.

There's something a little sad about late fall, too—melancholy, Emma calls it—but I even love that feeling. Late fall makes you want to hurry home. And that's exactly what I'm going to do as soon as I finish walking Pip.

Emma made me promise that I'd help Mrs. Bergson take care of him this year while she's gone, and I've tried really hard to keep that promise. Fortunately, Mrs. Bergson lives near Colonial Academy, so it's not a big deal for me to pop over there after school two or three times a week, plus I usually try and stop by once during the weekend, too.

Holding tightly to Pip's leash, I cross the Colonial Academy campus toward Witherspoon, the dorm I was in last year. I always stop and say hi to Maggie Crandall when I walk Pip over this way. Seeing him is one of the highlights of her week, which I guess makes sense when you're a toddler. I really miss the Crandalls, but this year I moved up to Elliott, one of the high school dorms, and my new houseparents are the McKinleys.

Mrs. Crandall greets me with a hug. Maggie goes straight for Pip, who busies himself licking graham cracker crumbs off her face and sweater.

"Hi, Maggie! Got a kiss for your favorite babysitter?"

She puckers up and toddles over to give me a smooch. I love babysitting Maggie. Like Cassidy's little sister, Chloe, she's totally adorable.

"Did you hear that the observatory is going to be open this weekend for the meteor shower?" says Mrs. Crandall. She knows I love astronomy. Actually, I love just about everything to do with science, and I still can't believe I go to a school that has a real live observatory.

I nod. I've been looking forward to seeing the Leonids for weeks.

Heather Vogel Frederick

"Yeah, but my mother and I already made plans to watch it together at home."

"That sounds even better."

It will be. Especially since my little brothers won't be there. This weekend is their big Cub Scout overnight at the Museum of Science in Boston. My dad's going along as a chaperone, so I'll have my mother all to myself, which hardly ever happens. I'm really looking forward to it.

Maggie chases Pip around the quad, squealing, and I let them play for a while until they both collapse on the grass, panting. Pip is a shelter rescue dog that we got for Emma as a birthday present last year. He's a yellow Labrador, and a real beauty. He's good with little kids, too, and never seems to mind when Maggie tries to climb all over him.

After a while, though, I can tell he's had enough. I let Maggie give him one final hug, then head for my dorm. Technically, animals aren't allowed upstairs in the bedrooms, but the McKinleys are both big dog lovers, and Pip is so well behaved they pretend not to notice when I bring him over once in a while.

"Pipster!" cries Adele, bounding off her bed and coming over to greet him as we enter my room. Adele Bixby and Francesca Norris—Frankie—and I are sharing a triple this year, which is really, really fun, especially after I got stuck with Savannah Sinclair last year. She and I patched things up over the summer, but we're not exactly close friends the way I am with Frankie and Adele and my book club friends. More like a tiny step up from frenemies.

"I wish you were staying this weekend," says Adele, her blue eyes wistful. She watches from beneath her dark bangs, while I stuff the things I'll need at home in my backpack.

Last year, I spent every weekend at home instead of here at boarding school. I wasn't sure I'd like Colonial, so that was how my parents and I compromised. This year, though, it's different. Homesickness isn't an issue anymore—I'm used to boarding school now, and I really like it—so I usually spend at least part of every weekend here on campus, and often I only get home for a brief visit. It's just more convenient, what with all the activities I'm involved in. Most of the equestrian team's events are on the weekends, and MadriGals, the invitation-only choral group I belong to, usually has a practice as well. This weekend is special, though.

"Don't worry, I'll be back in time for Movie Madness," I console her.

Our houseparents are crazy about movies, especially old ones, so Elliott has a tradition on Sunday nights where each hall takes a turn making dessert, and picking a movie from Mr. McKinley's collection for everybody to watch. It's kind of like book club, only with movies. There's a big-screen TV downstairs in the basement Rec Room, and a popcorn machine just like in the theaters. We all show up in our pajamas and robes. It's a blast.

People complained at first because most of the movies are black and white, but the thing is, they're really *good* movies. Great, in fact. Mr. McKinley says classic cinema is an education in and of itself, and I'm beginning to think he's right about that. We watched *Casablanca*

Heather Vogel Frederick

and *High Noon* and *To Kill a Mockingbird*, and *Top Hat* and *All About Eve* and *Rear Window*, which was actually in color. That one scared the socks off of us.

Mr. McKinley got wind of the fact that my book club is reading *Pride and Prejudice*, so this week we're watching an old black-and-white version of it starring Laurence Olivier and Greer Garson. I definitely don't want to miss that.

The door flies open and Frankie bounces in. She does a little pirouette, sending her curly dark hair flying. She didn't make MadriGals last year like Adele and me, which was upsetting for all of us at first. But she stuck it out in regular choir, and this year she joined the dance troupe and loves it.

Savannah crowds in behind her. "Hey, you guys, look what my mom sent." She holds out a tin of cookies. "They're from this bakery in D.C. that my family really likes."

Savannah's father is a Senator in Washington. We each take one of the chocolate frosted cookies and sit down on the edge of the beds.

"No, Pip, you can't have one," I tell him, reaching into the pocket of my fleece and pulling out a dog treat instead.

"I can't believe how much he's grown," says Savannah, leaning forward to pat him. As she does so, her long chestnut hair swooshes forward like a curtain and Pip barks. "He doesn't look like a puppy anymore." She glances at my backpack. "So you're heading home this weekend?"

I nod.

"Will you be at the shelter Sunday afternoon?"

I nod again. "Absolutely." Savannah and I volunteer together once a week at the Concord Animal Shelter. That's where we found Pip.

"Good. Maybe you can help me with my biology homework afterward."

Ever since last year, I've sort of been stuck in the role of Savannah's tutor. I don't mind, really. I've been tutoring most of my friends in math and science since about first grade.

"Me too," Adele chimes in.

"Me three," adds Frankie. "I just know I'm going to flunk that stupid test on Monday."

"You'll be fine," I tell them. "Just make sure you go over your notes beforehand, okay? If Savannah and I meet you here at four o'clock, that should give us plenty of time to study before dinner and Movie Madness."

"You should be a teacher," says Adele. "You're really good at it, you know?"

I shrug and grab another cookie, then shoulder my backpack and clip Pip's leash back onto his collar. "Maybe," I reply. "Who knows?"

"I'm going to be a dancer," says Frankie. "On Broadway." She shimmies across the room, her dark eyes aglow at the thought.

Savannah snorts, and the shimmy falters. I shoot her a look and she shoots me one right back, as if to say *"What?"* Savannah can be so clueless sometimes.

"That sounds awesome, Frankie," I say.

"I'm going to be a famous actress," says Adele, striking a pose, and Savannah snorts again, only quieter this time.

"How about you, Savannah?" I ask.

She shrugs. "I'd really like to run a horse farm, but my parents want me to be a lawyer."

Savannah's on the equestrian team with me. She's an amazing rider.

I leave my friends dreaming about their futures, and head out across town to Mrs. Bergson's house. Pip lives with her. She and Emma share him, because Emma's family has a cat who hates dogs. Besides making me promise to help with Pip, Emma asked me to keep an eye on Mrs. Bergson for her, too, which I told her I'd be happy to do. Mrs. Bergson's really nice.

There's a fire going in the fireplace when Pip and I arrive, and I make a beeline for it. I'm going to have to dig my down jacket out of my closet at home, especially before the meteor shower tomorrow night. It's gotten really cold out.

"Cocoa?" Mrs. Bergson asks, and I shake my head.

"No, thanks," I reply. "I just had some cookies back at the dorm and I'm kind of chocolate-ed out."

"Mint tea, then?"

"Sure."

"So, another year underway at Colonial Academy," she says, returning a few minutes later with a tray. "Is everything going well? How's Savannah?"

"Fine," I tell her. "I don't see all that much of her, except at the stable and at MadriGals. We're in totally different classes."

"That's probably a good thing," she says and we both laugh. Mrs. Bergson understands about Savannah. "So what do you hear from Emma?"

"She and her family are taking a trip to London this week. There's some kind of school holiday over there. She said she'd tell me all about it when we talk tomorrow." Emma and I have been videoconferencing on our laptops almost every Sunday right after church. That's dinnertime in England, and she's usually home by then, even if her family goes away for the weekend. They're trying to make the most of their year there and explore as much of the country as they can.

"Give her my love and tell her I'll look forward to hearing all the news at our next book club meeting. Oh, and tell her I just dropped a letter in the mail with some pictures of Pip. She should get it in a few days."

"Okay."

"Speaking of letters, do you hear anything from your pen pal?"

"Madison?" Last year, our book club teamed up with another mother-daughter book club in Wyoming, and our mothers made us write to each other. It was a pain at first, but eventually we got used to it and the habit kind of stuck. "She just sent me her new CD last week." Madison Daniels, my pen pal, plays guitar and has her own band.

"And how is her lovely mother?" Madison's mother is a professor at the University of Wyoming.

"Fine," I tell her.

Thinking about Madison and her mother reminds me of what my roommates said about me being a teacher. I've never really considered that. I've thought about a lot of other things, because I have a lot of interests. I love to sing; I love to ride; I love math and science. I love living on a farm, and I love animals. Everybody says I should be a veterinarian or a scientist or something. It's starting to bug me that all my friends already seem to know what they want to be. Emma has wanted to be a writer since she could hold a pencil. Megan's passion is fashion, as she likes to say. And Cassidy—well, Cassidy will probably end up being the first woman to play for the Boston Bruins.

But me? I really have no idea yet.

I'm still thinking about this when I say good-bye to Mrs. Bergson, and I'm still thinking about it while I play Sorry after dinner with my family, which we do almost every Friday night when I'm home, and I'm still thinking about it when I wake up the next morning.

It's just my mother and me for breakfast, because my father's already left to take my brothers to a swim meet. Mom makes French toast, my favorite, and we hang out for a while at the table reading the newspaper, something we almost never do because when you live on a farm, there's always work to be done. Actually, my mother reads the paper; I scan the comics. It's almost as good as watching Saturday morning cartoons, but I really am a little too old for that.

"Hey, listen to this," my mother says, pointing to an ad in the calendar section. "The Rec Center is offering a cake-decorating class this winter."

"Uh-huh," I murmur, not really paying attention.

"What do you think?"

"About what?"

"The class. It starts next month." She shoves the paper across the table at me.

I flick a glance at it. "Uh, sure, go for it."

"No, silly, I mean both of us."

"Cake decorating?" I look up, surprised. Doesn't she know me better than that? "Not really my thing, Mom."

"Oh, come on, it might be fun," she coaxes. "You and I need more fun in our lives. We work too hard. Plus, it would be nice to do something together."

"We're in book club together," I remind her.

"Yes, but this is different. I'm talking about something just for you and me."

She has such a hopeful look on her face that she reminds me of Sugar and Spice, our two Shetland sheepdogs, when they patrol the kitchen scouting for snacks. I almost burst out laughing. "Okay, I guess. But don't you think it sounds kind of old-fashioned? It's like something one of Jane Austen's characters would do, you know? Like embroidery and playing the piano or all those accomplishments for young ladies they're always talking about."

"All the more reason for us to take the class. It was meant to be." And she goes to the phone right then and there and signs us up for it.

We spend the day working together in the creamery. Half Moon

Farm's goat cheese has really taken off this past year, thanks in part to the fact that it was featured on an episode of *Cooking with Clementine*. My parents can hardly keep up with the orders from stores and restaurants. They say it's a good thing, but I can tell it's a lot more work for them and I feel really guilty for being away so much when I should probably be here, helping out.

"Don't be silly," my mother says when I tell her this. "Your education is much more important. Besides, we're thinking about hiring some part-time help."

"Really?" Somehow this makes me feel even guiltier. What's the point of a family farm if the family isn't pitching in to run it?

"Absolutely. We can afford it. You still do plenty around here, Jess, and you always have. And believe it or not, the boys are helping out a lot more these days too. They're setting their own alarm clocks and getting up to help with the milking without me having to nag them."

I stop in to visit Sundance, the goat I raised a few years ago for 4-H, and Cedar, her daughter. Cedar is nine months old now, and it won't be too long before she's ready for a kid of her own.

"You're quite the young lady, aren't you?" I tell her, scratching her behind her soft ears. "You don't have to worry about what you're going to be when you grow up, do you?"

The day passes quickly, and after a flurry of activity late in the afternoon getting my dad and brothers packed up for their overnight, the house is quiet again. The Leonid meteor shower won't peak until around midnight, so my mother and I have a lot of time to kill.

"How about we have dinner in the keeping room tonight?" my mother suggests. "We can eat in front of the fire."

Half Moon Farm is really old—it's been around since the Revolutionary War—and there are fireplaces in almost every room. The keeping room is my favorite, though. It's a cozy little nook off the kitchen, and would have been used like a family room back in Colonial times or for sleeping in when the rest of the house got too cold during the winter. I build a fire in the fireplace, and put a tablecloth on the coffee table.

"Can we use the good china?" I call.

"You bet," my mother calls back.

We hardly ever use our good china. The last time I remember besides the holidays was back in seventh grade, when we hosted an *Anne of Green Gables* tea party for our book club. Along with the china, I dig out two place settings of my grandmother's silver and polish them up.

"Jane Austen would definitely approve," says my mother, when I show off the gleaming result. "It looks fit for a ball at Netherfield."

I love the way all the houses in *Pride and Prejudice* have names. Netherfield. Longbourn. Pemberley. I guess it must be a tradition in England, because even the house where Emma is staying this year has a name—Ivy Cottage. Over here, people don't do that as much. Half Moon Farm is kind of unique that way.

My mother's had beef stew simmering on the stove all day, and she made homemade rolls to go with it. Afterward, for dessert, there's apple skillet cake hot out of the oven.

"My grandmother always told me that a cast iron skillet in the kitchen is the sign of a good cook," she tells me, dishing us each up a generous slice and adding a dollop of whipped cream.

We take our plates back into the keeping room and curl up on the sofa again. The fire has burned down, so I add another log.

"Shall we pay a call on the Bennets?" my mother asks, which is her way of saying let's read some more *Pride and Prejudice.*

Megan and her mom and Gigi are listening to the audio version of the book together, and so are Cassidy and her mom. My mother and I decided we'd try reading it aloud instead. So far, it's been really fun. Of course, it helps that my mother is an actress. She's every bit as good as the lady who reads it on the audio version. I try my best when it's my turn to read, but I'm nowhere near as good as she is.

We're at the part where Elizabeth Bennet's sister Jane catches a cold and has to stay at Netherfield—part of her mother's scheme to get Mr. Bingley to fall in love with her. Things are heating up because when Elizabeth comes to check on Jane, all of a sudden Mr. Darcy, who was so rude to her at the ball, seems a little interested. This makes Caroline Bingley mad. She's Mr. Bingley's sister and a total queen bee. You can tell she wants Mr. Darcy all to herself because she keeps trying to put Elizabeth down, but she only ends up making herself look stupid because Elizabeth is much, much smarter than she is.

"Elizabeth kind of reminds me of Cassidy," I tell my mother.

"Our Cassidy?" she replies, surprised.

"Yeah, you know, she's really feisty. She says whatever's on her mind."

My mother laughs. "Well, maybe a little. But somehow I can't picture Elizabeth Bennet playing hockey."

By now it's ten o'clock, but we still have a couple of hours to go so we watch some TV. Finally, it's time to head outside. The pasture behind the barn has the best view, and I get dressed in my warmest clothes while my mother rustles up sleeping bags for both of us. We bring along pillows, too, and a big beach blanket to spread underneath us.

People assume I get my interest in math and science from my dad, but I actually get it from my mom. She's always been interested in nature. When I was little she used to check books out of the library for us so we could learn about plants and animals and clouds and stars and stuff.

Scanning the pasture with our flashlights for a spot with no goat or horse droppings, we spread out the blanket and sleeping bags. Sugar and Spice are wild with excitement at this unexpected outing. When they're finished chasing each other all around, they trot over, panting frosty puffs of air.

"Settle down now, girls," my mother tells them, and they curl up by our legs.

Lying back, I cross my arms under my head. I love looking up at the night sky. If you stare at the stars long enough, it's almost as if you leave Earth behind. Everything fades into the background, and it's only you and the darkness and the stars. On nights like this, I

Heather Vogel Frederick

almost feel like I can wrap my mind around those questions like what's beyond the edge of the universe, and what exactly is infinity?

"Mom, when did you know you wanted to be an actress?"

"I don't know," she replies. "When I was around your age, I guess. Why?"

I tell her how it seems like everybody but me already knows what they want to do with their lives.

"Sweetheart, you can hardly expect to know that at fourteen."

"Almost fifteen. And you did, you just said so."

She sighs, and we stare at the stars again for a while. Then she continues, "Well, I suppose I had an inkling at your age that I wanted to be an actress, but I didn't know if I could actually do it or not. And then once I did, I still wanted more—marriage, and a family. Life took me in a different direction for a while, and then—well, I still had some sorting out to do."

I know she's talking about the year she moved to New York, to be on a soap opera called *HeartBeats*, back when I was in sixth grade. "Larissa LaRue," I whisper. That was the name of her character.

"Yeah," she says. "Good old Larissa. Anyway, the main thing is, you have plenty of time to decide. You don't need to start worrying about it now."

"Do you miss it?"

"What?"

"Acting."

She hesitates. "Sometimes. I've been thinking maybe I'd try out for some local theater, just to keep my hand in. But for the most part, not really. I love our life here on the farm."

I roll over on my side to face her. "I still wish I knew what I wanted to be when I grow up. It's just that I like so many things, you know?"

"What do you enjoy most of all?"

I have to think about that. "MadriGals, I guess." I love to ride, and I love my science classes, but I really, really love to sing.

"Why don't you just pour your heart into that right now, and see what happens. Didn't you tell me that tryouts are coming up for some solos?"

I nod in the darkness. "There's a choral competition after the holidays."

"And Jess, just because you're focusing on something now, at this stage of your life, doesn't mean that shuts the door on doing anything you want to do in the future, anything at all."

"What, like becoming a singing veterinarian?"

This makes her giggle. "Who visits her patients on horseback," she adds.

Now we're both giggling.

"And teaches math on the side," I finish. Our giggles turn to belly laughs, and even though it's not that funny, because it's late and we're tired, pretty soon we're howling. The dogs get excited and run around barking, and we have to settle them down all over again.

Overhead, the shooting stars are falling thick and fast now, and I

Heather Vogel Frederick

get tears in my eyes, but whether it's because it's cold out or because the meteor shower is so beautiful or because I'm just happy to be here with my mother, I'm not sure.

My mother starts to sing softly. *"When you wish upon a star . . ."*

I join in too. *"Makes no difference who you are . . ."*

We sing the next bit together: *"Anything your heart desires will come to you."*

I don't know the rest of the song, but my mother does, and I listen to her sing it, joining in again for the final refrain: *"When you wish upon a star, your dreams come true."*

We're quiet for a while after that, just watching the sky.

"Mom, can I ask you something else?" I say finally.

"Sure, honey."

"How do you know when somebody likes you?"

"You mean a boy?"

"Yeah."

"Anybody in particular?"

"Um . . ." I almost tell her about Darcy Hawthorne, but I'm still kind of keeping that to myself. A few people know—Emma, of course, and Savannah found out too, which makes me a little uncomfortable.

"It wouldn't be Darcy Hawthorne, would it?"

My mouth drops open. "How did you know?"

"Jess, I'm your mother! Besides, you do kind of start glowing when he's around."

I heave a sigh. "I just wish I knew whether he liked me or not. I've liked him for such a long time. Sometimes I think maybe he does, but he never says anything, you know?"

My mother reaches over and squeezes my hand. "I know, honey. This is a tough one, and I don't really have any answers for you. You're just going to have to wait and see."

"I feel like I'm stuck in a Jane Austen novel," I grumble. "You know, like one of those girls in long dresses who have to sit around waiting for a guy to ask them to marry them—not that I'm expecting Darcy to do that."

My mother laughs. "No, I don't suppose your Mr. Darcy will be doing that anytime soon. But I understand what you mean. You don't feel like you can be the one to say something first."

"Exactly! And it's so stupid! Here it is nearly two hundred years after *Pride and Prejudice* was written, and I'm in stuck in that same mold. I'm still waiting for Darcy—my Darcy, not Elizabeth Bennet's Darcy—to notice me."

"Oh, I have no doubt he notices you," says my mother, squeezing my hand again. "How could he not notice a beautiful creature like you?"

"You're my mother," I protest. "You have to say that."

"No, I don't."

"Yes, you do."

We start to laugh again.

"Maybe it's good for Darcy to be so far away," my mother says. "They say absence makes the heart grow fonder, you know?"

"Maybe," I reply, and we stop talking then and watch the stars.

Heather Vogel Frederick

The next day, my father and brothers arrive home after church, and the boys give us a blow-by-blow account of their night at the museum.

"Our den got to sleep in the dinosaur exhibit!" crows Dylan.

"It was awesome," Ryan adds.

"I'll bet," I tell them, envying them their uncomplicated lives. My brothers are only in fourth grade. They haven't started worrying about girls yet, or their future careers.

After lunch, I excuse myself and go upstairs to my room. One of the great things about Colonial Academy, besides the fact that they have MadriGals and horses and an observatory, is that every student, even the ones on scholarship like me, gets a laptop. I guess some wealthy alumna set up a fund for it, which was really nice.

I flip my computer open to find Emma online already and waiting for me.

"I am so glad that we can do this," I tell her when her video feed flashes onto my screen. "It's not the same as having you here in Concord—"

"—but it's pretty close," says Emma, finishing my sentence. "I know, I'm glad too."

"So how was London?"

"Amazing. Beyond amazing. Incredible. I want to live there some-day." She launches into an enthusiastic account of everything that they saw and did, from the B&B they stayed at in Notting Hill to their visits to places like the Tower of London and Kensington Palace and

Westminster Cathedral. "My dad posted a bunch of pictures on his blog."

"I'll check them out. How's everything going otherwise?"

Emma shrugs. "Okay, I guess. I wish you were here to help me with maths, though. Math, I mean."

"Anything new with Rupert?" I'm as fascinated with her nitwit of a neighbor as she was last year with Savannah Sinclair.

"Roooooo-pert!" she moos, and we both laugh. "Have you gotten to the part in *Pride and Prejudice* yet about Mr. Collins?"

I shake my head.

"Well, when you do, you're going to love him. I don't want to spoil it for you, but he's hilarious—really pompous and dull. My mother says he's a booby. Anyway, Rupert Loomis could be his little brother. You'll see what I mean."

"Sounds fun," I tell her.

Emma leans closer to the webcam, looks over her shoulder, and drops her voice. "Guess what? I think he likes me."

"Who likes you?"

"Rupert."

"WHAT?!"

Emma nods. "I know, isn't it horrible? It's way worse than Kevin Mullins's crush on you. I swear, every time I turn a corner at school, there he is. And he's always making excuses to come over here and check on Toby. I taught him—the parrot, not Rupert—to say '*ROOOPERT*' whenever he sees him."

"Emma, you are *bad*!"

Heather Vogel Frederick

She grins. "I know. But I've got to cheer myself up somehow. It's not fun having a wet blanket like Rupert Loomis mooning over me, you know?"

"Tell me about it. Kevin Mullins still won't take a hint. So what does Stewart think about your new crush?"

"Jess! He's not my crush!"

Now it's my turn to grin.

Emma shrugs. "I haven't said anything. There's no point."

We talk for a while about what's going on in her village—they just celebrated something called Guy Fawkes Night last week, which she tells me was when some plot to blow up parliament a zillion years ago was foiled.

"It was fun. There were fireworks, and we baked potatoes in a big bonfire, which was kind of weird but I guess it's traditional."

"Cool."

"So how's everybody over there doing?" Emma asks.

"Pretty good, I guess. Cassidy's hardly ever around because of hockey. You've read Megan's blog, right?"

Emma nods. "Isn't it hilarious? I especially love the Fashion Faux Pas."

Megan's been posting pictures online of random people, mostly at school, whose outfits she doesn't like, and having Fashionista Jane make snarky comments about them.

"She's getting really good at Austen-speak," Emma continues.

"I know!"

Emma coined that expression. It's what she calls the way Fashionista Jane talks, and the way we all do too, sometimes, when we're imitating *Pride and Prejudice*.

"I loved the picture of the guy in the suit wearing flip-flops," she says. "Sir Flops-a-lot?"

I laugh. "Yeah, that's the one. Cassidy says he's one of the teachers."

"I'm surprised she hasn't gotten into trouble."

"I don't think anybody but us knows who's writing it."

"Emma!" Mrs. Hawthorne's voice floats up the stairs.

"That's my mother. It's probably time for me to set the table or something."

"Go see, then come back and tell me. I still need to tell you something about MadriGals."

Emma leaves the room, and I turn away from my laptop to start getting packed up again for school. I don't want to be late for Movie Madness.

"Hey, Jess," says a familiar voice. My heart skips a beat. I look up to see Darcy smiling and waving at me on my laptop screen. I wave back, hoping that my hair doesn't look too dorky. I can't remember if I brushed it today or not.

"How's life?" he asks.

"Uh, okay."

"What are you up to these days?"

We talk for a while, and I tell him about the meteor shower, and about my brothers' trip to the Science Museum.

Heather Vogel Frederick

"I remember going there when I was a Cub Scout!" he says. "I'll bet they had a blast."

Darcy tells me about playing rugby, and some more about their trip to London, and I'm just starting to tell him about Movie Madness when he glances over at the door.

"I think I hear Emma," he says. "I'll say good-bye, I guess. Maybe we can talk again sometime."

"Sure," I reply, trying to sound casual. He leaves the room and a huge smile breaks out on my face. I sit there feeling stunned and happy. Was our conversation an accident, or did he plan it? Is it possible he likes me after all?

I think about the other Darcy, the Jane Austen one. He and Emma's brother couldn't be more different. Jane Austen's Darcy is always saying the wrong thing, always insulting Elizabeth Bennet and her family. He's a snob. My Darcy is the nicest guy in the world.

I'll take my Darcy over Mr. Darcy any day of the week.

But why, oh, why does he have to be three thousand miles away? Three thousand, three hundred and twenty-five miles, to be exact. Five thousand, three hundred and twenty kilometers. Metric or U.S., the measurement doesn't matter. Darcy Hawthorne might as well be in another galaxy with the Leonids.

WINTER

"*Young ladies of her age are sometimes a little difficult to manage. . . .*"

—*Pride and Prejudice*

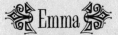 Emma

> *"Mr. Collins was not a sensible man, and the deficiency of Nature had been but little assisted by education or society."*
> —Pride and Prejudice

"Emma! Lucy and Rupert are here!"

"Be down in a minute, Mom!" I holler back.

I grab my backpack—regulation navy, of course, to match the regulation navy everything else of my Knightley-Martin School uniform—and sling it over my shoulder. I don't even bother looking at myself in the mirror. What's the point?

Clattering down the steep, narrow stairs, I'm careful not to bump my head on the low beam over the doorway at the bottom. People must have been midgets back in the 1600s, because I'm not all that tall and even I have to watch my head in a few places here at Ivy Cottage. Darcy's taken the brunt of it. His forehead was black and blue for about a month when we first moved in. But he's adjusted. We all have.

I poke my head into my dad's study to say good-bye. He's squinting at his laptop, absorbed, but waggles his fingers at me as I blow him a kiss.

My mother is sitting at the kitchen table with tea and toast and the morning paper. "Did you remember to feed Toby?" she asks.

"Oops."

"Allow me to be of assistance," says Rupert Loomis, startling me as he springs out of the alcove by the back door where he and my friend Lucy are waiting.

I protest, but it's too late. Toby spots him lumbering across the kitchen and flaps his wings. "MOOO," he squawks. "ROOOPERT!"

My mother shoots me a look.

Rupert, clueless as always, looks pleased. "He recognizes me! Good old Toby."

"MOOO," squawks Toby again.

"Don't forget I'm picking you up after school today," my mother tells me.

"I won't." I grab a piece of toast and lean down to kiss her good-bye.

"I cannot believe you taught that parrot to say that!" she whispers in my ear. "What were you thinking?"

I glance over at Rupert, who has finished feeding Toby and returned to his spot by the back door. The alcove ceiling is especially low, and he's standing there stiffly with his head tilted awkwardly to one side, scratching himself. I look back at my mother and grin. She shakes her head wearily and makes a shooing motion at me with her hand.

It's just me and Rupert and Lucy at the bus stop this morning. Darcy caught the early bus into town, because he's got rugby practice before school. It only took about two seconds after we arrived for him to get snapped up by the team. I guess jocks have special radar for detecting other jocks or something. And even though he's never played rugby before, he's brilliant at it, of course. My brother's a natural at every sport he's ever tried. Which is really annoying when you're not.

I'm not a natural at anything except reading books and writing. A couple of years ago, though, I decided not to let that stop me, and I started taking skating lessons with Mrs. Bergson. Once we determined that I probably wasn't future Olympics material—which took all of about thirty seconds—we just focused on working hard and having fun. And I do. I haven't been able to skate as much as I would have liked since we moved to Bath, because the rink is way on the other side of the city. Getting there means I have to change buses twice, so I've only been going once a week or so.

I'm still getting plenty of exercise, though, because we walk everywhere. Before it started getting dark so early—they don't have daylight savings over here, and this time of year it's dark out when we go to school and dark out when we come home—Lucy and Darcy and Rupert and some of the other village kids and I walked to school along the towpath by the canal. It's a long walk, but a really pretty one.

Mom calls Lucy Woodhouse an "English rose" because she's really fair-skinned, with rosy cheeks and a halo of strawberry blond curls. She lives across the street from Ivy Cottage in another super old house. Hers is a style called "half-timbered," with dark beams embedded in its whitewashed walls. It has a thatched roof too, and is even older than the Berkeleys' house.

I met Lucy the first day we got here. I guess Mrs. Berkeley told her about me, because she was on our doorstep before we were even unpacked. Lucy's an only child, like Megan. There are other kids in the village, but no girls her age. It turns out our birthdays are exactly two days apart. She was really excited to meet me, and it was great to have a ready-made friend. I think school might have felt a bit overwhelming without Lucy to help me navigate everything.

"I can't wait for Christmas, can you?" she says as we head to the bus stop.

"Nope," I agree.

Christmas is my favorite holiday. I'm a little sad we won't be spending it at home in Concord this year, but my parents are trying really hard to make it special for us anyway. We might even go back to London for New Year's.

"I trust you both received invitations to my great-aunt's holiday fete," says Rupert in his deep, formal voice. It's like he's practicing to be a radio announcer or something. "It's sure to be a festive event."

"Yes, Rupert," says Lucy, smiling at him. She's incredibly patient with Rupert. In fact, if his odd mannerisms didn't completely rule out the possibility, I'd say she actually liked him. "Ours came yesterday. I'm sure it will be a brilliant party, as always."

Rupert smirks. Or maybe it's just his normal smile. It's hard to tell.

Apparently his great-aunt's Christmas party is an annual tradition in the village. She has this huge old house—I mean like something-out-of-a-movie huge, open to the public for tours and everything—

Heather Vogel Frederick

and Lucy told me that it's always decorated to the hilt for the party, with live music and really good food. Our invitation came yesterday, in a thick cream-colored envelope.

"Fancy," my mother said, fingering the card inside with its printed border of holly leaves and berries. She propped it on the mantel. "It's not often you get an actual engraved invitation."

"We got ours, too," I assure Rupert, and one of his long arms suddenly shoots out toward me in an awkward high five.

"Uh, yeah," I say, reluctantly high-fiving him back. His palm is clammy and I edge away, relieved to see the bus approaching.

"Greetings!" Rupert booms to the driver as the door opens, and I cringe in embarrassment. Embarrassed is how I generally feel around Rupert. I try not to let Lucy see, though. She's kind of protective toward him. She probably feels a little sorry for him, being an orphan and everything. I guess anybody who was raised by his great-aunt would be a little south of normal, as my dad puts it.

My dad totally gets how I feel about Rupert. Maybe it's because he's a writer too. I'm always looking at people and thinking about how I could describe them, and I think he does the same thing. He calls Rupert Ichabod, after Ichabod Crane, the gangly schoolteacher in "The Legend of Sleepy Hollow." " 'With feet that might have served for shovels,' " he quoted to me under his breath the first time he met Rupert, who has enormous feet he's always tripping over. He has enormous ears, too, just like Ichabod.

My mother gets mad at us for talking about him behind his back.

"The boy just hasn't grown into himself yet," she protests, which is mom-code for "He's a total dork."

"Do you know yet what you're going to wear to the party?" Lucy asks me, after we take our seats. The two of us always sit upstairs on the bus. I still get a thrill out of riding a double-decker bus to school. Sometimes, living over here, it feels like I've fallen into a storybook or something.

"My mother's going to take me shopping this afternoon on Milsom Street."

My mother is in heaven, living near Bath. I guess Jane Austen used to shop on Milsom Street when she lived here two hundred years ago.

"Oh, there are some fabulous shops on Milsom!" says Lucy. "They're quite expensive, though. You might try that new mall down by the train station if you don't find anything."

Even though it doesn't have skyscrapers like Boston, Bath is still a full-fledged city, but it doesn't seem like the kind of place that would have a mall. It does, though. Of course, it's nothing like any mall I've ever seen before. For one thing, it's built out of the same honey-colored limestone as the rest of the city, and for another, it looks like it's ancient already, even though it's brand-new. The builders had to design it to match the existing historic architecture. My mom says they would have wrecked the looks of the city if they hadn't. Bath is something called a World Heritage Site, which is kind of like a National Park, only for cities and stuff too.

"Did you finish your maths assignment?" Lucy asks, and I nod.

Heather Vogel Frederick

It's funny, both countries speak the same language, but there are so many words that are different. Math is "maths," an elevator is a "lift," a truck is a "lorry," a flashlight is a "torch," and "crisps" are what they call potato chips, while "chips" over here means French fries.

Just as riding the double-decker buses thrills me, I get a thrill out of hearing people talk. I love the differences in the language, and I adore the British accents. And I love how beautiful the countryside is too. Concord is beautiful, but not in the same way that England is. England is so green, and there are sheep in practically every field you see. Plus, just about everybody has a garden, and there are villages scattered all over that look like maybe Hobbits live in them. Or Shakespeare.

What I don't get a thrill out of in England is Annabelle Fairfax.

Because as it turns out, they have queen bees in England, too.

As usual, Annabelle is already there when we get off the bus. She's by the front door of the school with her posse, waiting to pounce on her hapless prey, which could be just about anybody who strikes her fancy.

I've managed to stay on her good side so far this fall, mostly because I'm living at Ivy Cottage. Maybe she's hoping I'll invite her over so she can admire Tristan's trophies or something. She's always going on about what a great skater he is, and how handsome he is. I think she has a crush on him. Which is kind of creepy, considering he's her cousin and everything. Darcy just rolled his eyes when I mentioned this to him, though.

"Distant cousins, Emma," he reminded me.

At any rate, Annabelle and Tristan have been figure skating together since they were practically babies. I've seen her practicing at the rink a few times with their coach, and she's good. Really good. The problem is, she knows it. She swans around Knightley-Martin like she's minor royalty or something.

Even though she's been fairly neutral toward me so far, I smelled a rat the minute I met her. I've spent the last few years dealing with the likes of Becca Chadwick and Savannah Sinclair, plus I've also met some of the great queen bees of literature, as my mother and I call them, through my book club. Jenny Snow from *Little Women*. Josie Pye from *Anne of Green Gables*. Last year it was Julia Pendleton in *Daddy-Long-Legs*, and this year it's Caroline Bingley in *Pride and Prejudice*. I had Annabelle Fairfax's number before she even opened her mouth.

This morning she and her wannabees have one of the girls from my class cornered, and are twitting her about her *hijab*. Khalida is Pakistani, and like a lot of the other Muslim girls at Knightley-Martin, she wears a head scarf. It's part of their religion. At our school they're navy blue, of course.

I don't know Khalida all that well—she's in a couple of my classes, but she's quiet and reserved and we've only talked a couple of times. Seeing the miserable look on her face, though, I feel a hot spike of anger. I've been on the receiving end of Annabelle's brand of withering scorn too many times in the past few years, and I know exactly how she feels.

I hesitate, wishing Cassidy were here. She'd know exactly what to do. Taking a deep breath, and hoping that maybe I sound just a little

Heather Vogel Frederick

bit like her, I go over to Khalida and put my arm around her shoulders. "Put a sock in it, Annabelle."

Annabelle stares at me, shocked. "What did you say?"

"You heard me."

Lucy is looking at me like I've lost my mind, and Rupert has faded into the shrubbery. They're no more eager than I usually am to attract Annabelle's attention.

Annabelle glances over at her friends. "I guess that's American slang for 'I'm a twit.'"

Her friends laugh obligingly. I ignore them.

A crowd is gathering. Nobody but nobody at Knightley-Martin goes up against Annabelle Fairfax. I'm not sure where the words are coming from, but somehow they're welling up inside me and spilling from my lips. "You have no business picking on Khalida! And if you don't quit it, I'm going to tell one of the teachers."

She smirks at me. "Really? Go ahead. Miss Deane is right behind you."

"What's going on here, girls?"

I turn around to see the music teacher emerging from the door to the school. She's young and pretty and soft-spoken, and putty in the hands of someone like Annabelle Fairfax.

"Nothing, miss," chirps Annabelle, the picture of innocence. "We were just complimenting Khalida on her, uh, sense of style. Isn't that right, Khalida?"

With a quick, apologetic glance toward me, Khalida nods.

Miss Deane looks at us uncertainly.

"Well, you should be getting along to class, then. It's almost time for first period to start."

"Yes, miss," Annabelle replies meekly. She shoots me a *You were saying?* look.

Miss Deane heads back inside.

"Come on, Tink," says one of Annabelle's friends. "Tink" is short for "Tinkerbell," which is what they call Annabelle. They all have these stupid little nicknames for one another. Jemima Duff is "Puff," Sophie Miles is "Smiles," and Victoria Wesley is "Buttercup," for some unknown reason. Of course, nobody else is allowed to use these names. A new girl tried just last week and found herself locked in a stall in the boys' room as punishment.

Annabelle looks pointedly at Lucy, who is shaped like a straw, and Rupert, who is still trying to pretend he's a shrub. "Fly away then, Dorothy. And take your scarecrow and cowardly lion with you. Just remember, though, you're not in Kansas anymore."

And with that final parting blow, Annabelle prepares to flounce off in triumph. Except I don't let her.

"You must have forgotten what happened to the wicked witch at the end of that particular story," I retort. "You'd better watch your back. Plus, I'd rather be friends with Lucy and Rupert any day of the week than be stuck following you around, *Stinkerbelle*."

There's an audible gasp from the students around us, followed by a ripple of laughter. It's quickly stifled as Annabelle whips around. She opens her mouth, then snaps it shut again and turns haughtily to mount the steps behind us. Her friends quickly follow.

Heather Vogel Frederick

"You are dead," says Lucy faintly as Annabelle's rigid back retreats through the school's front doors. "Completely and utterly dead."

"Yeah, I know," I reply, rubbing my sweaty palms against my skirt. My heart is pounding like crazy. I'm still not sure where I got the courage to do what I just did. One glance at the relief on Khalida's face, though, tells me it was worth it.

"Thank you, Emma," she says softly. "I'm so sorry I . . . I—"

"Don't worry about it," I tell her. "I know the feeling, believe me."

Rupert emerges from his hiding place in the bushes, wearing a worshipful expression. My heart sinks. This is not a good sign.

"I can't believe how brave you were!" says Lucy, linking her arm through mine as the three of us head inside. "Wasn't she amazing, Rupert?"

"A veritable knight in shining armor," he agrees, stumbling over the doorsill.

Fabulous. I'm Rupert Loomis's hero.

I manage to make it safely to the end of the day without running into Annabelle Fairfax again. My mother is waiting for me when school lets out, and I get into the car with a sigh of relief. The Christmas holidays stretch out ahead like a nice big buffer zone between me and Stinkerbelle. I won't be seeing her for nearly three whole weeks.

My mother maneuvers nimbly through the city's clogged streets— she and my dad are getting really good at driving on the left—and manages to snag us a parking spot not too far from Milsom Street. We poke around in the boutiques for a while, but Lucy's right, everything's really expensive. Eventually we give up and head for the mall, where I quickly find just the thing for a holiday ball.

"I wish Stewart could see this," I say to the mirror in the dressing room. "It's too good to waste on stupid old Rupert Loomis and his great-aunt."

"What's that?" my mother calls through the door.

"Nothing, Mom. It's perfect."

It takes us a while longer to find just the right dress for her, but she finally settles on a dramatic dark burgundy velvet gown with long sleeves and a deep V-neck. My mother has similar coloring to mine— brown eyes and hair, only hers is straight and mine is curly, like Dad's and Darcy's. The fabric's color looks gorgeous on her.

"I don't think I've worn a long dress since my prom," she says. "Well, except for my wedding. But the invitation said black tie, so formal it is."

Back at the car, she slides in behind the wheel and turns to me. "I thought we'd stop and get some Bath buns for book club tomorrow."

"Sally Lunn's?"

"You bet."

Sally Lunn's is the oldest bakery in Bath, and it's located in one of the oldest houses in the city too. My mother manages to squeeze into a parking spot on the cobblestone street outside the narrow little four-story building.

"Hard to believe this shop has been around for over three hundred years," she says, sniffing the air appreciatively as we step inside.

"Just as long as their stuff isn't that old," I joke, eyeing the wares in the glass case.

"Not a chance, luv," says the round-faced woman behind the counter, laughing. "Everything's gobbled up too quick around here to get stale."

She boxes up our order, and my mother adds a container of their homemade cinnamon butter as well. I'm practically drooling by the time we get back in the car. Sally Lunn's is the best.

We make one final stop on the way home, for some takeaway fish and chips. Takeaway is what they call takeout here in England, and this has become our regular Friday night treat, the way pizza was back in Concord. They have pizza here too, of course, but we've gotten kind of addicted to fish and chips.

Dad and Darcy have the kitchen table set by the time we get home, and my mother and I distribute the food onto the plates.

"Mmmm," says my father, dousing everything with malt vinegar and digging in. "I just don't understand why this tastes so much better over here."

He's right. I've had fish and chips plenty of times before back home, but over here it's different. The batter on the fish is perfectly crispy, and inside, the fish is moist and hot. And the chips—French fries—are huge and delicious.

"Anything in here for us?" asks Darcy, snooping in the box from Sally Lunn's. My mother swats him away.

"Book club treats," she tells him, and he makes a face.

"You guys always hog the good stuff," he complains.

"It's for Jane's birthday," I explain.

Darcy looks mystified. "Jane who? Is there a new girl in your club?"

My mother and I both laugh.

"Duh," I tell him. "Jane *Austen*, of course."

"But these," says my father, whipping a tray of small mincemeat hand pies out of the pantry cupboard, "are not for Jane. They're for us."

"All right, Dad!" crows Darcy, grabbing one.

"I thought we'd put the tree up tonight," my father continues. "It's beginning to feel a lot like Christmas around here."

My father always makes mincemeat hand pies on the night we decorate our tree.

While my mother and I build a fire in the living room fireplace, he and Darcy bring in the Christmas tree and wrestle it into the stand. All of our decorations are at home, of course, so my parents' plan is to decorate it with Christmas cards instead. And, as we soon discover, homemade paper chains.

"Craft time!" announces my mother, passing out scissors and tape and construction paper.

"You're kidding, right?" says Darcy.

She shakes her head and grins. "Where's your holiday spirit?"

He sighs and picks up his scissors, but he's smiling and so am I. It's like being a kid again. The temperature has dropped outside, and the latticed windowpanes are rimed with frost. Mom puts some Christmas music on, and the four of us hum along to "Silver Bells" and "O Tannenbaum" and "Let It Snow" while we work on our paper chains. My father gets up after a while and wanders into his study, returning with a book in his hand.

"Look what I found," he says, holding up *The Wind in the Willows*. "Remember 'Dulce Domum'? That used to be your favorite chapter this time of year, Emma."

He settles into one of the armchairs by the fire and starts to read aloud: " '*The sheep ran huddling together against the hurdles . . .*' " I feel a shiver of delight as the story's familiar words wash over me.

There's something magical about being here in England, in this snug room, on this chilly winter night. It's like being inside a fairy tale, or Mole End itself. I practically expect to hear Kenneth Grahame's young field-mice caroling on our doorstep.

The following evening my mother and I bustle around getting ready for our videoconference. We hang a big sign that says, "Happy Birthday, Jane!" on the wall, and I set my mini-laptop on a table in front of our newly decorated Christmas tree so our friends can admire our handiwork.

It's December sixteenth—Jane Austen's birthday. And, as luck would have it, the only weekend afternoon in the entire month that Cassidy doesn't have a hockey game.

My father's holed up in his study again—he received the proofs of his novel, and has to do some final copyediting—and Darcy is off at a rugby match, which is going to disappoint Jess.

The appointed time finally rolls around, and the video call comes through and suddenly there they all are in Megan's living room.

"Hey, you guys!" I call to my friends.

"Hey, Emma! Hey, Mrs. Hawthorne!" they call back, waving.

My mother suggests that we sing "Happy Birthday" to Jane Austen to kick off our meeting, which is totally lame but we do it anyway.

"Let's start with Fun Facts this month," she continues, and onscreen I see Mrs. Wong scurry to distribute the handouts.

FUN FACTS ABOUT JANE

1) *Pride and Prejudice* was originally titled *First Impressions*. Jane Austen wrote an early draft of it, along with two other of her novels, before she was twenty-five. She once referred to the manuscript as "my own darling child."

2) The book was published in 1813 and met with instant success. It has been beloved by readers now for nearly two hundred years, and has been made into countless stage, audio, and film versions.

3) During most of her lifetime, Jane Austen's books were published anonymously, with "By a Lady" on the title page. Her identity as an author came to light only after the publication of *Mansfield Park* in 1814, when her brother Henry began proudly dropping hints in public.

Heather Vogel Frederick

4) Jane loved the character of Elizabeth Bennet. She wrote in a letter to Cassandra: "I must confess that I think her as delightful a creature as ever appeared in print, and how I shall be able to tolerate those who do not like her at least, I do not know."

5) Elizabeth Bennet and Mr. Darcy rank as one of literature's greatest romantic couples.

"What are your favorite things about the book so far?" asks my mother.

"Mr. Collins," Jess replies instantly. "He's a nitwit."

"Mooo," I whisper to her, but my mother still manages to hear me. She pokes me in the ribs.

"Wait until you meet Lady Catherine," says Mrs. Bergson. "She's an even bigger nitwit."

"I love the way no matter how many times I read the book, I'm always worried about how it's going to turn out," I admit. "I know it's ridiculous, but it happens every single time. Jane Austen's characters are just so real."

Mrs. Delaney nods. "She always hooks me, too. I suppose that's the sign of a good author."

"I'm starving," says Cassidy. "Can we eat first, then talk?"

"You're always starving," Becca tells her.

Cassidy flexes her arm. "Gotta keep my strength up."

My mother smiles at the webcam. "Shall we put our collective kettles on?"

We've planned a birthday tea in honor of Jane today, and as I place the box from Sally Lunn's on the table, I look to see what's being served at the Wongs. There are several plates of treats, including Mrs. Delaney's banana bread, and cupcakes and cookies as well.

"What are those things?" asks Cassidy, squinting at me onscreen.

"They're called Bath buns."

"Sounds like something you'd use in the shower," she replies.

"You can if you want, but I'd rather eat them," I tell her. "They're really good. They're a little sweet, but not sugary, and they're perfect with clotted cream."

"Ewwww," says Cassidy.

"I know, it sounds gross, but it's actually delicious." My mother returns with the teapot and I demonstrate, slicing a bun in half and spreading the clotted cream on it. "It's sort of halfway between butter and whipped cream." I spoon up some strawberry jam and plop it on top, then take a bite. "It's amazing."

"My mouth is watering just watching you," says Mrs. Chadwick, reaching for a cupcake.

"I know!" agrees Mrs. Sloane-Kinkaid. "I think I need to do an episode about a traditional British cream tea."

We start talking about *Pride and Prejudice* again.

"So why do you think Jane originally called it *First Impressions*?" my mother asks.

Heather Vogel Frederick

"Because in the story, everybody's first impressions are wrong," says Megan. "They make up their minds too quickly about each other."

"They judge a book by its cover," adds Becca.

"Exactly," says my mother, giving me a significant look and mouthing the word *Rupert*.

"What's that big card on your mantel?" asks Jess. "The one with the holly on it."

"Oh, we're invited to a Christmas party next weekend," I tell her. "It's kind of a big deal—they call it a fancy dress party, and we have to wear formal clothes and everything. It's at Rupert Loomis's great-aunt's house."

"Roooooopert!" my friends all moo on cue.

"Girls!" all the mothers chide right back.

I grin. It's almost as good as being there with them in real life.

The following week speeds by in a flurry of Christmas shopping and holiday preparations. Before I know it, it's Saturday again and time to get ready for the party.

"Hurry up, Darcy!" I call through the bathroom door, hopping from one foot to the other. The only problem with Ivy Cottage is that it has just one bathroom.

He flings the door open and strikes a pose. "How do I look?"

"Not bad," I tell him. "Now get out of my way."

In fact, Darcy looks great, but there's no way I'm going to tell him that. He has a big enough head as it is. My father looks great too, I notice a few minutes later when we all gather downstairs. Very distinguished. I don't think I've ever seen him in a tuxedo.

"Aren't you two just visions of loveliness," he says to my mother and me.

The burgundy dress really is perfect on my mother, and for once I don't think I look half bad myself. My dress is a shimmery sort of violet fabric, not exactly something you think of for Christmas, but it's gorgeous, and it matches my glasses. Plus I wanted to pick out something that I could wear again. Like maybe at senior prom next year, with Stewart Chadwick. If he invites me.

I've been growing my hair out—Mrs. Crandall, Jess's housemother last year, has curly hair like mine, and she wears hers shoulder length, which gave me the idea. Mine's not quite that long yet, but it's getting there, and I think it looks pretty good.

Loomis Hall is amazing. We get out of the car and stand there in the gravel driveway, gaping up at it. It's like something out of a Masterpiece Theatre program.

"Netherfield," my mother says to me.

"Or Rosings," I counter. "There's even a Lady Catherine in residence."

"What are you two babbling about?" says Darcy, annoyed.

"A little *P&P* humor," my mother tells him, and he snorts.

We enter through huge double doors into a vast foyer, complete with a footman in a white wig.

"Please tell me he's just an actor hired for the party, and doesn't work here all the time," I hear my father whisper to my mother, and she giggles.

Beyond the foyer is the grand hall. Really grand—I'll bet three Ivy

Heather Vogel Frederick

Cottages would fit inside. There's a gigantic Christmas tree in the center of the room, and a row of other, smaller trees lined up against the windows on the far wall.

"Robin Hood just called," my brother says dryly. "He wants Sherwood Forest back."

Enormous stone fireplaces blaze at either end of the room. A jazz quartet is playing in front of one of them, and footmen are setting out platters of food on the long tables that flank the other. We head toward the food.

"Behold ye olde Yule log," says my father in a fake English accent, gesturing at the blazing hearth with his punch cup.

My mother bumps him with her hip, sloshing his punch. "Hush, Nicholas," she scolds, but her eyes are twinkling.

He grins at us.

Rupert suddenly materializes. "Greetings," he says in his deep Eeyore voice. He actually gives a sort of stiff half-bow to my parents, sending his thick black bangs flying forward. My parents greet him politely in return. I can tell by the look on my dad's face that he's amused, and he's probably absorbing every detail so we can compare notes later. Preferably out of earshot of my mother.

"May I introduce my great-aunt, Miss Olivia Loomis." Rupert gestures toward an elderly lady in a dark blue evening gown sweeping toward us.

Rupert's great-aunt isn't as old as Mrs. Bergson or Gigi, but she could probably play the part of Lady Catherine de Bourgh any day of the week. Her silvery blond hair is swept up in an elegant style, giving her a regal air, and she holds out a thin, blue-veined hand covered with huge rings—diamonds and sapphires, mostly—to my parents.

"Delighted to make your acquaintance," says my father, shaking her hand. "I'm Nicholas Hawthorne, and this is my wife, Phoebe, and our children, Darcy and Emma."

A faint smile appears on Miss Loomis's lips. "Ah, yes, Darcy and Emma." She glances at my father. "You and your wife are Austen fans, I presume."

He nods toward my mother. "It's all Phoebe's doing," he says. "I can't take any credit."

"Perhaps Rupert has told you that we are distant relations of Miss Austen's."

My mother looks surprised. "Why, no, he hasn't."

"Yes, and I credit her with my father's interest in books. He was a publisher for many years—no doubt you've heard of Loomis & Sons. Although Loomis & Daughter would have been more accurate, as my brother had no interest in the family business and I was the one who stepped in. It's still a thriving concern. I sold it years ago after I retired, but they kept the name."

She turns and gives me a cool, appraising look. "So you are Emma," she says finally. "I've heard a great deal about you from my grand-nephew."

Rupert talks about me to his great-aunt? *Uh-oh*, I think. That can't be good. I smile weakly. I don't really know what to say.

My father does, thank heavens. "May I offer you some punch?"

Heather Vogel Frederick

He and my mother and Miss Loomis drift away, talking about Jane Austen and books and publishing. My brother sees some friends from school and crosses over to join them, leaving me stranded there with Rupert. He tugs on his giant earlobe, fishing around for something to say.

Please don't ask me to dance, I think.

"Would you care to dance?" he booms, giving a strange little leap.

Lucy appears just then, and I clutch her arm like a drowning person clutches a life preserver. "Let's go look at the decorations," I suggest, hustling her away from the buffet, and Rupert. "Maybe later, Rupert!"

But things only get worse. As we cross the room, I spot Annabelle Fairfax in the foyer.

"Oh, no," I groan. I drag Lucy behind the Christmas tree. "What's she doing here?"

"Her family always gets invited. They usually come with Tristan and Simon."

"Why didn't you tell me?"

Lucy's forehead puckers. "Didn't I? So sorry. You needn't worry, though, Emma, she never pays me any attention. She'll be too busy trying to impress the boys."

This looks to be true, because I see her make a beeline for my brother and his friends. Still, I edge my way around the Christmas tree, trying to keep it between the two of us. If I'm lucky, maybe I can manage to steer clear of her all evening. Unfortunately, I steer myself right into Rupert again.

He pounces. "Are you ready for that dance now?"

"Uh, I'm a really terrible dancer, Rupert," I tell him, which is true. I grab Lucy by the elbow and pull her forward. "I'll bet Lucy will dance with you, though."

She smiles at him, and he reluctantly offers her his arm. I swear, he acts like he's ninety. I stand there by the tree, keeping a wary eye on Annabelle as I watch the two of them waltz awkwardly around the far end of the room.

"I'd love a tour of the house," I say when Lucy and Rupert return, hoping to fend off another invitation.

"Happy to oblige," Rupert replies, leading us out of the grand hall to a door on the far side of the foyer. "This is the library."

"Oh, wow!" I exclaim. "Wow." I thought rooms like this only existed in books. It's two stories high, with a small balcony or walkway of some sort running around the top half. There are bookshelves stretching from the floor to the top of the very high ceiling, and ladders set up at regular intervals so you can reach the upper shelves. All around the room are tall windows with heavy red drapes, and tables topped with glowing lamps. Oriental carpets are scattered on the floor, along with deep leather armchairs. Every bone in my body wants to grab a book off a shelf and sink into one of them. I wish I'd brought a camera. Stewart would absolutely adore this room.

"I thought you'd like it," says Rupert, scratching himself happily.

"I have got to show my parents," I tell him. "This is their idea of heaven."

I head back through the foyer as fast as my new heels will let me, and run smack-dab into Annabelle Fairfax.

"Oh, it's you," she says. "And your pets."

Lucy flushes at this, and Rupert shuffles his enormous feet.

"Shut up, Annabelle."

Ignoring me, she flicks a glance upward at the chandelier, then back down at Rupert, who is standing directly beneath it. "Don't move," she tells him. Pretending to trip, she bumps against me, pushing me in his direction.

"Oh, look!" she cries in mock surprise. "How charming! Two turtle-doves under the mistletoe."

I look up and for the first time notice that there's a sprig of mistletoe tied to the base of the chandelier.

"No way," I tell her, stepping away from Rupert.

"Just another one of those rude Americans, aren't you?" drawls Annabelle. "I figured as much. We get so many of you over here."

"I'm not being rude!" I protest.

"Just ignorant, then, is that it?"

Stung, I start to sputter.

She laughs softly. "A Christmas kiss under the mistletoe is an old English tradition. And Rupert is your host, after all."

I glare at her.

"Pucker up, Emma!" she says sweetly.

Rupert has such a pathetically hopeful look on his face that I want to slap him. Over his shoulder I see Lucy watching us, her expression unreadable.

"Fine," I snap. "Let's get this over with."

I scrunch my mouth into as tight a knot as possible and raise my face reluctantly. Rupert's enormous ears are trembling in anticipation. He places his sweaty hands on my shoulders and leans in. I try not to grimace when his lips touch mine.

Click!

I pull back with a start and turn around to see Annabelle holding up her cell phone. "Oops!" she says. "My finger must have slipped. I didn't mean to do that."

Stinkerbelle just took my picture.

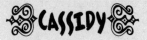
CASSIDY

"Happy shall I be when his stay at Netherfield is over!"
—*Pride and Prejudice*

Sleigh bells.

I pull the pillow over my head, trying to shut out the noise so I can keep dreaming. I don't want to wake up. I'm just about to score the winning goal for the U.S. Women's Olympic hockey team.

The jangling continues. Annoyed, I crack open an eyelid. My stepfather is standing in the doorway to my room, grinning. He's dressed in his pajamas and bathrobe. Chloe is in his arms. She's wearing her pajamas too, the green "Mini Grinch" footie ones that Courtney brought back for her from L.A. She wags her jingle bell rattle happily.

"Go away," I mumble. "I'm sleeping."

I roll over. The sleigh bells draw closer. They're not going to give up. I sit up. "Go bother Courtney," I growl, throwing the pillow at them. I miss. I'm not at my best early in the morning.

Stanley laughs. "She's already awake. Breakfast is on the table."

Suddenly I'm aware of a very good smell wafting into my room. Christmas morning coffee cake! My mother bakes it only once a year. I fling back the covers and scramble out of bed, reaching for my fleece robe and slippers.

Downstairs, Stanley plops Chloe into her high chair, plucks the rattle out of her chubby hand, and slips a "Santa's Little Helper" bib over her head. Then he and I slide into the breakfast nook where Courtney and my mother are waiting.

My mother lights a candle on the table. We don't usually have candles at breakfast, but it's Christmas and it's one of our traditions. She's big on traditions. The flame reflects in the yellow and blue and green of the stained glass window above the table, making the nook glow.

My mother beams at us. "Nothing makes me happier than having my family all together at the holidays."

And nothing would make me happier than knowing the Berkeleys had canceled out on dinner with us tonight.

No such luck, though. It was my mother's bright idea to invite them over, along with the Wongs. "It's Christmas," she said when I protested. "They're far away from home."

"The Wongs? They live in Strawberry Hill."

"No, silly, the Berkeleys. I thought maybe they'd like a taste of a typical American Christmas."

Typical American Christmas? That's a joke. This year's holiday special for *Cooking with Clementine* is called "A Victorian Christmas," and the way our house is decorated, the Queen of England would

Heather Vogel Frederick

probably feel more comfortable here than at Buckingham Palace.

I shove thoughts of Simon and Tristan out of my head and reach for the coffee cake. No point letting the Duke of Puke—my new name for Tristan—spoil the entire day.

"Chloe's first Christmas! Chloe's first Christmas!" sings Courtney, dancing the little Santa and Mrs. Claus salt-and-pepper shakers around the high-chair tray.

Chloe giggles and bangs her feet against the footrest, which gets Murphy all excited. He starts running laps around the kitchen, barking.

My mother is definitely feeling the holiday spirit because normally she'd be telling him to knock it off. Instead, she just laughs.

It's really, really great having Courtney home again. I missed her a lot, even though between hockey and school I've hardly had time to breathe this fall. We've stayed up late practically every night talking, and she's been to all of my practices and games. She's still the same old Courtney I've always known, but she seems different, somehow, too. More grown-up, I guess. And maybe I am too, because we aren't arguing all the time the way we used to.

"Let's open presents," I suggest, the minute I'm done with breakfast.

Mom and Stanley exchange a glance. "W-e-ll, I don't know," says my mother doubtfully. "I think maybe we should do these dishes first."

"And shouldn't someone walk the dog?" Stanley's trying to keep a straight face, but the smile lines around his eyes are working overtime.

Ever since my father died, Mom has kept up his tradition of torturing Courtney and me with delays before we're allowed to open presents, and it looks like Stanley is in on the game now too.

"C'mon, guys!" I holler in protest. I know I'm too old to be excited about opening presents—I'll be getting my learner's permit in a couple of months—but I can't help it. It's Christmas.

"Oh, all right," says my mother, pretending to give in. "I guess the dishes and Murphy can wait."

Stanley and I build a fire in the living room fireplace while Mom wipes Chloe off and gets settled with her on the sofa in front of the tree. The Victorian Christmas theme goes well with our house, actually, which really is a Victorian. The living room ceilings are ten feet high, which is perfect for a huge tree. It's covered with all the ornaments that my father gave my mother over the years. He traveled a lot on business, and would bring them back to her from all over the world. I miss my father, and I know I always will, but I don't feel like I have to choose sides any more—I can love him and still be happy to have Stanley as part of our family.

My stepfather and I have gotten a lot closer this fall. Probably because we spend so much time together. He drives me to the rink in Acton nearly every night for practice, and to the games and tournaments on the weekends as well. He brings work with him sometimes, and I often see him on the phone with clients and stuff, but he's always there.

We've had some good talks in the car too. Mostly about sports,

Heather Vogel Frederick

but sometimes about other stuff—school, friends, life. It was Stanley, in fact, who was the first person I told about my idea for a community service project.

I want to start a hockey club for younger girls in Concord. I figure there must be kids out there like me, girls who want to play hockey but don't because there aren't any girls' teams at the schools. I figure if I can get enough of them interested and trained, eventually there'll be so many potential players clamoring that the schools will have to finally expand their programs.

"I think it's a fantastic idea," Stanley told me when I ran it by him. "You should get Mrs. Bergson involved. She's got a lot of good connections."

I'm planning to talk to her tonight. She's coming for dinner too.

Tristan Berkeley's been taking lessons from her. He's training for some big competition in England next summer, from what his brother tells me. I haven't seen him skate yet, since I'm hardly at the Concord Rink anymore, but Stewart Chadwick has and he tells me he's good. Really good, in fact. I don't know, figure skating is fine and everything, but it's never interested me. And especially not ice dancing. Total waste of good ice, if you ask me. Plus, I never wanted to wear one of those sparkly costumes. I'd much rather suit up with pads and smack a puck around.

My mother puts some Christmas music on and passes the Santa hat to Courtney, since it's her turn to hand out presents this year. Chloe is pinging off the walls with excitement, and crawls around the floor chasing Murphy and trying to pull the bows off all the presents. When she pulls herself up on the coffee table and grabs a sheep and the baby Jesus out of my mother's antique nativity scene, Stanley steps in.

"Uh-oh, baby overload mode," he says, picking her up and prying the figurines out of her hands. "How about we rock around the Christmas tree instead?" And the two of them start dancing.

Chloe gets a ton of presents, of course—toys and clothes and a bunch of books, too. It's mostly clothes for Courtney and me, but I get the new hockey stick I've been eyeing and a biography of Cammi Granato and, from Courtney, a pair of silver earrings designed to look like tiny crossed hockey sticks and pucks.

"Aren't they cute?" she says. "I found them at a boutique in L.A."

"Uh, thanks," I tell her. I never wear jewelry. But I might make an exception for these.

After our present-opening binge, we go back for more coffee cake and then play one of our new board games while Chloe takes a nap. Board games on Christmas day are another family tradition.

I'm all for traditions at Christmastime—especially the food. Tonight's dinner is in the oven, and the smell is making me woozy. We always have ham at Christmas, and twice-baked potatoes and butternut squash and Caesar salad, plus my mother's homemade monkey bread with some of Half Moon Farm's homemade jam. There was a leftover mincemeat pie from Mom's Victorian Christmas episode, but Courtney talked me into helping her bake apple and pumpkin ones too. I'm not much for messing around in the kitchen, but it wasn't all that hard, especially since my sister did most of the work. She loves all that domestic goddess stuff. She's like a little carbon copy of my mom.

We've already set the table, so we pretty much just laze around all afternoon. I read some of my new book, and take a nap on the sofa, and then I head upstairs to find Courtney.

"So tell me about this family that's coming over tonight," she says as I wander into her room. She's lying on her bed texting her new boyfriend back in L.A.—Grant Something, from Santa Barbara.

"The Berkeleys? Oh, they're nice. Well, the parents are nice, and so is Simon. Tristan is a pain, though."

"How come?"

"He's stuck-up. He hardly ever talks to anyone, and he doesn't like me, that's for sure."

Courtney looks up from her phone. "Really? Why not?"

I shrug. "I don't know. Maybe he doesn't approve of girls playing hockey or something. He's English," I add, as if that explains it.

My sister laughs at this.

"Plus, he's a figure skater," I continue. "Ice dancing, actually. He probably thinks he's better than us hockey slobs, you know?"

"Cassidy!" my mother calls. "Megan is here!"

I jog out into the hall and lean over the top banister. "Hey, Megs! Come on up! I'm in Courtney's room."

My mother eyes my sweatpants and Lady Shawmuts hoodie. "Honey, you might want to change into something a little nicer."

"Why? It's Christmas."

"Exactly," she replies, and I notice that she's changed out of her pajamas and robe into black pants and a flowy red velvet top.

I look down at Megan. I can't see what she's wearing under her coat, but it's probably not sweats because I can tell that she's fussed with her hair and makeup. That's because she's got a crush on Simon Berkeley, though. I don't, so I don't particularly care how I look.

"Please, Cassidy?"

"Fine," I reply, and head reluctantly to my room. I'm rooting around in my dresser drawers when Megan comes in.

"How about I help you pick something out?" she offers.

"Good luck," I mutter.

She stands in front of my closet with her hands on her hips. I press my lips together to keep from laughing. I don't own a skirt, and the last time I wore a dress was at my mother's wedding nearly a year and a half ago. But Megan is determined. "This is nice," she says, pulling out a gray satin shirt and holding it up. I frown. I can't even remember ever wearing that. Did it get stuck in here by mistake?

"I think that belongs to my mother," I tell her.

"Well, it will definitely fit you, then. You'll look great—it's the same shade as your eyes." She digs around in the closet again, emerging this time with a pair of black velvet pants.

"I wore those back in sixth grade," I protest, holding them against my legs to prove my point. They come halfway up my shins.

"So why are they still in here?"

I shrug.

Courtney sticks her head in. "Hopeless, isn't it?"

Megan nods, smiling. "We have half an outfit so far. This shirt is gorgeous. It would look really nice with these pants, but Cassidy says she's outgrown them."

"So sue me," I grumble. I outgrow everything. At this rate I'm going to be taller than my mother.

"I might have something that will work." Courtney isn't as tall as I am, but we're kind of built the same. She disappears into her room, returning a minute later with a black skirt and a pair of black tights.

Megan's face lights up. "Perfect!" They both look over at me expectantly.

I sigh and stick out my hand. "Gimme." I retreat into the bathroom to change. The skirt is short, and even though I'm wearing tights, my legs feel exposed. Skirts are way different than shorts, somehow. I always feel comfortable in shorts.

I shuffle back to my room, plucking at the hem of the skirt to try and pull it down.

"Stop that," Megan orders. "It looks great. What do you have for shoes?"

I point wordlessly at the row of sneakers on the floor of my closet.

"You're kidding, right?"

"Well, I suppose I could wear these," I suggest, pulling my suede moccasin slippers out from underneath my bed.

Megan shakes her head in disbelief. "Don't you ever go to the mall?"

"Not if I can help it."

"Hey, didn't I hear Mom saying that you two wear the same shoe size now?" asks my sister.

I shrug. "Maybe."

"Give me a second," she tells Megan, and disappears again. This time, she comes back with a pair of high heels.

"As if," I say, eyeing them.

"No arguing. This too." Courtney passes me a wide black belt with a rhinestone buckle.

I sigh, but I do as she says.

"Oooh," they both chorus when I'm done.

"Cassidy, you look fantastic!" Megan pulls out her cell phone and snaps a picture.

"Hey! No blogging about me, remember?"

"They won't see your face," she promises.

"But everybody else here tonight will, so we need to fix it up a little." Courtney takes my hand and leads me back out into the hall. I teeter after her into her room, where she plunks me down at her desk and starts rounding up stuff for my hair and makeup.

"Eye shadow?" I recoil as she leans in. "Get out!"

"Shut up, Cass," she says cheerfully. "Your eyes are beautiful, and you never do a thing with them."

"I don't want to do anything with them but see out of them!" I protest, but I surrender to the eye shadow, and to mascara and blush, too.

Megan roots around in her purse and pulls out some lip gloss.

Heather Vogel Frederick

"Okay, that's it." I leap to my feet. "I draw the line at lip gloss. I am not Becca Chadwick."

"It's Christmas," says Courtney, grinning. "Think of this as your final present to Mom."

I sigh, and allow her to dab some on my mouth.

"There," she says. "Perfect."

They both look so pleased with their handiwork that I want to laugh. Instead, I tell them to hang on a sec and teeter off to my room in search of the hockey earrings Courtney gave me.

"Nice touch," says Megan when I return.

"Maybe you aren't so hopeless after all," adds Courtney.

"Gee, thanks."

A joyful bark from the front hall means Pip and Mrs. Bergson are here. As we head downstairs to greet them, my mother turns and spots me. Her mouth drops open.

"Oh. My. Goodness." She grabs my stepfather's arm. "Pinch me."

He and Mrs. Bergson both turn around too.

"Who are you and what have you done with my stepdaughter?" Stanley teases.

"You look beautiful," says Mrs. Bergson.

"All three of you look absolutely gorgeous," my mother agrees, smiling at Courtney and Megan, too.

For some reason, I feel ridiculously pleased. Ducking my head, I squat down to pat Pip, who is wearing a little Santa hat.

"Emma sent it from England," Mrs. Bergson tells me.

The doorbell rings and behind me I see Megan peek at herself in the mirror over the front hall table. As she tucks a strand of her dark hair behind her ear, she catches me watching her and grins sheepishly. I wink.

My mother and Stanley usher the Berkeleys inside. Stanley takes everyone's coats and hangs them up as my mother introduces Courtney and the Wongs.

"And you've met Mrs. Bergson and my daughter Cassidy," says my mother.

"Of course," says Mrs. Berkeley, smiling at us.

Simon smiles too. Tristan's eyebrows go up slightly when he sees me, then he quickly rearranges his face into its usual bored expression.

Fortunately, we're seated at opposite ends of the table for dinner. My mother thought he'd enjoy sitting next to Mrs. Bergson, since she's filling in as his skating coach this year. I watch them out of the corner of my eye. Tristan is talking and laughing like a normal human being, for once. I didn't think he had it in him. He's always so cool and distant at school. On the other hand, why should I care how he behaves?

After dessert, we all go in by the fire. The Christmas tree lights are on, and the room looks really pretty.

"You have a lovely home, Clementine," says Mrs. Berkeley.

"Thank you," my mother replies.

"Thank *you* for including us," says Professor Berkeley. "That was an amazing meal."

I spot Megan and Simon setting up a board game on the table

Heather Vogel Frederick

in the window alcove, and I cross the room to join them. Just as I sit down, Tristan drifts over.

"We're going to play Sorry," Megan tells him. "We need four people—are you interested?"

His dark eyebrows knit themselves together as he frowns. "Um, no, thanks. Sorry."

I snort. "Bad pun."

Looking offended, he drifts off again, and Gigi joins us instead.

Tristan spends the rest of the evening talking to my sister and Mrs. Bergson and the other adults, and playing with Pip and Murphy. I keep my distance. No point getting my feelings squashed again, although I'm still not sure why anything he says or does should bother me.

Finally, the Berkeleys and the Wongs leave and I get a chance to talk to Mrs. Bergson by myself. Mom is upstairs putting Chloe to bed, and I can hear Stanley and Courtney talking and laughing in the kitchen, where they're doing the dishes. Pip and Murphy are sacked out by my feet on the hearth. Only Mrs. Bergson and I are left in the living room, sipping cocoa.

"Mrs. Bergson, you know how everybody at Alcott High has to do community service?"

She nods. "So I've heard."

"Well, I've been thinking, and I want to do something different. You know, something besides recycling or volunteering at a nursing home."

"What did you have in mind?"

"I want to start a hockey club."

Mrs. Bergson nods thoughtfully. "Interesting. Go on."

"It seems to me that there should be a whole lot more girls in this town trying out for hockey. Enough that the schools would think seriously about having separate teams for them. So I thought, what if I started a club? Volunteer my time—"

"Do you have any free time left?"

"Not a whole lot, but Mom says as long as my grades don't start to slip, I can give it a try. I'd just do it once or twice a week to start."

"I think it's an excellent idea, Cassidy."

"Do you think the rink would let me have some ice time?" I ask her. "I couldn't pay them or anything."

"Let me talk to the manager. He might be persuaded, especially when I point out that your club would bring in new skaters, and that means more business for the rink store, and for concessions, and for freestyle and stick time."

I'm glad Stanley suggested I talk to her. "Thanks, Mrs. Bergson."

"Have you thought of a name for your club?"

"Chicks with Sticks."

She laughs. "Perfect. I think you'll get a lot of interest."

"Now I just have to figure out how I'm going to raise money for the equipment. It can be expensive and I don't want anybody not to be able to join because they don't have enough money."

"Have you thought about asking Mr. and Mrs. Wong? They're always donating money to good causes, and I'll bet Wong Enterprises would love to sponsor your club." Mrs. Bergson sets

Heather Vogel Frederick

down her cocoa mug. "And now I have a favor to ask you, Cassidy."

"Sure."

"I have an exceptional student this year, someone who has been skating with a partner he had to leave behind when he moved here. He's been practicing with me and with one of my protégés, but she's quite petite and he's quite tall, and it's presenting difficulties. He has an important competition coming up this summer, and it's vital that he keep up his skills. He and his partner back home are currently among the top-ranked athletes in their age bracket, you see."

My heart sinks as I realize who she's talking about.

"How would you feel about stepping in as Tristan Berkeley's practice partner?"

For a few moments all I can hear is the loud ticking of the grandfather clock out in the hall.

"Ice dancing?" I manage finally. "Me? I don't know if I could squeeze anything more in." What I really want to say is, *Over my dead body*.

My mother comes in the room. "What was that about ice dancing?" She perches on the arm of the sofa beside me as Mrs. Bergson explains her proposition. When she's done, my mother turns to me.

"Of course you'd be happy to help out, wouldn't you, sweetheart?"

I shoot her a desperate glance. "But I don't know anything about ice dancing! I'm a hockey player."

Mrs. Bergson smiles. "You'd be surprised how much the two sports have in common. Footwork, balance, strength. And what you don't know, I can teach you."

"Sounds like an offer you can't refuse," says my mother.

I press my lips together tightly, squelching the protest that's trying to burst out. My mother has a point, especially since Mrs. Bergson just offered to help me launch Chicks with Sticks. I guess it's only fair that I return the favor.

"Deal?" she says.

I nod reluctantly. "Deal."

Two days later I'm at the rink as promised. I stand by the door for a few minutes, watching Tristan warm up. Stewart is right—he's really good. Phenomenal, in fact.

Mrs. Bergson spots me and motions me over. "There you are," she says. "I was worried you weren't coming."

"A deal's a deal." I try not to sound too grumpy.

"That's the spirit!" She smiles. "I have some good news for you. I've managed to carve out some ice time for your new club on Tuesday and Thursday afternoons after school. And the manager is willing to waive the rink fee. He's even going to put an ad in the newsletter for 'Chicks with Sticks.'"

"Wow!" My grumpiness melts away at this news.

Mrs. Bergson holds up a pair of skates. White figure skates. I haven't worn anything but hockey skates for about a hundred years. "A present for you, for being such a good sport."

I sit down on a nearby bench to lace up, then step tentatively onto the ice. Figure skates are different from hockey skates—they have toe picks on the front of the blades, for one thing. Hockey is all about speed, not jumps and twirls. We don't need toe picks.

I push off and glide—and although I stumble a few times, I quickly start feeling confident. I speed up a little, and try a few crossovers, hoping Tristan's watching. Out of the corner of my eye I can see that he is. Unfortunately, he's also watching a few seconds later when I trip over my left toe pick and go sprawling.

He gives me one of his cool glances, then turns to Mrs. Bergson. "I thought you said she could skate." His words are as clipped and hard as the ice I'm sitting on.

Furious, I scramble to my feet. Mrs. Bergson puts a restraining hand on my arm.

"Cassidy is one of the best skaters I've ever seen," she tells him, which is high praise coming from a former Olympic champion.

Somewhat mollified, and determined not to make a total fool of myself in front of Tristan, I push off again and this time I make it all the way around the perimeter of the rink without stumbling once.

"Backward this time," calls Mrs. Bergson. "And pick up the speed."

Piece of cake, I think, and instantly find myself facedown on the ice again, thanks to the idiotic toe picks.

"Can't I just wear my hockey skates?" I plead.

Mrs. Bergson shakes her head. "Don't worry about it, Cassidy, you'll adjust. Now, let's try some side-by-side work." She positions Tristan to my left, with his right hand on my waist and my left arm extended across his chest. He crooks his left elbow, and takes my hand in his. His fingers are rigid with disapproval.

"This is called the Open Killian position," Mrs. Bergson tells me. She cocks her head to one side and gives us the once-over. "You're certainly well matched," she says. "You make a very good-looking couple."

I stiffen. Tristan inhales sharply, a sure sign he doesn't like this idea any more than I do.

"Now, Tristan, partner her around the rink."

As we move awkwardly forward, I glance up at the bleachers, hoping that none of my hockey buddies are around to see me.

Our first practice is a disaster. I'm not picking the basics up at all, and I feel clumsy and uncoordinated. It's so different from hockey! I spend half the time sitting on my butt on the ice, and Tristan doesn't make it any easier. He just looks at me like I'm some kind of science experiment gone very, very bad.

By the end of the hour I'm frustrated, sore, and close to tears, which is not a normal feeling for me where sports are involved.

"I can't believe she ever thought this would work," Tristan mutters under his breath as we skate over to where Mrs. Bergson is waiting.

"I'd like to see you in a scrimmage, Mr. Fancypants Berkeley!" I snap back at him, wishing I had my hockey stick so I could smack him with it. "You wouldn't last thirty seconds." Furious, I stomp off the rink.

Mrs. Bergson follows me. "Cassidy," she says gently.

"What?"

"Don't be so hard on yourself. It's going to take some work to get you up to speed, but you, my dear, are a natural athlete and a fine

Heather Vogel Frederick

skater. You have exceptional balance and lovely, crisp footwork, and best of all, you're strong."

The tears spill over and I lean down and unlace my skates, hoping she won't notice. "I don't feel strong—I feel stupid. I can't do this."

She pats me on the shoulder. "Never say 'I can't.' 'I can't' is a limit, and life is about breaking through limits. Say 'I will' instead." She passes me a tissue. "This sport is simply ballroom dancing on ice. All we're going to do is develop your grace and rhythm and style."

She doesn't think I have grace? She doesn't think I have rhythm or style? Has she never seen me do a triple deke? I'm poetry in motion.

"Come back Thursday afternoon after school," she tells me. "I'll help you with 'Chicks with Sticks,' and then we'll try again."

I blow my nose. This whole thing is the worst idea in the history of the world. Why on earth did I say yes? The problem is, I can't back out now. Not with Mrs. Bergson being so nice about helping me with my community service project. I have no choice but to stick it out.

Final score: Mom, Mrs. Bergson, and Tristan Berkeley: 1. Cassidy: another big fat zero.

Jess

It starts as a single whisper and quickly spreads, like ripples from a stone dropped in a pond. *The solo list is posted*. In a flash the music room is buzzing with excitement. Mr. Elton, our choir director, pretends not to notice.

"From the top, ladies," he says, tapping his baton on the music stand in front of him.

Obediently, we burst into the opening notes of *"Lirum bililirum."* It's an Italian madrigal, and the upbeat tempo and cheerful tune don't really match up with the lyrics, which are all about waiting for love. As I dutifully sing my part, I can't help thinking, *I can totally relate.* I close my eyes as the melody soars, imagining myself singing it to Darcy Hawthorne.

"Le ses an che t'vo mi ben"—I have loved you for six years. Well, okay, maybe it's not been six whole years that I've had a crush

on Emma's brother, but still, it's been a long time. *"Ma t'aspet che l'so ben"*—I've been waiting for you so long—*"Ch'al fin sclopi per amor"*—that I shall end by bursting with love.

Oh, yeah. That about covers it.

Between thinking about Darcy and wondering if my name is on the list, rehearsal seems agonizingly long. The minute the final bell rings I find myself in the middle of a very undignified herd of MadriGals, all stampeding for the door.

We race for the bulletin board down the hall where the list is posted. My voice teacher and I worked for weeks on my audition piece, which I thought was as good as anything I've ever sung. The MadriGals enter a big regional choral competition every year—this time around it's down in New Haven—and the winning groups go on to nationals. Colonial Academy usually places pretty well, and about ten years ago they actually made it to nationals. Mr. Elton is hoping for a repeat victory. I'm hoping for a chance to sing a solo onstage at the Civic Opera House in Chicago.

"Yes!" says Savannah, punching her fist in the air.

Okay, I think, *so Savannah made it*. She deserved to. I heard her audition, and it was flawless. But I'm pretty sure mine was just as good. Maybe even better. I crane my neck to see over her shoulder, but she's a lot taller than me and everyone's pushing and shoving and I get bumped out of the way.

Two seniors and a sophomore start jumping up and down when they spot their names, then Adele lets out a whoop and throws her arms around me. My heart leaps. Does that mean I made it?

No, it means *she* made it.

I hug her back anyway.

A brief image flashes through my mind: me, standing by the piano in the auditorium, singing "O Waly, Waly" for Mr. Elton. It's one of my favorite madrigals. I loved it even before I knew it was a madrigal—it shares the same melody as the Scottish ballad "The Water is Wide." My mother has a recording of Eva Cassidy singing it, and the haunting melody gives me goosebumps every time I listen to it. It gave me goose bumps during my audition, too. I poured my heart into the words that afternoon: *"The water is wide, I cannot get o'er, and neither have I wings to fly. Give me a boat that will carry two, and both shall row, my love and I."*

Mr. Elton had smiled and thanked me when I finished, and scribbled some notes on his pad of paper. That must have been a good sign, right? That must have meant that I earned a solo spot.

The crowd surges again and I'm swept up right next to the wall this time. I scan the list.

I scan it again.

My name isn't on it.

There has to be some kind of mistake! I just know I was as good as Savannah and Adele. But it's true. I wasn't picked for a solo, or even for a duet.

Tears sting my eyes and I blink them back, trying not to let my disappointment show. There's a swarm of girls around Savannah and

Heather Vogel Frederick

Adele and the other girls whose names are listed, and I join them to offer my congratulations.

"I'm so happy for you guys," I tell them, and I mean it. But at the same time it's hard not to feel crushed. Ever since my mother and I had that talk the night of the meteor shower, I followed her advice and threw myself heart and soul into working on my audition. I really truly tried my best. This time, though, my best wasn't good enough.

I turn away and head for the door. Nothing seems to be going right for me this year, at school or anywhere else. I'm not good enough at the thing I love to do more than anything else in the whole world, my best friend is three thousand miles away, and her brother barely knows I exist. Mom keeps telling me it's just growing pains, and that everything will settle down eventually, but it sure doesn't feel that way right now.

I hear footsteps behind me and turn to see Adele running down the hall. She links her arm through mine. "Come on, roomie," she says. "I'm taking you downtown for ice cream."

"Why?" I say miserably, once we're out of earshot of the others. "I didn't make it."

"You deserved to," she says loyally. "And you really, really helped me. When I think of all those hours you spent listening to me practice my audition piece—you deserve at least an ice-cream cone for that." She gives me a sidelong glance. "Maybe even a sundae."

I know she's trying to cheer me up, so I muster a smile. We grab our jackets from the rack by the door and step outside to find that it's snowing again.

"Uh, maybe ice cream isn't such a good idea," I tell her.

She laughs. "What are you talking about? It's never too cold for ice cream."

We swing by the dorm to get Frankie, who is furious when she hears that I didn't make the cut and that Savannah did.

"It's obviously a conspiracy," she says darkly. "You have a much better voice than she does. Her father probably pulled some strings in Washington."

Somehow, this makes me feel a lot better even though I know it's not true.

As the three of us shiver our way across the quad, we decide that maybe it really is too cold for ice cream, and opt for the café on Main Street instead, where we plop into a trio of cozy armchairs and order hot chocolate from the coffee bar.

"I thought March is the month that's supposed to come in like a lion, not January," Adele complains. She's from San Francisco, and they don't get much snow there.

Ever since school started again we've been blasted with one storm after another. Usually we have two more class periods after MadriGals, but they closed school early today so that all the teachers and administrators who don't live on campus could make it home.

"Hey, Beauty!" I hear a voice behind me and turn to see Zach Norton coming through the door with Ethan and Third and Simon Berkeley.

I smile. "Hey, Beast!"

Zach and I were in a play together back in middle school, and we've

Heather Vogel Frederick

been friends ever since. He came with me to the Founder's Day dance last spring, so Frankie and Adele already know him, but I introduce them to the other boys.

"Adele Bixby and Francesca Norris, meet Ethan MacDonald and Third—excuse me, *Cranfield Bartlett III.*"

He bows, and Frankie and Adele both laugh.

"And this is Simon Berkeley. Simon and his family are living at Emma's house this year."

The boys crowd onto the couch across from us.

"How's Melville?" I ask Simon.

"Moping," he says. "He misses the Hawthornes."

"I know the feeling."

"Hey, we're going sledding tomorrow morning at Nashawtuc Hill," says Zach. "You three should come."

"Sounds like fun," says Adele.

"It'll be wicked fun if this snow keeps up," Zach replies.

Simon looks puzzled.

"Wicked is a good thing," Zach assures him.

"It's New England-speak for *really*," I explain. "Wicked fun equals really fun."

Simon's face clears. "Got it."

Zach pokes me in the arm. "Cassidy said she'd try and get there between hockey practice and her, uh, workout with Simon's brother. Did you hear about her ice-dancing gig?"

I nod.

Simon looks down at the floor. Apparently his brother and Cassidy aren't exactly hitting it off.

"So will you come too?"

I shake my head. "I wish I could, but I can't."

"Why not?"

I sigh. "My mother signed the two of us up for a cake-decorating class," I admit sheepishly. "Tomorrow's the big finale. While you guys are having fun tobogganing, I'll be decorating a wedding cake at the Rec Center."

"Ooh," says Ethan. "Lucky you."

"Shut up, Tater."

Ethan shoots a glance over at Adele and Frankie and reddens. I grin. He totally hates being reminded of his old nickname, especially when there are girls around. He earned it, though. He's the one who used to like to eat stray Tater Tots off the cafeteria floor back in elementary school.

Zach grins and puts his finger to his lips, as if to assure him that his secret is safe with us.

"Jess makes killer frosting roses," says Frankie, her dark eyes sparkling mischievously over the rim of her mug. She has a whipped cream mustache, but Zach doesn't seem to notice. He grins back.

The bells over the door jangle and Peyton Winslow parades in with a new friend in tow, some girl from Phoenix named Beatrice. Peyton and Savannah were friends last year in eighth grade, but from what Savannah tells me they've had kind of a falling out this year, which

Heather Vogel Frederick

is awkward since they're roommates. It's not because of any one big thing, really—although I guess Peyton got her feelings hurt when Savannah didn't invite her along on her family's Christmas trip like she did last year. Mostly it's just that Savannah wised up and stopped being so mean, plus she's working harder at school and at MadriGals and everything. Peyton's jealous that Savannah has other friends and activities, and isn't as interested anymore in her favorite hobby—boys, with being snarky running a close second.

Peyton and Beatrice place their orders and drift over toward us, eyeing Zach and Simon. Not that I blame them. Let's face it, they're both cute guys. Wicked cute, in fact.

"Aren't you going to introduce us, Jess?" says Peyton.

"No," I tell her. "Go away."

Adele and Frankie both start to giggle. I know I'm being rude, but I don't care. I'm not afraid of Peyton Winslow. If I can survive a whole year of Savannah Sinclair, I can survive anything. I've been permanently cured of queen bees.

Simon stands up and holds out his hand. "I'm Simon Berkeley," he says politely. In addition to being wicked cute, he has really good manners. Megan's always gushing about that.

Peyton and Beatrice pull up a couple of chairs and we all sit there for a while awkwardly, making small talk. Finally, I check my watch.

"Gotta go," I tell everybody. "My dad's coming to pick me up."

"Can he make it in this snow?" Simon asks, sounding concerned. He is *really* polite.

I smile. "I live on a farm, remember? We have a truck."

"That's right," Peyton sneers. "You raise goats, don't you?"

"Yup," I reply cheerfully. "And chickens, too. They call me Goat Girl, and Princess Jess of Ramshackle Farm."

Zach, who has just taken a sip from his mug, sputters out a laugh, spraying the table with hot chocolate. I laugh too, feeling pleased with myself. No way am I going to let Peyton get my goat. Literally. I really have come a long way in the last few years.

The storm continues through dinner, and all night I hear the scrape and clank of snowplows up and down the road in front of Half Moon Farm. Come morning, though, I wake up to sunshine and a sparklingly white world. The thermometer has shot up, and everything is melting. The January thaw has finally arrived.

Although I'm still disappointed over not getting picked for a MadriGals solo, it's hard to be droopy on such a beautiful day, and I'm in a much better mood by the time my mother and I arrive at the Rec Center.

Frankie is right, actually. I do make killer frosting roses. And a lot of other things too. It turns out I have a knack for cake decorating.

"I knew all those science and math classes would come in handy someday," my mother teases, as I squeeze a final pink curl of frosting ribbon onto the top of my masterpiece. "That pastry bag is a precision instrument in your hands."

I grin at her and wipe a stray smudge of buttercream off the cake plate, then carry it to the display table. Ours is the only cake that isn't round. When we were first given this assignment, I got to wondering

Heather Vogel Frederick

why people didn't pick other shapes for wedding cakes—triangles, maybe, or ovals or octagons. My mother explained that round cakes are like round wedding rings, meant to symbolize eternal love. I guess that makes sense, but still, it's kind of boring, the same old tower of round tiers every time, with a cascade of frosting flowers winding down the side. Sometimes it's just fun to be different.

So our cake is square. The base is made of three layers of chocolate cake covered in pale green fondant frosting. Fondant is cool stuff— you can roll it out and drape it over things for a really smooth look, almost like wrapping paper. On top of that base we heaped a pile of smaller squares—we found a square muffin pan online and used it to make square chocolate cupcakes—and decorated them to look like presents too, each with fondant frosting and "ribbons" of contrasting colors tied neatly in a bow. We had fun picking out the designs—polka dots, stripes, zigzags, that sort of thing.

And because I really do love making frosting flowers, I scattered a few pale pink roses in among the presents, and just for fun, a white marzipan mouse peeking out from under a curl of ribbon.

The teacher finds something nice to say about every cake on the table, but when she gets to ours, she stops and just looks at it for a while, smiling.

"Now, this," she says, "is really original. I love the strong geometrical lines, the color scheme, and the whimsical touches. Well done, Team Delaney!"

"It was mostly Jessica's idea," my mother tells her.

"Then Jessica, this is for you to take home with you." And she hands me a blue ribbon.

Later, in the truck on the way home, my mom turns to me. "Aren't you glad I signed us up for that class?"

"Yeah," I have to admit, fingering my ribbon. Our cake is balanced on the seat between us. I've made my mother promise she won't let the boys or Dad at it until I get a chance to show Emma tomorrow. I haven't videoconferenced with Emma for nearly two weeks, because she and her family have been off on another road trip.

I give my mother a sly glance. "Maybe I have a future career as a singing veterinarian who runs a bakery."

"And makes deliveries on horseback," my mother adds.

"And teaches math on the side," I finish, and we burst out laughing.

The following afternoon, I get the cake from where we hid it in my mother's closet and carry it down the hall to my room.

"Ta-da!" I cry, holding it up in front of my laptop's webcam.

If I was expecting an enthusiastic response from Emma, though, I don't get it.

"Cool," she says listlessly.

I set the cake down and peer at her, concerned. "What's wrong?"

Emma bursts into tears. "My life is over!" she wails.

"What happened?"

Between sobs, she spills out her tale of woe. "Remember what happened under the mistletoe?"

I nod.

"Well, Annabelle Fairfax sent the cell phone picture to half the students at Knightley-Martin," she continues. "Worse, to make sure the other half didn't miss out, she blew the picture up to poster size and plastered it all over the halls."

"Oh, no!"

"Now everybody thinks I'm dating the biggest dork in Bath!" Emma finishes, blowing her nose. "Everywhere I go at school, people make smooching noises when they see me. I pretended to be sick two days this week just so I wouldn't have to go."

"Oh, Emma," I tell her. "How horrible! I wish there was something I could do!" There's no way I'm telling her about MadriGals. Compared to her disaster, mine is nothing to complain about.

She shakes her head sadly. "There's nothing anybody can do."

"Can you sic Darcy on her?"

Emma frowns. "He just tells me to quit worrying about it. He says it'll blow over."

We talk for a while longer, and then Emma tells me she has to go because her parents are taking them out to dinner. I don't get a chance to talk to Darcy, but tonight I don't feel like it anyway. I'm kind of mad at him for not sticking up more for his sister.

As soon as I shut my computer, I grab my cell phone and send a text to Cassidy and Megan and Becca: HELP! EMERGENCY MDBC MTG!

MY HOUSE—4:00 Cassidy texts back.

We rendezvous in the turret. Cassidy or her mother must have been up there reading, because there's a copy of *Pride and Prejudice* lying open on the window seat.

Cassidy is the last one up the stairs. She enters carrying a tray. "Mom sent up French Silk Chocolate pie for everybody. She's testing recipes for the show."

We each take a plate and sit down.

"So what's going on?" asks Megan.

My eyes slide over to Becca. "You all have to absolutely promise not to tell anyone," I say sternly. "Especially you, Becca."

"Whatever," she replies, forking up a bite of pie.

"I mean it," I say.

She sighs. "Okay, fine, I promise."

I tell my friends about Annabelle Fairfax. They all laugh when I get to the "Stinkerbelle" part, but they stop laughing when I tell them about the cell phone picture and the mistletoe.

"Do you think maybe she's making a mountain out of a molehill?" asks Becca, carefully avoiding looking at Megan. The two of them were involved in a cell phone picture prank a couple of years ago, and it almost cost Becca Megan's friendship.

"Molehill?" My voice rises. "Just imagine how you'd feel if you got tricked into kissing, say, Kevin Mullins, and somebody took your picture and showed it all over school."

Becca bites her lip. "I guess I see what you mean."

"We have to do something!" I tell them. "Lucy's the only good friend she's got over there. Emma needs us."

Heather Vogel Frederick

"What did you have in mind?" asks Cassidy.

I shrug. "I don't know. I thought maybe you guys would have some bright ideas."

"Can Emma get me a picture of Stinkerbelle?" asks Megan. "I could blog about her."

"That's a great idea," says Cassidy, who's always up for a good prank.

"I wasn't really thinking about getting even with Annabelle Fairfax at this point," I tell them. "Not that it isn't a good idea. I just want to do something to cheer Emma up."

"Too bad we can't put Pip in a box and mail him to her," says Cassidy. "All she has over there to keep her company is the Berkeleys' stupid parrot."

"Too bad we can't put Emma in a box and have her parents mail her back here to Concord," says Megan.

"Yeah," Becca agrees. "I know Stewart would really like to see her too."

That's admitting a lot, for Becca. It totally grosses her out to think that her brother likes her book club friend.

"Why not?" I ask.

"Why not what?" says Cassidy.

"Why not bring Emma home? Spring break's coming up soon—maybe we could send her an airplane ticket."

"Round trip from England's got to cost a ton of money," says Cassidy.

"Not as much as saving Half Moon Farm," says Becca. "This would be a piece of cake in comparison to what we did back in seventh grade."

Two years ago, we held a fashion show to help raise money for the Delaneys' property taxes. Becca turns to Megan. "You must have a bunch saved up from Bébé Soleil. Can't you pay for it?"

Megan shakes her head regretfully. "My mother makes me put it all in a special savings thing at the bank. It's for college, and you know my mom and college. She'd kill me if I got into it."

I make a face. "There's always babysitting, I guess."

"We'd have to do a whole lot of babysitting to afford a plane ticket from England," Megan points out.

We're quiet for a while, thinking. Cassidy takes another bite of pie. She smiles. "Maybe we could do what they do at school, and have a bake sale," she jokes.

That makes us laugh. Then Becca looks down at her plate. "You know, that's not a totally stupid idea, Cassidy."

"Thanks a bunch."

"You know what I mean! This pie is incredible. All your mom's pies are incredible. I'll bet she has a zillion great recipes." She turns to me. "And you and your mother just took that cake-decorating class. We could start a little business, and sell pies and cakes and cupcakes. Our own private bake sale."

"Who would we sell stuff to?" asks Cassidy. "Restaurants?"

Becca shakes her head. "Too complicated, and I'll bet there are all sorts of health laws we'd have to know about."

"She's right," I tell Cassidy. "I know, because we sell cheese to restaurants."

"I was thinking more like selling to neighbors, and friends of our parents, that sort of thing. People are always having parties, and word gets around."

We nod slowly, thinking it over.

"This could really work," I say, starting to get excited.

"No kidding," Megan agrees. "It could be fun, too. But where are we going to do all this?"

"We can't use my house," says Becca. "My mother has all her stupid worm bins on the counters. It's disgusting."

"The kitchen's a no-brainer," says Cassidy. "Ours is commercially licensed because of the TV show. I'm sure my mother would let us—I mean you guys—bake there. I don't have a whole lot of extra time these days. But I can pass out flyers and help with the marketing."

"And I have my food handler's license already, because of our creamery," I tell them. "You have to have one for selling cheese and stuff to the public. It's not a big deal to get one. There's this test you study for—"

"A test?" Becca protests. "Don't we get enough of those at school?"

"Becca! This is Emma we're talking about."

She sighs deeply, as if making a huge sacrifice. "Okay, count me in."

"Me too," says Megan.

"Didn't you tell me Stewart has his driver's license now?" says Cassidy, and Becca nods. "I'll bet he'd be willing to help with the deliveries."

Becca nods. "Probably. I'll ask him."

"We need a name," I say. "For the flyers and menus and things."

Megan whips out her sketchbook and a pen. "You're good with names, Cassidy. Everybody loves 'Chicks with Sticks.'"

"How about 'Chicks with Sweets'?" Becca suggests.

I shake my head. "That sounds too much like Easter."

We brainstorm for a while. Pie-a-palooza. Chick-a-licious. Sweet Treats. Have Your Cake and Eat it Too. Everything's either too dumb, too bland, or too silly. Then my gaze falls on the window seat, and Cassidy's copy of *Pride and Prejudice*. "Hang on a sec," I tell them. "I've got it! Pies and Prejudice."

"Perfect," Becca decrees, giving it her stamp of approval.

Megan bends her head over her sketchbook. With a dozen or so strokes of her pen, a lady in a Jane Austen–style dress appears, holding up a pie in one elegant hand. Above this little sketch Megan writes "Pies and Prejudice" in fancy script. Then she erases the "and" and changes it to "Pies & Prejudice." "Behold our logo," she says, holding it up.

"Way to go, Wong!" says Cassidy admiringly.

"We're probably going to have to tell our moms this time," Becca cautions. "We can't keep it a secret, the way we did the fashion show. We're going to need too much help."

Megan nods. "Gigi will definitely want in."

"The more the merrier," I tell her. "Only don't let your mom get any ideas, okay? Seaweed pie is not an option." Cassidy snickers, and

Heather Vogel Frederick

Megan kicks her in the shin. "Let's keep it a secret from Emma, though. A surprise would be more fun."

We all agree that this is a good idea.

I turn to Cassidy. "Let's go talk to your mom."

Downstairs, we find Mrs. Sloane-Kinkaid in the kitchen with Fred Goldberg. He's the producer of her TV show, and they're bent over some paperwork on the island counter.

"Hi, girls," says Cassidy's mother as we troop in. "What did you think of the pie?"

"Two thumbs up," says Becca, and we all nod in agreement.

"And speaking of pie, can we talk to you for a minute?" Cassidy asks.

"Sure, sweetheart. Fred and I are just wrapping up here. Why don't you girls put your dishes in the dishwasher, and Cassidy, could you check on Chloe for me? It should be about time for her to get up from her nap."

Cassidy returns a couple of minutes later carrying her baby sister, who is rubbing her eyes with her fists. Her hair is mussed and her plump little cheeks are all pink from sleeping, but she breaks into a big grin when she sees us.

"Check this out," says Cassidy, setting her down on the floor. Chloe holds tightly onto Cassidy's hands and takes two wobbly steps before siting down with a thud.

"Yay!" We all clap and cheer for her, and she claps and cheers too.

We play with her and help her practice walking while Mrs. Sloane-

Kinkaid and Mr. Goldberg finish their discussion about a show they're planning—a tribute to Julia Child, from the sounds of it.

"So, what's up, girls?" Mrs. Sloane-Kinkaid says finally, after her producer leaves.

I explain about what happened to Emma.

"Ouch," she says when I'm done.

We all nod. "We want to send Emma a ticket home for spring break," I tell her. "We think it would really cheer her up."

Cassidy's mother frowns. "That's a lovely thought, girls, but a present like that is pretty expensive."

"We know," says Becca. "That's why we need your help."

Mrs. Sloane-Kinkaid listens thoughtfully as we outline our plan.

"You know, that just might work," she says when we're done.

Megan passes her the piece of paper with our logo drawn onto it. Mrs. Sloane-Kinkaid smiles. "Pies & Prejudice. Catchy." She smiles at us. "Jane would approve, and so do I. I have a feeling the rest of your moms will too. If it's okay with them, it's okay with me, and you may certainly use our kitchen, as long as you work around our filming schedule. Just let me know if there's anything else I can do to help."

With a rising sense of excitement, we race back up to the turret to make more plans. Our new business is off and running!

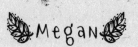

Megan

> *"Good apple pies are a considerable part*
> *of our domestic happiness."*
> —*Letter from Jane Austen*
> *to her sister Cassandra, October 1815*

I love Saturday mornings.

For one thing, there's no school. For another thing—well, I guess it's really the no-school part I love best.

Not that I don't like high school. *Au contraire*, as Gigi would say. (That means "on the contrary." My grandmother adores everything French, including the language.) Alcott High started off kind of rocky for me, but now I really like it. It's just that on Saturday mornings I get to sleep in, and there's nothing that I absolutely have to do. Oh, sure, maybe a little homework, maybe a few chores, but that's about it. On Saturday mornings, the whole weekend stretches out ahead of me like yards and yards of smooth white silk. I wake up happy because I know that I have hours of time to do the stuff I want to do—sketch, sew, read fashion magazines, watch movies with Gigi, hang out at the mall with Becca and Ashley, that sort of thing.

But that was before Pies & Prejudice.

My alarm goes off and I groan, fumbling for the snooze button. It's not even seven o'clock yet. I start to roll over, then stop. Reminding myself that I'm doing this for Emma, I force myself out of bed and into the shower. I'm due at Cassidy's house in an hour.

This bake sale idea is starting to take off. We sold only two pies the first week, one to Cassidy's grandparents and one to Mrs. Bergson, but in the month since then, word has gotten around.

Cassidy enlisted her sister Courtney to help us create a website using my logo. We put it on our business cards too, which we've posted on just about every bulletin board in town. Plus, our parents have been handing them out to all their friends and clients too. We take orders up through Thursday night, finalize the list on Friday morning, then on Friday after school Jess and Becca and I take turns buying the ingredients. Saturday is baking day, since weekends are the only time that the kitchen at Cassidy's house is available. During the week, the film crew is there for *Cooking with Clementine*.

When we told our moms about the whole Pies & Prejudice idea, they were all for it, but on one condition.

"You have to have adult supervision," Mrs. Delaney told us. She said she wished she could be the one to mentor us, but she couldn't take on any more projects with all that she's got going at the farm plus the twins plus she just got a part in a play at some theater in Boston. Between her TV show and taking care of Chloe, Mrs. Sloane-Kinkaid was way too busy to help us out too, and the weekends are Mrs. Bergson's busiest time at the rink. Becca's mother is up to her eyeballs with her landscape design classes, especially with spring just around the corner, and my mother is president of the Concord Riverkeepers this year plus she's on the school board plus she's thinking seriously about running for office next fall, so she couldn't help us either.

That left Gigi.

Fortunately, my grandmother loves to cook and she loves to boss people around, so helping us with Pies & Prejudice is a perfect combination. Plus, my mother says Gigi needs a project.

My grandmother has tons of energy. I overheard my mom and dad talking about it, and my mom said Gigi is like one of those dogs that's supposed to be out herding sheep or cattle all day or something, and when they're cooped up inside instead they get into all kinds of trouble. That's Gigi, all right.

The first six months after she came from Hong Kong last year to live with us she kept herself busy cooking up a storm, which was great except my dad had to keep buying new pants in bigger sizes. After Mom put her foot down, Gigi busied herself rearranging the furniture instead. She even painted a wall of our living room one weekend when my parents were away. Mom hit the roof when she came home. Personally, I think that fire-engine red looks fantastic with all our white carpet and furniture, especially the white baby grand piano. My mother eventually admitted it did too, but I guess she's right, Gigi should have asked first.

It's a little after eight when Becca and Jess and I shuffle into Cassidy's kitchen, yawning.

"Okay, girls," my grandmother says, clapping her hands together sharply. "Time to wake up and get to work!"

This weekend we have nearly two dozen pies to make, and we scored in the cake department, with two birthdays and a wedding shower. On top of that, we got our first order for organic whole wheat banana blueberry bread. My mother is ecstatic about that. When we first told her about this whole idea, her forehead got that worried pucker it always tends to get whenever sugar is mentioned.

"Shouldn't you offer some healthy treats on your menu too?" she asked us.

We managed to convince her that nobody but nobody would want to buy her tofu cheesecake, and finally compromised on Mrs. Delaney's banana bread, which is fabulous. To make my mom happy we promised to use all organic ingredients and whole wheat flour instead of white flour. Mrs. Sloane-Kinkaid is the one who suggested adding blueberries, to help keep it moist. I guess whole wheat makes things kind of heavy and dense. That would explain my mother's pancakes, which you could use as skipping stones at Walden Pond.

"Hi, everybody!" Mrs. Sloane-Kinkaid pokes her head in the door. Chloe is in her arms, and she waves at us. The two of them are dressed in matching workout clothes—navy stretch pants with white piping down the side seams, white T-shirts, and identical navy warm-up jackets with a white daisy motif around the collar and cuffs. Cute but classy. When it comes to fashion, Mrs. Sloane-Kinkaid is amazing. "I left some muffins and fruit salad out for you in the breakfast nook," she tells us. "And please help yourself to juice and tea and whatever else you want, okay?"

"Where's Cassidy?" I ask her.

"Big game this morning up in Nashua. She and Stanley left at the crack of dawn, but they'll be home after lunch." She glances at her watch. "I'd better get going or I'm going to be late for our 'Baby and Me' yoga class."

We say good-bye and I help myself to a blueberry muffin as Gigi hands out aprons.

"So how's our bottom line?" she asks.

Jess consults her notebook. Since she's the math whiz, we made her the accountant. Cassidy's stepfather, who actually is an accountant, showed her the ropes and got her set up with a system for tracking our sales and expenses—ingredients, gas for deliveries, advertising, all that sort of thing.

"It looks like we've netted almost two hundred dollars so far, after expenses," she says.

Gigi purses her lips thoughtfully. "Well, it's a start," she says. "I'm sure we'll get more orders as more people taste our goods." She turns to Becca. "You and I are going to be in charge of the pies this week, and Megan, I want you and Jess to handle the rest."

We all nod and head to our workstations—Gigi and Becca at the kitchen island, Jess and I at the far counter—to get set up.

"So what's your plan?" I ask Jess. She always has a plan. It must be the scientist in her.

"I'm thinking chocolate cupcakes with white frosting for the pirate birthday party." She passes me some black construction paper and a white gel pen. "I thought maybe you could draw little skull-and-crossbone flags?"

"Piece of cake," I tell her, then grin. "Sorry, bad pun."

"We'll stick them on toothpicks," she continues, ignoring me. "Plus, I picked up some gold foil-wrapped chocolate coins we can stick in the frosting as well."

"They'll love it," I tell her. "How about the princesses?" The other birthday party has a princess theme.

"Yellow cupcakes with pink icing, and lots and lots of sprinkles and sparkles." She holds up a bag of plastic rings that look like tiny tiaras. "And we'll top each one with one of these."

"Perfect. And the wedding shower?"

"The bride wants carrot cake with cream cheese frosting, and purple is her favorite color. I'm thinking of tinting the icing a pretty lavender, and then I thought we could outline a big purple umbrella on top of that." She pauses, glancing over at me. "You know, since it's a *shower*?"

"Got it. Cute."

"Only instead of raindrops, we'll have it raining frosting violets instead."

It's fun to see Jess so into this. Fooling around with color and design

Heather Vogel Frederick

comes naturally to me, but it's kind of unexpected in Jess. She's so focused on science and math most of the time. I mean, I know she loves music, and that's creative, but cake decorating? We all think it's a riot.

"Let's get to work, girls!" says Gigi.

She cranks up the music while we set up an assembly line. Old musicals are my grandmother's favorite, and my dad made her a mix of all her favorite songs. I grab a whisk to use for a microphone, and Jess sings into her spatula. We pie-ify each song that comes on, cracking each other up.

"The pies are alive, with the sound of music!"

"Oklahoma, where the pies come sweeping down the plain!"

"Somewhere, over the piecrust!"

Becca tries to pretend it's too stupid at first, but pretty soon she's singing just as loudly as the rest of us.

Jess and I start by making the batters for the carrot cake and cupcakes. By the time they're ready to go into the oven, Becca and Gigi have finished making the piecrusts, so we pitch in to help them peel apples. We have half a dozen pie choices on our menu—lemon meringue, apple, blueberry, cherry, French silk chocolate, and coconut cream— but for some reason this week nearly everybody ordered apple.

We bake all morning. Lunchtime comes around, and Mrs. Sloane-Kinkaid pops in with pizza to keep us going. She returns a couple of hours later when we're finished, to help us box everything up. Jess found this bakery supply store that has inexpensive white boxes, and Cassidy enlarged our business card to make labels to stick on them. It was cheaper than getting the boxes professionally printed, and they look great.

The back door bangs open, letting in a gust of cold air. "Hey, guys!" It's Stewart. He's wearing his Alcott Avengers hockey jersey. He's really proud of the fact that he finally made the high school team. He's been playing rec hockey forever, which Cassidy says takes anybody that breathes. But she's been coaching him privately for the past year or two, and I guess he's gotten a lot better.

"Almost ready to go, Mr. Delivery Boy," says Gigi. "We're down to the last cake."

Cassidy and her stepfather arrive home while Jess is finishing up the frosting violets.

"How'd your team do, honey?" her mother asks.

Cassidy scowls. "It was a tie for most of the game, but we lost in sudden-death overtime."

She hates to lose.

"You'll have another whack at them later in the season before play-offs," Stanley consoles her, giving Mrs. Sloane-Kinkaid a kiss. "Where's Chloe?"

"I put her down for a nap."

He yawns. "I could use one too."

"Maybe you should lie down for a while too, Cassidy," says her mother. "You were up so early."

Cassidy shakes her head. "I'm supposed to meet Mrs. Bergson and Tristan at the rink." She doesn't look too thrilled at this prospect.

Heather Vogel Frederick

"Sweetheart, are you sure you're not overdoing it?" Mrs. Sloane-Kinkaid looks worried.

"I'm fine, Mom. Quit worrying about me."

We box up the carrot cake for the wedding shower and load everything into the Chadwicks' SUV. Stewart slides into the driver's seat, then rolls down the window and sticks his head out.

"I forgot to tell you guys—some of us are going to the movies tonight. Anybody want to come?"

"Who is 'some of us'?" asks Becca, who is pretty particular about who she's seen with these days.

Her brother mentions the names of a couple of his hockey teammates, then adds, "Oh, and Zach Norton and Simon Berkeley too."

"Could be fun," says Becca, trying to sound casual. She'd walk over hot coals to do anything with Zach Norton.

"Is Tristan going to be there?" asks Cassidy.

Stewart nods. "I think so."

"Forget it, then."

Cassidy may be Tristan Berkeley's practice partner, but she doesn't even try and hide the fact that she doesn't like him. Behind his back, she calls him stuff like "Tristan Jerkeley" and "His Majesty" and "the Duke of Puke."

"I wish I could go, but I can't," says Jess. "I've already got plans with Adele and Frankie."

Stewart looks at me. "How about you, Megan?"

"I'll come," I tell him, trying not to sound too eager. To be fair to Becca, I'd pretty much walk over hot coals too, only not for Zach Norton. He's been eclipsed this year by Simon Berkeley.

"Great! Becca and I will pick you up around seven, okay?"

I nod. My parents have said that I can't go on solo dates until I'm sixteen, which I think is ridiculous, but I'm allowed to do stuff in groups. Normally, they'd insist on driving me too, but Stewart is so responsible he's like a junior grown-up, and I know they won't mind if he drives.

Stewart heads off with our deliveries, and we go back inside to clean up. When we're done, we pile into Cassidy's family's minivan. Mrs. Sloane-Kinkaid is going to drop Cassidy at the rink first, then take us all home.

A few minutes later we pull into the parking lot in front of the arena, and Cassidy hops out and grabs her skating bag. As she heads inside, Mrs. Bergson pulls up alongside us.

"I hope you have my pie in there," she says, smiling.

"One French silk chocolate, coming right up," says Jess, handing her a white box.

"Why don't you all come inside and watch for a few minutes?" Mrs. Bergson asks, after she puts the pie in her car. "You too, Clementine. I think you'll be interested to see a different side of your talented daughter."

We get out and follow her into the rink, then find seats in the bleachers while she goes over to where Cassidy and Tristan are lacing up their skates. The three of them stand there talking for a few minutes, then Cassidy and Tristan head out onto the ice.

Heather Vogel Frederick

"What the heck is he wearing?" whispers Becca.

I take out my cell phone and flip it open. "Not sure, but Fashionista Jane will definitely be interested." Speeding around the rink, Tristan switches directions and skates backward toward us with his rear sticking out. I zoom in on it and snap a picture, then slip my cell phone back in my purse.

Fashionista Jane, my alter ego, has been having a lot of fun over the past couple of months. She loves lurking the halls of Alcott High, cell phone in hand, and secretly snapping shots for her Fashion Faux Pas, as she calls them. She's blogged about other stuff too—how to organize your closet, Accessories 101, that sort of thing. But people are especially crazy about the Fashion Faux Pas.

Everybody at school is buzzing about Fashionista Jane's real identity, especially the people whose pictures I've posted. They're not too happy about that. I figure I'm doing them a favor, though. If they can see themselves the way we all see them, maybe they'll make better fashion choices.

Take Tristan Berkeley, for example. Here he is, out in public wearing a blue spandex jumpsuit. Sure, I know, he's an ice skater. But still—spandex? Not only is it skin-tight, it's *shiny*. Plus, he's been so rude to Cassidy I figure he has it coming.

Too bad he doesn't take his fashion cues from her. I never thought I'd say this, but out there on the ice right now, Cassidy Sloane actually looks good. She's wearing black leggings—non-shiny, non-Spandex leggings—and a black turtleneck. Simple. Chic. Stunning.

"Like Audrey Hepburn, only taller and with red hair," says my grandmother, nodding her approval. She elbows me. "You should put her on your blog."

Gigi's in on my secret. She thinks it's hilarious, and is always trying to give me ideas. She knows a lot of designers—she goes to Fashion Week in New York and Paris every year, and spends a lot of money on clothes—and her latest brainstorm is that I should host interviews with people in the fashion industry. I can't imagine that any of them would want to talk to me for my blog, but as my grandmother points out, you never know until you try.

Some music comes on—a waltz, I think. Cassidy moves into position beside Tristan, and he reaches around and puts his hand on her waist and the two of them skate away from where we're sitting, their feet moving in unison as they step from one foot to the other in a series of graceful turns. Then Tristan swings her around so that she's facing him, and she puts one hand on his shoulder and reaches out to clasp his free hand, and suddenly they're waltzing around the rink.

"Oh, my," says Mrs. Sloane-Kinkaid. Her hand wanders up to her throat, and her eyes are bright as she watches the two of them. "Oh, my."

"She's really growing up, isn't she?" says Gigi softly, patting her knee.

"I thought you'd like to see this," says Mrs. Bergson, who has come over to join us. She leans against the railing, her eyes following the pair. "Her height gives her beautiful lines. She's like a thoroughbred."

Heather Vogel Frederick

"She's good," says Jess.

"She's starting to get the hang of it," says Mrs. Bergson diplomatically. "The waltz is the easy part."

We watch for a while longer, and then Mrs. Sloane-Kinkaid reluctantly tells us she needs to get back to Chloe. After she drops Gigi and me at home, I head to my room for a nap. It's been a long day, and I want to be rested up for tonight. Afterward, I spend some time coming up with a suitably snarky post about Tristan Berkeley (Fashionista Jane titles it: "Spandex Fannies? Just say 'Non'!). Then it's time to take a shower.

I picked out my outfit earlier—a powder blue V-neck sweater over skinny leg jeans tucked into black boots—and as I'm getting dressed, there's a knock at my door.

"Come in!"

My grandmother pokes her head in, her dark eyes sparkling. "Ready for your big date?"

"Gigi! I told you, it's just a movie, not a date!" I protest.

"Mmm," she murmurs, arching an eyebrow. "Then I don't suppose you need these." Extending her hand, she opens her fingers. Her enormous diamond earrings are sitting on her outstretched palm.

I draw in my breath sharply. "Really?"

She nods. "Diamonds go with everything. Especially my beautiful granddaughter."

"Thank you so much!" I give her a hug, and kiss her soft cheek. She smiles at me. What would I do without Gigi?

Stewart and Becca show up promptly at seven.

"The others are going to meet us at the theater," Stewart tells me, after promising my parents that he'll drive carefully, make sure everyone's seat belts are buckled, obey the speed limits, and do everything else he's supposed to short of making us wear safety helmets.

"Sounds good," I reply.

Zach is already there when we arrive, and Becca trots over to him and starts talking his ear off. He doesn't look too annoyed, for once, though he does seem a little disappointed when he learns that Cassidy isn't coming. I think he still kind of likes her.

Stewart's hockey friends trickle in as we buy our tickets, but there's no sign of Simon and Tristan yet, and I start to worry that maybe they're not going to show.

They do, though, just as we're lining up for popcorn.

"Hi, Megan," says Simon, coming right over to stand by me.

"Hi."

"Pretty earrings."

"Thanks," I reply shyly. "They're my grandmother's."

His eyebrows shoot up. "You mean they're *real*?"

I nod.

"Wow, nice grandmother."

"She's the best."

"Hey, what's up with your brother?" asks Zach.

We all turn around to look at Tristan, who's standing by himself at the end of the line. His face is like a thundercloud.

Heather Vogel Frederick

Simon shrugs. "He's got his knickers in a twist."

Zach looks puzzled, and Simon grins. "Let's just say that he's 'wicked' unhappy, as you all put it. That idiot blogger—you know the one I'm talking about, Jane somebody-or-other—put an unflattering picture of him on the Internet. He's been brooding about it since dinner."

Idiot blogger? I turn away to hide my flaming face, his words ringing in my ears. What if Simon finds out it was me? And how on earth did Tristan discover the picture so quickly? I only posted it a couple of hours ago.

My gaze slides over to Becca. She's wearing what my mother calls a cat-who-ate-the-canary smile.

"Did you tell him?" I whisper furiously.

"Stewart asked me to e-mail them the movie time, and I figured I'd tip Tristan off while I was at it," she whispers back. "He was going to find out eventually anyway. What's the big deal? Besides, it serves him right. Look at him standing there, like he's not even part of our group. Talk about Mr. Stuck-Up."

Honestly, sometimes Becca is so clueless.

I feel a tug on my arm and turn back around to see Simon smiling at me. "Do you mind if I sit with you?"

Do I *mind*? Is he kidding? Sitting with him is all I've been thinking for hours.

Except now the evening is ruined, and I have nobody to blame but myself.

SPRING

"*Obstinate, headstrong girl!*"

—*Pride and Prejudice*

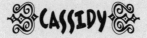

CASSIDY

"There is a stubbornness in about me that never can bear to be frightened at the will of others. My courage always rises with every attempt to intimidate me."

—*Pride and Prejudice*

"Time out!"

I blow my coach's whistle and a dozen little girls skate over to me, huffing and puffing. The chicks in my Chicks with Sticks club range in age from seven to eleven, and I tower over all of them. I squat down so they don't have to tilt their heads back to look at me.

"Way to go!" I tell them. "That was much better."

This is a lie.

We've been working on speed drills this afternoon, and they're moving like slugs out there. I don't care, though. They're trying really hard, and they'll get better. I did. Plus, I remember how patient my father and my coaches were with me when I was first learning to play. I blow my whistle and tell them to go line up again.

I really like working with kids, which surprises me. I've never spent much time with younger kids before, aside from occasionally teaching skating lessons. I never even babysat before my sister Chloe came along. I never had time, and I wasn't interested. But coaching Chicks with Sticks is just about the most fun thing I've ever done. It's almost as much fun as playing hockey. I love to play hockey—I mean *really* love to play hockey—but getting these little girls excited about chasing after a puck even rivals that.

"Stop at the blue line!" I call to them as they dash off—well, if you can call what they're doing a dash—across the rink. "Keep your heads up!" Responding to my whistle, they sprint and stop, sprint and stop from one line to the next all the way down the ice.

Which is where I just about live these days. There and in the car. Monday through Thursday nights I practice with the Lady Shawmuts out at the rink in Acton. Saturdays and most Sundays we have games—some of them as far away as Rhode Island and Connecticut. The only ice time Mrs. Bergson could wangle for Chicks with Sticks was on Tuesdays and Thursdays right after school, so I book on over here from Alcott High, then stay afterward to practice with Tristan until dinnertime. The two of us also practice on Monday, Wednesday, and Friday mornings before school, and we usually squeeze in at least one session on the weekends, too, depending on when and where my hockey games are scheduled.

Oddly enough, I'm not the only one who practically lives at the rink. Tristan puts in just as much time on the ice as I do, and some of the girls on my U16 team are working this hard too. A lot of them go to schools that have hockey programs for girls, and they're doubling

Heather Vogel Frederick

up, playing for their high school teams and for our Division 1 team. I guess when you love to skate, you love to skate, it's as simple as that.

My mother was really worried at first about me overextending myself, as she calls it, but, for the most part I'm the happiest I've been since my father died. I'm in better shape than I've ever been too. I'm even working harder to keep my grades up, since Mom told me if I don't she's pulling the plug on the whole shebang. I worked out a deal with Stewart Chadwick, who tutors me when I need help in exchange for free hockey coaching. So far, it's going really well. I doubt I'll ever be the kind of student that Jess and Emma are, but there are a lot more B's than C's on my report card this year, and I even managed an A in Spanish.

The only thing I'm not so happy about is Tristan.

I would have quit after that first practice except for Mrs. Bergson. She's been so great about helping me out with the hockey club and everything—assisting me with drills, and taking the girls who need extra work on the basics aside for extra coaching, not to mention getting the rink for us for free—I didn't want to let her down. And actually, even though I hate to admit it and I'm not all that good at it yet, I kind of like ice dancing. It's completely different from hockey, that's for sure. But it gives me that same feeling that nothing else on earth does—that sense of complete freedom when I'm soaring across the ice. Only this time, I'm soaring to music.

The other reason I'm sticking with it is that I have a stubborn streak, and I don't want to give His Majesty the satisfaction of seeing me fail.

Out of the corner of my eye I catch a glimpse of Mr. Fancypants himself stepping onto the ice. He's early. This annoys me for some reason, and I pretend I don't see him. At least he ditched the blue Spandex. He was mad for a solid week after Megan's blog post, but it did some good because he went out and got himself some plain black workout pants.

"Cassidy!" Mrs. Bergson calls to me from the side of the rink, pointing to her watch. "Time to wrap it up out there. Your girls are looking good!"

My girls. I like the sound of that. I smile to myself as I motion them over. They're adorable, all bundled up in their giant hockey pads with their faces barely showing under their helmets. Did I look that cute when I was their age?

As she passes Tristan, tiny Katie Angelino slips and falls. She's my youngest "chick"—only seven—and the weakest skater. She lies there for a minute, then bangs her glove on the ice in frustration. Poor kid. I remember that feeling only too well. Heck, I still struggle with it when I'm ice dancing.

Before I can skate over to her, though, Tristan scoops her back onto her feet. He pulls a tissue out of his pocket and hands it to her, then squats down and talks to her softly while she blows her nose.

He glances up at me and our eyes meet. I want to mouth the words *thank you*, but something won't let me. Pride, I suppose. I press my lips together instead and look away.

Tristan Berkeley is a puzzle. He's one of the rudest, most stuck-up

Heather Vogel Frederick

people I've ever met, but I know he's close to his brother, who's the nicest guy in the world. Simon obviously worships him, so there must be something good there. Darned if I can figure out what, though. Tristan barely says two words to me, and when he does, they're usually critical. Not once has he thanked me for stepping in to be his practice partner. Practice doormat is more like it. He doesn't bother trying to be friendly, and at school he mostly ignores me, even though we spend hours and hours together every week.

Tristan gives Katie a gentle push and she slip-slides over in my direction, but when she tries to stop she can't. She bursts into tears again as she barrels into me.

"I can't do anything right!" she wails.

"That's not true," I tell her, handing her another tissue. I've learned to come armed with a bunch of them. "A month ago you couldn't even stand on those skates, and now look at you! You're getting stronger all the time, and I'm really proud of how hard you're trying."

Sniffling, she swipes angrily at her tears. I put my arm around her shoulders. I want to laugh, because she looks so much like Chloe does when she's dressed in her snowsuit, like a puffy little marshmallow. But I don't, of course. I keep my coach face on. "Listen, Katie, when I was first starting out, I was way worse than you are."

She looks up at me suspiciously. "Really?"

I nod. "Uh-huh. But I didn't give up, and you're not going to give up either, okay?"

Her forehead puckers as she thinks about it. She nods. "Okay."

I slap her a high five. "That's the spirit. Now go tell your mom that your coach thinks you're awesome."

As she toddles away toward the side of the rink, I notice Tristan watching me. For some reason, I feel my face flush.

"Cassidy! Tristan!" calls Mrs. Bergson. "Time to start warming up! Cassidy—take a five-minute break, then change your skates and join us."

I head for the bleachers and my sports bag, where I down some water and check my cell phone. There's a message from Dr. Weisman. He wants me to call him.

"Cassidy Sloane!" he says when I do. "Purveyor of world-famous pies."

I laugh. "Dr. Weisman, world-famous shrink!"

He laughs too.

Amazingly, I've made it through almost three quarters of a school year without being dragged into Dr. Weisman's office. He's a family therapist really, not a shrink, and my mother made me go to him a lot when we first moved here and I was having a tough time dealing with that, and with missing my father. She marched me down there last year too, after the incident with the goat cheese in Savannah Sinclair's suitcase. And he was a big help when I found out Mom was expecting Chloe, which kind of knocked me for a loop. This year, I still see Dr. Weisman, only not in his office. He and his wife are big hockey fans, and they often turn up at my games. Plus, they're regular customers of Pies & Prejudice.

"What can I get for you this week?" I ask him.

"We have friends coming to lunch on Sunday, and we need something that says sunshine, warmth, and everything that Mud Season is not."

Mud season in New England is a total pain. It happens when winter's not quite over and spring's not quite here, and it's cold and wet and drizzly and the snow is melting and slushy and the ground turns to sludge. We never had anything like it back in Laguna Beach, where I used to live. This is the time of year I miss California the most.

Thinking about California reminds me of Courtney. I make a mental note to text her as soon as I finish with Dr. Weisman's order.

"What you need is lemon meringue pie," I tell him. "My mother calls it summer in a piecrust."

"We'll take two."

After we hang up, I call in the order to Jess, who keeps track of everything, then send a text to my sister: AT RINK WITH DUKE OF PUKE.

She texts me right back: POOR YOU!

MUD SEASON. YUCK, I tell her.

HA HA, she texts back. HOT AND SUNNY, HEADING TO THE BEACH. COME VISIT.

I was hoping to go see her over Spring Break, but that was before our big plan to surprise Emma with a plane ticket home. Now I'm thinking maybe some weekend in May instead. Hockey will be well over by then, and I can probably talk Mom into letting me take an extra day or two off school, especially if I continue to keep my grades up.

"Cassidy!" calls Mrs. Bergson.

"Coming!" I call back, lacing up my skates.

Tristan's coach in England sent over a DVD of the programs he's supposed to be practicing for the competition this summer, and we watched it last night at Mrs. Bergson's. It was my first glimpse of his cousin Annabelle. Emma told us that she's pretty, and she's right. I guess I'd been kind of hoping she was exaggerating. But Annabelle looks like a ballerina, with really good posture and sleek dark hair and dark blue eyes just like Tristan's.

The compulsory dance looked simple enough—it's a waltz—but the free dance was a lot more complicated, with a ton of fancy footwork. There were some pretty tricky-looking rotational lifts too, including one where Annabelle did a handstand on the coach's bent leg while he spun around.

Unlike pairs skating, there aren't any throws in ice dancing, but there are a few lifts. We've attempted only the easiest ones so far, like the one where I face Tristan and put my arms around his neck, and he locks his forearms underneath my shoulder blades. The momentum of the spin does most of the work, leaving me to concentrate on bending my knees back in a graceful arc, which sounds a lot easier than it is. The other lift we've mastered is the one where Tristan puts his arm around my waist and swings me off my feet. That's simple enough.

That handstand lift, though? Good luck with that. Tristan is strong, but lifting me is going to be like lifting Led or Zep, one of the Delaney's Belgian draft horses. I'm nearly six feet of solid muscle.

"So," says Mrs. Bergson as I skate over to where she and Tristan are standing. "I've broken the programs into bite-size pieces for you, Cassidy—"

Tristan snorts at this, and I glare at him.

"—which I think will help make them easier to learn."

"Let's hope so," says Tristan under his breath, and I squelch the urge to kick him.

The next two hours fly by in a confusing flurry of chasses and twizzles, slip steps and rocker turns, Mohawks, Choctaws, jumps, hops, and spins. I push myself to the limit, grimly wondering how on earth I'm ever going to memorize all this stuff.

"What's the matter with you?" says Tristan as I manage to get out of sync yet again during a side-by-side spin. He frowns at me in exasperation. "Weren't you watching the way Annabelle did it?"

I cut my blades sharply to the side, sending up a shower of ice shavings as I come to an abrupt stop. "Will you shut up already about your stupid girlfriend!"

"Distant cousin," says Tristan stiffly.

"Whatever! I don't care! Look, I get the fact that I'm not as good at ice dancing as your precious cousin, but I'm trying my best here, okay?"

"There's no need to get snippy about it," he replies, clearly offended.

"All right, then," interjects Mrs. Bergson. "I think that's probably enough for today. I want you both to go home and get a good night's sleep, and I'll see you back here in the morning."

As Tristan skates off in a huff, Mrs. Bergson takes me aside. "Cassidy, two things," she says. "First of all, don't let Tristan get under your skin. He's doesn't have my perspective. He's too close to you—quite literally. The two of you are rarely more than a foot apart out there on the ice, and he can't see the forest for the trees. You're improving by leaps and bounds, my dear, leaps and bounds."

"It doesn't feel that way," I grumble.

"Trust me, it will. And secondly," she continues, "I've been meaning for some time to tell you what a good job you're doing with Chicks with Sticks. You're a natural at coaching, Cassidy. Those little girls just adore you. I know you want to play pro hockey someday, and there's no reason you can't, but I hope you think seriously about pursuing a career in coaching at some point too."

I look over at her, surprised. "Really?"

She nods. "Coaching is a wonderful job. It's one of the most rewarding things I've ever done professionally. There's nothing like helping others learn to do something you love."

I feel a warm glow inside from her praise. Leaning down a minute later to unlace my skate, I smile to myself. Mrs. Bergson, a former Olympian, thinks I'm coach material! I'm floating on air as I leave the rink.

Then Tristan completely ruins it.

"Cassidy!" he says, as I emerge into the parking lot.

"What?" I snap, surprised to find him waiting for me.

"Um, I was talking to Stewart Chadwick at lunch the other day, and he says you're in a book club with Emma Hawthorne, the girl whose house we're living in."

"Yeah," I admit cautiously, wondering where he's going with this.

"He says you do some sort of videoconference bookclub meetings with her."

"That's right."

"Well, perhaps we could set up a videoconference with Annabelle and our coach back at home," he suggests. "They could watch us skate, and then give us some pointers."

I stare at him in disbelief. "Forget it," I tell him flatly. "It's bad enough that you criticize me all the time, I don't need Sti—uh, Annabelle—putting her two cents in as well."

"That's not what I meant!" he protests. "Look, I'm sorry if I hurt your feelings back in there. I just wanted to—"

"To what?" I holler at him, all my wounded pride and resentment for the way he's treated me these last few months boiling over. "Make me feel like a big loser? Well, you've done a great job of that, trust me!"

We stand there, eye to eye, glaring at each other.

"Have it your way," he says finally. "I just wanted to help." He turns on his heel and so do I, and we both stalk away in a snit.

Final score: Who cares?

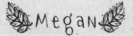

Megan

I think Simon Berkeley likes me.

I mean really, truly likes me.

I don't think I'm making this up—ever since we all went to the movies a while ago he's been acting differently. He almost always sits next to me at lunchtime, and sometimes I catch him staring at me when he thinks I'm not looking. Last night he called to ask a question about our biology homework, and we ended up talking for, like, half an hour.

I can't stop thinking about him. I haven't said a word to anyone—not even Becca. Now I understand why Jess hasn't told any of us, besides Emma, how she feels about Darcy. It's something I just want to hug close.

"You're in a good mood today," says Gigi when I waltz into the kitchen for breakfast.

"Yup," I say, giving her a hug and a kiss. I hug my parents, too, who are sitting at the table reading the paper.

"What's up?" says my dad. "You're awfully cheerful for a Monday morning."

"It's spring," I tell him. "I like spring."

Which is totally true. Spring is my favorite season. I love the way the air smells, and the way you can practically hear things growing. I love spring colors, too, all those Easter egg shades and pretty pastels. Fall is the important season for fashion—lots of coats and sweaters and serious clothes, and magazines that weigh about ten pounds— but spring styles have always been my favorite.

Adding to my good mood are the pancakes my grandmother slides onto my plate. Not a speck of whole wheat in sight, just fluffy golden-brown buttermilk pancakes loaded with blueberries and drenched in butter and real maple syrup. I attack them hungrily.

"I talked to Shannon Delaney last night," my mother tells us. She's picking at a bowl of the new organic cereal she bought made of something called spelt, but she keeps sneaking bites of pancake off my father's plate when she thinks he isn't looking. "She is planning to call Phoebe today with an update."

Mrs. Hawthorne has been in on our secret from the beginning. We had to tell her about Pies & Prejudice so that she wouldn't plan any trips for their family during spring break week.

"So are you girls going to surprise Emma when you talk next

weekend?" asks my dad. He winks at me as my mother's fork darts over to his plate again.

I smile. "Maybe," I reply. "I hope so. I guess it all depends on our sales this week."

He gets up from the table and kisses the top of my mother's head, then slides his plate with the remaining pancakes on it over in front of her. She grins up at him sheepishly. Turning to me he asks, "Want a ride to school this morning, pumpkin?"

"Sure." It's always nice to get driven to school. I polish off my breakfast, then head to my room to brush my teeth and grab my stuff. I pause to hop online really quick and see if anybody commented on my latest blog post.

I have to admit I'm kind of addicted to Fashionista Jane. I get a kick out of trying to mimic what Emma calls Austen-speak, and I love the way I can be as creative as I want with my postings. It's kind of like having a magazine of my own. The only downside is I'm still worried that Simon will find out that Fashionista Jane is me. He and his brother are really close, and I guess Tristan was upset for weeks about that photo of him I put on my blog. At the moment, though, this worry is the only tiny rain cloud hovering over my happiness.

I haven't posted any more Fashion Faux Pas since the Spandex smackdown, even though readers are begging for them. I've been sticking to stuff like Closet Makeovers—Becca and I tackled Ashley's closet last week—and last night I put up a new Wardrobe Remix with odds and ends scrounged from my own closet.

Heather Vogel Frederick

I scroll down to the picture: Last year's short black denim skirt; a wide, stretchy faux satin black belt I bought almost three years ago; and—this is a first for me—a T-shirt I borrowed from my mother. Gigi brought it home for her from France last year, and I love the skinny black-and-white stripes, and the white satin piping around the boatneck collar.

Sure enough, below it there are a ton of comments waiting for me. Becca and Ashley both gave the remix a thumbs-up, someone who calls herself Angelfire said, "Satin + denim = oh yeah!" and there's a comment from Emma, too, who wrote, "Fashionista Jane's gentle readers abroad are greatly indebted to her for keeping them attuned to the latest fashion trends in the colonies." That is so Emma. She's really good at Austen-speak.

There are a bunch more comments from people I don't know, including one from a blogger named "Wolfgang." I pause when I see that one.

I know a Wolfgang, but he's the fashion editor of *Flash* magazine and its teen spin-off *Flashlite*. Could it be him? But how would he know about Fashionista Jane? I read the comment: "Love your blog, darling! Refreshingly snarky, with a pinch of sweet. FABULOUS! Big things ahead for you—contact me!"

It's got to be the Wolfgang I know. He writes exactly the way my Wolfgang talks.

But what if it's some weirdo? My mother's always lecturing me about the dangers of the Internet, and she's got a point. Frowning, I debate on whether to take a chance or not. There's no e-mail address, just his blogger name: WOLFGANG.

I decide to risk it. Making sure not to include my phone number or e-mail address or anything, I type a quick reply, and sign it "*Flashlite*, Vol. 1, Issue 1, p. 21." If it's my Wolfgang, he'll know exactly what that means, because that was the issue of *Flashlite* magazine that featured an interview with me. If it's not, well, no harm done, I'll just delete his comments.

Hoping that it is the Wolfgang I know, I gather my things for school and head out to the car. What could he want to talk to me about, though? I'm still mulling over all the possible answers to that question when my dad drops me off at Alcott High.

As I climb out of the car, I spot Simon Berkeley standing by the flagpole, watching the buses unload. He runs a hand through his curly blond hair and my heart gives a happy lurch as I realize he's watching for me. I can tell by the way he perks up as my bus pulls in, and then droops in disappointment when the last kid gets off and it isn't me.

I sneak up behind him. "Hey!"

He spins around and his face lights up. "Megan!"

We stand there grinning at each other.

"My dad drove me to school," I tell him.

"Oh! That explains—I mean, uh—how nice."

We smile at each other some more, then he says, "I guess I'll see you this afternoon in biology."

"Okay," I reply. *Smooth, real smooth.* Why is it I can never think of anything to say around him? "Did you finish your homework?"

"Yes, finally. That question about DNA codes and proteins was beastly."

I love the way he says that. *Beastly*. It's so British. The bell rings and we head across the parking lot.

"You have ceramics today, right?" he asks.

He knows my schedule!

I nod.

"Well, I guess I won't see you at lunch, then. Too bad." We get to the door and he holds it open for me, which is like something my dad would do. "Until biology, then."

"See you!" I reply.

"See you."

I float down the hall toward math class, smiling to myself. What other high school guy would be polite enough to hold the door for a girl? It's kind of a dad thing to do, but it is nice, and Fashionista Jane would definitely approve. "*Such happy manners the young gentleman displayed!*" she'd probably say, or something like that. I should do an Austen-speak blog post about etiquette.

"What's up with Simon Berkeley?" Becca whispers as I slide into the seat beside her. "I saw you guys outside. What were you talking about?"

I can feel myself turn bright red. I really don't want Becca poking at this. It's too . . . new.

"Nothing."

"Oh, c'mon," she says. "You can't tell me he doesn't like you. Sheesh, Megan, he lights up like a Christmas tree every time you're around."

"You really think so?" I ask eagerly. So much for not discussing my crush with Becca.

"Absolutely."

The happy feeling stays with me all morning. I have a hard time keeping my mind on school and the only class that benefits is ceramics, because all the joy flows down my arms and out my fingers and I make my best creation ever, a stout little pitcher with cheerful curves and a sleek handle. I put a sunny yellow glaze on it. It will make a perfect birthday gift for my mother. She loves handmade stuff.

Afterward, I eat lunch with Kevin Mullins because he's sitting by himself again and because it's the right thing to do. He asks me why I'm "overflowing with the milk of human kindness" today—his exact words; I swear the kid is destined never to be normal—and I tell him I'm just happy because it's spring.

Finally, it's time for biology class. We're watching a PowerPoint presentation today about DNA, which means we don't have to sit with our lab partners. There's an empty chair next to Simon where Zach usually sits, but he's off at an away baseball game, and Simon pats it encouragingly. I shoot Becca an apologetic look and cross the room to slide in next to him.

"How was ceramics?" he whispers.

"Great!" I whisper back. "I made a birthday present for my mom."

The slideshow is incredibly boring—who besides Jess Delaney and Kevin Mullins could possibly care how genetic information is transmitted?—and Simon must think so too, because he keeps slipping me these funny little cartoons of our classmates and Ms. Bates, our teacher. I have to stifle my giggles.

My mother is always going on about how teachers are underpaid, overworked, and underappreciated public servants who deserve our respect, but honestly, Ms. Bates desperately needs a makeover. She dresses, well, like my mother. Lots of stretch pants and natural fibers and comfortable, ugly shoes. Today she's got on these hideous sandals with cork soles and thick suede straps, and unbelievably, she decided to accessorize with toe socks. Toe socks! And worse, there are smiley faces on them. I can't resist—I wait until Simon isn't looking and sneak my cell phone out of my purse, then snap a picture of her feet.

"Um, I was wondering," Simon says to me as we're walking out of the classroom together afterward.

"Uh-huh?" I reply eagerly, hoping that maybe he's going to ask me out. Not that I could go if he did—my parents have decreed that I can't date until I'm sixteen. Another whole year to go. But still, it would be amazing to be asked.

"Here." He hands me an envelope.

"What's this?"

"An invitation. Next Sunday is my birthday, and I'm having a party."

"Sounds like fun," I tell him, trying to keep from jumping up and down with excitement. An invitation to a party isn't a date, exactly, but it's close.

I don't remember a thing about the bus ride home. I skim up the driveway and into the house to find a note on the kitchen table letting me know that Mom is at a Riverkeepers meeting and that Gigi and Mrs. Bergson have gone into Boston to have tea at the Ritz. It's Mrs. Bergson's birthday treat from my grandmother.

I think about calling Simon to officially RSVP, but decide I'd better wait until I ask my parents first, just to be sure. So I go online instead. There's a message waiting ("Call me!") from Wolfgang. He includes his real e-mail address—wolfgang@flash.com—this time, along with his phone number. Just to be sure, I google the number, and sure enough, *Flash* magazine pops up. It's my Wolfgang. I pick up the phone and call.

"Megan WONG!" he cries when he hears my voice. "I can't believe it's YOU, darling! Such a FABULOUS coincidence! I should have known—you're a genius!"

I'd forgotten how much fun it is to talk to Wolfgang. All of his sentences end in exclamation points. It turns out he's been hunting for teen bloggers, and is interested in having me do a guest blog once a month for *Flashlite* online.

"Don't change a thing, just be your fun snarky-sweet Fashionista Jane self, and it will be FANTASTIC!"

We agree on my first deadline and I hang up the phone, dazed.

"So what did you do today?" my mother asks at dinner.

"Well," I hesitate, wondering if I should tell them. But it's too exciting not to share. "I got asked to be a guest blogger for *Flashlite* online."

"Wow," says my dad. "That's really great."

"You have a blog?" says my mother.

"I told you about it a few months ago, remember?"

"This is wonderful news," says Gigi, beaming at me. "My talented granddaughter."

Honestly, I could make a mud pie and Gigi would think it was the most amazing thing anybody had done, ever. I love her for that.

My mother's forehead crinkles. "Do you think you'll have time for all this?" she asks. "Blogging, Bébé Soleil, Pies & Prejudice. You're in high school now, Megan. The grades you get these next four years will go on your permanent record. You need to be thinking about college."

My mother's been thinking about college for me since kindergarten.

"It's not that big a deal, Mom," I assure her. "It's only once a month. My fashion blog is just what I do for fun—Wolfgang told me not to agonize over it."

Two days later, though, I'm at Becca's house after school, agonizing over it.

"I can't believe I said yes," I moan. "Thousands of people are going to be reading this stupid thing."

"Thousands of people could already be reading your blog," Becca points out. "Which isn't stupid, by the way. Your wardrobe remix totally saved my life. I bought that identical belt back in seventh grade, remember? I dug it out and I'm going to wear it tomorrow."

"You know what I mean," I tell her. "Plus, what if Simon finds out?"

We're holed up in Becca's room, hiding from her mother. Mrs. Chadwick has taken over the dining room as her office, and the table is piled high with books and catalog and big sheets of graph paper. She spent all winter in there, happily studying for her landscape-design classes and sketching new plans for their yard. Now that spring has arrived, she's corralled Becca and Stewart into helping her with the clipping and pruning and digging and planting. She put me to work last time I was here too, spreading manure with Mr. Chadwick. Not exactly my idea of a fun Saturday afternoon.

"It's going to look like Versailles," Mr. Chadwick said sadly, shaking his head. "Our neighbors will run us out of town. We'll have to go into the witness protection program."

"Don't be such a drama queen, Henry," Mrs. Chadwick scolded. "It's going to be perfect."

"Mark my words," he whispered to Becca and me. "We'll be sent to live someplace in North Dakota, and our name will be Oinkelmeyer instead of Chadwick."

Mr. Chadwick is really funny. I guess you'd have to have a good sense of humor to be married to Becca's mother.

Becca tells me that there's no way Simon will find out—"like he's going to be reading *Flashlite* online," she scoffs—and that I need to stop worrying and concentrate on coming up with a debut blog post. She helps me brainstorm, and I go home with a lot of ideas.

I can hardly keep my mind on school the rest of the week, though, and by Saturday I'm a bit of a wreck. I nearly dump twice the amount of salt into the apple pies that Gigi and I are assembling—Becca is helping Jess with the cupcakes this time around—and I accidentally put whipped cream on the lemon meringue pies and meringue on the French silk chocolate pies.

Heather Vogel Frederick

"Megan, what is the matter with you today?" my grandmother says, exasperated.

"Sorry, Gigi," I apologize, and help her switch them back.

That night I realize that I have something new to agonize over as well—namely, what am I going to wear tomorrow to Simon's birthday party?

The next afternoon, while my mother and Gigi and Mrs. Chadwick are visiting in the kitchen—it's the Chadwicks' turn to bring snacks to our book club meeting, and it looks like Becca's mother went all out to try and redeem herself from last year's cornmeal mush episode, because she brought a yummy-looking Kentucky Derby pie—I get the equipment ready in the living room. Becca watches as I set up the webcam and microphone and connect my laptop to the TV.

"You should join the A/V Club," she says. "I hear Kevin Mullins is president."

I grin. "Technical expertise comes with the territory when your father is a computer whiz."

"So did you decide on a blog post for *Flashlite* yet?"

I nod. "Want to see it?"

I open the Fashionista Jane file on my computer and read it aloud to her: " 'Gentle readers, today your faithful fashion guide embarks on a new journey. Parasol gripped firmly in her gloved hand, she steps out of her carriage and into the glamorous world of . . . New York fashion! In celebration of this, her first guest blog for *Flashlite* online, she has assembled for you an all-new selection of Fashion Faux Pas, many of them spotted on the fair streets of the Big Apple itself.' "

"You're doing Fashion Faux Pas again!" Becca cries. "But I thought you'd sworn off them since the Tristan meltdown?"

"I know, but they're the part of my blog that Wolfgang likes best. Besides, what you told me is probably true, Simon will never read *Flashlite*, right?" I keep my voice light, but what I don't tell her is how much I want my guest blog to be a big success. This is *Flashlite* we're talking about!

I send the pictures to our TV screen and she starts to laugh. The first one is of some guy wearing a little kid's propeller hat. I took it in Central Park last time I was in New York. The caption reads, "Mobile headgear is simply not acceptable on anyone over the age of six." The next one shows a businesswoman who looks normal enough from the ankles up—she's wearing a suit and carrying a briefcase and everything—but instead of the kind of shoes that would go with her outfit, she's got a pair of those ridiculous giant plastic shoes on. My mother has a bright orange pair, and I totally hate them.

Becca laughs when she reads the caption: "Why is this otherwise dignified gentlewoman wearing dishpans upon her feet?"

"Dishpans!" she cries, delighted. "That describes them *perfectly*. Wait until I use that on mom."

Becca's mother has a pair too. Hers are green. I happen to know this because I was with my mother when she bought them for her. She

Heather Vogel Frederick

thought they'd be perfect for Mrs. Chadwick's new gardening venture.

"Um, I still haven't decided if I'm going to use this one or not," I tell Becca as another picture flashes up onto the screen.

"Omigosh, I forgot about that!" squeals Becca.

It's Tristan Berkeley again. He's squatting down to pick up an apple that rolled off his cafeteria tray, and his sweater is scooched up in the back. You can see the waistband of his underwear. MANCHESTER UNITED is printed in big letters across it.

"What would you use for a caption?" asks Becca.

"I was thinking something like, 'A true gentleman never reveals the purveyor of his undergarments.'"

Becca grins. "Perfect. You definitely have to use it."

I gnaw on a corner of my fingernail. "You think?"

"Absolutely. For one thing, Simon's never going to see it, and for another, even if he did, you can't tell it's Tristan."

"Yeah, I guess you're right. There's one more." I click on the final picture and our biology teacher's feet flash onto the screen.

Becca stares at them, and then recognition slowly dawns. "Are those Ms. Bates's smiley-face socks?"

"Yep," I reply smugly. "And here is what Fashionista Jane has to say about them: 'If a lady is bold enough to reveal her ankles in public, it were better not to draw attention to them with inappropriate or boisterous hosiery.'"

Becca collapses on the couch. "*Boisterous hosiery?*" She gasps, clutching her sides.

I grin. "I used a thesaurus. I wanted something more Austen-ish than 'loud socks.'"

"Wolfgang is going to die laughing! *I* might die laughing!"

I grin at her, pleased.

The doorbell rings and I quickly close the Fashionista Jane file as the rest of the book club arrives. I'd rather surprise them once it's posted on the *Flashlite* website.

"So girls, just a reminder," says my mother as everyone settles into their seats. "Don't spoil the secret!"

"Mom!" I scoff. "As if we're going to forget."

"I'm just saying." She turns to Jess. "Any updates from the treasurer?"

Jess pulls a small notebook out of her book bag and consults the figures. "We're getting closer, you guys," she tells us.

"Close enough to tell Emma?" asks Cassidy.

Jess shakes her head. "Not quite. We could use a few hundred more dollars."

"But spring break is less than a month away," I say.

"Yeah, I know." Jess looks a little glum.

"I'm sure Jerry and I could—"

"No way, Mom," I tell her. My mother is always eager to open up her checkbook for a good cause. Not that it isn't nice of her and everything. But this is different. "We really want to do this ourselves."

Jess and Cassidy and Becca nod in agreement.

"What we need is a big sale," says Becca. "Anybody know someone who wants to buy, like, fifty pies?"

The room is quiet for a moment, then Mrs. Bergson speaks up. "Didn't you tell me you have a spring concert coming up, Jess?"

"Uh-huh."

"What if you were to ask Colonial Academy if Pies & Prejudice could cater the refreshments?"

Jess perks up at this. "That's a good idea. I'll ask tomorrow."

"I'm just curious," says Mrs. Chadwick, with a quick glance at Gigi. "What's the best-selling pie so far?"

It's no secret that she and my grandmother have a little rivalry going with their pie recipes—namely Gigi's apple streusel and Mrs. Chadwick's coconut cream.

Jess grins. "Sorry, ladies, but this month it's lemon meringue all the way."

"Summer in a pie crust," says Mrs. Sloane-Kinkaid smugly.

My mother looks at her watch. "It's time," she tells us. "Places, everyone. And remember, not a word about all this." She gives me a thumbs-up, and I click the icon on my laptop to place the videoconference call to England.

"Hi, everybody!" Emma and her mother chorus a minute later as they appear on our giant TV screen above the mantel.

"Hi!" we chorus back. We chat for a little while and they show us some pictures of their latest trip—a weekend in Edinburgh, Scotland—and then it's time to officially start our book club discussion.

"I've got a question," blurts Cassidy, before anybody has a chance to say anything else.

"Let me guess," says Mrs. Hawthorne dryly. "You want to eat first."

Cassidy grins. "Nah, I'm good. Here's the thing. I like this book okay, and it's really funny in some parts—that Lady Catherine De Bourgh is a pill, isn't she?—but why was Jane Austen so obsessed with people falling in love and getting married?"

"Good question," Mrs. Hawthorne replies. "*Pride and Prejudice* is much more than just a love story, however."

"Yeah, it's only the best love story *ever*," says Emma.

"I wouldn't disagree," says her mother, who I suddenly notice is wearing an I ♥ MR. DARCY T-shirt. "But back to your question, Cassidy—while love is at the center of all of Jane Austen's novels, they are also notable for their keen social criticism and gentle satire."

Cassidy's face clouds.

"That means she pokes fun at everything," Emma explains. "Like the way Mr. Collins is always sucking up to Lady Catherine, just because she's richer than he is."

How does Emma *know* all this stuff?

"And because she's higher up the social ladder," adds my mother. "The class system back then was very rigid."

"Still, it's the love stories at the heart of her books that have kept people coming back to them for two centuries now," Mrs. Bergson notes.

"That's because it's love that makes the world go round," says Mrs. Delaney.

Becca nudges me with her elbow, and I shoot her a warning glance.

Heather Vogel Frederick

The last thing I need is for her to blab to everybody how I feel about Simon Berkeley.

"So was Jane Austen ever in love?" asks Jess.

"Funny you should ask!" Mrs. Hawthorne replies, holding up this month's handout.

FUN FACTS ABOUT JANE

1) Although she fell in love on several occasions and was once briefly engaged, Jane Austen never married and never had children of her own. She was said to have been "a particularly agreeable aunt," however. She had twenty-four nieces and nephews and enjoyed spending time with them.

2) Once, when she was young, she invented a list of husbands for herself, none of whom were real people, and wrote their names down in her father's parish register—Henry Frederick, Howard Fitzwilliam, Edmund Arthur William Mortimer, and Jack Smith.

3) Historians disagree over who was the love of Jane's life. Some say it was Tom Lefroy, a young Irishman she flirted with when she was twenty and wrote about to her sister, others that it was a student at Cambridge named Samuel Blackall, or a mysterious suitor she mentioned meeting at

the seaside in the summer of 1801. Unfortunately, none of these crushes ended in engagement or marriage.

4) Her sister Cassandra was also disappointed in love. She was engaged to a former pupil of her father's, a young clergyman who traveled to the West Indies before their marriage to try and make his fortune. Tragically, while there he caught yellow fever and died. Cassandra remained single for the rest of her life.

5) Jane was engaged briefly once, when she was twenty-six. Harris Bigg-Wither, whose sisters were close friends of Jane's and Cassandra's, proposed one evening while she was visiting at their home. She accepted, then changed her mind and broke off the engagement the following morning.

6) Harris was heir to a comfortable estate, and as Mrs. Bigg-Withers, Jane would have been mistress of a large, elegant home and could have helped take care of her family financially. While no one is entirely sure what happened, toward the end of her life she wrote to her niece Fanny, "Anything is to be preferred or endured rather than marrying without Affection." It's not unreasonable to assume that she called off the engagement because she didn't love Harris Bigg-Withers, and didn't want to settle for anything less than love.

Heather Vogel Frederick

I reread Fact #2 and feel myself blush. Just this morning, I practiced writing *Megan Berkeley* in my sketchbook. Not that I'm in love with Simon or anything, or thinking of marrying him.

"Why would someone as smart as Jane Austen even think about marrying someone she didn't love?" Cassidy asks. "Especially somebody named Harris Bigg-Withers." She looks over at Jess. "Don't withers have something to do with a horse?"

Jess snorts. "Yeah. It's the part at the base of their neck."

"Jane Big-Neck," quips Cassidy, and we can't help but giggle. "No wonder she didn't want to marry him."

"Does anybody remember which character in *Pride and Prejudice* married someone she didn't love?" asks Mrs. Hawthorne. She grabs Emma's hand, which had started to shoot up. "Anybody *besides* Emma?"

"Charlotte Lucas!" says Becca triumphantly, and her mother slaps her a high five. Becca's been coming on strong in book club this year.

"I still don't get why she'd do that," says Cassidy. "Especially that stupid Mr. Collins, too."

"Remember, things were different in those days," Mrs. Bergson tells her. "Either you got married, or you lived at home with your parents forever."

We all look at our mothers, and then at one another, and then we burst out laughing. It's obvious from the looks on our faces that we're all thinking the same thing—*no way!*

I glance at my watch. Only an hour and a half until I have to leave for Simon's party. "Isn't it time for snacks?" I ask.

"Good idea," says Gigi, hopping up off the sofa. "I'll bring out the pie."

"What is it with you guys and pie this year?" says Emma from onscreen as my grandmother trots off. "I swear, every time we have a book club meeting, you're always eating pie."

Becca and Cassidy and I start to snicker.

"What's so funny?" she demands.

"Nothing," I reply.

By the time we finish eating and wrap things up and everybody finally leaves, I barely have half an hour to get ready.

I change about four times. Even Mirror Megan is starting to get annoyed by the time I finally settle on an outfit. It's just a pizza party, so I don't want to overdo it, but still, I want to look good. It may be spring but it's not all that warm out, so I opt for jeans instead of a skirt, these cool vintage black flats covered with black sequins that I found at a thrift store, and a soft cotton shirt with gathers around the scooped neckline. I like how feminine it is, plus the turquoise color looks dramatic against my pale skin. I grab the wide black belt from yesterday's wardrobe remix at the last minute and add that, too.

Mirror Megan gives me the nod of approval. Festive, a little bit sophisticated, but not over-the-top.

"You're too young to date," says my mother grumpily when I reappear in the kitchen.

"It's not a date, it's a birthday party, remember?" says my grandmother. "Pizza, Ping-Pong, a DVD. That's what Mrs. Berkeley said when you and Jerry called."

Embarrassingly, my parents grilled Simon's parents about the party before they agreed to let me go.

My mother nods, but she's watching me with a funny expression on her face.

"What?" I ask, pulling a Cassidy and sniffing my armpits in case I somehow forgot deodorant.

She smiles wistfully. "Nothing. It's just that you're growing up so fast."

I roll my eyes. "Mo-om!"

"I know, I know." She jumps up and grabs her keys. "Come on, I'll drive you into town."

Cassidy and her mother pull into the Hawthornes' driveway right behind us. Cassidy is behind the wheel—she got her learner's permit last week—and she grins and waves. I give her a big thumbs-up.

She got invited because of being Tristan's skating partner, and I guess this time she decided to put up with his company. I thought maybe there would be a few other girls here as well, but there aren't. It's a really small party—just a few guys from the soccer team, one I recognize from biology class, and Zach Norton and Stewart Chadwick and us.

"Hi, Megan!" says Simon when Cassidy and I come to the door. He beams at me—well, at both of us, really. "Cassidy—so glad you could make it too."

He leads us out to the kitchen, where everybody's clustered around the table. There are a lot of jokes about the paint color. I'm used to it, but

I guess there aren't a lot of pink kitchens in the world. Tristan stands apart, leaning against the counter and looking uncomfortable. He barely glances at Cassidy, who seems to have put a little more effort than usual into her outfit. She's wearing jeans, like me, and a pale green hoodie that looks great with her hair, which she's obviously fussed over as well. And is that mascara I see? Her mother must have gotten ahold of her. Or maybe not, I think, noticing how often her gaze drifts over to Tristan.

Tristan, meanwhile, is watching me and Simon, like he's trying to figure something out. Or it could be that I'm just imagining the whole thing.

Professor Berkeley comes in the back door carrying a stack of pizza boxes, and Mrs. Berkeley passes out paper plates and we all dig in. Cassidy starts to relax and ignore Tristan and be more her usual funny self, and pretty soon everybody's laughing. The Hawthornes' house is small, but they have a rec room in the basement, and we take our food down there to start the Ping-Pong tournament. I'm eliminated almost immediately and so is Stewart, but the rest of Simon's friends are supercompetitive, and the rallies are fast and furious.

"Go, Cassidy!" I cheer as we gather around the table to watch. One by one she takes out the remaining players, including Zach. Finally, only Tristan is left.

"It's showtime, Ice Dancer," says Cassidy, twirling her paddle. "Put up or shut up."

"What's that supposed to mean?" asks Tristan.

"Just that you are so going down in flames."

"Don't count your chickens," Tristan retorts, but the corners of his lips are quirked up and for once he looks as if he's enjoying himself.

The two of them are closely matched, and the little white ball flies back and forth, back and forth in a series of really long rallies. Cassidy's got that look on her face I've seen before at her hockey games when she's driving toward the goal—focused, intense, serious. Tristan's face mirrors hers.

In the end, though, she destroys him with a smash shot he just can't return. I'll say this for Tristan, he's not a sore loser. As Simon awards her a can of root beer as a prize, Tristan lifts his paddle in a salute.

"Well done, m'lady," he says with a mocking bow.

"Thank you, Your Majesty." She dances around the room, holding her root beer up like a trophy.

Simon picked *Revenge of the Space Bugs* for our movie, which is more sci-fi than what I usually go to see but I don't care, especially when he plops down beside me on the couch. He doesn't hold my hand or anything, but so many people are crowded onto the sofa we're kind of squashed together, and his knee and shoulder are pressed against mine. I notice he doesn't try and move away, and that makes me really happy.

After the movie is finished, Mrs. Berkeley comes downstairs carrying a birthday cake. We sing to Simon, and then he blows out the candles. His eyes meet mine when he finishes, and I can't help wondering what he wished for. I notice Tristan watching us again.

I give Simon a gift certificate to the local movie theater for his present, in hopes that maybe he'll decide to ask me to go with him. He looks pleased when he opens it, and says that it will definitely come in handy, which sounds pretty promising.

We're just getting set up for a game of Risk when Professor Berkeley opens the basement door and pokes his head in. "Megan!" he calls. "Your father is here!"

"It's too early!" Simon protests. "We're just about to start a board game."

I glance at my watch. Nine o'clock on the dot. "Sorry," I tell him. "My parents are kind of strict."

"I understand," he says, "but it's still not fair."

I say good-bye to everyone and Simon follows me up the stairs. I can hear his parents laughing with my dad in the front hall. As I start to head out of the kitchen, he puts his hand on my arm.

"Wait," he says. "I want to thank you for coming."

"Thanks for inviting me," I reply shyly, and he leans over and kisses me on the cheek.

I smile all the way home.

I think I might finally have a boyfriend.

Jess

*"Let us hear what has happened
to you all, since you went away.
Have you seen any pleasant men?
Have you had any flirting?"*

—*Pride and Prejudice*

"Hurry up, Jess! We're going to be late!"

I take one final look in the mirror—long black skirt and white shirt, Colonial Academy's regulation concert dress—and tuck a stray strand of hair behind my ear. "Coming!" I call back, and grabbing the folder of sheet music off my bed, I jog down the hall of my dorm.

Adele and Savannah are waiting for me at the bottom of the stairs. They're dressed in identical outfits to mine, and the three of us race across the quad to the auditorium. A crowd is already gathered outside. I spot my parents and wave. Senator and Mrs. Sinclair have flown in from Washington and are sitting with them. They wave too.

Tonight's the night of Colonial Academy's spring concert. It's always a popular event, but even more so this year since the MadriGals did so well at regionals. We didn't quite make the cut to go to nationals, but we were really, really close. Mr. Elton says there's always next year.

The orchestra plays first, then the jazz band, and after the choir it's the MadriGals' turn. As we file onto the risers, I look out at the audience. The book club is here, of course—they have to be, to man the table in the lobby afterward. Mr. Elton loved the idea of having Pies & Prejudice cater the refreshments, and he arranged everything with Colonial Academy. Baking six dozen pies kept us all incredibly busy the past few days, but we managed, thanks to my mom and Mrs. Wong, who jumped in at the last minute to help Gigi finish up while we were all in school. The money was just what we needed to put us over the top for Emma's plane ticket.

I wish I'd had a picture of her face when we told her.

We sprang the news last Sunday. The two of us were supposed to do our usual videoconference, but instead of setting up my laptop in my room the way I usually do, I set it up in our kitchen instead. The rest of the book club hid in the dining room waiting for my signal.

Emma knew right away something was up. I'm hopeless at keeping secrets from her.

"Go get your mom," I told her, when she asked why I had such a funny look on my face.

"What? Why?"

"Don't ask questions—just go get your mom."

She shrugged and left the room, then returned a minute later with her mother, who was grinning hugely.

"Mrs. Hawthorne," I said, "could you give Emma the envelope, please?"

As she handed it over three thousand miles away in England, Cassidy started drumming on the dining room door. Emma looked up, mystified.

"Open it!" I told her.

As she did, I counted "one, two, three" under my breath, and then everybody piled into the kitchen and we all shouted in unison: "You're coming home for spring break!"

Emma stared at the plane ticket in her hand, then let out a shriek.

We all started to talk at once. I explained how we wanted to do something to cheer her up after the incident with Stinkerbelle and the mistletoe, and then Becca and Cassidy and Megan leaped in and told her about Pies & Prejudice.

"So *that's* what all that pie stuff was about," Emma replied. "Now it makes sense." She turned to her mother. "Have you known all along?" she said accusingly.

Mrs. Hawthorne raised her eyebrows. "Mmm," she replied. "Maybe." When we all finally quieted down, she added, "I have an announcement to make too. Nicholas and I have been talking, and we've decided to chip in and send Darcy home along with Emma!"

All the breath had whooshed out of my body. Darcy was coming back to Concord too? Then Becca started to squeal, and onscreen Emma's eyes slid over to me. I knew exactly what she was thinking. *Chadwickius frenemus.* That's the Latin name I made up for Becca, when she's in frenemy mode. Becca doesn't know that I like Darcy—I've been good about keeping that secret—but it's no secret that she likes him too. Of course, she likes a lot of boys, including Zach Norton. She's kind of like Elizabeth Bennet's boy-crazy younger sisters Lydia and Kitty that way.

Right now, *Chadwickius frenemus* is sitting in the audience at Colonial Academy, waiting to hear the MadriGals sing. So is Kevin Mullins, who is sitting next to her.

"Hope dies hard," my father always says whenever Kevin's name is mentioned.

I've tried to convince Kevin that I'm not interested, but he just doesn't take a hint. Sometimes I wish I could explain to him about Darcy.

They're both smiling at me. I smile back, wishing again that I'd gotten a solo part. It would have been nice to sing a solo in front of my family and friends.

I also wish the concert could have been scheduled for next weekend instead, when Emma and Darcy will be here. They could have seen my mother's play, too, but it closes tomorrow night. She's been starring in a revival of *I Remember Mama* at a small theater in Boston. She got paid for it and everything. Not as much as she did when she was on the soap opera *HeartBeats* a few years ago, but enough to make her feel like a professional, she says. Plus, she's had a lot of fun. She says she might try out for a play every winter, now that my brothers are a little older and we've hired an assistant for our cheesemaking business.

Mr. Elton taps his baton, and the audience grows quiet. Even though it's still April we start with "Now is the Month of Maying"— *"The spring, clad all in gladness, doth laugh at winter's sadness"*—

Heather Vogel Frederick

and then segue into "Of All the Birds that I Do Know," my least favorite song in our repertoire. It's about a pet sparrow called Philip who's really a girl, and the lyrics are totally stupid. We sing in French—*"Il est bel et bon"*—and in Italian—*"Lirum bililirum"* again, the one that always reminds me of Darcy, and then Savannah and Adele team up for a duet of "Greensleeves," which is always an audience favorite. Their voices blend beautifully together, and when they finish, Senator Sinclair pulls his handkerchief out and blows his nose.

We end with "My Bonnie Lass She Smileth," another crowd-pleaser. I try not to catch Adele's eye while we're singing this one. Her dad sent us a recording of it that changed the opening line to "My Bonnie Lass She Smelleth," and we just howl every time we listen to it. I'm trying so hard not to look at her, that I make the mistake of looking out at the audience again, where I spot Cassidy holding her nose and grinning at me. I have to quickly turn my gaze to Mr. Elton so I don't crack up.

Afterward, I make a beeline for the dessert table, where my book club friends are already gathered, getting ready to serve the pies. Gigi hands us each a gift bag.

"What's this?" I ask, peering in.

"A little something to celebrate your spring concert and our success."

We reach into our bags and pull out matching aprons. They're hot pink, and the Pies & Prejudice logo is emblazoned on the front.

"Oh, how cute!" says Mrs. Sloane-Kinkaid. "Put them on, girls, and stand behind the pies. I'll get a picture."

"Dude, it's *pink*," Cassidy protests. She hates pink.

Her mother raises her eyebrows and nods toward Gigi, who is busy bossing Mrs. Chadwick in how best to cut the pies into slices. Cassidy heaves a dramatic sigh. "Fine," she snaps, and pulls the apron on.

We line up behind the table and put our arms around one another. People are trickling in from the auditorium now, including the Sinclairs, and as they line up for refreshments they watch us curiously.

"Say 'pie'!" jokes Cassidy's mother. We do, and she snaps our picture. "I'll frame it for Emma," she tells us.

"So this is the business you started?" says Mrs. Sinclair, as the line moves forward and she reaches for a plate and fork. "The one Savannah told us about?"

I nod. Savannah and I have gotten along a lot better this year now that we're not roommates. I don't see her all that much at school— we're in completely different classes, except for choir and MadriGals— but we spend nearly every Sunday afternoon together at the animal shelter, and she's heard plenty about Pies & Prejudice, and about Emma's run-in with Annabelle Fairfax.

"Well, I think y'all are brilliant," says Mrs. Sinclair. She nudges her husband. "Don't you agree, darling?"

"Yes, Poppy," says Senator Sinclair absently. He's busy eyeing the pie selection.

"A slice of all-American apple pie for you, Senator?" asks Gigi, offering him a plate.

Mrs. Chadwick sticks her arm out in front of Megan's grand-

Heather Vogel Frederick

mother. In her hand is another plate. One with a piece of *her* pie on it. She gives Senator Sinclair a coy smile. "Didn't Poppy tell me that coconut cream is your favorite?"

Savannah's father looks from her to Gigi and smiles. "Actually, ladies, tonight I'm hungry enough to eat a slice of both." He tucks a twenty-dollar bill into our tip jar and helps himself to their offered plates.

Gigi laughs. "Spoken like a true politician."

"Well done, dear," says Mrs. Sinclair. Seeing the disappointed look on Mrs. Chadwick's face, she leans across the table and whispers, "But if it makes you feel any better, Calliope, it's true that he's especially fond of coconut cream."

Later, I say good-bye to my parents and friends and head back to the dorm with Frankie and Adele. The three of us stay up until after midnight talking in our room. Hanging out with my friends is the best part about boarding school. I don't know what I would have done without the two of them this year, with Emma away in England.

The next night it's my turn to sit in the audience, this time to watch my mother. She's a great actress, and it's really fun to see her onstage. Even my brothers, who usually won't sit still for more than about three seconds, are completely mesmerized. The Norwegian accent she had to learn for the part has them discombobulated, and when we go backstage afterward they hang back shyly and keep looking at her as if she's a stranger.

Since it's closing night, there's a cast party. Someone offers to drive Mom home afterward, so Dad and I and the boys head back to Concord without her. It's late, and Dylan and Ryan quickly fall asleep in the back.

"Does it bother you that Mom's acting again?" I ask my father in the quiet darkness.

"Not a bit," he replies. "Why should it?"

"You know." I pause. "Like maybe she'll decide to run away from home again." That's what the two of us called it the year she went off to New York for *HeartBeats*.

He reaches over and pats my knee. "Jess, your mom and I are on the same page about this. We both love running Half Moon Farm, but acting makes your mom happy too. It's what she was born to do. I'm glad she's found a way to do both."

I stare out the window at the highway. *What was I born to do?* It's the same question that's been nagging me all year. My parents just laugh when I try to talk to them about it. I'm fifteen, they say. I shouldn't be worrying about this—I have plenty of time to figure things out.

They're right, of course, but the thing is, I do worry about it. And the MadriGals concert this weekend just dredged up those worries all over again. I used to think that music was what I was born to do, the way acting is for Mom. But ever since I didn't get picked for a solo, I've started doubting myself. Maybe it just means I should keep practicing and try harder. Or, maybe it means I'm meant to do something else, like a career in science or math. How am I supposed to know?

It's just so confusing. I don't know why I feel like I need to know the answer now. Telling myself firmly to knock it off, I push the niggling thoughts away and focus on thinking about Emma and Darcy instead.

I can hardly wait until next weekend. Emma's going to stay at Half Moon Farm with us, and Darcy is going to stay with his best friend Kyle Anderson. I hope I get to see him a lot too, though.

The next day, after church and lunch, I kick around the farm for a while helping my father. Things are always busy for us in the spring, and I throw myself into my chores, glad for the chance to help out. With all that's going on at school, I don't feel like I'm holding up my end of things at home anymore. I give the equipment in the creamery a thorough scrub, and supervise my brothers as they clean out the chicken coop, and check in on Sundance and Cedar, who are both pregnant and close to their due dates. After that, it's time to head over to the animal shelter for my volunteer shift. I want to get there a little early, because with her parents in town this weekend Savannah won't be able to come, and that means extra work for me. I don't mind, though—Savannah would do the same for me if I couldn't make it. She's a really good sport that way.

It's funny to think that we were such enemies last year. She's changed a lot. She can still be a little prickly sometimes, sort of the same way that Becca Chadwick can be prickly, but for the most part we're good friends. I feel sorry for her, stuck rooming with Peyton Winslow. That can't be much fun.

"Oh, Jess, I'm so glad to see you," says Janice, the new weekend receptionist, when I walk in the door. She looks upset.

"What's going on?"

She points to a box on the counter. "I'm not sure what to do. Someone just dropped this off. He was pretty shaken up, and kept saying he didn't mean to hurt it."

My heart sinks. I peek into the box. At first I think it's a puppy or a small cat, but then I see the ears. I suck in my breath sharply. A fox! It's a young one too. I've never seen one this close before.

"I don't know what's wrong with it," Janice says. "The man who brought it in said he was mountain biking in Estabrook Woods when he hit it. It was shivering, so I put a towel over it. I think it's in shock."

"Have you tried to get ahold of Ms. Mitchell?"

Ms. Mitchell is the shelter supervisor.

Janice nods. "I left her a voice mail. She hasn't returned my call yet."

"How about the Audubon Society?"

"Good idea."

She dials and I hear her saying, "uh-huh, uh-huh" while she scribbles down some information. She hangs up and turns back to me. "They gave me the name of a local wildlife rehabilitator here in Concord. I'll go ahead and give him a call."

She does, but he's out of town for the weekend, so she leaves another voice mail. "I'm not sure what to do now."

I glance in the box. The fox hasn't moved. "I think we should probably have a vet take a look at it," I tell her. "Dr. Gardiner takes care of all the animals on our farm, and she's really nice. I could call home and get her number."

Janice thinks this is a good idea, so I do.

"Well, hi there, Jess," Dr. Gardiner says when I reach her. "What can I do for you? Is everything okay with Sundance and Cedar?"

I assure her that my goats are fine, and then I explain about the injured fox.

"A fox, huh? I've treated raccoons and possums and even a skunk once, but never a fox. Why don't you bring it over here to my office and I'll take a look."

Janice has to stay and hold down the fort, so I call my dad again, who agrees to drive me. We put the box with the injured fox in it onto the front seat of his truck between us. The fox is still motionless under the towel, and I can't tell if it's sleeping, or unconscious, or what. I hope it's not "or what." But it looks like it's still breathing.

Dr. Gardiner greets us at the door. She's wearing a pair of heavy leather gloves. "Very important when you're dealing with wild animals," she tells us, holding up her hands and wiggling her fingers. "They can be unpredictable, and even the babies have needle-sharp teeth."

She takes the box from my dad and we follow her inside to one of the examination rooms. Very gently, she picks the fox up and lays it on the stainless steel table.

"It looks like she—it's a she, by the way, a vixen—got lucky," she says. "No major injuries, but I want to take an X-ray of this back leg of hers. It looks like it may be broken."

She wheels the table out of the room, and returns a few minutes later.

"Just as I suspected," she tells us. "The leg is fractured, but in the grand scheme of things it shouldn't be difficult to mend. I'm going to sedate her and set it, but she'll need weeks of care. Have you been in touch with a wildlife rehabilitator?"

I tell her about the man that the Audubon Society recommended.

"Walter Mueller?" says Dr. Gardiner. "He's a good guy. Really knows his stuff. She'll be in good hands with him."

"He won't be home until tomorrow, though," I tell her.

Dr. Gardiner frowns. "Someone needs to keep an eye on her overnight."

"Can't she stay here?"

She shakes her head. "The office is unsupervised at night, and I don't want to leave her by herself." She turns to my father. "Could she stay at Half Moon Farm, Michael? I have a pet carrier you could borrow to keep her in."

My dad rubs his chin. "I'm not sure," he says doubtfully. "It's not that we don't have the room, but I'm worried that her scent might send our flock of chickens into a tizzy. Sugar and Spice, too. And with Sundance and Cedar being so close to term, I hate to risk unsettling the animals like that."

Dr. Gardiner nods. "I understand."

"I have an idea," I tell them. "There's an empty storage room in the stable at Colonial Academy. Maybe I could ask if we could keep her there."

Heather Vogel Frederick

"That could work," says Dr. Gardiner. "Especially since it's only one night. But there absolutely, positively has to be adult supervision."

We call my dorm and Mrs. McKinley answers. After I explain what happened, she asks to speak to my dad.

"She's going to talk to the stable manager," he tells us, and Dr. Gardiner heads off to set the fox's injured leg.

"Is she okay?" I ask when she returns. The fox's leg is now in a cast, and she's lying limp in the bottom of a pet carrier.

"Don't worry," the vet tells me, "it's just the anesthesia. She'll be hungry when she comes around."

"What do I feed her?"

She scribbles out a list. "I don't know if she's been weaned yet, so you might offer her a bottle. I'll give you one, along with some canine replacement formula and puppy chow."

"Thanks."

"The main thing to remember when taking care of a wild animal, Jess, and I know the rehabilitator will tell you the same thing, is that they are exactly that: wild. And it's your job to keep them that way. Don't try and make a pet out of her, as tempting as that may be."

My housemother calls back, and says that it's okay with the stable manager if we keep the fox at Colonial Academy overnight, as long as she stays in a carrier and is closely supervised. Mrs. McKinley tells Dr. Gardiner that she's willing to help keep an eye on things, and after Dr. Gardiner gives us some final words of advice, my father and I head off, swinging home first to round up a heating pad and blankets, along with some grapes and hard-boiled eggs and a few other things on Dr. Gardiner's list.

"What are you going to call her?" asks Dylan, peering at the fox through the mesh grate on the carrier. I can tell by the way his fingers are twitching that he's itching to pat her. But Dr. Gardiner made me promise—as little human contact as possible.

"Her name is Lydia, because she's a wild girl," I tell him. Lydia Bennet is Elizabeth Bennet's little sister. She's boy crazy and disobedient and gets the Bennet family into a whole lot of trouble in *Pride and Prejudice.*

"Lydia?" Ryan scoffs. "That's a stupid name. You should call her Ruby or Foxy or something better than dumb old *Lydia.*"

I grin at him. "She's my fox, and I'm calling her Lydia. If you guys are really good and do your chores around here, though, I'll let you come visit her in a few days."

Back at school, Mrs. McKinley meets us at the stables.

"Oh, isn't she darling!" she says as I lift the carrier out of the truck. "She looks like something out of Beatrix Potter."

The little vixen really is cute. She's snuggled in the fleece blanket that I tucked in around her, and she's got one paw curled over her nose, like a cat.

After the stable manager shows up, my father gives me a kiss good-bye and heads home to Half Moon Farm.

"Just until tomorrow afternoon, right?" says the stable manager, unlocking the storage room.

Heather Vogel Frederick

I nod, and my housemother puts her arm around my shoulder and raises three fingers of her right hand. "Scout's honor," she tells him. "I promise to keep a close eye on things."

Satisfied, the stable manager hands us the key and leaves. We make sure Lydia is settled, then we lock up and head back to the dorm. It's Movie Madness night, but as I sit there with my friends watching *How Green Was My Valley*, I find it hard to keep my mind on the movie. I keep worrying about Lydia. When it's over, I ask Mrs. McKinley if we can go check on her again.

"Of course," she tells me. "Let me grab a flashlight."

"I wish I could spend the night with her," I say as the two of us head out the back door.

She pauses on the doorstep. "Hmmm," she replies. "I have a couple of sleeping bags in the basement. Why don't we both stay with her?"

"Really?"

Mrs. McKinley nods. "I hate the thought of her waking up in the middle of the night and crying for her mother, and nobody being there to comfort her. She's just a baby."

"Exactly!"

We go back inside and I run upstairs to get my pillow and a few other things I'll need. Frankie and Adele beg to join us when they hear about the plan, but I remember Dr. Gardiner's instructions and shake my head. "Too much human contact isn't good for wild animals," I tell them. "But you can come down and see her tomorrow at lunchtime."

I grab an extra jacket, a warm hat, and my alarm clock. I want to make sure I'm up early enough to shower before school. "Goat Girl" was bad enough—I don't need to add "Fox Girl" to the list.

Lydia is still sound asleep when we get to the stable. Being careful not to wake her, Mrs. McKinley and I spread our sleeping bags on some straw and settle down for the night. I lie awake for a while, listening to barn noises—the creak of wood timbers, a low whinny now and then from one of the horses, and a rustle or two that's probably one of the barn cats on the hunt for mice or rats—and then, breathing in the comforting scent of horses and saddle leather, I finally fall asleep.

Lydia doesn't make a peep all night, but my alarm wakes her. I hear her stirring in the dog carrier, and then she starts to cry these pathetic little mewling cries.

"Poor baby!" I whisper. "You must be starving."

Crawling out of my sleeping bag, I fix a bottle of the special puppy formula that Dr. Gardiner gave me. Mrs. McKinley raises herself up on one elbow and watches as I pull on the heavy leather gloves.

"Careful now," she cautions.

I've been around farm animals all my life, and the trick is to handle them gently but confidently. Feeding Lydia isn't really all that different from feeding a baby goat. I pick her up, being careful not to disturb her leg, and holding her firmly in the crook of my arm, I offer her the bottle. She sucks it down greedily.

When she's finished, I offer her some grapes and a little chopped-

228   *Heather Vogel Frederick*

up hard-boiled egg, but she's not interested. She snuggles in my lap instead and goes right back to sleep.

"Would you look at that!" exclaims Mrs. McKinley. "The little angel."

"Can I skip classes and stay with her here instead today?"

My housemother smiles. "Nice try. How about I check in on her for you later this morning?"

"That would be great." Very gently, I move Lydia back into her carrier and gather up my things to return to the dorm.

While I'm showering I have a brainstorm, and after breakfast I make a beeline for the science labs.

"Mr. Turner!" I call, spotting my AP biology teacher in the hallway up ahead.

He turns around. "What's up?"

I quickly tell him about Lydia, and then launch into my idea. "I'd like to help rehabilitate her, and I'm wondering if that could count as my science project." For the life of me I haven't been able to think of something interesting to do as a project, until now.

"I don't see why not," he replies. "As long as you document everything carefully. I think it would make for a fascinating project, in fact."

He agrees to meet me at the stable at lunchtime, and I head off to my first class. The morning drags on endlessly. I keep looking at my watch, wishing that noon would arrive. When it finally does, I run to the stable to find Mr. Turner already there, along with Mrs. McKinley and a handful of students, including Frankie and Adele, who are practically hopping up and down with excitement.

"Looks like word has gotten out," says my housemother.

While I'm feeding Lydia again—more formula, and a little chopped egg this time—I explain my plan to Mr. Turner in more detail. "I already checked online this morning, and you have to be eighteen to be a licensed rehabilitator," I tell him. "There's nothing that says I can't help with the rehabilitation, though, so if Mr. Mueller says it's okay, would it be okay with you?"

My biology teacher nods. "If he agrees to allow you to apprentice with him, I'll approve your project," he says. "I think this is a wonderful opportunity for you, Jess. Keep me posted, okay?" He squats down by the carrier. "Cute little thing, isn't she?"

Back at the dorm, I call Walter Mueller.

"Jessica Delaney?" he says. "I knew your grandparents. Sure, I'll take your fox—and I'm happy to have you help out, if you want to."

I offer to pay for Lydia's care, but he says no, adding, "But I wouldn't mind some of Half Moon Farm's wonderful goat cheese, if you can spare it."

Afternoon classes seem like they'll never end. When 3:00 finally rolls around, I race down to the stable again. My father is already there with the truck. We load Lydia in and head off to the address that Mr. Mueller gave me.

"Looks like his property backs up to Estabrook Woods," my dad remarks as we pull into a driveway a short while later.

Estabrook Woods is this big wildlife preserve here in Concord, the one where Lydia was hit by the mountain biker.

Heather Vogel Frederick

A deep voice floats across the yard from the barn as we get out of the truck. "I'm out here!" As we enter the barn with the pet carrier, an old horse pokes his head over one of the stall doors.

"New friends, Milo," says a spry-looking elderly man, patting him on the neck. He gives me a wink. "Milo supervises things around here." He extends his hand. "I'm Walter Mueller. You must be Jess."

Nodding, I shake his hand. Mr. Mueller looks over my shoulder and spots my father. "Mikey Delaney!" he exclaims, breaking into a wide grin. "I haven't seen you since you were in short pants."

My father laughs and shakes his hand. "Nice to see you again too, Walter. I can't remember the last time anyone called me 'Mikey.'"

"Probably back when your father and I used to go duck hunting," Mr. Mueller replies. He turns back to me. "That was a long time ago, young lady, when I used to chase 'em instead of care for 'em." He jerks his thumb toward a big cage on the floor next to Milo's stall. Inside it is a mallard whose wing is hanging limply at its side.

I glance around the barn, curious. There are a number of other cages scattered around too, not all of them occupied. But I spot a raccoon, another duck, and a couple of rabbits.

"Business is picking up now that spring is here," Mr. Mueller tells us. "I often get fox kits this time of year. Your little vixen may have company eventually." He gives me a keen look from under a pair of shaggy white eyebrows. "I'd be glad of some extra help, if you're still interested."

I nod eagerly. "I can ride my bike over every day after school."

"Jess got a full scholarship to Colonial Academy," my father tells him proudly.

"Is that right?" says Mr. Mueller. "Apple didn't fall far from the tree then, did it? Your grandmother had more smarts than just about anybody I ever met. She could add a list of numbers as long as your arm, all in her head."

I never knew my grandparents. They died before I was born. But I smile and nod anyway.

Mr. Mueller takes a good look at Lydia, who is awake and alert and sitting right next to the wire mesh on the front of the carrier, observing her new surroundings curiously. He tells me it looks like I did everything just right so far, which makes me happy. "Main thing now is just to see that she gets plenty of rest and food, so she'll heal fast and get strong again," he says.

I've never known a week to fly by so fast. Fortunately, the weather holds, and every day after school I ride my bike over to check on Lydia and document her progress. Often when I arrive I find her pacing back and forth in her cage, and she makes little puppylike yips and squeals when she sees me.

"She knows me!" I tell Mr. Mueller proudly.

"She knows you're going to feed her," he says, with a chuckle.

I'm still careful to wear the heavy leather gloves when I touch her—I've seen her teeth and Dr. Gardiner is right, they're really sharp. And I try not to pat her and stroke her too often, as tempting as it is.

"I know just how much you'd love to make a pet of her, Jess," says

Heather Vogel Frederick

Mr. Mueller one afternoon toward the end of the week. "I've had the same feelings myself with other animals over the years. In fact, I tried to keep a raccoon for a pet once, but it only made us both unhappy. Wild creatures belong in the wild, and our goal as rehabilitators is to release them back there safely. That won't happen if she grows too attached."

I nod. "I understand."

And I do, really. But the urge to cuddle her is almost irresistible. Her fur is incredibly soft, and she looks at me with such trust when I feed her. I can't help but think about how cool it would be to have a tame fox for a pet, and I fantasize about having her follow me around our farm, and sleep at the foot of my bed at night.

Lydia has been moved to a bigger cage by now, and I squat down beside it and call to her softly. She limps right over, poking her nose through the wire mesh and sniffing my jeans. She cocks her head and watches me, intelligence shining in her bright golden eyes. She's lovely, with her sleek coat and black markings on her tawny muzzle and legs.

"You're going to be a beauty," I whisper to her. "Just like Lydia Bennet. All the boy foxes will be chasing you before long."

On Thursday afternoon I bring Adele and Frankie and Savannah with me. We stop at the bakery for fresh buttermilk donuts, which I have learned are Mr. Mueller's favorite.

"Look how adorable she is!" squeals Frankie when she sees Lydia. "She's really grown!"

"Wait until Emma gets here," adds Adele. "She'll go nuts."

"No kidding," says Savannah.

I suddenly realize that I've been so busy with school and taking care of Lydia I've hardly thought of Emma all week. She'll be here the day after tomorrow. And so will Darcy!

Friday night is my last night in the dorm for nearly ten days, and it's abuzz with excitement. Some students are heading out tonight, others first thing in the morning. My friends are scattering to all points of the compass. Frankie is going home with Adele to San Francisco—I got invited too, but had to say no because of Emma and Darcy. Adele said not to worry, she'd invite me again another time. Savannah is going skiing in Switzerland again. Peyton Winslow is not going with her this time. Savannah told me no way did she want to be cooped up in a hotel with Peyton for a week, not after being stuck with her for a roommate. I guess Peyton practically turned herself inside out trying to wangle an invitation, but Savannah just kept pretending she didn't get the hints.

Savannah and I have made a few awkward jokes about goat cheese, but I've been careful not to overdo it. Even though I know she's totally forgiven us for the prank we pulled last year, it's still kind of a touchy subject.

On Saturday morning, Mom gets up early and rides over with me to Mr. Mueller's.

"So you're Mikey's bride," he says. "I used to love watching you on *HeartBeats*."

Somehow, Mr. Mueller doesn't seem like the soap opera type to me. But I guess you really can't judge a book by its cover.

"You bring your friend Emma on over here real soon, okay?" he says as we get back on our bikes to head home. "Her mother's been a big help to me at the library over the years, with research and such, and I'd love to meet her daughter."

I promise I'll bring Emma as soon as I can, and my mother and I pedal off. We ride quickly because we're picking Emma and Darcy up at Logan in a few hours and both of us still need to take a shower and change.

"Don't expect to do too much this afternoon," Mom warns me. "They'll have been flying for hours, and they're going to be wiped out."

I'm too excited to eat lunch, but my mother says I have to eat at least half of my turkey sandwich before she'll take me anywhere, so I force it down. Then we drive over to Cassidy's house to meet the rest of the book club so we can caravan to the airport. Mom and I hop into the Sloane-Kinkaid's minivan with Cassidy and her mother and Mrs. Bergson, while the Wongs and Mrs. Chadwick and Becca and Stewart cram into the Chadwick's SUV, which smells like manure, unfortunately.

I know this because Mrs. Chadwick came over to Half Moon Farm the other night to get some horse droppings to spread around her new rose garden, and because I can see Megan and Becca inside, gagging. Cassidy and I start laughing as they roll the windows down and stick their heads out, gasping for air.

"Suckers!" Cassidy calls to them. "See you at the airport!" Her stepfather and Chloe wave to us from the front porch.

Forty-five minutes later we pull into the parking garage. We find the waiting area outside international arrivals, and Becca and Megan unfurl the big banner we made—the one with WELCOME HOME EMMA AND DARCY! painted on it in huge blue letters. They're going to be embarrassed when they see it, but that's the point.

Stewart is pacing up and down. His hair is still wet from the shower, and I can tell he just shaved because there's a smear of shaving cream behind his left ear. He smells good too. I wonder fleetingly whether Darcy will smell good too, and what it would feel like to have a boy be nervous enough about seeing you that he'd take a little extra care getting ready. It must be nice.

"Hey, isn't that Simon Berkeley?" says Becca, pointing across the waiting area.

I frown. "Yeah. I wonder what he's doing here?"

Simon is with his brother and parents, and they all come hurrying over when they spot us. Megan lights up as she sees Simon, which makes me wonder if I'm as obvious about the way I feel about Darcy. The two of them start chattering away while Cassidy and Tristan make stiff conversation with Mrs. Bergson.

"We tried to call, but you'd already left," Mrs. Berkeley tells Mrs. Sloane-Kinkaid. "The boys' cousin—well, my second cousin's daughter, actually—decided at the last minute to accompany your young friends on their flight."

Cassidy and I exchange a glance. She can't be talking about Annabelle, can she?

She can.

Heather Vogel Frederick

"Annabelle's coach thought it would be an excellent idea for her to spend the week over here with Tristan, practicing for this summer's competition," Mrs. Berkeley continues. "She's never been to the U.S. before, and she's very excited to visit. We thought we might take her and the boys to New York and Washington for a few days."

"I'm sure our girls will enjoy getting to know her," says my mother.

Cassidy turns slightly so that her back is toward our mothers and Mrs. Berkeley, then mimes sticking her finger down her throat. Before we can discuss this horrible new development further, though, Stewart suddenly gives a shout.

"There they are!" he cries, waving wildly. I see a hand fluttering above the heads of the oncoming crowd in response.

It's Emma!

I start waving wildly too. If it hadn't been for our video chats, I would hardly recognize her. She's grown her hair out, and it's down to her shoulders now. It's really pretty, and makes her look different—more grown-up. She breaks into a run and flings her arms around me.

"BFBB," she whispers in my ear, and I grin. *Best friends before boyfriends.*

I shove her toward Stewart. "Your turn," I tell him, and he swoops her up in a bear hug.

Darcy is making his way down the mom reception line, politely hugging everybody, including Becca, who kisses him on the cheek while she's at it. Cassidy gives him a high five. Megan, who is still standing next to Simon Berkeley, does the same.

Then it's my turn. Darcy looks at me with those deep brown eyes of his, and I feel myself melt, like the inside of a warm chocolate chip cookie.

"Hey, Jess," he says softly.

"Hey," I whisper back, feeling shy all of a sudden. He leans down to hug me and I have to stand on my tiptoes to reach around his neck. He smells just as good as Stewart. He squeezes me tight, leaving me breathless. And happy.

"It's really good to see you," he says.

"You too."

"You guys have accents!" Becca squeals. "How cute is that?"

Mrs. Sloane-Kinkaid crosses over to where Mr. and Mrs. Berkeley are standing with Tristan and his cousin. "Welcome," she says warmly. "You must be Annabelle."

"Stinkerbelle," Cassidy mutters to us under her breath.

"I would have warned you guys, but we only found out at the last minute!" Emma whispers as our moms cluster around Annabelle, chattering away about what a fun week she's in for. She's all warmth and sparkle talking to them, but when she's introduced to us she goes all cool and formal. She's very pretty, with her long dark hair and blue eyes, and I notice the way she sticks to Tristan, hanging on his arm possessively.

"What's up with that?" I whisper. "I thought they were just ice dancing partners. And cousins. Eww."

Heather Vogel Frederick

Emma shrugs. "Distant cousins, as she always reminds me. I think she's got a crush on him."

Cassidy watches them, a thoughtful expression on her face.

Annabelle is watching us all, too, and I realize with a jolt that she's sizing us up. She looks directly at Cassidy for a long minute, then her gaze falls on each of us in turn, Megan and Simon, Emma and Stewart, and Darcy Hawthorne before finally settling on me. I look away quickly.

Why do I feel like a fox who's just been sighted by a hound?

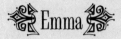

 Emma

"What an eventful week!"
—*Letter from Jane Austen to her sister, Cassandra, 1801*

It's so good to be home again!

I really missed Concord. I absolutely adore living in England—I love Ivy Cottage, and I love our village and the city of Bath and the beautiful countryside, and I never get tired of listening to the way people talk over here. But there really is no place like home.

I still can't believe that my friends got me a plane ticket to Boston. And I especially can't believe that they started a whole business in order to earn the money for it. That day they surprised me with the news that I was coming home for spring break and told me about Pies & Prejudice, it didn't really hit me just what a big deal it was. It wasn't until later, when I got to thinking about all those weekends of work, baking pies and delivering them, that I started feeling kind of overwhelmed, like there was no way I could ever repay them.

"They're not expecting you to repay them," my mother said when I told her how I was feeling. "They're your friends, and they did this just because they love you."

The best friends anyone could ever ask for, I think, glancing across the room at Jess, who's still sound asleep in her bed. I've been awake for a while now, because I'm jet-lagged and because it's almost lunchtime back in England.

The spare bed in Jess's room is right by a window, and I prop my chin on the sill and look outside at the world waking up. England is beautiful, but Concord is beautiful too. Especially Half Moon Farm in the springtime. It's light enough to make out the front yard, and the split-rail fence by the road with the wide swath of daffodils that stretches along its entire length. Mrs. Delaney loves daffodils, and she planted them all around the farm. They look gorgeous in the spring.

I yawn and squint at my watch. I'm dying to call Stewart but there's no way I'm going to do that at five o'clock in the morning.

The good thing about jet lag is that I'll be wide awake for the first time ever tomorrow morning for Patriot's Day. We're having a book club meeting tonight at Megan's house, and she's organized a sleepover for all of us. Tomorrow, we're going to get up early and go to the battle reenactment and pancake breakfast at the Old North Bridge. That's been my family's tradition forever, but most of my friends skip it and sleep in. The last time we all went together was back in sixth grade.

A few minutes later, Jess's alarm goes off. She leaps out of bed, wide awake. I don't know how she does that, but I guess it has something to do with growing up on a farm. Plus, I think she's excited about introducing me to her fox. I promised I'd ride over there with her before church.

"I still can't believe you named her Lydia!" I whisper, pulling on my jeans.

Jess grins at me. "You've got to admit it's perfect, though, right?"

We try and suppress our giggles as we get dressed, but it doesn't really matter because her parents are already up. Mornings start early for the Delaneys. Dylan and Ryan stumble downstairs as we're having breakfast, giving me shy smiles.

"Do you guys remember me?" I ask.

"Duh," says Dylan, rubbing his eyes.

"You talk funny," adds Ryan. "How come?"

I shrug. "I don't think I talk funny, but perhaps it's because I've been living in England." My friends told me that my brother and I picked up English accents, and I thought they were imagining it, but as I reply to Ryan I hear myself say "bean" instead of "been," so maybe they're right.

After we eat, the boys head out to the barn with Mr. Delaney to start their chores, while Jess and I grab our jackets and hop on our bikes. Mine has been in storage in their barn while I was away. The streets are deserted this early in the morning, and we ride side by side into town.

"I want to show you something!" Jess calls over her shoulder. She turns down Main Street and I follow, gliding to a stop behind her in front of the bookshop.

"Check it out," she says.

"Oh, wow!" I exclaim. My father's new novel, *Spring's Reckoning*, is displayed prominently in the window. It's set during the Revolutionary War, so publication was timed to coincide with Patriot's Day. "I've gotta come back later and take a picture. Dad will be thrilled."

"It's so cool he got his book published," Jess replies. "Have you read it yet?"

I nod. "It's really good."

"What's it about?"

"This family who lives here in Concord. The father and sons are patriots, and go off to fight in the war. But the daughter falls in love with a British soldier."

"Sounds really good." She smiles at me. "Someday *your* books will be in that window too."

"You think so?"

"I know so."

I haven't told Jess yet about the new story I'm working on. It's different from the kinds of things I've written before. It's for little kids, for one thing, like Chloe's age or a little older, and for another thing, it's funny. My stuff is usually more serious. Especially my poetry. Anyway, I want to keep it a secret until it's finished. I haven't even told Stewart.

We mount our bikes again and swing back toward Monument Square and then on down Lowell Road. It feels weird to ride past my house and know that other people are inside, sleeping in our beds. I'm dying to stop and visit Melville, but it's still too early. Plus, I'm not keen on running into Annabelle.

We cross over the Concord River and turn up Liberty Street. As we pass the entrance to Minuteman Park and the Old North Bridge, my eyes start to sting a little—it's just so good to be back in my hometown!

Like the Delaneys, Mr. Mueller is up early too.

"Jess told me you'd be coming," he says. "I made coffee cake."

"So how did you figure out what a baby fox will eat?" I ask, settling onto a battered wooden stool. I watch as Jess prepares a bottle of something that looks like milk, but comes in a can.

"Dr. Gardiner got me started, and Mr. Mueller knows absolutely everything about everything else," she replies.

"I don't know about that," says Mr. Mueller, his eyes crinkling around the edges in a smile. He reminds me a little of Mrs. Bergson. He hands me a paper plate with some coffee cake on it.

Lydia has been moved from her cage to a nearby stall that the Muellers have fitted out especially for injured animals. I can hear her pacing back and forth in anticipation, making little yipping sounds.

"She knows you're here," I say to Jess, who nods.

"Foxes have a really good sense of smell. Plus, she recognizes my voice."

She pulls on big leather gloves, then crosses to the stall and opens the door. A small creature about the size of Melville bounds out and stretches up toward Jess, nuzzling hungrily at the bottle.

"That's right, baby," she murmurs, picking her up. "Drink up. I've got you."

Lydia turns her head from time to time to peer at me. She's a curious little thing, with a long pointed nose and huge ears.

"She's adorable!" I whisper.

"Isn't she? She's going to be a real beauty, too. I can't believe how bushy her tail has gotten in the past few weeks."

"And that leg is healing up nicely too," says Mr. Mueller. "She's barely limping at all anymore. Her cast will need to be taken off soon."

"Can I pat her?" I ask, already knowing what the answer will be. Jess explained everything to me last night about wildlife rehabilitation.

"I hate to say no, Em," says Jess, "but I'm really, really trying to do this right."

"And you're doing a crackerjack job," says Mr. Mueller. "I hope you'll think about getting your license in a few years. You're a natural."

Jess smiles.

Watching Lydia, I don't know how Jess will be able to let her go. I had a hard enough time leaving Pip behind this year, knowing he'd be safe and happy with Mrs. Bergson. But Jess said that as soon as the fox's leg was healed and she was strong enough, they were planning to release her back into the wild.

We watch Lydia for a while, then ride home and get ready for church. Afterward, Mr. Delaney drops Darcy and me at Mrs. Bergson's before taking Jess back to Mr. Mueller's. He left a message that someone just brought in an injured red-tailed hawk, and wanted to know if Jess was interested in helping him get it settled.

Cassidy organized a special session of Chicks with Sticks this afternoon with Darcy as the guest instructor, and I've got a skating lesson—an early birthday present from Mrs. Bergson. But first, it's time to see Pip.

He recognizes me instantly.

"I was so worried you'd forgotten me, boy!" I tell him, as he flings himself through the doorway of Mrs. Bergson's condo and covers me with frantic doggie kisses.

"No chance of that," says Mrs. Bergson. "I show him your picture all the time."

I stand up and wipe the slobber off my face, then give her a hug. "Thanks."

We visit for a little while, then she gets her coat and we take off for the rink. Pip is pulling hard on his leash. It's a gorgeous afternoon, almost warm enough to go without a jacket. Sometimes in New England there can still be snow on Patriot's Day weekend, but not this year. It's supposed to be sunny all week.

Stewart is planning to meet us at the rink and take Pip for me while I'm skating, then walk me back to Half Moon Farm. I'm hoping maybe we can detour through Sleepy Hollow Cemetery. There's a secluded spot on a bench under a willow tree I'd really like to revisit. I haven't had any time alone with Stewart since I got here, and just thinking about it makes my heart beat a little faster.

When we reach the parking lot at the rink, I do a double take as I see our old car pull in. Then I remember—it's the Berkeleys. We did a car swap as well as a house swap with them. I stiffen as Annabelle gets out of the car, followed by Tristan.

Heather Vogel Frederick

"Hullo, Darcy," she coos, ignoring me.

"Hey, Annabelle."

I squat down next to Pip. "Stinkerbelle," I whisper to him, then aloud to Tristan I say, "By the way, Toby is doing fine."

He smiles, the first smile I've seen from him. "He's a handful, isn't he?"

I nod. "Yeah."

"We especially like the way you trained him to say, 'UNITED!' whenever there's a soccer game on TV," adds Darcy. "Nice touch, dude."

Tristan laughs. "Melville is doing fine too," he replies. "You guys should stop by and see him."

"Listen to you, with your 'you guys,'" Annabelle teases. "What happened to 'you lot'? You sound like a real American."

Tristan ignores her, and squats down next to me. "Hullo, boy," he says, scratching Pip behind the ears.

"I'll see you kids inside," says Mrs. Bergson. "Don't be long."

As she heads into the rink, Stewart trots around the corner into the parking lot. He stops short when he sees me and Tristan. I stand up quickly and smile at him. "Hey, Stewart."

"Hey, Emma." He crosses the parking lot and takes my hand, glaring at Tristan.

Annabelle watches us, a smile playing on her lips. I try to ignore her as I give Stewart the leash. "Thanks for walking Pip," I tell him. "I should be done in an hour or so."

"No problem," he tells me, shooting Tristan another sharp glance. "Have fun." He leans over and kisses my cheek.

Stewart Chadwick is jealous! I smother a grin. How funny. Especially since he has absolutely no reason to be.

Inside, as Darcy and Tristan and Annabelle and I sit down to lace up our skates, Cassidy skates over. "Hey, guys!" she says. "Thanks for helping me out, Darcy. The girls will be here in about an hour, after Tristan and I are done, and after Emma's lesson."

"No problem," Darcy tells her. "I haven't skated much this year—I'll just warm up and stay out of everybody's way."

He steps out onto the ice and skates away. Annabelle stands up. She's taller on her skates, of course, but nowhere near as tall as Cassidy. Annabelle is like one of the bantam chickens that the Delaneys raise, though, the little ones who think they're a whole lot bigger than they really are. She crosses her arms and looks Cassidy coolly up and down. "So Tristan tells me you play hockey. What was it he called you? Big, bad Cassidy Sloane?"

A hurt look passes over Cassidy's face, and her eyes slide over to Tristan, who frowns at his cousin but doesn't say anything.

"Come on, Tris, let's skate," says Annabelle. She grabs his arm and drags him past Cassidy and me onto the ice.

We watch as they skate off. "Do you think that's really what he told her about me?" says Cassidy in a low voice. "I mean, I know I'm kind of a moose and everything. . . ."

"You are not a moose!" I reply hotly. "Besides, what do you care what the Duke of Puke says? He's a jerk, you told me so yourself."

"Yeah, I know, and I don't care. Not really. It's just—" She pauses,

Heather Vogel Frederick

and her voice trails off. She takes a deep breath. "It's just when I think of all the hours I've spent helping him practice, hours I could have spent doing something I really wanted to be doing—when I think of all the weight-lifting and crunches and running—I even took a couple of ballet lessons! And for what? So that he can trash talk me to that, that—"

"Stinkerbelle?" I offer.

"Exactly!" she fumes.

"Forget it, Cassidy. She's not worth it and neither is he."

Cassidy stomps off to round up the equipment for Chicks with Sticks, and I glide out onto the ice to warm up for my lesson. I haven't put in a whole lot of ice time in England, and I've gotten pretty rusty, but Mrs. Bergson sets me back on track. I'll never be anywhere near as good as Cassidy, or my brother, or Tristan and Annabelle—who are almost impossible to ignore, since first of all they're hogging the rink and second of all they're really amazing to watch—but I love love *love* being out on the ice. And that's all that matters, I tell myself loftily as I stumble and land on my backside once again.

After my lesson is finished, Mrs. Bergson tries to get Cassidy to skate with Tristan so that Annabelle can see what they've been working on. Cassidy refuses, using her chicks, who are starting to arrive, as an excuse.

"Tomorrow, then," says Mrs. Bergson.

"Sure," says Cassidy. "Tomorrow."

She mouths the words *NO WAY* to me as she skates over to help

Darcy set up the cones for their hockey drills. I grin and give her a thumbs-up, then go to change back into my shoes.

Outside the rink, Stewart is waiting for me with Pip. On our way back to Half Moon Farm we make a detour through Sleepy Hollow Cemetery, just like I'd hoped.

"What are you smiling about?" Jess asks, when we knock on her door a while later.

"Nothing," I tell her, wiping a telltale smear of lip gloss off Stewart's cheek.

Jess hasn't been kissed yet. We don't talk about it much, and it's not like I've done a lot of it so I'm not some big expert or anything. But I know she's still hoping that Darcy will be her first. My brother, Darcy, not Jane Austen's Mr. Darcy, of course. Sometimes I think that between book club and my family, there are just too many Darcys.

Mrs. Delaney drives us to the store to pick up the ingredients for our bake-a-thon tomorrow. Pies & Prejudice is closing down, my friends told me, but they have one last order to fill, and it's a big one. The British-American Society of Concord is having their annual Patriot's Day dinner dance, and Pies & Prejudice is providing the desserts. I'm looking forward to helping out. It's the least I can do to help repay my friends for all they've done for me. Even though, as my mother said, they're not expecting me to repay them.

We drop everything off at Cassidy's and then hop into her van to drive over to Megan's for our book club meeting and sleepover.

"Go ahead into the living room," Mrs. Wong tells us when we

arrive. "Becca and Calliope aren't here yet, and Megan's just now hooking up the computer, so there's no rush."

I left my mini laptop back in England with my mom so she could videoconference with us. It's late there, but she said she didn't care, she didn't want to miss out.

"Okay, here we go," says Megan a couple of minutes later. She clicks on the icon to make the call, and a few seconds later my mother appears onscreen.

"Bonjour!" she trills.

My parents are actually in Paris this week. It's their twentieth wedding anniversary, and they wanted to do something special.

"Don't you mean *bonne nuit*?" says my dad from somewhere offscreen. "It's eleven o'clock over here."

My mother waves her hand at him. "Whatever." She leans in toward the webcam. "You have to see our view! This hotel is phenomenal!"

The image onscreen gives a lurch as she picks the laptop up and turns it around. I get a quick, blurred view of my dad. He's sitting in an armchair with—what else?—a book, reading. Then the image settles, focusing on a set of French doors open to a balcony, and beyond that, the twinkling lights of Paris.

"Ooooooooh," everyone sighs.

"It's so romantic!" says Gigi. "Paris in the spring! And look—you can see the Eiffel Tower."

"I know!" says my mother, pulling a chair over so we can see both her and the view. "It couldn't be more perfect."

"Happy anniversary," I tell her, and everybody else wishes her a happy anniversary too.

The front door bangs open and we all flinch.

Becca comes in, her face as white as the Wong's carpet. Before anyone can ask what's up, her mother marches in behind her. She's clutching a copy of my dad's book, *Spring Reckoning,* and she's clearly on the warpath.

She glares at the video screen. "Phoebe Hawthorne, is that husband of yours around?"

"Nick? He'd better be—it's our anniversary."

Mrs. Chadwick doesn't think this is funny. "Would you be good enough to get him for me?"

My mother turns the laptop around, and my dad waves at us from his cozy seat in the corner of their hotel room.

"What is the meaning of this?" Mrs. Chadwick demands furiously, waving the book at him.

He gives her a blank look. "What's the meaning of what?"

"Don't play games with me, Nicholas Hawthorne. You know exactly what I'm talking about."

My dad shakes his head. "Sorry, Calliope. I'm in the dark here."

"*Hepzibah Plunkett* is what I'm talking about." She flips opens his book to a bookmarked page and starts to read:

"'*Hepzibah Plunkett waddles into the tavern. Her sharp gaze rakes the room, settling finally on a small, balding man perched on an overturned ale cask. 'Ezekiel Plunkett!' she screeches. 'I demand*

Heather Vogel Frederick

that you leave here at once! These rabble-rousers are nothing but trouble, and will be the ruin of us all.' 'Hepzibah, my sweet—' her husband demurs, but his wife holds up her hand. 'I will not hear another word!' she tells him. 'Will you bring shame upon our family? Risk everything, and for what—a wild dream of freedom? Come home with me now, or not another morsel of food shall you receive from my hand, and you shall bed in the barn from this day forward.' As her husband rises meekly to his feet and obeys, Hepzibah flings a triumphant look at the gathered patriots. She marches out behind him, her enormous posterior bringing up the rear like a defiant lady-in-waiting. The door closes and the tavern erupts in raucous laughter.'"

Mrs. Chadwick slams the book shut and glares at the TV screen. "How *dare* you!"

We're all open-mouthed, including my father.

"Calliope," he protests, "You don't— I mean you can't possibly think that I, that you—"

I stare at Mrs. Chadwick, horrified. She thinks that Hepzibah Plunkett is *her*.

My father shakes his head. "Calliope, I assure you, I would never, ever—"

"Don't you tell me what you'd never ever!" she retorts, tapping angrily on the cover of the book. "Here it is, in black and white. And to think I thought you were my friend!"

"Calliope, hold on a second!" says my mother.

"I will not," Mrs. Chadwick fumes. "Come along, Becca."

"But Mom!" she prostests, "the sleepover!"

"Emphasis on *over*." She grabs Becca by the hand and drags her, protesting, out the front door, slamming it shut behind her.

There's a long silence in the living room.

Beside me, Megan gives a tiny snort of laughter. "I really like that line about her bottom being like a defiant lady-in-waiting," she whispers to me, and I have to smother a grin because I was thinking the same thing. But the situation isn't funny, otherwise. Not at all.

"I don't know what to say," says my dad finally.

My mother appears onscreen, crossing the hotel room to perch on the arm of his chair. "I doubt there's anything you could do tonight to mollify Calliope, so I suggest we let her cool off, and try and turn this into a useful discussion for our book club. Do any of you think that some of the characters in *Pride and Prejudice* were based on people Jane Austen knew?"

My father starts to get up and leave, but my mother puts a restraining hand on his arm. "Stay and talk with us, Nick. Your perspective will be valuable."

"I don't know about the characters," he says cautiously, "but I do recall some advice she once gave her niece Anna, who also wanted to be a writer." He turns to my mother. "Do you know the quote I'm talking about, Phoebe?"

She darts offscreen again, returning a second later with a book. "I think I remember reading it in this new Austen biography."

"Who but Phoebe Hawthorne would bring a book about Jane Austen on an anniversary trip to Paris?" says Mrs. Sloane-Kinkaid dryly.

My mother ignores her. "Here it is. She wrote this in September, 1814, after Anna sent her some chapters of a novel she was working on. Jane wrote back: 'You are now collecting your people delightfully, getting them exactly into such a spot as is the delight of my life. Three or four families in a country village is the very thing to work on.'"

"That's the one," says my dad.

"Wow," I say to no one in particular. "Lucky Anna." How cool to have Jane Austen for your aunt—and your editor. I would kill to have her read some of my stuff.

"So what's your point, Nicholas?" asks Mrs. Wong.

"Just that I followed her advice in writing my novel—it's set in a small town, and while there's a large cast of minor characters, for the most part I focused my writer's lens on just a handful of families."

My mother pats him on the shoulder. "Jane Austen would approve."

"But Calliope doesn't," says my father glumly.

"I wonder if people ever thought Jane modeled her characters after them?" asks Jess.

"Probably," says Cassidy. "Lots of people in *Pride and Prejudice* remind me of people I know. Caroline Bingley, anyone?"

"Stinkerbelle," I reply.

"Bingo."

"And how about Rupert Loomis?" I add. "He is *such* a Mr. Collins."

"Emma!" my mother warns.

"Well he is. Dad thinks so too—ask him!"

She turns to my father, who grins. My mother swats him.

"By the way," says Cassidy. "I'm really mad at Elizabeth Bennet."

"Why, honey?" asks her mother.

"I can't believe she's actually starting to like that stupid Mr. Darcy! That's not like real life at all. Who would ever like such a stuck-up creep? I mean, he actually said he wouldn't dance with her because she's not pretty enough. How did he put it? That she's 'not handsome enough to tempt me'? Gimme a break."

I can tell Cassidy's still stinging from Annabelle's "big, bad Cassidy Sloane" remark.

We start talking about famous couples in books who start off not liking each other.

"How about Anne Shirley and Gilbert Blythe from *Anne of Green Gables*?" Megan suggests.

"That doesn't count," I point out. "Gilbert liked Anne from the very beginning, but she didn't like him. With Elizabeth and Darcy, the dislike is mutual."

"Some scholars think Jane Austen got the idea for Elizabeth and Darcy from Shakespeare," says my mother. "They say she was inspired by Beatrice and Benedick from *Much Ado About Nothing*, or by Kate and Petruchio from *The Taming of the Shrew*."

"Kate and Petrooshee-who?" asks Cassidy.

Heather Vogel Frederick

"You'll get to them eventually in school," her mother tells her.

"Such a fun play!" sighs Mrs. Delaney. "I played Kate in New York once, a long time ago."

My father, who has been leafing through my mother's Jane Austen biography, starts to laugh.

"What?" my mother asks.

"Listen to this quote," he says. "It's from *Pride and Prejudice*, and it's perfect. I should e-mail it to Calliope: *'For what do we live, but to make sport for our neighbors, and laugh at them in our turn.'*"

We all laugh too, but a little uneasily. I glance over at Mrs. Wong, thinking of all the stuff I've said about her behind her back. And about Becca and Mrs. Chadwick, too.

"On that note," says my mother, "perhaps we should wrap this up with a handout."

FUN FACTS ABOUT JANE

1) Jane was most productive as a writer when she had peace and quiet and a settled routine. During her early years at Steventon, she wrote prolifically, but that stopped when her parents abruptly announced that they were retiring and moving to Bath. For the most part, Jane preferred country life to the bustle of the city, especially when it was time to write.

2) The years at Bath were tumultuous ones, as her father died and she and Cassandra and her mother were forced to move to ever-smaller quarters, and eventually to Southampton, where they lived for a time with her brother Frances and his wife. Her writing routine was constantly disrupted, and her productivity declined.

3) Eventually, Jane's brother Edward, who had been adopted by wealthy, childless relatives when he was twelve (common practice in those days, to ensure that property stayed in the family), offered them a cottage rent-free in the village of Chawton, where he had inherited a grand home. There, Jane enjoyed the most prolific years of her life.

4) The hinge on the door to the sitting room where Jane wrote at Chawton squeaked, and according to family lore she specifically asked that it not be oiled, so that she'd be alerted to interruptions.

5) Jane's niece Marianne Knight recalled how her aunt, as she was doing needlework, "would mysteriously burst into laughter and hurry across the room to write something down, then return to her place."

6) Jane never had a study of her own, a desk of her own (besides

Heather Vogel Frederick

a tiny lap desk she'd prop on a table), or even a room of her own—she shared a bedroom her entire life with her sister Cassandra. When someone entered the sitting room where she was working, she'd quickly cover the pages of her manuscript or slip them into her lapdesk.

As I place the handout into my notebook, Jess's mom and Mrs. Sloane-Kinkaid leave to take Mrs. Bergson home. While Gigi and Mrs. Wong clear away the dishes, Megan and Jess and Cassidy head down the hall to Megan's room, leaving me alone in the living room with my parents onscreen.

My father blows me a kiss. "Go ahead and talk to your mom for a bit, sweetheart. I'm going to get ready for bed. It's nearly midnight here."

He pads away, and my mom and I smile at each other.

"Mom," I whisper, "do you really think Dad based Hepzibah Plunkett on Mrs. Chadwick?"

My mother pauses before she answers. "I don't know, Emma," she says finally. "I don't fully understand how the creative process works for a writer. Perhaps a little bit, unconsciously."

"I mean, it's kind of a coincidence and everything, her having a big, uh—"

"I know."

My mom and I start to giggle.

"I wish you were here," I tell her.

She smiles. "Me too. But a person's twentieth wedding anniversary only comes around once in a lifetime."

I blow her a kiss. "I know. Happy anniversary!"

A little while later, as we're getting our sleeping bags all spread out downstairs in the Wongs' enormous family room—it has a media center with actual movie theater seats and a soda machine—the door flies open and Becca comes in, breathless.

"What did I miss?" she asks.

Megan looks at her, surprised. "But I thought your mother said—"

Becca flings her sleeping bag onto the floor and flops down on it. "You guys you should have been there! My dad rocks! He and my mom got into this big argument when we got home. He said it wasn't fair for her to punish me for something that's between her and your dad, Emma, and besides, he thinks she's being ridiculous. So he drove me back over."

I never thought I'd actually be glad to see Becca Chadwick, but I am. Our evening felt sort of incomplete without her.

"You've got to admit it's pretty funny," says Cassidy. "Hepzibah Plunkett, I mean."

Becca nods. "Yeah, but my mother's kind of touchy about her, you know—"

"Hindquarters?" says Cassidy.

"Caboose?" says Megan.

"Nether regions?" I offer. "Haunches? Keister?"

"Gluteus maximus?" adds Jess.

We all dissolve in laughter, even Becca.

Heather Vogel Frederick

It's so good to be home with my friends! I've never even tried to explain the synonym game to anyone back in England. Not even Lucy.

The five of us stay up way too late talking and laughing, and everybody groans when Mrs. Wong comes down at four the next morning and flips on the light.

"Rise and shine, girls! Big day ahead!"

Somehow, we manage to get up and drag ourselves over to the Old North Bridge.

"Oh, great," mutters Cassidy. "Stinkerbelle is here. Figures."

The field is crowded with onlookers milling around, waiting for the battle reenactment to start.

Annabelle is standing with Tristan and Simon and their parents, along with some other people I don't recognize. They're young, though, and look like students, so I figure maybe they belong to Professor Berkeley. Simon told Megan he's always dragging his history classes to famous sites around Boston.

I see the Chadwicks arrive, and I wave to Stewart. He doesn't see me. "Hey, Stewart!" I call, waving again. He turns and frowns, then turns away, pointedly ignoring me. The enthusiasm drains out of my wave and I lower my arm, feeling puzzled and hurt.

"What's going on?" asks Megan. "Did you two have a fight?"

"Not that I know of."

The Chadwicks stroll over to join the Berkeleys, and Annabelle starts talking to Stewart. He pretends he doesn't see me watching them. Mrs. Chadwick points at something a little closer to the bridge, and as she heads off toward it everybody but Stewart—who's squatting down to tie his shoe—follows her.

I grab Cassidy by the arm. "I may need backup," I tell her. "You guys too. Come on. Let's go see what's up."

Cassidy and I start across the field, with Megan and Jess and Becca right behind us.

"What's going on, Stewart?" I ask when we reach him.

Wordlessly, he holds up his cell phone. On it is the picture of me with Rupert Loomis under the mistletoe. My heart sinks, and I get a sick feeling in the pit of my stomach. I don't even have to ask where he got it. Stinkerbelle is obviously still bent on revenge.

I force myself to laugh. "Stewart, come on! That's *Rupert Loomis*. Remember? *Moo?* The one who's kind of like Mr. Collins Junior? I've told you about him a zillion times! The whole thing was a joke. I can explain."

"Explain what, exactly?" he says coldly.

"I was tricked into kissing him. Annabelle pushed me under the mistletoe and snapped the picture."

"The overall impression is not that you were unwilling to be kissed."

Stewart is going into his weird, stiff little version of Austen-speak, which is not a good sign. This always happens when he's nervous or upset.

The problem is, he's right. From the angle that the picture was taken, you can't see my scrunched-up mouth, or the revolted expression that I know was on my face. All you can see is Rupert's obvious delight, and his giant hands on my shoulders.

Heather Vogel Frederick

"Honestly," I tell Stewart. "It's not what it looks like."

"Stewart, don't be a dork," Becca scolds. "Emma's telling the truth. She told us all about it months ago."

"So how come she didn't say anything to me?"

"I was embarrassed," I admit.

"Wouldn't you be?" Jess points out. "It's like me getting tricked into kissing Kevin Mullins."

"I don't want to talk about it anymore," Stewart replies, and stalks off.

Openmouthed in disbelief, I watch him go, feeling completely and utterly humiliated. I can't believe this is happening! My boyfriend just broke up with me, in front of all my friends, on Patriot's Day! At five o'clock in the morning!

Across the field, I can see Annabelle watching us. She looks like the cat who ate the canary. *Too bad the pancake breakfast hasn't started*, I think. If I had a full plate in my hand right now—or even a pie—I'd start a battle reenactment of my own.

"I hate Annabelle Fairfax!" I blurt out. "I can't believe she did that!"

"You know what they always say—don't get mad, get even." Megan holds up her cell phone. "Stinkerbelle is about to get a taste of her own medicine."

She flips it open to reveal a picture of Annabelle that she must have snapped earlier. Nobody looks their best at five o'clock in the morning, and Annabelle is no exception. She obviously hasn't taken a shower yet today, and her hair is stuck to one side of her head. Plus, her mascara is smeared and she's wearing what looks like some ratty old soccer jersey of Tristan's or Simon's. The expression on her face—her eyes are narrowed and her mouth is all twisted up in a smirk—makes her look like she just drank a quart jar of pickle juice, as my dad likes to say.

"I think I feel a blog post coming on," Megan tells us. "Let's go home."

We find her mother and convince her that I'm jet-lagged and not feeling well and need to leave. She says it's a shame that we're going to miss out on the festivities, especially since we managed to get up early, but that she understands.

Mrs. Wong drops us off at Megan's house, and after she leaves again, we all crowd around the coffee table in the family room and watch as Megan uploads the photo onto her laptop.

"We're counting on you," says Jess.

"Never fear, Fashionista Jane is here," Megan replies. Squinting at the picture, she blurs the face slightly so that Annabelle isn't instantly recognizable. Then she turns her attention to the caption. *"It is a truth universally acknowledged,"* she begins, talking out loud as she types, *"that a young lady—if one can indeed call her a lady—who is not in possession of a shower, a hairbrush, suitable garments, or—"* she hesitates, drumming her fingers on the desktop, thinking.

"Or a brain?" suggests Cassidy.

"Manners?" I offer.

Megan shakes her head. "Nope. Hang on, I've got it." She continues typing and talking: *"or a genteel upbringing would do well to remain at home, rather than risk becoming an object of public mirth."*

Heather Vogel Frederick

I stare at her. She's gotten really good at Austen-speak. "Megan, you're a genius!"

"That's what Wolfgang says," she replies smugly, and with a click of her mouse, she posts it.

"Are you sending it to your blog, or to *Flashlite*?" asks Becca.

"Both," Megan replies. "This one deserves maximum coverage."

We go back to bed for a while after that, but of course I can't sleep because I'm too worked up about Stewart. I send him about a zillion texts and leave him half a dozen voice mails, but he doesn't respond. Finally, I crawl out of my sleeping bag and into the shower.

"Looks like you're feeling better," says Mrs. Wong a little later, when she comes back downstairs to check on us and sees me already up and dressed. "Traveling always takes a lot out of me, too. Just take it easy today."

But of course I don't. I can't—not with three dozen pies to help bake and Stewart to worry about. And first, there's the parade. The Berkeleys invited us over to watch, which we do. It feels weird, standing in my own front yard where I've stood for what feels like a million April mornings before, knowing that they're living in our house and driving our car around our town. I give Annabelle a wide berth. She's obviously gloating, and I have no intention of giving her the satisfaction of knowing how upset I am. I plaster a smile on my face and leave it there as Darcy marches by with Kyle Anderson, both of them dressed as Minutemen and playing their fifes. Darcy's been dressing up as a patriot for the parade ever since he was in sixth grade. Usually he marches with Dad, but this year he and Kyle are with Mr. Anderson.

"Your brother looks delicious in knee breeches," says Annabelle, sidling up beside me. "Don't you think so, Jess?"

We both ignore her. *Just wait until you see what we have in store for you,* I think to myself.

After the parade, Mrs. Wong drives us over to Cassidy's house. Gigi is waiting in the kitchen, and she hands me a pink apron that matches the others.

"Welcome to Pies and Prejudice," says Gigi. "This is your honorary uniform."

"Sweet!"

It takes us all day to bake the pies. We barely finish in time to get them over to the country club before the dinner dance starts. People are already starting to arrive as we pull into the long gravel driveway.

"Perfect timing!" says the caterer as we troop into the kitchen. "Line them up over there." She points to a stainless steel countertop, and we line the pies up in three rows—a dozen cherry, a dozen blueberry, and a dozen coconut creams piled high with whipped cream.

"Red, white, and blue," says Mrs. Chadwick, swooping in through the swinging door that leads to the dining room. "In honor of the Union Jack and the Stars and Stripes."

Mrs. Chadwick, whose ancestors fought with the British, is president of the British-American Society this year. Tonight, her gardening clothes are nowhere in sight. She's wearing a long formal gown the same pale robin's-egg blue as her eyes, dangerously high heels, and

Heather Vogel Frederick

diamond earrings almost as big as the ones Gigi sometimes lends to Megan.

As Mrs. Chadwick goes over to talk to the caterer, Cassidy pokes her head into the dining room. "Uh-oh," she says. "Stinkerbelle alert."

"What?" I take a look too. "What's she doing here?"

"Professor Berkeley is giving a talk before dinner," says Mrs. Sloane-Kinkaid, coming in with more pies. "See? It's on the program."

She passes one to Megan, who reads it aloud. " 'The Rebel Uprising: A British Perspective.' "

"That should go over really well here in the cradle of liberty," I reply.

Mrs. Chadwick brushes past us on her way out to the dining room, then sails back in almost immediately with Mrs. Berkeley and Annabelle trailing in her wake.

"And this is our kitchen," she announces grandly.

"Look at all those pies!" says Mrs. Berkeley. "You girls have been busy, haven't you?"

Annabelle surveys our handiwork. "Mmmm," she chirps. "Look at all that lovely whipped cream! Such a favorite amongst"—she pauses dramatically—"young ladies of genteel upbringing."

Mrs. Chadwick and Mrs. Berkeley and Mrs. Sloane-Kinkaid all laugh at this, thinking it's a joke, but Annabelle's eyes are very bright and her face is flushed and she's staring at Megan.

"I've been reading *Flashlite* for years," she whispers, as the adults drift off to tour the patio. "So have my friends. Jemima sent me a text the minute she spotted my picture. I knew it had to be one of you, and

Simon was gushing just yesterday on the way home from the airport about your keen interest in fashion, Megan."

I glance over at Megan, who's looking stricken, and realize that this could get much worse.

It already has.

"Simon wasn't at all pleased, when he saw how upset I was," Annabelle continues. "And of course I had to confide in him my suspicions as to who did it. Oddly enough, it's the same person who ridiculed his brother." She leans toward Megan. "Nobody but nobody does that to me and gets away with it."

The color drains from Megan's face. She turns and runs blindly outside. Annabelle starts to follow her, but Cassidy grabs her arm.

"Back off, Stinkerbelle," she warns. "You don't want to tangle with big, bad Cassidy Sloane." Annabelle sniffs, then retreats through the swinging doors back into the dining room.

My friends and I go in search of Megan, who has taken refuge in the back of the Sloane-Kinkaid's minivan. She's crying.

"We'll get it all sorted out, don't worry," I tell her, as Becca hands her a tissue. I'm not nearly as certain as I sound, though. This is a real mess.

It quickly gets messier. It seems Annabelle isn't done with us yet.

Mrs. Sloane-Kinkaid takes us all to Burger Barn for dinner, and afterward, we go back to her house for dessert—leftover pie. The phone is ringing as we walk through the door. Mrs. Sloane-Kinkaid, who's balancing Chloe on one hip, presses the speakerphone button.

Heather Vogel Frederick

"Hello?" she says.

"Is this some kind of a joke?" replies a cold voice. It's Mrs. Chadwick.

Cassidy's mother gives an exasperated sigh. "Now what, Calliope?"

"'Now what?'! We just served the pies, and it turns out that my coconut creams are topped with *shaving cream,* not whipped cream, that's what!" Mrs. Chadwick hollers. "How dare you make me look like a fool in front of the entire British-American community?"

I feel something vibrating in the pocket of my jeans. It's my cell phone. My heart leaps—it's got to be Stewart! But it's not. It's someone else, using his phone.

A picture flashes onto the tiny screen. It's Annabelle Fairfax. She's holding up a piece of coconut shaving cream pie and waving her fork cheerily. The message beneath it reads: SEE YOU BACK IN ENGLAND!

SUMMER

"Next to being married, a girl likes to be crossed in love a little now and then. It is something to think of, and gives her a sort of distinction among her companions."

—Pride and Prejudice

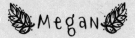

Megan

"*Adieu, sweet you.*"
—Letter from Jane Austen to her sister, Cassandra, January 1809

My mother hangs up the phone, then turns around to face me, eyes narrowed and hands on hips.

"What?" I ask.

"That was Mr. Flanagan."

Mr. Flanagan is the principal of Alcott High School.

"And your point is?"

"Don't you sass me, Megan Rose Wong! You are in big trouble, young lady!"

My father backs slowly out of the kitchen. Gigi suddenly decides the pantry needs reorganizing. Nobody wants to be caught in the crossfire when my mother gets like this.

I try for a more respectful tone. "I honestly have no idea why he was calling, Mom." Which isn't entirely true. I actually have a pretty good guess.

"I have two words for you: Fashionista Jane."

Uh-oh. My guess was right.

Today was our first day back at school after Spring Break. Word is out about my blog, and while I got my fair share of high fives and "Way to go, Wong"s, I was also on the receiving end of a lot of dirty looks. Mostly from people I poked fun at in the Fashion Faux Pas.

"Boisterous hosiery?" Ms. Bates had said, arching an eyebrow at me as I entered the biology classroom.

I shot her a guilty glance. "Sorry," I replied. But as I took my seat I couldn't help noticing that she was wearing regular shoes for once, and normal-looking socks.

"Mr. Flanagan says his phone has been ringing nonstop, and several parents are threatening lawsuits," my mother continues.

"*Lawsuits?*" I gulp. "For what?"

"Cyber harassment."

"Harassment? Gimme a break! All I did was make fun of stupid stuff like silly socks and bad haircuts and highwater pants."

"Well, obviously people don't like being ridiculed!" My mother sighs wearily and slumps into the seat across from me at the table. "Where did I go wrong? I'm obviously a failure as a parent."

Here we go again. My mother loves to trot this line out. Just to remind me that I was probably switched at birth with the perfect Chinese-American daughter she was meant to have, the one who is never in trouble, always gets straight A's, and plans to go to Harvard.

Gigi pokes her head out of the pantry. "I think Megan's blog is very funny. And so does Eva Bergson."

"Mother!" my mother snaps. "You are not helping!"

"Sorry." The pantry door closes again.

"One thing's for sure," my mother tells me, drumming her fingers on the table. "You are pulling the plug on Fashionista Jane. Tonight."

"But Mom—"

She holds her hand up, silencing me. "No ifs, ands, or buts. I promised Mr. Flanagan."

"What am I going to tell Wolfgang?"

"Tell him the truth—that you acted irresponsibly and that your blog is inappropriate and inconsiderate. In fact, maybe I should call him. Shame on him for egging you on! And paying you to do it!"

I can't help it; I start to cry. The thing is, I'm not even crying because of my blog. I'm crying because of Simon Berkeley. At lunchtime, he sat with his brother instead of at our table, and he barely even looked at me in biology class. As he passed me in the hall, all he said was, "Badly done, Megan." He looked so disappointed that I just wanted to disappear.

But I can't tell my mother that. She doesn't know how I feel about Simon and I don't need her poking her nose in, especially not tonight, and especially not when she's in this kind of a mood.

I go to my room and call Becca instead.

"Poor baby!" she says sympathetically. Becca has been extra nice to me since the Patriot's Day fiasco. She's feeling pretty perky these days, and when Becca's perky, everybody around her benefits. Over the break, Zach Norton asked her to go to Spring Formal. I was really happy for her, because she's had a crush on him just as long as I have, and because I thought Simon was going to ask me and we'd all go together. But now that's not going to happen and I'm feeling nothing but sorry for myself. Plus, part of me is jealous that she has a date, and an even teenier part is wishing that I'd stuck to Zach instead of falling for Simon. Then maybe I'd be in her shoes.

"I'd like to get my hands on Annabelle Fairfax," I tell her bitterly. "This is all her fault."

Even though we told our mothers that it was Annabelle who added a layer of shaving cream to the top of the coconut cream pies, she got off scot-free since no one had actually seen her do it. When Mrs. Chadwick questioned her, she went all wide-eyed and innocent and said, "Why on earth would I do such a thing? Besides, where would I have gotten shaving cream?"

"Duh," said Cassidy when she heard about it afterward. "It's a *country club.* Hasn't anybody ever heard of locker rooms? And she had plenty of time to prank the pies while her father was giving his dumb talk."

It was Mrs. Sloane-Kinkaid who saved the reputation of Pies & Prejudice. After Mrs. Chadwick's frantic phone call, she drove right back over and set up this thing called a chocolate fountain. I guess it was a big hit, and she even managed to get all the guests laughing about the shaving cream pies, too.

Heather Vogel Frederick

Everybody but Mrs. Chadwick. She's still ticked off, and she's still not talking to Mr. Hawthorne, either.

"How's Stewart doing?" I ask. "Have you talked to him about Emma?"

"Yeah, but he won't listen," Becca replies. "He's being really stubborn. My dad says it's wounded male pride, whatever that is."

Jess and Cassidy and I have tried talking to Stewart too, with no luck. Emma's just crushed about their breakup. She probably feels a whole lot worse than I do, since Simon wasn't even officially my boyfriend.

After I finish talking to Becca, I send Wolfgang an e-mail, explaining what happened and why my mother is making me quit blogging. He e-mails me right back. "Too much snark, not enough sweet?"

"Exactly," I reply.

"You're still FABULOUS!" he writes back. "TTFN, darling—I look forward to other brilliant projects together in the future!"

And that's that.

The week goes downhill from there. The next morning, I get hauled into Mr. Flanagan's office, where my mother has arranged for me to apologize in person to the parents who wanted to sue, along with their kids. Feeling totally humiliated, and with my mother's eyes burning twin holes in the back of my new yellow tank top and matching cardigan, I make it worse by apologizing in Austen-speak.

"I am sincerely regretful of having caused anyone distress," I begin. It's like I can't help myself. I'm nervous—three sets of parents, my mother, and the principal all staring at me with their arms folded across their chests—and the words just come tumbling out. "Fashionista Jane was never meant to harm, only to enlighten and provide mild amusement for her readers."

My mother hustles me out of there pretty quickly after that.

Simon continues to ignore me, even after I slip him a note apologizing—not in Austen-speak this time—and trying to explain.

By Friday afternoon, I'm a wreck.

"Let's go shopping!" says Becca. "I need something to wear to Spring Formal."

Great, I think. *Just what I need to cheer me up*. A reminder that I am so not invited to the dance. But it's better than sitting home alone brooding, so I allow myself to be talked into going along.

We end up taking the train into Boston with her mother. Mrs. Chadwick wants to go to some fancy gardening store on Newbury Street, right near this awesome thrift store I discovered the last time I was downtown with my grandmother.

I have Gigi to thank for getting me interested in vintage stuff. It started last year, when she gave me this beautiful material she brought from Hong Kong. It was practically antique, and completely unique. People went nuts over anything I made out of it, and I'm pretty sure it's what got me in the door at Bébé Soleil.

I used to make fun of thrift stores, but now I think they're cool. Shopping at them is like going on a treasure hunt—you never know what you're going to find. And at the fancy ones in Boston, you can find some really great stuff. Like the '60s prom dress I pull off the rack a little while later to show Becca.

"Look at this!" I tell her. "Doesn't it remind you a little of that dress of Jackie Kennedy's we saw at the Smithsonian last year?"

She wrinkles her nose. "I don't know. Maybe."

"Try it on," I urge.

"You don't think it will make me look too old or out of style or something?"

"No way. Vintage is always in style. Besides, check out the color—peach is gorgeous on you. And, it's strapless." I waggle the hanger enticingly.

Becca has been dying to wear something strapless.

While she goes to try it on, I dig through a big basket of purses on the floor. Some of them are tacky—just your basic used stuff—but I unearth a lime green designer clutch that I know Gigi will love. Plus, it's only $9.50, which is another reason thrift stores totally rock.

Becca comes out of the dressing room and twirls in front of the mirror, beaming at her reflection. "You're right, it's gorgeous."

"Told you so," I tell her smugly. "Zach will faint when he sees you."

"I hope not—that would be awkward."

She laughs, and as I catch a glimpse of myself standing next to her, I'm struck as always at how different the two of us are. Becca has what my mother calls "girl-next-door looks"—she's blond and blue-eyed and a classic beauty, like Mrs. Sloane-Kinkaid. With my dark hair and eyes and ivory skin, I'm like night to her day. Plus, she's a cheerleader and super outgoing, and I'm more on the quiet side.

"Yin and yang," says Gigi.

Somehow, though, our friendship works.

Becca's mother comes to get us as we're ringing up our purchases. She's loaded down with packages and bags, and there's a small trellis sticking out of one of them. I ask her what it's for.

"Clematis," she tells me. "It's a climber and needs something to scramble up. I thought I'd put it back by the shed, as the centerpiece of the new seating area I'm planning."

Despite Hepzibah Plunkett and the Patriot's Day pie fiasco, Mrs. Chadwick seems a lot happier these days. She really loves all this landscape design stuff. And actually, Mr. Chadwick's dire predictions haven't come true. Their yard looks really good, especially now that everything's starting to bloom. The neighbors love it, and a bunch of them have asked her to help them with their gardens too. My parents have told her that as a graduation present, they want to hire her to completely redesign our property, and Mrs. Sloane-Kinkaid has invited her to do a guest spot on her show.

"I vote for dinner here in town," she says, and takes us to a really nice restaurant down near the Public Gardens. It's warm enough that we can eat at a table on the sidewalk, and we sit and watch the Swan Boats floating around the pond across the street. I feel very grown-up, and wonder if this is what Paris is like. My parents have promised I can go there next year with Gigi, when I'm sixteen.

By the time our train pulls into the Concord Depot, it's nearly nine

Heather Vogel Frederick

o'clock. Both my parents are there waiting for us, which strikes me as a little odd. I thought Mrs. Chadwick was planning to drive me home.

"How was your shopping trip?" my mother asks.

"Great! Becca found a fabulous dress, and I got a present for Gigi." I open the bag I'm carrying and pull out the lime green clutch.

"That's so thoughtful of you, sweetheart."

There's something wrong with my mother's voice. And when I look more closely at her face, I can tell she's been crying.

"What's the matter?" I ask.

"Calliope, hang on a second," says my father. "You and Becca need to hear this too."

Mrs. Chadwick frowns, and Becca and I exchange a glance.

"We have some sad news," he continues.

All of a sudden I can't breathe. I look around wildly. *Where's my grandmother?*

"Is it Gigi?" I blurt out. "Is something wrong with Gigi?"

My mother shakes her head. "No, no," she says quickly. "Your grandmother is fine, honey. It's Mrs. Bergson."

"What happened?" asks Mrs. Chadwick.

"She passed away this afternoon."

Mrs. Chadwick and Becca and I stare at her blankly.

"But I just saw her at the rink yesterday, when we went to pick up Stewart!" Becca protests. "Are you sure?"

My father nods. "Mrs. Sloane-Kinkaid called us with the news. I guess it happened shortly after Cassidy's practice session earlier this evening with Tristan Berkeley."

"You mean she died at the rink?" My voice cracks.

"It was very quick," my mother replies. "Apparently she sat down to take off her skates, and then she was just—gone."

I stand there, stunned, trying to absorb this news. "Does Cassidy know?"

My mother nods. "I guess she's taking it pretty hard. So is Tristan."

"Why didn't you call us?" asks Mrs. Chadwick. "We would have come straight back."

"We didn't want to spoil your girls' day out," says my father. "And there wasn't anything you could do. There wasn't anything any of us could do."

I can't believe it. *Mrs. Bergson?* I mean, I know she's kind of ancient and everything, but she's so vibrant. So *alive.* Tears well up in my eyes and spill over.

My mom puts her arm around my shoulders. "Let's go home," she says. "Gigi really needs some support. Mrs. Bergson was her best friend here in Concord."

"Who's going to tell Emma?" I ask.

"Jess and her mother called the Hawthornes a couple of hours ago. You might want to give Emma a call, too—but not until tomorrow, since it's the middle of the night in England. I'm sure she's needing lots of extra love right now. Mrs. Bergson was like a grandmother to her."

All the way home I stare out the window of our car. Why do people

Heather Vogel Frederick

have to die? It's horrible. I'm really, really going to miss Mrs. Bergson. Plus, part of me can't help worrying about Gigi, too. She's always talking about how she wants me to have her jewelry and stuff someday when she's gone, but I just took it as a joke. I've never really thought about it seriously—I mean, my grandmother seems ageless. But she's not, she's the same age as Mrs. Bergson. Tears slide down my cheeks again as I realize I'm going to lose her someday too.

"You okay back there, Megs?" my father asks, his eyes flicking worriedly to the rearview mirror.

I nod, and my mother reaches over the back of the seat and pats my knee, then wordlessly passes me a tissue. I wonder if she's thinking about Gigi too.

The memorial service is set for a week from Sunday. It's going to be held at the rink, which was what Mrs. Bergson requested. There's a note from her in the paper and everything. "No sad faces, no glum clothes," she wrote. "Think of it as a going-away party."

The Mother-Daughter Book Club takes her at her word, and at the appointed time we show up in our brightest, cheeriest clothes. My grandmother is dripping with diamonds—"ice in honor of the queen of the ice," as she puts it—and so am I. Well, my earlobes are at least. Gigi lent me her diamond earrings again. She didn't say a word this time about her wanting me to have them someday when she's gone. I think she knows that I don't want to think about that right now.

The bleachers around the rink are packed. Over the years she lived in Concord, Mrs. Bergson taught hundreds, maybe thousands, of people how to skate, including her minister, who talks about how much fun he had with her when he was a little boy.

"Whenever I think of Eva Bergson, I think of Paul's first letter to the Corinthians," he says. A carpet has been placed in the center of the rink, and he's standing at a podium in the middle of it. He glances down at his Bible and starts to read: "'*Love is patient and kind; love is not jealous or boastful; it is not arrogant or rude. Love does not insist on its own way; it is not irritable or resentful; it does not rejoice at wrong, but rejoices in the right. Love bears all things, believes all things, hopes all things, endures all things. Love never ends.*'"

Beside me, Gigi is sniffling into a hankie. I see my mother reach over and squeeze her hand.

The minister's words really do sum up Mrs. Bergson. I think about how patient she was with Emma when she wanted to learn how to skate, and how kind she was in giving Pip a home when it looked like we were going to have to take him back to the animal shelter. Pip must be missing her too, even though he's got plenty of company at Half Moon Farm, where the Delaneys are keeping him for now.

I glance over at Cassidy. She's leaning her head on her mother's shoulder, and Mrs. Sloane-Kinkaid has her arm around her. I'd forgotten all about Chicks with Sticks! Mrs. Bergson put so much time and effort and love into that project too. And all those pies she bought from us this year! She really was one of the kindest people my friends and I have ever known.

A lot of other people think so too. After he finishes his eulogy, Mrs. Bergson's minister invites people to share their memories of her, and

Heather Vogel Frederick

there's practically a stampede. Cassidy wipes her eyes, blows her nose, and joins the long line on the red carpet that stretches from the side of the rink to the podium. When it's her turn, she talks about how generously Mrs. Bergson volunteered her time and energy helping launch Chicks with Sticks, and she smiles wryly as she recalls being asked if she'd consider being Tristan Berkeley's practice partner.

"I'm a hockey player," she tells the gathered listeners. "Not an ice princess—oops, I mean ice dancer." She flashes a grin at Tristan, who shakes his head as a ripple of laughter runs through the crowd. "So her idea came as a bit of a shock. In fact, I actually thought maybe Mrs. Bergson was a little nuts at first. But she helped me see another side of myself that I didn't even know was there. She told me I should never put limits on myself, and I will always, always be grateful to her for that."

I notice Tristan nodding in agreement as she finishes, and I'm hoping that's a good sign. If he thaws, maybe Simon will eventually, too. Right now they both still seem pretty disgusted with us.

Afterward, while a slideshow of scenes from Mrs. Bergson's life is projected onto a giant screen at the far end of the rink, the skating party begins. This was another of Mrs. Bergson's requests, along with a full selection of desserts from Pies & Prejudice, which we spent all day yesterday baking.

"I'm so glad we have this one last chance to show people we really can bake," I tell Jess as we start serving the crowd. "I think they wondered, after the shaving cream incident."

She laughs. "No kidding."

"Hey, have you talked to Emma this weekend?"

She nods. "She really, really wanted to be here, but there was just no way she could."

"I know Mrs. Bergson would understand."

"I promised I'd videoconference with her later, and tell her how everything went," Jess adds, glancing at her watch. "I wonder how long people will stay."

I cut into another apple pie, which looks like the hands-down favorite this afternoon. Comfort food to comfort those that mourn, I guess. "I think the program said that the skating party ends at three. Hey— how about Stewart? Has he called her or anything? Maybe this will be the push he needs to get over his stupid wounded pride. Which had no reason to be wounded in the first place." I snort. "Rupert Loomis! As if!"

Jess shakes her head.

"Wuss."

My mother comes running over. She really made an effort to look good this afternoon, ditching her usual yoga pants for a crimson wool skirt of Gigi's and matching sweater set. Red is a great color on my mother. The pearls—also Gigi's—are the perfect accessory. "Girls!" she says. "I just ran into Eva's lawyer, and he wants to meet with us after the party."

"With you and me and Jess?" I ask, puzzled.

"No, silly, with the entire book club." She glances down at the business card she's holding. "His office is just down the street. I've got to find Shannon and Calliope and Clementine. Have you seen them?" I point across the rink to where they're standing, talking with the manager. As my mother trots off, Jess and I look at each other and shrug. Neither of us have a clue what that was all about.

By the time the rink clears out, though, we're all abuzz with curiosity.

"I'm sure you ladies are wondering why I've asked you here," Mrs. Bergson's lawyer says as we file in and take seats. "Eva was a good friend as well as a client. She told me all about your book club. She thought of you as family, you know."

He peers over his glasses at us and smiles. "Eva came to me earlier this year and made some changes to her will. Although she left the bulk of her modest estate to the U.S. Figure Skating Association, there are also a few individual bequests. I have a letter here that she gave me to read to you, her Mother-Daughter Book Club friends."

He unfolds it and clears his throat, but before he can start, Mrs. Delaney interrupts him.

"Wait!" she says. "Does your a computer have a webcam?"

"Uh, yes, I believe so."

"Two members of our group aren't here," Jess's mother explains. "They're living in England at the moment."

His brow furrows. "Yes, I'm aware of that. I was planning to call them tomorrow."

"My daughter was supposed to videoconference with Emma right about now," she continues. "Perhaps—"

His brow clears as he catches her drift. "Ah! Excellent idea."

I scoot around his desk and set things up, and a minute later Emma appears onscreen. I can tell she's been crying. She looks surprised to see all of us gathered in front of the computer. Mrs. Delaney quickly explains what's happening, and sends her off to get her mother. When the two of them return, Mrs. Bergson's lawyer clears his throat again.

"Everybody here now?" he asks, and we give him a big thumbs-up.

He starts to read:

"*It is a truth universally acknowledged, that an elderly woman in possession of no relatives of her own must be in want of some friends. That was certainly my case a year and a half ago, when Emma invited me to join your book club. What a wonderful chapter in my life it has been! Spending time with all of you was truly one of the most enjoyable things I've ever done.*

Now, I don't want you to be sad, my dears. I've had a full and extraordinary life, doing something I loved every single day. I wish each of you that same gift as you make your own journeys through life. And speaking of gifts, I have a few surprises for you. First, I've set up a fund to help care for Pip until it's decided where his next home will be.'"

"He's safe with us for now," says Jess's mother, and Emma blows her a kiss.

"*I've also set up a fund to keep Chicks with Sticks going for many years to come.'*"

Cassidy looks surprised to hear this.

Heather Vogel Frederick

"'Your idea is such a splendid one, Cassidy, and this is a way of giving it the support it deserves after you have moved on to college, and beyond that to a shining career that I have no doubt will involve a skating rink. It may even involve a coach's whistle, and for that reason I'm leaving you the sterling silver one that my husband, Nils, gave me when I first began to teach. Wear it with pride; you've earned it. Oh, and I've made separate arrangements for my trophies and medals—including my Olympic gold medal—to be permanently displayed at the Concord rink, to inspire young skaters. Perhaps you can have your little chicks look at them now and then, and tell them my story, okay?'"

Tears are trickling down Cassidy's face. "Okay," she whispers.

"'Emma,'" the letter goes on, and onscreen I see Emma lean in closer, not wanting to miss a word, "'I'm leaving you my skates—the ones I wore when I won my Olympic medal. They aren't your size, and they're shabby and worn, but it's my hope that you'll cherish them anyway, and that they'll serve as an inspiration to you to follow your dreams, wherever they take you. And always remember, by the way, that the pen is mightier than the sword!'"

Emma is crying too—we all are, by now—but we have to laugh at this last line.

"'And Gigi, my dear Gigi, what delight your friendship has brought to this late season in my life! I will miss my fellow 'wise old owl,' and I'll miss our little jaunts and our visits over tea. I have been very sad at the thought that Pies & Prejudice is to be no more, and I

have a proposition for you. I'd love it if you would sell my condomin-
ium, and take the proceeds and start a tea shop. Concord needs a good
tea shop, and I think Pies & Prejudice deserves a permanent home.
Perhaps you could serve dim sum on the weekend, who knows?'"

My grandmother perks up at this. She wipes her tears away, and a little of the sparkle comes back into her dark eyes. I can tell that the wheels are already turning. A new project!

"'And finally, I'm leaving a bequest to the Mother-Daughter Book Club itself. I want you to take this money and do something extravagant and fun—once-in-a-lifetime kind of fun. Nothing sensible or dull, and for heaven's sake no plaques or statues of me or anything like that. Go somewhere, do something, and have a wonderful experience, with my blessing. I love each of you dearly and wish you lives as long and happy as my own. Farewell, Eva.'"

The lawyer finishes reading, and sets the letter down on his desk. Now it's his turn to wipe his eyes. "She was one-of-a-kind," he says, shaking his head.

"Absolutely," agrees Mrs. Sloane-Kinkaid.

"She was a treasure, and I know exactly what we should do with her gift," says Mrs. Hawthorne.

We all turn and look at the computer screen.

"What could be more extravagant and fun than a Mother-Daughter Book Club jaunt to Jane Austen country?"

There's a collective gasp as her words sink in, and she smiles at us. "I think you all should come to England!"

Heather Vogel Frederick

Jess

> *"No one who has ever seen you two together,*
> *can doubt his affection."*
> —*Pride and Prejudice*

I knew this day had to come, but it doesn't make it any easier.

My dad reaches across the front seat of the truck and squeezes my shoulder. "You did a fine job with this little fox of yours," he tells me. "I'm proud of you, honey."

A slender red foreleg with black markings pokes through the grate of the pet carrier between us and bats at my denim-covered knee.

"See?" my father adds. "Lydia agrees."

I manage a wobbly smile.

"Are you sure you don't want me to drive?"

I shake my head. I got my permit a few weeks ago, and I need all the practice I can get. Besides, setting Lydia free is something I want to do all by myself, start to finish.

A couple of weeks ago, Mr. Mueller and I took her to see Dr. Gardiner, who gave her a clean bill of health.

"That leg has mended nicely," she says, holding up the X-ray. "She's obviously thriving."

It's true. Lydia is beautiful. It's been nearly two months since that afternoon she was brought into the animal shelter, and she's grown a lot. She's put on weight and her coat is soft and shiny, and her tail has grown bushy and full. I love the white splash on the end of it that looks as if she dipped it in a pot of paint.

After Lydia got her cast off, I helped Mr. Mueller move her outside to a nice big enclosed dog run so she could start getting more exercise. I could tell how much she loved getting rid of the cast and being out in the fresh air again by the way she scampered around in there, as full of energy as my twin brothers.

Then last week we started leaving the dog run open at night. I was really worried the first time, so Mr. Mueller invited me and my dad to stay over. We watched from the window in the kitchen as Lydia stepped out and sniffed the air cautiously, then wandered around the yard checking everything out. She eventually headed for the stone wall at the far edge of their property, and we lost sight of her. She must not have ventured too far, though, because when we went to check the dog run around midnight, she was already back again, curled up fast asleep on her blanket in the little doghouse we put in there for shelter.

Every night after that, she was gone a little longer until finally, two days ago, she didn't show up until after breakfast, and instead of being starving she wasn't much interested in food, which meant she must have either hunted or foraged for herself.

"It's time," Mr. Mueller told me when I rode over that afternoon. "She's ready."

Of course, it's been the plan all along to set Lydia free, but the news struck me like a thunderbolt. Which is why I'm driving down Estabrook Road right now with a lump in my throat the size of a softball.

I originally wanted to set her free in the woods behind Half Moon Farm, so she'd be close by and could maybe stop in for a visit now and then, but my parents said absolutely not, on account of our chickens.

"We have enough predators in these woods already," my mother told me.

Mr. Mueller recommended releasing her in Estabrook Woods. For one thing, it's where she was found, so there's a chance she could be reunited with her parents and littermates. Plus, it's secluded and safe, with over a thousand acres of protected land for her to run around in.

Up ahead, I see the turnoff for the parking area and I slow down, preparing to pull in. I cut the corner a little sharp, though, and the pet carrier goes sliding across the seat toward my father.

"Whoa!" he says, and Lydia gives a worried little yip.

"Sorry, guys." I'm not the world's best driver yet.

My science fair project on Lydia was a huge success. I couldn't bring her to school for it and I didn't want to, anyway—there was no way I was turning her into a circus sideshow—so I borrowed a video camera from the Wongs and made a film about her instead. I showed her getting fed, and curled up asleep, and getting her cast off and running around the stall and then, later, the dog run. I filmed myself putting on the leather gloves and explaining the need for safety when working with wildlife, and why it's important not to try and turn an injured wild creature into a pet. I shared information about all the research I did on red foxes—I know more about them now than I ever expected to—and I interviewed Mr. Mueller, too, and got him to explain the process of getting a rehabilitator's license and tell stories about some of the animals he's rescued. And of course, I included a video tour of all the current guests in his barn.

Helping to rehabilitate Lydia has been the most rewarding thing I've ever done so far in my life. I've enjoyed it more than volunteering at the dog shelter, more than helping on our farm, and more, even, than raising Sundance for 4-H, although that's a close second. While it's not something a person could do for a career, exactly—it's a volunteer job—I could definitely see combining wildlife rehabilitation work with something else someday, and I'm thinking seriously about working toward getting my license. Until then, Mr. Mueller has told me that he'll always be glad to have my help, and that I can consider myself his official apprentice.

I pull into a parking spot and turn the engine off.

"I guess this is it," says my dad.

I don't reply. I can't. I'm afraid the tears might spill over.

Instead, I open the cab door and climb out of the truck. My father does too, then carefully lifts the pet carrier out and sets it on the ground. Lydia starts pacing back and forth, sniffing the air and making excited fox noises.

"Are you sure you can carry this?" my father asks me, and I nod.

"Okay, then." He gives my shoulder another squeeze. "I'll be right here if you need me."

Picking the carrier up by its handle, I head off on the trail into the woods. Mr. Mueller and I decided that it would be best to release Lydia right in the center of the sanctuary, near one of the ponds. I wanted to be sure she was as far away as possible from any of the roads.

People often walk their dogs along the trails, but it's dinnertime and I pass only one jogger. We figured dusk would be the best time of day to release her, since she's nocturnal and that would give her the whole night to explore her new home.

I continue walking for a quarter of an hour or so, the carrier bumping lightly against my leg. Finally, rounding a curve by a large boulder, I see the clearing that I'm looking for. It's a pretty spot, and Emma and I ride our bikes out here sometimes in the summer and bring a picnic lunch. When I reach it, I set the carrier on the ground. I know I should put my leather gloves on—Lydia has nipped me twice, accidentally, in her eagerness to get to the food I was offering her, making me glad I was wearing them—but since this is the last time I'll ever get to touch her, for once I break the rules and leave them in my pocket.

I open the mesh door and she trots out, all her senses on full alert. She circles the clearing, panting, then comes back and stands beside me, pressing herself against my leg. She stands motionless for a minute, only her long nose and ears twitching.

I squat down beside her and run my hands over her soft fur, then scratch her behind her ears. She looks up at me and gives me a little fox grin, just the way our dogs Sugar and Spice do, then takes a few steps forward. She pauses, looking back over her shoulder.

"That's right, girl," I tell her softly. "You can do it."

And she bounds off into the woods, a streak of pure joy.

"Good-bye, Lydia," I whisper.

I'm still missing her a week later when we get on the plane to England.

After we met with Mrs. Bergson's lawyer, Mrs. Wong and Mrs. Hawthorne took charge of planning our trip. At first we weren't sure Mrs. Chadwick would want to go with us—my mother says her nose is still out of joint over Hepzibah Plunkett and *Spring Reckoning*—but I guess the prospect of visiting the gardening capital of the world was too hard to resist.

"When she heard the roses would be in full bloom, she caved," Becca told us.

The money Mrs. Bergson left us was enough to cover plane tickets and hotel rooms and all that stuff not only for our book club, but for our families, too, if they wanted to come. Mr. Wong and Mr. Chadwick couldn't, because of work, and my dad stayed behind too.

"Somebody's got to keep an eye on the farm," he told my mother and me. "Besides, you'll want to visit tea shops and gardens and all that girl stuff. The twins have their Cub Scout camping trip coming up, and I know they don't want to miss that, so I'm perfectly content to stay

Heather Vogel Frederick

home with them. We'll eat lots of he-man food and watch inappropriate movies, right, boys?"

"Right!" my brothers shouted in agreement. They loved the idea of being he-men, and ran around flexing their skinny little arms for days.

Gigi's coming, of course, and so is Cassidy's stepfather. Mrs. Sloane-Kinkaid said she needed him to help watch Chloe, who is walking on her own now and into everything. The other person who's coming is Stewart Chadwick, which I think is a good sign. He says Darcy needs reinforcements, but I'm hoping it's because he wants to see Emma.

The flight is long and boring. We leave shortly after dinnertime, but I'm too excited to sleep, mostly because I can't wait to see Darcy. My mother and I have seats together by a window, and while she puts on one of those eye mask things and dozes off, I watch a movie and then reread the last few chapters of *Pride and Prejudice*, hoping that maybe some of Elizabeth Bennet's magic dust will rub off on me.

It's nearly midnight Boston-time when we land in London, but over here the sky is streaked with pink clouds and it's tomorrow already. I'm still not tired, though. I can hardly stand still as we wait to collect our bags, and I'm on pins and needles as we inch our way through the line at customs. I keep craning my neck and trying to see over the heads of the people in front of us to the waiting area beyond. Finally, we get our passports stamped—I had to get my own passport for the trip, which is pretty cool—and head through the big double doors.

I spot Emma right away. She and her mom are holding up a huge sign that says WELCOME MOTHER-DAUGHTER BOOK CLUB! Emma is bouncing up and down with excitement, but there's no sign of Darcy.

"He's at a football game," Emma whispers in my ear as she gives me a hug. "I mean soccer—they call it football over here. He said to say hi."

She and Stewart greet each other awkwardly, shaking hands.

"I wish someone would give your brother a kick in the pants," mutters Megan to Becca, watching them.

Outside in the parking lot, Mr. Hawthorne is standing proudly in front of a small bus. A very fancy bus.

"It's called a luxury mini-coach," he informs us. "Mrs. Bergson said extravagant, and we're taking her at her word."

We climb aboard, cramming our luggage into the overhead bins and what Mr. Hawthorne calls the "boot" way at the back. There are pairs of leather seats on either side of the aisle, so Emma and I sit together. Megan and Becca are across from us, and Cassidy and Stewart plop down behind us and start jabbering away about hockey.

There's a lot of traffic leaving London, and it's weird to be driving on the left, but Mr. Hawthorne doesn't seem bothered by it at all. I guess he's used to it by now.

Emma and I can hardly stop talking. We have so much to tell each other! I tell her all about letting Lydia go, and how hard it was, and I show her the picture that I keep in my wallet of me feeding the little fox. She tells me about how she's been working really hard on something to submit to her school's literary magazine, and about a trip she took with her friend Lucy's family to Lucy's grandparents' farm in Yorkshire.

Heather Vogel Frederick

"They have this amazing border collie named Mitzi—you would have loved her, Jess. She's incredibly smart. All they have to do is say, 'Fetch the cows in, Mitzi!' and she's off like a shot. She runs all the way out to these fields way at the far end of their property and rounds up the cows by herself, then brings them back to the barn."

"Cool."

Emma glances across the aisle at Megan and Becca and lowers her voice. "So tell me about Alcott High's spring formal," she says. "Cassidy says that Becca went with Zach Norton?"

I nod. "Yeah. He asked her that week you were home in Concord on spring break."

We're quiet for a moment. Emma had a crush on Zach all the way from kindergarten through seventh grade, when she got to be friends with Stewart. I wonder whether she's feeling any twinges now.

But apparently not. "I'm really glad for Becca," she says, then gives me a mischievous smile. "I guess it's her turn for Zach attacks." That's what Emma used to call it when she got all fluttery over him. She wrote a poem about it once, and Becca found it and read it out loud to Zach and completely humiliated her.

I smile back. "Yup."

"So what did Megan do? Since Simon didn't ask her to the dance, I mean."

"She thought about going stag, but I guess in the end she stayed home."

"Did Simon go?"

I shake my head. "He stayed home too."

"Maybe that's a good sign," says Emma. "I mean, if he really didn't like Megan, wouldn't he have asked somebody else?"

I lift a shoulder. "Maybe. I don't know. I'm not an expert at this stuff."

"Me neither."

Cassidy's head pops over the back of our seat. "What are you two whispering about up here?" I glance back and see that Stewart has conked out. His head is resting against the mini-coach's window, and he's snoring softly.

"Nothing much," Emma tells her. "Spring formal. Did you go?"

"Do hockey players wear tutus? Of course I didn't go."

"But you were asked," I prompt her.

She reddens, and Emma lets out a quiet squeal. "You *were*? Who?"

"Tristan Berkeley," Cassidy admits reluctantly, and Emma squeals again. Stewart's head jerks forward and he makes this weird snuffling sound, then relaxes back into sleep.

"So why didn't you go with him?" Emma whispers.

Cassidy shrugs. "He's been a little nicer to me and everything since Mrs. Bergson died, but I still think dances are stupid." Her face is bright red by now.

"Cassidy! You should have gone."

"And have people think I like him? You sound like my mother."

"Okay, okay. Never mind." Emma changes the subject. "How was California?" Cassidy flew out to visit her sister at college a few weekends ago, right after hockey season finished.

Heather Vogel Frederick

Cassidy brightens. "Awesome!"

"Did you go to any classes?" I ask her.

"Right, like I take a couple days off school so I can fly across the country and go to *more* school. Duh."

"I was just asking," I reply, stung. "You were at UCLA, after all."

Cassidy grins. "I was in L.A.—forget the U.C. part. Actually, I thought the dorm was pretty cool, and so is the campus. But we went all over the place. We borrowed Courtney's roommate's car and drove to Hollywood—"

"Did you see the sign on the hill?" Emma asks eagerly.

"Of course. And we went to Grauman's Chinese Theater and saw all the stars' handprints and footprints in the sidewalk, and afterward we drove down to the Santa Monica pier and rode the Ferris wheel, and then on down the coast to Laguna Beach, where we used to live." A wistful tone creeps into Cassidy's voice. "I hardly recognized our old house," she continues. "The new owners painted it blue."

"Did you go surfing?" I ask.

"Yup. It was fantastic. And we went to Crystal Cove, this great beach our dad used to take us to, and had shakes at the Shake Shack, and on the way back to UCLA we took the little ferry over to Balboa Island and got frozen bananas at Dad's."

Emma and I have no idea what she's talking about, but it's obvious she had a great time so we smile and nod anyway. The three of us continue talking for a while, and then at some point I must have fallen asleep because I'm surprised to find myself jolted awake when the mini-coach pulls up to a stop in front of our hotel.

"Here we are, ladies and gents!" Mr. Hawthorne announces into the microphone. He's speaking in a fake English accent, which I bet we'll be hearing a lot of over the next week. I can tell he's having fun already. "Your hotel was once a private residence," he goes on to explain.

"Dude, you'd have to be way rich to live in a house like this," says Cassidy, staring out the window.

"Believe me, this is nothing," says Mr. Hawthorne. "Wait until you see some of the 'private residences' we're going to visit this week."

We pile out of the mini-coach and stand in the driveway, stretching. Our hotel is an enormous brick house perched on a hill in the outskirts of Bath. There are gardens and terraces everywhere, and a long, sweeping hillside at the back that leads down to a river.

"That's the Kennet and Avon Canal," says Emma. "The one I told you I walked along everyday to school, remember? Our village is about ten minutes upstream."

"I picked this place for you because the owners love books," says Mrs. Hawthorne, who's as excited about everything as Emma and her father are. "You'll see what I mean in a minute."

Inside, there's an entry hall with black and white tiles on the floor. Mr. Hawthorne checks us in, and we're each handed a room key. Stewart is staying by himself in the Charles Dickens room, and Cassidy's mom and stepfather and Chloe are in William Wordsworth. Cassidy and Becca and Megan and me are all in the Percy Shelley suite, next door to my mother, who's staying in the Jane Austen room.

Heather Vogel Frederick

"I made sure your mom got the best one," Emma whispers to me. "It has a view of the gardens and the canal, and there are two beds, so maybe one night you can stay with her."

Mrs. Chadwick will be down the hall from us in the Charlotte Bronte room, and Mrs. Wong and Gigi are beside her in a suite named after George Eliot.

"That was actually the pen name of a writer by the name of Mary Anne Evans," Mrs. Hawthorne tells us, as we grab our suitcases and start up the sweeping staircase.

"Why would a girl change her name to George?" asks Cassidy. "Sheesh."

"She wanted to be taken seriously as a writer, and it was difficult for women back then," Mrs. Hawthorne replies. "Remember how Jane Austen had to publish her novels anonymously?"

There are oohs and aahs as we all open the doors to our rooms. Each one is unique, with different color schemes and high ceilings and windows that stretch all the way to the floor. There are plump, comfortable armchairs and pretty lamps and beds with lots of pillows piled on them.

"Wow!" exclaims Becca as Cassidy unlocks our door. "It looks like Snow White and the Seven Dwarves live here."

She's right. Our suite has four beds lined up in a row, and each one has a canopy of drapes over it. My mother pops her head in and smiles when she sees the delighted looks on our faces.

"Pretty great, huh? Have fun, girls!" And she disappears again.

Mrs. Hawthorne tells us to unpack and take showers and naps if we want, and that Mr. Hawthorne will be back to get us in a few hours. "We don't have anything planned for today but getting you rested up and settled in. I thought we'd tour our village and hang out at Ivy Cottage this afternoon, then go out to dinner. There's a charming old pub by the canal."

Becca flops backward onto the bed she's claimed by the window. She nearly disappears into its fluffy comforter. She sighs happily. "Heaven," she says. "Pure heaven."

Megan heads for the shower, reappearing a second later with the hotel's fancy toiletries. "Look at the label!" she says, holding up a tiny bottle of shampoo. "Gigi's gonna be thrilled."

"Tea, anyone?" says Emma, plugging in the electric kettle that's sitting on one of the dressing tables. There's a stack of teacups and saucers beside it, along with a plate of homemade cookies, and she gets busy preparing a snack for us.

"I can't believe we're really here!" I say, hugging my knees to my chest. "We're in England, you guys!"

"Yeah, it's cool, but I need a nap," says Cassidy. She glares at Emma and me. "Somebody kept me awake on the ride over here, yakking." She lies down on her stomach on her bed and pulls the pillow over her head.

Emma and I look at each other and start to laugh. Cassidy is always crabby when she's tired.

Becca and Megan decide they want to nap too, but since I got some

Heather Vogel Frederick

sleep in the car I'm not tired. After our tea and cookies, Emma and I decide to walk over to Ivy Cottage. She leads me through the hotel's back door to a wide stone terrace, then through the formal gardens to a narrow track down the hillside. Crossing through a sheep meadow— complete with real sheep—we end up on a gravel path that runs along the length of the canal.

It feels really good to stretch my legs after sitting on the plane and in the bus for so many hours. I jog around and swing my arms in big circles, breathing in the fresh air.

"Oh, great," says Emma, spotting a distant figure on the path ahead.

"What?"

She sighs. "Rupert Loomis."

"Good afternoon, ladies," he says as he reaches us.

"Hi, Rupert," Emma replies, without enthusiasm. "This is my friend Jessica Delaney."

He extends a large, sweaty hand, and I shake it, sizing him up. Rupert isn't as tall as Stewart or Darcy, but he's gangly, which makes him look taller. He's very pale, like someone who spends most of his time indoors, and he has a shock of limp dark hair that hangs over his forehead. He keeps brushing it away with annoyed flicks of his hand.

"Very pleased to make your acquaintance," he says in perfect Austen-speak. Rupert's eyes are a pale, watery blue, and over them, like a parabola, arches a dark unibrow. Emma wasn't exaggerating about his ears, either—they're huge.

So are his feet, which scuff at the gravel as he stands there awkwardly.

"So," says Emma finally. "Are you heading into town?"

"My great-aunt thought that some exercise would be beneficial," he explains, sounding so much like a character out of a book that I have to press my lips together to keep from giggling.

"Mr. Collins lives!" I whisper to Emma as he walks away.

"Didn't I tell you?" she whispers back.

We continue on, looking at each of the canal boats and wondering what it must be like to live on the river, and in another ten minutes or so we reach Emma's village.

"This place is like something out of a movie," I say, spotting the row of tidy cottages that line the narrow main street.

"I know! Isn't it amazing? I can't wait until Mrs. Chadwick sees the gardens. She's going to go bonkers."

I shoot her a questioning look, and Emma laughs. "That means nuts," she explains.

We stop in front of the prettiest house of all. The front garden is framed by a waist-high hedge, and there's a small sign that says IVY COTTAGE attached to the gate.

"This is us," says Emma, unlatching it.

I drift in behind her, wondering if I'm in a dream. "I can't believe you actually live here."

"Tell me about it. I've been pinching myself all year."

"Hi, girls!" Mrs. Hawthorne calls, spotting us through the kitchen

Heather Vogel Frederick

window. "I thought you might be coming back with Emma, Jess. I picked up some orange squash on the way home."

Puzzled as to why she's telling us this—does she think we're hungry? And if so, why would we want to eat butternut squash this time of year?—I follow Emma into the kitchen. The mystery is solved when she pulls a liter-size bottle of soda out of the fridge.

"Behold! Orange squash," she says.

I shake my head. "Football means soccer, squash is soda, bonkers is nuts—I'm going to need an interpreter or something."

"Nah," she replies. "You'll pick up the lingo quickly." She pours us both a glass and crosses the kitchen. "Hey, do you want to meet Toby?"

"Of course."

The Berkeleys' parrot rocks back and forth on his perch, hopping from one foot to another in excited anticipation as Emma opens a bag of bird treats.

"Who's a good bird?" she asks him.

"TOBY!" he squawks.

"That's right," she replies, and hands him a treat through the bars of his cage. With a pang, I wonder what Lydia is doing right now.

Mrs. Hawthorne checks her watch. "I'm going to take a quick nap myself," she tells us. "Darcy should be home soon, and after he cleans up from soccer I'll send your father back to the hotel to round up everyone else."

"Okay, Mom," Emma replies. She waits until her mother leaves the room, then grins mischievously at me. "Want to see something funny?"

"Sure."

She pulls open a lower drawer of the big cupboard where the dishes are displayed and riffles through the phone books and loose papers stacked inside, then plucks out a photograph from the very bottom of the pile. It's a professional shot of someone posing in a sequined ice skating outfit—Annabelle Fairfax.

"Watch this," says Emma. She holds the picture up in front of Toby's cage.

"STINKERBELLE!" the parrot shrieks.

I stand there in shocked silence, then collapse against the table behind me, howling with laughter. "I can't believe you taught him to say that!"

"I figure it will give Tristan and Simon something to talk about next time Annabelle comes over."

Still laughing, we sit down at the table to drink our soda, and a couple of minutes later Toby makes us jump when out of the blue he shrieks, "GO RED SOX!"

Darcy Hawthorne walks into the kitchen.

My heart stops.

His legs are covered in mud, his face is streaked with sweat, and his curly brown hair is matted down against his head. He looks amazing.

"Jess!" he cries, spotting me, and my heart starts again, racing this time because he sounds genuinely thrilled to see me.

Heather Vogel Frederick

"Hey, Darcy," I reply shyly.

"I'd give you a hug but I smell terrible," he says cheerfully.

I wouldn't mind, I want to tell him, but of course I don't.

"It's so great that you're here!" he continues. "How was your flight?"

"Fine."

"Emma's really been looking forward to your visit," he says.

How about you? I want to ask him, but of course I don't say that, either. "Me too," I reply instead.

"Mom says to hurry up and take a shower," Emma tells him, holding her nose. "Dad's going to drive over and pick everybody up and we're going to go to dinner in a little while."

"Okay. Good to see you, Jess," he says, and he tugs on my braid as he passes the table.

I smile a little wistfully. I was probably imagining that he was thrilled to see me. I need to stop getting my hopes up, stop dreaming of something that's never going to happen. Darcy Hawthorne still just thinks of me as his little sister's best friend.

A while later, Mr. Hawthorne brings the rest of the book club over, and we spend a fun couple of hours checking out Ivy Cottage and exploring the village. Emma's right, Mrs. Chadwick does go bonkers when she sees all the gardens, and embarrasses Becca by making her pose for a picture in front of every single one of them. We get to meet Lucy Woodhouse really briefly—she's just as cute and nice as Emma said she was—and then afterward, we walk to the George Inn for dinner, heading back down the canal path the way Emma and I came this afternoon. I notice Stewart is still keeping his distance. He's walking ahead of us with Darcy and Mr. Hawthorne and Mr. Kinkaid.

"Where's Rupert Loomis when you need him?" I ask Emma. "There's no way Stewart can stay mad at you after he meets him."

"I sure hope not," she replies glumly.

My mother comes over and links her arm through mine. Her eyes are sparkling, and she looks relaxed and happy. She works really hard on our farm, and doesn't get to take vacations very often. Especially ones that involve nice hotel rooms instead of tents filled with Cub Scouts.

"Having fun, sweetheart?"

I nod enthusiastically.

"This is amazing, isn't it? I feel like I'm on the set of a Jane Austen movie."

"I know just what you mean, Shannon," Mrs. Wong chimes in. "I expect to see Elizabeth and Darcy come walking around the corner any minute."

How about Jess and Darcy? I think to myself. I'd settle for that.

The sun is low in the sky now, and its slanting rays light up the green meadows and give the stone houses we pass a warm golden glow. Mrs. Hawthorne explains that they're made of a special honey-colored limestone that's found only in this part of England.

"Wait until we take you into Bath tomorrow," she adds. "The whole city is made of the same stone, and it's absolutely stunning."

The George Inn is right on the canal, a low building with half a

Heather Vogel Frederick

dozen chimneys sticking out the roof. It's half-buried in ivy, and looks like something from *The Hobbit*.

"It's been around since the twelfth century," Mr. Hawthorne tells us, holding open the door. "It was originally a monastery."

Inside, there are bunch of connected rooms, with whitewashed walls and dark exposed beams across the low ceilings just like at Ivy Cottage. Stewart and Darcy and Cassidy and her mother all have to duck their heads in some spots. We pass fireplaces and tables tucked into the building's nooks and crannies as our waiter leads us to the private room that Mrs. Hawthorne has reserved for us. We place our order, and Emma and I both get fish and chips. So does Darcy.

"Careful, they're addictive," he says, smiling at me.

For once, Becca is stuck down at the other end of the table, next to Mr. Kinkaid. Even though she's technically interested in Zach Norton these days, with Becca, you never know. And with Zach of sight, he might be out of mind, too.

Emma and her brother and I talk and laugh all through dinner. Darcy is really interested to hear about Lydia, and he agrees with Emma that I should definitely work toward getting my wildlife rehabilitator's license.

"Eighteen seems like a long time from now," I tell them.

"It's going to fly by, you watch," Darcy replies. "I can't believe I'm going to be a senior next year. I'm going to have to start thinking about college." He throws a French fry—excuse me, a "chip"—at Cassidy, who catches it neatly. "Hey, Sloane, heard anything from your sister lately? How's she liking UCLA?"

I stare down at my dinner. Cassidy's sister Courtney is really, really pretty. I mean model pretty. She looks just like Mrs. Sloane-Kinkaid. A person could hardly blame Darcy for liking her.

"I went out to visit her a couple of weeks ago," Cassidy tells him. "We had a blast. UCLA is huge, but it's pretty cool. I got to meet her boyfriend, too."

I perk up at this: I didn't know Courtney had a boyfriend.

Darcy turns back to Emma and me. "I think I probably want to go someplace a little closer to home," he tells us. "Dartmouth, maybe, if my grades are good enough."

I smile. My aunt and uncle live near there, in New Hampshire. And Darcy's grades are definitely good enough from what Emma tells me. Plus, he's a star athlete. He'll probably get all sorts of scholarships.

Dessert arrives—a large cake with "Welcome, Mother-Daughter Book Club!" written on it in wobbly script. I guess they're not much into cake decorating at the George. As the waiter slices it for us, Mrs. Hawthorne taps her knife against her glass.

"I'd like to propose a toast," she announces. "To Eva Bergson!"

"Hear, hear!" replies my mother, lifting her glass. We all lift ours, too.

"To a wonderful friend and fairy godmother—many thanks for bringing us all together here for what I know will be a magical week in England!" says Mrs. Hawthorne.

"To Eva!" says Gigi, and we all echo her words.

Later, outside the pub, Mrs. Hawthorne roots around in her purse. "It stays light late over here in the summer," she says, "but the canal path is a bit uneven so I brought torches."

I watch her, curious to see if flames suddenly shoot out of her purse. But it turns out that torches are just what they call flashlights in England. Great. Another vocabulary word to add to the list.

"I don't have enough for everyone," she adds, passing them out. "You'll have to share."

We split up into groups of twos and threes. Emma winks at me and drifts over to where Cassidy and Megan are standing. Mrs. Chadwick, who is complaining loudly about how tired her feet are, and how she's not sure she can make it back to the mini-coach, has Stewart firmly by one arm and Becca by the other. The rest of our parents and Gigi are happily chatting together.

Darcy materializes, holding up a flashlight. "Want to walk with me?"

I nod, smiling.

"It's pretty amazing here, isn't it?" he says as we walk along.

I nod again. "It's like time stood still or something."

"I know. There are places at home in Concord that feel that way to me—the Old North Bridge sometimes, and Kyle Anderson's house, with that bullet hole from the Revolutionary War—but here it's just about everywhere. You don't even have to half-close your eyes to imagine the past."

"You do that too?" I ask, surprised. I thought I was the only one who used that trick.

"Sure. I love history. I'm thinking I might major in it at college."

We talk for a while about what we might want to be when we grow up. I always figured Darcy would want to do something with sports, since he's such a jock, but he tells me he thinks he'd like to be a professor.

"I was talking to Tristan and Simon's father over spring break, and he's a really cool guy. He loves his job and says I should think seriously about a career in academics." He kicks a stone into the canal, and it lands with a plunk. "How about you, Jess? What do you want to be?"

"I don't know," I reply honestly. As I think it over, I realize that ever since taking care of Lydia, though, I've stopped worrying about it.

We walk along in silence for a while. A few faint pinpricks of light twinkle against the inky blue darkness of the sky, reflecting in the calm water of the canal. Darcy starts whistling. I recognize the tune right away. It's the same one my mother and I sang in our back pasture that night last fall, during the Leonid meteor shower: "When You Wish Upon a Star." I hum along under my breath, looking up at the sky. *When you wish upon a star, makes no difference who you are . . .*

I haven't felt this happy in a long, long time.

"I'm really glad you came," says Darcy suddenly.

"Me too," I tell him.

And as we round the bend toward Ivy Cottage, he tugs my braid just the way he always has ever since I was six, and then he reaches down and takes my hand.

Maybe sometimes dreams really do come true.

Heather Vogel Frederick

*"To be fond of dancing was a certain
step toward falling in love."*
—Pride and Prejudice

The sun wakes me up.

I glance over at the trio of beds lined up beside me. Megan and
Becca and Jess are still asleep. I yawn and glance at my watch, then at
the alarm clock on the bedside table. It's the middle of the night back
in Concord, but it's nearly seven over here.

I decide I might as well get up and go for a run. Mom told me that
back when she was working as a model and flying all over the world
for photo shoots, the way she used to handle jet lag was just to force
herself onto the same schedule as whatever country she was in.

So since the sun says it's morning out, it's morning out.

I change into shorts and a T-shirt and tiptoe out of the room, carrying my running shoes. Heading downstairs, I hear the clink of dishes
and silverware in the hotel kitchen. Something smells good. I'll definitely be hungry for breakfast by the time I get back.

I stretch a little on the terrace, then make my way down the hillside through the wet grass to the canal path, where I start jogging in the direction of Ivy Cottage. It's nice out, with mist rising off the water and birds chirping in the trees and hedges that line the gravel path. There are only a few people out and about—I see one other jogger and a couple having coffee on the deck of one of the canal boats. They wave to me, and I wave back. Emma says that people live on the boats year-round, and that some of them are for rent, too, for visitors who want to explore the canals on vacation. Sounds like fun to me.

As I get closer to Emma's village, I spot another jogger heading toward me. It's Darcy Hawthorne.

"Hey!" he says, doing a U-turn so he can run beside me.

"Hey, yourself!"

"Where are you headed?"

I shrug. "Wherever. I just needed a stretch. We're supposed to meet for breakfast soon."

He laughs. "Wait until you see what my mother has planned."

Mrs. Hawthorne and Mrs. Wong have been really mysterious about what we're going to be doing for the next week. I guess they want to surprise us.

We run along side by side until we reach the village, then double back along the canal.

I slant a glance at Darcy. I don't think anybody else noticed, but I saw him holding hands with Jess last night when we walked back to

Heather Vogel Frederick

the hotel after dinner. I'm glad for Jess, but this whole boy/girl thing is still kind of a mystery to me. When I'm hanging out with my friends somewhere and they start drooling over a guy, I look at him and think one thing: *I bet I could beat you at hockey.*

What was Zach Norton thinking when he kissed me out of the blue a year ago? Why me? We managed to get it all straightened out eventually, and we're good friends again, but still. And Tristan Berkeley inviting me to Spring Formal—what was that all about? I thought he hated me. Honestly, I just don't get it.

I've gotten a few letters from my pen pal Winky Parker's brother Sam this year too. He's hilarious, and I had a lot of fun hanging out with him at his family's ranch in Wyoming last summer. And maybe I liked him a little, too. Maybe I still like him. It's confusing. Can you like only one person at a time? Do I even want to like anybody? If I think about it all too much, it makes me mad. I don't want to things to change, including me.

"I got an e-mail from Tristan this morning," Darcy says, jolting me out of my daydream. Or maybe further into it. My mixed-up feelings toward Tristan Berkeley are another whole subject.

"He and his family are flying to London tomorrow."

Tristan and Annabelle's ice dancing competition is later this week. It kind of slipped off my radar screen in all the excitement of getting ready for the trip. We're supposed to go London to watch them, which is just about the last thing I want to do. If I never see Annabelle Fairfax again it will be too soon.

I say good-bye to Darcy at the turnoff, then scramble up the steep hillside path to the hotel. Back in our room, I find Becca and Megan and Jess up and showered and getting dressed.

"Where were you?" asks Megan.

"Out for a run."

"Everybody else is at breakfast already," Jess tells me. "We'll see you there, okay?"

I shower quickly and get dressed, then go downstairs to join them. They're sitting in a room off the dining area that the waitress tells me is called the conservatory. It looks sort of like a greenhouse. A very fancy greenhouse made of glass panels and white wrought iron.

"Homemade croissants," my mother says, waving one in front of my nose as I take a seat.

"I thought croissants were French," I reply. "We're in England."

"The cook is from Paris," she says, licking her fingers. "Lucky us."

"Darcy and Nick will be bringing the bus around in half an hour or so," says Mrs. Hawthorne. "Please eat up. Meanwhile, Lily and I have a little something for each of you."

Mrs. Wong goes to stand next to her. "Ladies and gentlemen, presenting the one and only, first-time-ever, not-to-be-missed, Jane Austen Commemorative—"

"Tour Packet!" Mrs. Hawthorne finishes with a flourish, holding up a pink folder. On the front is a large sticker with a silhouette of Jane Austen on it, and a name written in calligraphy. "This one is for you, Gigi," she says, handing it over. "There's one for each of you."

Heather Vogel Frederick

As Mrs. Wong starts passing them out, Emma groans. "Mo-om! Can't we ever do anything without handouts?"

"Handouts?" cries her mother, pretending to be offended. "These are not mere handouts! We're talking an informational extravaganza here, complete with postcards, historical and biographical sketches, background reading material—"

"Don't forget maps," adds Mrs. Wong, who has a thing about maps.

"Maps, too. In short, everything a budding Janeite could possibly want to understand a bit about what she's going to be seeing and doing over the next week."

"Um," says Stewart Chadwick. "I'm not so sure I want to be a budding Janeite."

"Me neither," agrees my stepfather. "I carry around enough pink stuff as it is. Right, Chloe?"

My little sister gives him a jam-covered grin.

"You said it, monkey face," I grumble, and my mother shoots me a look.

"Fear not," says Mrs. Hawthorne, riffling through the stack and pulling out two blue folders. "Behold the Commemorative Tour Packet's Manly Edition." She hands them over, then asks us all to take a look at our itinerary.

"Our schedule," she adds, seeing the puzzled look on my face. "We're going to be taking a chronological tour of Jane's life this week."

I scan the page. Today and tomorrow—museums, tea shops, historic houses, gardens, walking tours. It's not that I'm not interested, because actually I think Jane Austen is pretty cool, especially the way she wrote books back when most women didn't do that sort of thing. It's kind of like me playing hockey on the middle school boys' team. In fact, I'll bet Jane Austen would have made a great hockey player.

I look back at the schedule, wishing that they'd planned some other stuff too. Stuff that really interests me. Like maybe watch a cricket match or something.

My mother sees me frowning. She taps her finger on the word "Stonehenge," listed as a side trip for this afternoon. "You'll love it, I promise," she whispers. "And check out page two."

I do, and am relieved to see that things get better. Wednesday: *Sea-bathing at Lyme Regis.* Cool, we're going swimming in the ocean. And then we're heading to London that night to go hear—

"*Led Zeppelin?*" squeals Jess. "You got us tickets to hear them?"

I'm not a huge music freak, but even I've heard of them. Mostly because of the Delaneys' horses, Led and Zep. Mr. Delaney is a huge fan.

"Yes!" crows Darcy, and he and Stewart slap each other a high five.

"It's a one-night only reunion concert," Mrs. Hawthorne says. "You can thank your father for this, Jess. He said our itinerary needed more than just petticoats and bonnets."

"Hear, hear!" says Mr. Hawthorne, and my stepfather nods enthusiastically.

"Hyde Park is very historic, right?" asks Mrs. Chadwick, frowning at her itinerary. She always likes to make sure we're getting educated, even if it's at an outdoor rock concert. I notice Becca

Heather Vogel Frederick

rolling her eyes at her brother, who suppresses a grin.

"Really historic, Mom," he replies. "Almost as historic as this band performing together again."

After the excitement dies down, I look over the rest of the schedule. Thursday looks good—we're going to the Tower of London, for one thing, and Emma says they have lots of cool suits of armor and dungeons and stuff—but Friday squats on the page like a toad. We're meeting the Berkeleys for lunch, then spending the rest of the day with them at the Junior Ice Dancing Championship.

I am so not looking forward to that.

"What's this?" asks Emma, pointing to the words "Chawton Surprise" on Saturday's schedule.

"We-ell," says her mother. "Do you think we should tell them, Lily?"

"I suppose we have no choice." Mrs. Wong sighs.

They're both grinning their heads off, so I figure it's gotta be something amazing. Like maybe they've signed us up for private polo lessons. Or at the very least, we're going to Buckingham Palace to meet the queen.

"That, my dear daughter, is the best part of the whole week," says Mrs. Hawthorne. "As Mrs. Bergson's parting gift to us, we are all going to attend the Regency Ball at Chawton House!"

Everybody seems to think this is great except me. And my stepfather. While they're all applauding and cheering, Stanley leans over and whispers in my ear, "Too bad they didn't have Regency BASEball back in Jane Austen's day."

"No kidding," I whisper back.

It turns out we're expected to show up for this thing dressed the way they used to dress in Jane Austen's day, so tomorrow afternoon we're going to be fitted for costumes at some rental place.

"Me too?" asks Stewart, looking nervous.

"Yes, and Darcy, and Nicholas, and you too, Stanley," Mrs. Hawthorne replies. "Our dance partners need to be as stylish as we are, right, ladies?"

I notice that Stewart Chadwick is carefully avoiding looking at Emma, whose face is a deep shade of pink. So is Jess's, but for a completely different reason. It's that stupid boy/girl stuff again. It just messes everything up! Life would be so much easier without it.

We get lost a few times on the way to Steventon, which is even tinier than Gopher Hole, Wyoming, where our pen pals all live. Our mini-coach barely fits on the narrow country roads, and I notice that all the moms close their eyes and grab the back of the seat ahead of them whenever a car approaches and Mr. Hawthorne squeezes over to let it pass.

The house where Jane Austen grew up doesn't exist anymore, but the church where her father preached is still there, so that's where we're headed. When we finally find it—a small stone building stuck out in the middle of nowhere surrounded by fields of sheep—we pile out of the bus and crowd around Mrs. Hawthorne. Since she's the Jane Austen expert, she's our official tour guide.

"All right, gang, listen up," she says. "This church is almost eight hundred years old."

"Even older than me," says Gigi, which gets a laugh.

"It was built at the beginning of the thirteenth century. The steeple was added later, during the Victorian era—"

"Same time period as our house," my mother murmurs to me.

"—and I'd like you all to notice the weather vane."

We crane our necks. "Cool!" I say, spotting it. The Delaneys have one shaped like a rooster on top of their barn, but I've never seen one that looks like a quill pen before.

"There are more tributes to Jane inside," Mrs. Hawthorne continues. "See if you can spot them."

We do. There are silhouettes of Jane on the needlework kneelers in the pews, and a plaque on the wall about her too. And by the guest book there are Jane Austen bookmarks and stationery for sale.

Emma rubs her arms and shivers. "It's cold in here."

"Let's go back outside," I suggest.

We wander around to the graveyard behind the church and find some Austen tombstones.

"Is Jane buried here?" I ask, figuring Emma will know.

She does, of course. "Nope. These are other relatives. She's buried at Winchester Cathedral."

Emma and I take pictures of each other with the church in the background, then get back on the bus to wait for our friends.

Stonehenge is on the way back to Bath, and my mother was right, it's awesome—probably about the coolest thing I've ever seen before in my life. I brought my good camera, the one my father gave me a long time ago, and I take a ton of pictures so I can show Courtney. She really wanted to come with us on this trip, but she's working as a camp counselor this summer up in Maine to help earn money for college, so she couldn't.

Stonehenge is a big circle of gigantic standing stones stuck out in the middle of an empty plain. It has nothing to do with Jane Austen, but Mrs. Hawthorne said it's one of the most famous landmarks in the world, and no way were we going to skip seeing it since it was so close by. No one really knows who built it or how or why, exactly, but it's been around since, like, 3000 B.C. It's like visiting the pyramids or something.

I see Darcy and Jess wandering around the path that circles it together. They're not holding hands or anything—I guess they don't want everybody to know about them yet—but they're both sort of squinting at the stones, with their eyes half shut. Weird.

When we get back to the city, we go to this place called the Pump Room for tea. Bath is almost as amazing as Stonehenge, but in a different way. I don't know a thing about architecture, and never thought it would interest me, but even I can tell that it's pretty spectacular. There's this cool bridge over the river with shops built right into it, and cobblestone streets everywhere, and Mrs. Hawthorne reminds us that all the buildings are made of that special kind of golden limestone that's only found in this part of England. They were all built in the same style around the same time period too.

"Georgian," says Darcy. "That's George the first, second, third, and fourth," he rattles off, then grins. "I took English history this year at Knightley-Martin."

"And who was on the throne in England when the Revolutionary War broke out back in Concord?" says his mom.

Emma starts to wave her hand, then pulls it down and mimes zipping her lip.

"I actually know the answer to that question," says Becca, sounding shocked. "George the Third."

"Good girl," says Mrs. Hawthorne. "So while our own hometown was fighting the British, they were building this amazing city. Which, by the way, was a Roman resort thousands of years before that."

The Pump Room is built over some ancient Roman ruins where a hot spring bubbles up. I guess people have been coming here forever to sit in the water, thinking it would cure them of all sorts of illnesses. It's kind of like a hot tub. They drink the water too—well, not while they're sitting in it. It's pumped up here to the Pump Room, to an old stone fountain that's been around since Jane Austen's day.

"Just think—she drank this very water," says Mrs. Hawthorne, passing us each a glass.

I take a sniff. "Nasty," I say, passing it right back to her. No way am I drinking that.

Fortunately, tea is pretty great—those triple-tiered trays that my mother and Courtney go gaga for, piled with sandwiches and scones and cookies and cakes. And endless pots of tea, of course. We finally get to try clotted cream, too, which really is delicious, just as Emma said.

"This was where everyone came to see and be seen," says Mrs. Hawthorne. "They'd promenade around the room—they called it 'taking a turn about the room'—gossiping about who everybody was with and what they were wearing."

I yawn. If that was what they did for fun back then, I'm glad I live now. I pick a currant out of my scone and toss it at Stanley. He's looking as bored as I feel. He bats it back at me, and we get a little game of Ping-Pong going until my mother tells us to knock it off.

By the end of the day I'm exhausted, and so is everybody else. Jess and Megan and Becca and I were going to stay up and play cards, but we all fall into bed practically the minute we get back to the hotel room.

The next day is more of the same—wandering around Bath, taking pictures, trotting after Mrs. Chadwick as she wades into the gardens. Becca's mother loves England. The only time she stops smiling is when she sees Mr. Hawthorne. She's still ticked off about Hepzibah Plunkett.

We tour the Jane Austen Centre, which explains all about Jane's life—the tour guide is surprised to find out how much we already know about it—and afterward, we stop in the gift shop. Stewart and Mr. Hawthorne and Darcy and my stepfather take one look at all the doilies and tea towels and bolt for the door. I want to go with them but my mother asks me to pick something out for Courtney. I can't imagine my sister actually wanting any of this stuff, but I know she likes Jane Austen so I try to be a good sport and pick something halfway decent. I settle on a sterling silver locket that's shaped like a book. *Pride and Prejudice* is engraved on the cover in tiny letters. I figure she can stick a picture of her boyfriend in there, or of Chloe and me, or Murphy or something.

Gigi buys everybody mugs with the opening line from *Pride and Prejudice* on them, and Mrs. Hawthorne spots some Elizabeth and Darcy paper dolls and holds them up.

"Remember when you sent the girls *Little Women* paper dolls, Shannon?"

Mrs. Delaney nods, and I groan. "Don't remind me."

My friends all laugh.

I see Jess buy an "I ♥ Darcy" keychain, and my mother buys a bunch of flowery bookmarks and a complete set of Jane Austen novels.

"In case you want to try a few more," she tells me.

Our last stop of the day is the costume fitting.

"There is absolutely no way I am wearing this dress," I tell my mother flatly, glowering at the mirror. "I look like Little Bo Peep."

"You do not, sweetheart!" she says, adjusting one of the many frills. "You look lovely. Besides, how often in your life do you get to do something like this?"

"Never," I tell her. "That's the whole point."

She tries a different tack. "This is a very, very exclusive ball. The tickets were enormously expensive."

"So?"

"So aren't you being just a little bit ungrateful? Remember what Mrs. Bergson said—she wanted us to do something extravagant and fun. A once-in-a-lifetime experience."

"Why don't we go bungee jumping, then? Anything would be better than this."

"Cassidy," she warns, pulling out her Queen Clementine voice.

"Fine," I snap. "Just please don't make me wear the bonnet."

She laughs. "It's a deal. But it looks cute on Chloe, don't you think?"

Of course Chloe looks cute in the bonnet. My baby sister would look cute wearing a garbage bag. Especially the way she's toddling all over the place now. Her chubby little legs are adorable. I still can't believe my mother's actually going to dress her up and bring her along to the ball, but Mrs. Wong and Mrs. Delaney have promised to help babysit so Mom can dance with Stanley.

My stepfather comes strutting out of the dressing room a moment later. He's got these really tight pants on, which aren't a great look since he could stand to lose a few pounds, and a white shirt with a high ruffled collar, and a jacket with long tails in the back, and boots that come up to his knees. He looks even more ridiculous than I do.

"What do you think, Clemmie?" he asks, striking a pose.

"I think I'm going to call you Mr. Darcy from now on," my mother gushes, kissing the top of his bald head.

I dive back into the dressing room. Some things you just don't want to have to witness, especially where your parents—or stepparents—are concerned.

By Wednesday, I'm really ready for something besides "petticoats and bonnets," as Mr. Hawthorne puts it. Fortunately, Lyme Regis is on the schedule. We leave the hotel early, because it's a long drive to the coast, but it's so worth it. Lyme Regis is a cool old resort town, with something called the Cobb that sticks way out into the water, like the jetty does in Dennis, on Cape Cod. The water is cold, but no colder than we're used to at home, and we have a great time swimming and hanging out on the beach and exploring the town.

After lunch, it's time to head to London. We'll be staying there until after the ice dancing competition Friday night.

"I'm officially tired of driving," Mr. Hawthorne announces as we pile onto the bus.

"You're doing such a good job of it, though, sweetheart," says Mrs. Hawthorne.

"Absolutely," agrees Mrs. Delaney. "How about a round of applause for Nick?"

Everyone but Mrs. Chadwick claps.

We arrive in London in time for a quick dinner, then we set out for Hyde Park. It's not far from the hotel, and on the way we pass Buckingham Palace, which looks just the way a palace should.

The concert is amazing. Beyond amazing. I'm giddy. It's my first rock concert ever, and I can't imagine anything topping this. The Led Zeppelin reunion has drawn a massive crowd, spilling out of the park and onto the streets, which they've had to close. People are pushed up against one another, but everybody's having so much fun that nobody minds. The music is so loud I can feel the thump of the beat vibrating through my entire body. Mr. Delaney snagged us unbelievable tickets, and we're standing practically right next to the stage, so I manage to take some sweet pictures to send to Courtney. I had no idea these guys were so ancient—Jimmy Page and Robert Plant are as old as my grandparents—but they sure don't act their age. They can totally rock. The whole band plays and sings the way I play hockey: all out. It's awesome.

Mrs. Chadwick decided not to come—"I'm not a fan of rock music," she sniffed—and Gigi said she was just too tired, so the two of them stayed back at the hotel with Chloe. But my mom and Stanley are here, and they're acting like teenagers, dancing and singing at the top of their lungs. It's incredibly embarrassing. Emma's parents are doing the same thing, so I don't feel quite so stupid. And in the end I start dancing too; I can't help it. Nobody can. The music picks you up and carries you away.

It's really late by the time the concert is finally over, but we're all wired so we go for a long walk down by the Thames past the Houses of Parliament and Big Ben, which are all lit up and look as spectacular as Buckingham Palace.

"This whole country is like one giant postcard," I tell my mother.

She slips her arm through mine. "Isn't it great?" she agrees. "I used to love to come to London when I was modeling. It's one of my favorite places in the whole world."

We're tired by now, so we hop a bus back to the hotel. Jess falls asleep with her head against Darcy's shoulder, and I see Mr. Hawthorne waggle his eyebrows at Mrs. Hawthorne, who smiles over at Mrs. Delaney. I guess I'm not the only one who's noticed what's going on.

Heather Vogel Frederick

Thursday is just as good as Wednesday. London is huge, as big as New York or bigger, maybe, only without all the skyscrapers. There's no way we can see it all, Mrs. Hawthorne tells us. We take a tour in the morning to give us an overview of the city, sitting on top of a double-decker bus with a really hilarious tour guide. After lunch, we split up, to allow people to see the things they're really interested in. I go with my stepfather and Darcy and Jess and Stewart to see the Tower of London. Emma's right—there's tons of armor there, and old weapons, plus the Crown Jewels. I'm not a big fan of jewelry, except for my hockey earrings, but these things are in a league of their own. I've never seen such enormous gems.

While we're touring the tower, Mrs. Chadwick and Mrs. Delaney and my mother and Mrs. Wong all head for the Royal Botanic Garden. Gigi and Megan and Becca make a beeline for some store called Harrod's, and Emma and her parents join a walking tour of literary London, what else.

We sightsee until dinner time, when we meet up at the hotel again. Then it's time to go to the theater—*Romeo and Juliet*, at the Globe Theater, where we spend the evening standing again. Like the concert last night, though, it's worth it. The play is amazing.

"I'm so glad that Jane Austen believed in happy endings," says Mrs. Hawthorne, afterward. "Shakespeare can be so darned depressing."

"But so darned wonderful, too," says Mrs. Delaney.

"Can't argue with you there," says Emma's father.

"I can't believe how much we're cramming in," says my mother, yawning.

"But wouldn't Eva be proud of us?" says Gigi. "We're certainly being extravagant."

We have one last Jane Austen stop on our schedule here in London—the British library. After breakfast on Friday morning, we take the tube (that's what they call the subway over here, like Boston calls it the "T"), and head for something called the treasure room. I'm expecting gold doubloons at least, but instead it's mostly books, of course. Well, and stuff that belonged to writers and composers.

"Look! It's Jane's writing desk," says Emma, her eyes shining behind her glasses. "Wow." She's standing so close that her breath is clouding the glass case. "And look—original manuscript pages from one of her novels."

"*Persuasion*," says her mother.

"That's her *handwriting*," Emma continues. "See how she crossed stuff out and scribbled things in the margin? Just the way I do!"

Emma looks like she's going to start hyperventilating. I see Stewart is hovering nearby, like maybe he wants to say something to her. He catches me watching him, though, and drifts away.

"Amazing, isn't it?" says Mrs. Hawthorne, and I nod. Nothing to get that excited about, maybe, but still, pretty cool.

We're due to rendezvous with the Berkeleys for lunch at the Victoria and Albert Museum, so after we're done looking at Jane's stuff, the tube whisks us off again. I've been dreading this part of the trip, and unfortunately it's just as awkward as I expected. At the café, Annabelle ignores us, pretending like nothing has happened. Simon is busy trying to avoid Megan, and our parents are all completely clueless.

I'm surprised when Tristan comes to sit next to me. I didn't see much of him after I turned him down for the spring formal. I had that trip out to California first of all, plus even though we tried to practice together after Mrs. Bergson died, it was pretty hard without a coach. And then school was over and he and his family took off to explore America.

"Hullo," he says.

"Hey," I reply.

"Having fun?"

I nod. "Yeah. England is great. How was the Grand Canyon?"

"Brilliant."

"So are you ready for this?" I ask him.

He nods. "I think so. Annabelle and I are still having a little trouble with those synchronized twizzles, but our coach has been working with us all week and I think we've got the programs down."

Annabelle sees us and frowns. She gets up and comes around the table and plunks herself into the empty chair next to Tristan. I swear she sticks to him like tape on a hockey stick. I can tell that she considers him her own private property. Well, if he's stupid enough to want that, he's welcome to her. Not that I really care, anyway.

After lunch, it's time to go to the rink. I suck in a big lungful of cold air as we enter the main doors. I love the smell of ice. It makes every nerve in my body tingle. Everything about me comes alive in a rink. Different things do it for other people—an art studio, maybe, or a science lab or a kitchen or a bookstore, but for me, it's always been a skating rink.

Tristan skates over when he sees me standing by the edge. I slap him a high five.

"You're gonna do great," I tell him, going into coach mode. I owe that much, at least, to Mrs. Bergson. No point being snippy with him here, right before his competition. I take something out of my pocket and pass it to him.

"What's this?" he asks.

"Mrs. Bergson's silver whistle," I tell him. "Stick it in a pocket or something for good luck. I want it back afterward, though."

"Right. Got it. No pinching the silver." He smiles and gestures at his costume. "I don't have a pocket, though. Spandex, remember? Mr. Fancypants?" He passes it back. "How about you hold it for me. It'll be doubly lucky that way." He places it on my palm and closes my fingers around it. His hands are warm, and I feel my pulse start to race.

Annabelle comes skating over. Her eyes narrow when she sees his hands wrapped around mine. "Tristan!" she says in a shrill voice. "Thirty-minute warning! You should be warming up."

"I heard," he tells her. "I'll be right there."

She glares at me and skates off.

"Good luck," I tell him, and I mean it, feeling suddenly shy. "I wish Mrs. Bergson was here to see you."

"Me too," he replies, his deep blue eyes serious all of a sudden.

Heather Vogel Frederick

He lets go of my hand and heads back out onto the ice. I sit down slowly, feeling a little light-headed.

A couple of minutes later I hear the clack of skate guards against cement, and look up to see Annabelle Fairfax standing in front of me with her hands on her hips.

"Stay away from my cousin."

"Distant cousin," I correct her.

"I mean it. Hands off."

It takes every ounce of restraint that I can muster not to lay into her, but I think about the fact that Annabelle has to get out there in less than half an hour and perform in a competition, and I think about what Mrs. Bergson would want me to do. It wouldn't be fair of me to rattle her cage. "Whatever," I tell her, and start to walk away.

"Promise me!" she calls, her voice rising.

Without looking back, I flap my hand at her. If I stop now, I don't think I'll be able to keep myself from saying something I'll regret. I really, really don't want to be responsible for messing this day up for Tristan.

I hear the quick clack of skate guards behind me again, like someone's running, followed by a scraping sound and a shriek. I whip around just in time to see Annabelle go sprawling on the cement floor.

Things get jumbled after that. Her coach comes running over, and Annabelle's holding her ankle and hollering that I pushed her, which is obviously not true since I'm nowhere near her, plus Tristan saw the whole thing.

"Annabelle was running after Cassidy," he tells their coach. "She was reaching out to grab her arm, and she slipped. Cassidy never touched her."

It turns out Annabelle's ankle is sprained. Her coach goes ashen-faced when the rink doctor gives him the news.

"This is it, then," he says to Tristan. "A whole year of hard work down the drain. If you don't place in this competition, you don't go advance to the European Junior Championship. You're out."

Tristan's eyes slide over to me. "What are the rules about last-minute substitutions?"

Half an hour later I'm out on the ice. I still don't know how it happened. They practically had to cut Annabelle out of her costume, she was so determined not to let me use it, and then Megan and Gigi had to do some last-minute alterations to get it to fit me since I'm so much taller. They scrounged up a needle and thread and somehow managed to let out the shoulder seams, though, and I squeezed into it.

Finding skates were a little harder. I have big feet. But we managed that, too, thanks to a Dutch skater who had to bail out because of the flu.

I had exactly five minutes to warm up. Five minutes! And I haven't been on the ice for over a week.

The thing is, though, once I am out on the ice, nothing else matters. Ice is my native element. When I'm out here, I don't hear the crowd, I don't see the people in the stands, I only see that gleaming expanse of frozen liquid stretching out in front of me. And whether I'm wearing hockey skates or figure skates, whether I'm in Concord or London, I am never more me, Cassidy Sloane, than I am when I'm in the middle of a rink.

Tristan skates over. "Ready?" he asks. I nod. He holds up his forefinger, and I smile. One minute. That's all it takes to complete the compulsory dance.

The music starts and I feel my tense muscles start to relax. It's Strauss—Mrs. Bergson's favorite. I think about the rock concert last night, and I let the music pick me up and carry me. One-two-three, one-two-three, step glide release, step glide step, the moves are in my bones, just like the music. Practice makes perfect, Mrs. Bergson always said, and she's right. I've practiced this a million times at the rink back home. This waltz is in my DNA. I look over at Tristan and see it on his face too. *He gets this.* He loves the ice as much as I do.

We finish to wild applause.

"That was the easy part," I tell my mother, who's waiting for us at the edge of the rink with Stanley and Chloe and the rest of the Mother-Daughter Book Club.

"Cassidy, *nothing* you do is easy," she tells me. "I don't know anybody who works as hard as you do, or who has as much gumption or flat-out determination as you do." She gives me a hug. "I'm so proud of you! I wish your father could be here right now to see this."

That brings tears to my eyes. She's right—my father would be thrilled. Then I see my stepfather standing a little ways apart with Chloe, giving my mother and me a little space and pretending he can't hear every word of our conversation. I think of all those early mornings when he got up to drive me to practice, and all those weekends he gave up to haul me around New England to games and tournaments.

"I know, but I'm glad Stanley's here, at least."

My stepfather's face lights up at this. I smile and blow him a kiss, and he smiles back. My mother hugs me again. "Thank you," she whispers.

A minute later our results finally flash up on the screen, and they're solid. Not stellar, but solid. I didn't disgrace myself out there, and we're still in the top six. We still have a chance to place.

A few rows up in the stands, I spot Annabelle sitting with her parents. She's changed into her warm-up suit, and she does not look happy. Tough. She has no one but herself to blame.

And then it's time to change into my costume for the free dance. Back in the dressing area, Megan and Gigi are working overtime to somehow remake this outfit too. It's a black and white number that fits the mood of the music, which is a very dramatic Flamenco piece.

"We added a ruffle here," Megan says, pointing to the bodice. "And I sliced off a strip from the bottom of the skirt to use as extenders for the shoulder straps."

I wedge myself into it and stare at the mirror. Then I turn to her and grin. "All I can say is, I'm glad Fashionista Jane has gone into retirement."

Back out on the ice again, Tristan is waiting for me. He holds out his hand and I take it, aware that my palm is sweaty. This is much, much different from the compulsory dance. Most of our score rides on this free dance, and it's a whole lot more complicated than the waltz. I try not to think about the handstand lift in the middle of the program. That's the one move that's been giving me fits since we started this whole practice partner thing. I'll just have to trust my training. We skate out into the middle of the rink and take our starting position—a reverse Kilian. I take a deep breath. I'm not doing this for Tristan; I'm not doing it for me; I'm doing this for Mrs. Bergson. This is my thank-you to her. My final farewell.

The music starts with a flourish. Tristan and I toss our heads back and fling our right hands into the air, and then we're off. I match him step for step, turning and gliding. He pulls me close and pushes me away, lifts me up and swings me around and spirals by my side. I don't think about the steps—I don't have to. My body is doing what it was trained to do, what it practiced and practiced and practiced again. What I do think about is the *music*.

In hockey, I hear the music of the crowd. I hear the music of adrenaline pumping, of the drive for the puck and the goal. Out here, today, I hear the music of the Rodrigo Concerto, and as I surrender to its drama and passion, it carries me forward.

My palms grow slick with sweat as we approach the lift, though. *Keep it together, Sloane*, I tell myself sternly. *You can do this.*

I nail the forward inside mohawk leading into it, and the energy from that move sends me soaring as I place my hands onto the upper part of Tristan's bent leg and throw myself into a handstand. His right arm encircles my waist, giving me the stability I need, and we pivot, my legs extended in the air above our heads, his left arm flung triumphantly upward.

The crowd loves it.

Seconds later I'm upright on my feet again, and with this hurdle overcome, we sail through the final section of the free dance with ease.

The arena explodes in applause as we finish with a dramatic twin knee slide. Tristan gives me a huge hug. People throw flowers. I could get used to this.

We come in third.

Third is just fine. It's enough to keep Tristan in the running for his next competition, and it means I'll be taking home a trophy to add to Mrs. Bergson's display case at the rink.

After a celebration dinner, we drive from London back to Bath. On the way to our hotel, we stop by Ivy Cottage to pick up the rest of the Hawthornes' things. They've moved into the hotel with the rest of us now that the Berkeleys are back, and we'll all be heading directly to the airport from Chawton after the ball.

"Come in!" Mrs. Berkeley calls out the kitchen window, as our mini-coach pulls into the front drive. "I just put the kettle on."

We crowd into the kitchen, where the rest of the Berkeley family is seated around the table. It's obvious they're happy to be home again.

"Wasn't that exciting?" says Mrs. Delaney. "You and Cassidy were wonderful, Tristan."

"Shhhh!" whispers Mrs. Berkeley, pointing to the ceiling. "Annabelle is asleep upstairs."

"Gotcha," says Jess's mom.

Mrs. Hawthorne starts talking about the Regency dance thing we're supposed to go to tomorrow night. "I have a few extra tickets," she says. "We thought Michael Delaney and Henry Chadwick and Jerry Wong would be able to come, along with my daughter Courtney. I thought about offering one to Rupert Loomis—"

"MOOO!" squawks Toby from the corner, making us all jump.

"How odd," says Mrs. Berkeley, frowning at the parrot. "I wonder what made him do that?"

The Mother-Daughter Book Club tries really, really hard not to giggle.

"—but then it occurred to me that you all might like to come." Mrs. Hawthorne continues. "We'd love to have you join us if you can."

"I'd like to go," says Tristan, looking straight at me.

I feel my face flush and I look away. Across the room, Toby is gnawing at a carrot.

"Me too," says Simon with a smile. I notice Megan perk up at this.

"I do so wish I could say 'me, three,' but alas I'm leaving in the morning for a conference in Edinburgh," says Professor Berkeley. "But you should go too, darling. It's quite the affair, from what I've heard."

"I'd love to," says Mrs. Berkeley.

"Perhaps Annabelle would like to go as well," says Mrs. Hawthorne. "Not that she'd be able to dance, but still, it might help cheer her up after her disappointment."

"Here she is now," says Mrs. Berkeley. "Why don't you ask her?"

Annabelle comes stumping into the kitchen on crutches.

Behind me, I hear the thud of a carrot against the bottom of a bird cage.

"STINKERBELLE!" squawks Toby.

There's a shocked silence in the kitchen. Then Tristan starts to snicker. Pretty soon his brother joins in, and then my friends and I are laughing, too. Mustering as much dignity as she can, Annabelle Fairfax stalks out of the kitchen.

I smile.

Life is good.

So good, in fact, that sometimes you don't even need to keep score.

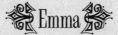 Emma

"Excuse me, miss, but a packet came for you earlier this morning." The hotel desk clerk holds out a thick envelope.

"For me?"

"Boy about your age delivered it. Bit of a gawky fellow."

Rupert. Who else?

I glance into the breakfast room. No sign of Stewart yet. Too bad. He's been in England nearly a week and still hasn't met Rupert Loomis.

"Thanks," I tell her, and duck into the sitting room to open it. Inside are two copies of a big magazine-size booklet with a glossy cover. The Knightley-Martin Literary Anthology! In all the excitement of having my friends here I'd completely forgotten about it. There's a note attached: *Your story is the best one*. It's signed *Your friend, Rupert Loomis.*

My story made it into the collection? How come no one told me?

Heart pounding, I flip the anthology open and thumb through the pages. There it is! *Stinkerbelle the Bad Fairy*. And right beneath it, my name: *Emma Jane Hawthorne*. My byline for the middle school newspaper back home was always "E. J. Hawthorne," but when I submitted this story I decided to use my full name, since it would be my official literary debut. I run my finger over it. It looks good in print.

I turn the pages, happy to see that they used Lucy's clever illustrations of Stinkerbelle and her helper fairies Puff, Smiles, and Buttercup too. The two of us had a whole lot of fun with this project, and I think it shows. The judges must have thought it did, anyway, otherwise they wouldn't have decided to include it.

I hope my father thinks so too. Stuffing the extra copy back into the envelope, I head for the breakfast room to find him. I told him a while ago that I was thinking of submitting a story, but I didn't give him any more details.

"Come sit by me," he says, patting the chair beside him. "Your mom's sleeping in this morning. Too much excitement yesterday." He gives me a wink.

My mother was not happy with the whole Stinkerbelle thing, and apologized profusely to the Berkeleys last night after Toby's outburst. "I had no idea that Emma trained Toby to do that," she told them. She made me apologize too.

My father thought it was funny, though.

"Serves her right, the little blister," he'd said.

I pass him the magazine. I can only imagine what my mother

will say when she sees it. It was so worth risking her wrath, though. Annabelle deserves every ounce of comeuppance she gets, after all the mean things she's done this year. Most people aren't going to have a clue that she's Stinkerbelle, and besides, I'm leaving the country in two days, and with any luck I'll never see her again after the ball tomorrow night.

My father glances at the cover, then looks up at me. "Did your story make it in?"

I nod, smiling, and watch as he opens to the page I've marked. He chuckles at the title. As he starts to read the chuckle blossoms into full-blown laughter, until finally he has to take his glasses off and wipe his eyes.

"Brilliant," he tells me when he's done. "Just brilliant."

"What's brilliant?" asks Cassidy, her mouth full of scone.

My father passes her the magazine, and her eyes widen when she sees the title. "Way to go, Hawthorne!" she crows, spraying the table with crumbs. "Check it out, you guys!"

My story makes its way around the table to much hilarity and congratulations. I try and look humble, but I can't help it, I'm grinning like a jack o' lantern. Now I know how my father felt last summer when he got that call from New York about his book. It's really, really great to finally have something officially published.

If only Stewart were here so he could see it, too. I'm dying to ask him what he thinks about it. He's been my best literary critic for two years now. But just like my mother, he's sleeping in this morning, which means I'd have to go knock on his door and give it to him face to face, and that's just too awkward right now.

I only wish he'd had a chance to see Rupert while he was here in England. I know Stewart, and he has just as keen a sense of the absurd as I do. One look at Rupert Loomis and he'd instantly know that I was telling the truth about the mistletoe kiss.

After breakfast, we all head back upstairs to finish packing. Since the Berkeleys are home again, and since we're flying back to Boston this weekend anyway, my family and I moved out of Ivy Cottage and into the hotel last night with our friends. My parents and Darcy are in the Lord Byron suite, and I piled in with my friends on a roll-away bed.

"I can't believe how fast this week has gone by," sighs Becca, unzipping her suitcase. "I'm not ready to go home yet."

"Me neither," says Megan. "I could spend another week just in London, easily. Their stores are amazing."

"Well, we still have all day today and the ball tonight," I remind them.

Megan takes her rented ball gown out of the closet. It was delivered to the hotel yesterday with the rest of our costumes, while we were at the skating competition. It's pale blue, with short puffed sleeves and a scoop neckline, and there's a wide ribbon of white satin under the bodice, accentuating the high, Empire-style waist. It's stunning. *"Tonight, tonight,"* she sings, hugging the dress to her as she dances around the room. *"Won't be just any night!"*

Megan's happy because Simon is speaking to her again. I guess his brother set him straight about Annabelle's little schemes, and helped patch things up between the two of them.

"Wrong musical," says Jess. "'Tonight' is from *West Side Story*. A Regency ball is more—I don't know, more like a fairy tale, don't you think? How about 'Someday My Prince Will Come,' from *Snow White*?" Humming the tune, she takes a turn around the room with her own dress, which is pale pink with lace inset at the bodice.

Becca grabs her choice—daffodil-yellow, with a ruffle around the bottom—and jumps up on her bed. "Or how about, 'I Am Sixteen Going on Seventeen' from *The Sound of Music*?" she suggests, and the four of us burst into a chorus of "I am fifteen going on sixteen," which is closer to the truth.

"How about put a sock in it already?" says Cassidy, who's still grumpy at the prospect of having to wear a long dress in public. We've told her a zillion times that lavender looks great with her red hair, and that she absolutely does not look Little Bo Peep, but she's still convinced she's going to make a fool of herself.

I carefully pack my dress—a soft peach with a crossover V-neck—back into its plastic bag and carry it down with my suitcase to the mini-coach.

"I'll take that, milady," says my father, stuffing the suitcase in the compartment underneath and hanging the dress up in the boot with the rest of our clothes for tonight. I see Stewart's name tag on one of the suit bags, and wonder briefly how he'll look dressed up like Mr. Darcy. As good as he looked in that tuxedo a couple of years ago at our fashion show, I'm willing to bet. In other words, pretty fabulous.

"Good-bye, Bath!" I call out the window softly a few minutes later, as we pull out of the hotel parking lot. "Good-bye Ivy Cottage, and Knightley-Martin, and Lucy and Toby and fish and chips and Sally Lunn's and everything else I love about this place!"

My brother is sitting across the aisle with Jess. He smiles at me. Despite all our misgivings last summer when our parents sprang the idea of living abroad on us, it's been an amazing year, and I know he's going to miss England just as much as I will.

This morning we're headed to Chawton, and the Jane Austen House Museum. Chawton is also where the ball will be held tonight. We're staying at a nearby inn since it's closer to London and the airport. It's hard to believe we fly back to Boston tomorrow.

I didn't think anything could top the British Library, but I'm wrong.

It's a little misty when we pull into Chawton, the village where Jane Austen spent the last years of her life. I look out the window, eager for a glimpse of her house. This is where the magic happened, after all. This is where she wrote her books.

Oddly, this is my first visit to Chawton. I'd been to all the other Jane Austen sites we visited this week except the British Library, and I was supposed to come to Chawton earlier this spring with my mother, but that was the weekend I ended up going with Lucy's family to Yorkshire.

My stomach flutters as we get out of the bus. How often do you get to visit the home of your favorite writer? Back in Concord, I've toured Orchard House, where Louisa May Alcott lived when she wrote *Little Women*, a zillion times before, but this is different. This is *Jane Austen.*

I stand in the parking lot, looking across the street at the big brick house with the walled garden. It's newer than the Berkley's house, my mother tells us, built in the seventeenth century, but the front door is white, just like Ivy Cottage, and there's a climbing rose scrambling up the wall around it.

"Isn't it beautiful?" says Cassidy's mom with a sigh.

I nod. Jane's family always referred to it as a "cottage," but it's bigger than our little house back in Concord. It's not grand, though, and it reminds me a bit of Half Moon Farm—a little shabby and worn but as comfortable as an old shoe. Inside, the likeness to Half Moon Farm is even stronger. Just like Jess's house, this one has uneven floors and creaky stairs and fireplaces in nearly every room. And there are views of the garden from nearly all the windows.

There's a piano in the drawing room, with music books displayed on it that were Jane's. You can see her handwriting and everything. I linger by a display case that has a lock of her hair—brown, like mine—and some of her jewelry, including a blue beaded bracelet and a topaz cross necklace her sailor brother Charles sent her from Spain.

"She mentions that necklace in one of her books," my mother tells me. "Remember?"

I nod. "Mansfield Park. Fanny Price gets one from her brother William. Only it's amber, not topaz."

My mother laughs. "Spoken like a true fellow Janeite," she tells me, putting her arm around my shoulders and giving me a hug.

The two of us have actually read all of Jane Austen's novels together this year. We didn't tell the rest of the book club, though, because they already think I'm an overachiever where books are concerned.

Upstairs, I spend a while in Jane's bedroom, the one she shared with her sister, Cassandra. It's tiny—about half the size of my room back home. There's a canopy bed, and a fireplace with narrow closets on either side. One is for clothes, and in the other there's a china wash-basin and a blue bowl on the shelf underneath.

"What's that for?" asks Cassidy, pointing to the bowl.

"It's a chamber pot," my mother tells her.

"Huh?"

I give my friend a significant look. "Um, they didn't have indoor plumbing back then, remember?"

"Eeew," she says.

"Beats running to the outhouse in the rain," my mother points out.

"I guess." Cassidy doesn't look convinced.

We wander into another bedroom where there's a patchwork quilt on display that Jane and Cassandra and their mother made. It's faded, but pretty. Megan takes a picture of it.

"For Summer?" I ask, and she nods. Summer Williams is Megan's pen pal from Wyoming. She's absolutely mad about quilting.

Megan takes pictures of the mannequins in Regency clothes that are standing in many of the rooms, and of the lace shawl one of them is wearing. Gigi points to a lace collar that's framed and hanging on one of the walls.

"Be sure and take a picture of that," she says. "Can you believe Jane actually made it?"

"Pretty cool," agrees Becca. "They must have had a lot of time back then, though, to sit around doing something like making lace."

"Well, they did," says Mrs. Wong. "Just imagine—no TV, no radio, no computers, no malls."

Becca makes a face.

I head back downstairs, where I've saved the best for last. Pausing on the landing, I look out the window and see that the mist has burned away. Stewart is sitting on a bench, soaking up the sun. At the far end of the garden I spot Jess and Darcy, admiring the flowers and each other, from the looks of it. I smile. I've had plenty of time to get used to the idea of my brother liking my best friend, and it's just fine with me.

My father is in the parlor, standing by a small, round, twelve-sided table under a window.

"Humbling, isn't it?" he says.

I nod. The plaque on the wall above explains that this is where Jane worked.

"To think that she wrote six of the world's greatest novels sitting at this tiny table! I'll never complain about my office at home again," he says.

My father's always grumbling that he needs more bookshelves. "At least you *have* an office!" I tell him, and he grins.

"What are you fussing about, laptop girl?"

It's true. I love my new laptop. It's really fun to write on.

He takes a picture of me standing by Jane's writing table, and on the way out we test the door to see if the hinge still squeaks—it does. I totally understand why Jane was so private about her writing. I am too.

Leaving my parents in the gift shop, I head outside, pausing briefly in the doorway to gaze at the garden with its low brick wall. I try and imagine for a moment that I'm Jane, getting ready to go for a walk. I can see why she loved living here. Thatched roof cottages line the town's narrow streets, and beyond them stretch the green fields and woods of the Hampshire countryside. No wonder Jane wrote as much as she did here. She was happy. I can just feel it.

Across the lawn, Mrs. Chadwick is kneeling on the grass, her large bottom sticking up into the air. She's taking close-up shots of all the flowers in the border.

"Looks like Hepzi—I mean Calliope—has found her calling in life," says my father, coming up to stand beside me.

I turn around and stare at him, openmouthed. "Dad!"

He grins sheepishly. "Busted!" he says. "I guess somehow she did manage to wander onto the pages of my book. What can I say, Calliope Chadwick is just larger than life. You know how that goes, right?"

"Right," I reply, thinking of *Stinkerbelle the Bad Fairy*.

He holds up his pinkie. "This will just be our little secret, okay? Writer's honor?"

I hook my finger around his. "Writer's honor."

Heather Vogel Frederick

Lunch is soup and sandwiches across the street at Cassandra's Cup, the little café named after Jane's sister, then we climb back onto the mini-coach for the short drive to the inn where we're staying tonight. Tomorrow morning, we'll drive directly from Chawton to Heathrow Airport.

We're going home! It's hard to believe a whole year has flown by. So much has happened. Most of it was very, very good, like my father getting his book published, and just about everything here in England besides Stinkerbelle, and Jess rescuing Lydia the fox, and me getting my story published. Some of it wasn't so good, though, especially this misunderstanding with Stewart, and of course Mrs. Bergson's death.

I still really miss her. She wrote me faithfully every week from Concord, and sent me pictures of Pip and told me about funny things that happened around town and at the rink. Her letters were fabulous. I've kept them all, and I reread them often. Somehow, I expected them to keep coming after she died, but of course they didn't. Her passing left a hole in my life and my heart that I can't imagine anyone else filling.

Even though Mrs. Bergson is gone, it's still going to be good to be back home in Concord. England has been amazing, but I can't wait to sleep in my own bed again, and to be reunited with Melville and Pip. My father finally caved and said that Pip can come live with us. Melville will just have to get used to the idea.

But I'm not ready to think about home quite yet. I just want to enjoy my last day in England.

"Are the Berkeleys staying here at the inn too?" asks Megan as we pull into the parking lot. She's trying to sound casual, but I know how eager she is to see Simon again.

My mother shakes her head. "No, they're coming directly from Bath to the ball." She glances at her watch. "Speaking of which, we need to leave for Chawton House in about three hours. Shall we rendezvous down in the lobby at six? That should give everyone time for naps, showers, last-minute wardrobe adjustments, and what-have-you."

We find our rooms—Jess and I are in one together, and Cassidy and Megan and Becca are right next to us, with an adjoining door— and get settled. The inn serves tea and cookies, so Cassidy and I go downstairs and bring up a tray for everybody. We talk for a while, and then it's time to get ready.

"You girls look absolutely adorable," says Mrs. Sloane-Kinkaid, poking her head into Cassidy and Megan and Becca's room where we're all gathered to help one another with zippers and hair and makeup.

"Gee, thanks, Mom," says Cassidy, who is watching us from an armchair across the room.

Our mothers all crowd in behind Mrs. Sloane-Kinkaid. They look great in their gowns too, and I can tell they're as excited as we are because they're all chattering away and taking pictures.

"Remember that first year of book club, when we had the *Little Women* Christmas party and everybody got dressed up as their favorite characters?" says Mrs. Wong.

"And remember how all of you came as Marmee?" I remind them, which gets everybody laughing.

"Check this out," says Megan, twitching up the hem of Cassidy's dress to reveal her sneaker-clad feet. "She did the same thing when she dressed up as Jo March. Some things never change."

"Cassidy Anne!" cries her mother.

"Hey!" Cassidy protests. "They do too change!" She turns her head back and forth, showing off her silver hockey stick earrings.

Gigi enters carrying an armload of lacy somethings, which she proceeds to pass out.

"Mother! This is beautiful," says Mrs. Wong, holding hers up. It's a lace shawl.

"I got one for each of you at a gift shop back in Bath," says Gigi. "A true lady would never attend a ball without one."

"You sound like Fashionista Jane," says Megan.

"I miss Fashionista Jane," says Gigi.

"Mother," warns Mrs. Wong.

Gigi shrugs. "I'm just saying."

As we leave the room, I grab something from my suitcase and wrap it discreetly in my shawl, then follow my friends and their mothers downstairs.

Our fathers and brothers are waiting for us in the lobby. My eyes are drawn instantly to Stewart. As I suspected, the dark jacket and white high-necked shirt look very dramatic on him. Our eyes meet briefly, and I think I see a flicker of admiration on his face, but then we both look away, embarrassed. I try not to let this dampen my spirits, but it's hard. I miss him terribly.

"Mrs. Bergson has one final surprise for us," my mother announces, once we're all gathered. "Ladies and gentlemen, your coaches await!"

My father opens the inn's big double doors to reveal three horse-drawn carriages standing on the gravel drive.

A collective gasp goes up, and the other guests go scurrying for their cameras. I guess it's not often that a whole group of people magically appear in the hotel you're staying at looking like they just stepped out of the pages of *Pride and Prejudice*. Add carriages ready to whisk them away to a ball, and it's an instant photo opportunity.

Cassidy and Jess and Megan and Becca and I all climb into the first one. Mrs. Sloane-Kinkaid passes Chloe up to her big sister. "Let her ride with you, honey," she says. Chloe is dressed all in white, and seems to be enjoying herself just as much as the rest of us are.

"Horsie!" she squeals, bouncing up and down in Cassidy's lap.

"Oof," says Cassidy. "Careful, monkey face."

"Cassidy Ann!"

Cassidy grins sheepishly. "Sorry, Mom."

"What a picture you two make," Mrs. Sloane-Kinkaid continues. "Stanley? Are you getting this?"

Behind her, Stanley nods, not looking up from his video camera. "Say 'monkey face,' girls."

"MONKEY FACE!" We all chorus gleefully.

Cassidy's mother throws up her hands in surrender. "I give up."

As we clip-clop through the streets of Chawton, I try to engrave every second on my memory. Like my first kiss from Stewart—

Heather Vogel Frederick

who's in the carriage behind us, with his mother and Darcy and my parents—this is a moment I don't ever want to forget. It's going in my permanent memory book.

"I feel like Cinderella right now," says Becca dreamily.

"It's like riding in your sleigh, Jess," says Megan.

Jess shakes her head. "No," she says. "This is much, much better."

It's an absolutely perfect summer night, warm but not hot, with a whisper of a breeze. As we turn onto the long gravel drive that leads up a gentle rise to Chawton House, the Elizabethan manor where Jane Austen's brother Edward once lived, it's not difficult to imagine that we've stepped back two centuries. The slow clop-clop of the horses hooves; the crunch of gravel under the wheels; the flickering torches that light our way past the stables and the old stone church where Cassandra Austen and her mother are buried, all add to the mood. And when we finally round the corner of the circular drive, light spills from the big stone house's casement windows, and the faint strains of music can be heard coming from a white marquee on the lawn beside it. I whoosh out my breath. It's magical.

"Want a piece of gum?" asks Cassidy, holding out a pack and completely shattering the mood.

I have to laugh because there's no point getting annoyed. Megan is right about Cassidy—some things never change.

But on the other hand, I think, spotting Tristan Berkeley waiting for us, maybe sometimes they do.

Like Stewart and, I have to admit, my own brother, Tristan looks incredibly handsome. It's as if he was born to wear Regency gentleman's clothing. As Cassidy passes Chloe to me and gathers up her skirts, preparing to leap over the door of the carriage to the ground, Tristan holds out a gloved hand. She hesitates for a long moment, looking at him from beneath her bangs, then releases her gown and takes his hand, allowing him to open the carriage door and guide her down its steps. Tristan tucks her hand in the crook of his elbow and leads her inside. As she passes through the doorway, she throws a glance back over her shoulder at the rest of us as if to say, "Sorry, guys." We just sit and stare.

"Would you look at that," says her mother, taking Chloe from me. "Sneakers and all. Life is never dull with that daughter of mine around."

"You can say that again," says Stanley Kinkaid.

The two of them follow Cassidy into the house, and then it's my mother and father's turn. Mrs. Chadwick is next. She takes Stewart's arm, and my heart gives a twinge as he escorts her inside without so much as a backward glance at me. I'm going to have to get over my feelings for him eventually, but right now it's still really hard.

My brother helps Gigi and Mrs. Wong out of the carriage, then extends his hand to Jess.

"Wait a minute! Are they—" says Becca, staring at their clasped hands as they follow Megan's mom and grandmother inside.

I nod. "Uh-huh."

For once, Becca is speechless.

Heather Vogel Frederick

"There you are!" says Simon Berkeley, smiling at Megan. Megan happily takes his offered arm, and the two of them disappear inside as well, chattering away.

"Well, girls, I guess that leaves just us," says Mrs. Delaney, holding out one elbow to Becca and another to me. She grins. "*We're off to see the wizard!* Oops, wrong time period."

"We're off to see Mr. Darcy," says Becca.

The entrance hall to Chawton House is imposing, with dark, wood-paneled walls and a high ceiling. Staff dressed as footmen usher us into the Great Hall, where our hosts for the evening, two actors dressed up as Mr. Fitzwilliam Darcy and Mrs. Elizabeth Bennet Darcy, greet us politely.

"Welcome to Chawton House," says the fake Mr. Darcy. "Or, just for this one special evening, my own humble abode, Pemberley."

A ripple of laughter goes through the crowd. I lean over and whisper to my mother, "Did Jane really base Pemberley on this house?"

She shakes her head. "No. But some scholars think it might have been the model for Donwell Abbey, Mr. Knightley's estate in *Emma.*"

There are about a hundred people milling around. I spot Annabelle Fairfax on a sofa in the far corner of the room between two elderly ladies. Her leg is propped up on a footstool, and there's a big white bandage wrapped around her ankle. I flutter my fingers at her and she quickly looks away.

"A light collation will be served shortly," says our hostess. "You'll find the food, as well as music and dancing, under the marquee on the lawn. Meanwhile, please feel free to join one of our guided tours inside if you'd like, or simply enjoy the pleasure of your fellow guests."

She curtsies to us, and Mr. Darcy bows. We all clap politely.

"Emma!" I turn around. It's Jess. She points to one of the windows. Rupert Loomis is leaning against it, or rather drooping like a wet sock. "You didn't tell me Eeyore was going to be here."

"I didn't know he would be!" I look around frantically for Stewart. This is my chance. It's now or never. "Jess, you're my best friend in the entire world, right?"

"Absolutely."

"You've got to do something for me, then. Go find Stewart and introduce him to Rupert."

"I was about to go dance with your brother," she says, then smiles at me. "But he'll just have to wait. BFBB, right? Tell Darcy I'm on an errand of mercy if he comes looking for me."

She melts into the crowd and I stand there, waiting. Inside my white gloves, my palms start to sweat.

"Aren't you going to get something to eat?" asks my father, who's been talking with Rupert's great-aunt and the fake Mr. Darcy.

"In a minute," I tell him. I don't want to move until I see what happens with Stewart.

Cassidy and Tristan walk by. Her hand is still tucked under his arm, and they're laughing about something. Annabelle sees them too, and looks like she wishes the floor would open up and swallow Cassidy. I smother a grin. Chalk one up for big, bad Cassidy Sloane.

Jess reappears, towing Stewart. I hold my breath as she takes him over to Rupert, who is busy scratching himself. I can't hear their conversation, of course, but it's brief. Rupert gives one of his stiff little half-bows and launches into what I assume is a windy greeting, tugging at a giant earlobe. Stewart stands there looking stunned until he's finished, then turns and walks straight across the room to me.

He doesn't say a word. He doesn't have to. I can read his face like a book.

"Told you so," I say smugly.

He grabs my hand and pulls me out of the room, down the hall, and into another big room with a stone fireplace. This one is empty, though, except for the portraits of elegant ladies lining the walls. Shutting the door firmly behind us, he pulls me close and kisses me.

It's another one for the memory book.

"Just for the record, you're a much better kisser than Rupert Loomis," I tell him when we come up for air.

He grins. "That's a relief. Listen, I'm really, really sorry, Emma. I was a jerk."

"Yup," I reply. "A big one. But I forgive you."

He glances around the room at the portraits. "Who are all these people?"

"Famous women writers," I tell him. "The library here specializes in books written by women between 1600 and 1830."

With Stewart, I never need to worry about him thinking I'm a show-off. Besides, we both love literary trivia.

"Cool," he says.

"Hey, can I show you something?"

"Sure."

I unwrap the Knightley-Martin Literary Anthology from my shawl and hand it to him. "Check out page thirty-two."

He flips to my story and starts to laugh the second he spots the title. He sinks down into a nearby armchair and reads the whole story straight through, laughing the entire time.

"Emma, this is fantastic! It's funny and clever and I love the way it ends, with Stinkerbelle and her little fairy posse's spell boomeranging and turning them all into toads."

"You really like it? You're not just saying that?"

He nods. "It's really, really good. And I'm really, really proud of you." And to prove it, he jumps up and kisses me again.

"I need you to help me with something," I tell him when we finish.

He laughs when he hears my plan, then gives a mock Rupert-like bow. "At your service, milady."

Hand in hand we return to the Great Hall. Annabelle hasn't moved from her perch on the sofa. I guess when you have a sprained ankle, you aren't going anywhere fast.

"Hi, Annabelle!" I say brightly. "You met my boyfriend, Stewart Chadwick, back in Concord, I think. And he was at the ice dancing competition, when you, well, you know."

She glares at us. "What do you want?"

"I just wanted to see if you needed assistance going out to the tent," says Stewart politely.

Annabelle perks up at this.

"I'll get your things," I tell her, picking up the tote bag with her sweater and left sneaker in it.

Stewart helps her up from the sofa and puts an arm around her waist as she hobbles out of the room, leaning on him. I trail behind them, and as Stewart glances back at me over his shoulder, I hold up the copy of the literary anthology, then slip it into her bag and smile. That should give her a little something to think about when she finds it later.

The marquee—a big white tent similar to the one Mrs. Chadwick scrounged for us back in seventh grade, when we put on a fashion show—is breathtaking. The sides have been rolled up and are open to the surrounding gardens and lawn, where a parquet wood dance floor has been set up. Inside, round tables covered in white cloths are scattered about, some with chairs around them for seating, others bearing platters of delicious-looking finger food—strawberries dipped in chocolate, deviled eggs, little sandwiches, and all sorts of cheeses and things. The tent's central pillar is twined with fresh flowers, and there are flower arrangements on each of the tables. At the far end, a beautifully decorated cake is on display, and I notice Jess and her mother examining the workmanship.

Stewart and I get Annabelle settled at one of the tables, then offer to bring her some food and punch. I figure it's the least we can do for poor Stinkerbelle. She's in for quite a shock when she reads my story. I make sure and pop a couple of little tarts onto her plate and add a dollop of whipped cream to each one.

"Not the kind of cream that you like best, but it will have to do," I tell her as I hand her the plate.

She gives me a poisonous smile.

The dancing is about to start, so Stewart and I grab a quick bite ourselves and then head out onto the dance floor. An instructor is lining everybody up to teach us the cotillion and quadrille. It's a teeny bit like square dancing, only without a caller or fiddler. It's fun, especially being outside like this, with the candles and the music and the torches.

"I keep wanting to pinch myself," whispers Jess, who is dancing next to me with Darcy. My brother Darcy, not the fake actor Mr. Darcy.

"I know," I whisper back.

After we've danced two or three sets, Rupert materializes. "Might I have the pleasure?" he asks me. "If you don't mind, that is," he adds, bowing to Stewart.

"Don't mind at all," says Stewart, cheerfully handing me over and ignoring the black looks I'm shooting in his direction.

One thing about these old-fashioned dances is that there's the opportunity to talk to your partner while you're out there on the floor.

The music starts and we raise our hands and touch our gloved palms together. "I hope you have a good trip home," says Rupert stiffly.

"Thank you," I reply. We retreat and advance, retreat and advance, then do a little do-si-do-like move around the person to our left. Rupert looks so entirely pathetic, lumbering in every direction but the right one, that I suddenly feel a rush of pity. "You know," I tell him, when the dance brings us together again, "I probably shouldn't tell you this, but I think Lucy Woodhouse likes you."

"Lucy?" Rupert's deep baritone swoops up to a squeak.

I nod. We dance away in separate directions, Rupert stumbling over his feet but managing to catch himself before he crashes into Gigi, who's dancing with Mr. Kinkaid.

"Do you really think so?" he asks as we touch palms again and rotate in a circle. His normal pallid color has been replaced by a deep brick red.

"I really do," I reply solemnly.

It's true. I've been watching Lucy all year, and I'm convinced of it. I don't know why, and I don't know how it's possible, but I'm pretty sure she does. Lucy is a bright girl, so I figure there must be some hidden gold in Rupert's character that nobody else sees.

The dance finishes, and I leave a very thoughtful Rupert on the dance floor to return to Stewart.

We sit the next one out with my mother. "Looks like your mom has finally called a truce, Stewart," she says, pointing to the dance floor, where Mrs. Chadwick is stepping her way through a quadrille with my father.

Stewart grins. "About time," he says. "Dad says that we Chadwicks have a tendency to hold on to grudges long past their expiration date." He reaches over and gives my hand a squeeze. My mother smiles and looks discreetly away.

"I'm going to go inside for a minute," I tell them, and excuse myself.

It's quiet and cool inside the stone house, and I wander the empty halls, looking for the tour guide. Figuring the group must have gone upstairs, I creak my way to the top, then along a long corridor that I recognize as the gallery. My mother has been here before, to use the research library, and she says that in the olden days when the weather was poor, the ladies of the house would walk up and down this corridor for exercise.

It's a little creepy up here, especially with all the portraits watching me. I hear footsteps ahead, and quicken my pace. It must be the tour. But when I turn the corner, no one is there.

The hair on the back of my neck begins to prickle. Where *is* everybody?

"Hello?" I call.

There's no reply. Then I hear footsteps again, only this time in the opposite direction. I turn around and break into a jog. My arms are covered in goose bumps by now. I don't believe in ghosts, but if ever there was a place for one, Chawton House is it. All this dark wood paneling and creaky floorboards! I can't wait to get home to Concord and our little house with its cheerful pink kitchen.

My imagination is working overtime by now. Jane Austen used to visit her brother and his family here all the time. What if her ghost is wandering about? I turn the corner again and see a flash of silk as someone—or something—whisks through an open doorway.

Slowly, reluctantly, I draw closer to the doorway. The room beyond

Heather Vogel Frederick

is dimly lit, and the someone—or something—is sitting in an arm-chair in shadows. Could it be Jane herself?

But no, it's just Rupert's great-aunt Olivia.

"Ah, Emma Hawthorne," she says. "Just the girl I wish to see. Do come in."

She cocks her head and studies me as I obey. "She loved this room, you know," she tells me.

"Who?"

"Why, Jane Austen, of course. They call it the Oak Room now, but it used to be the Ladies' Withdrawing Room. It's my favorite room in the house. Jane and her female relatives and friends would gather here in the afternoons and after dinner, to read and talk and do their nee-dlework." She points to an alcove in the far wall, where there's another armchair. "They say she sat right there and worked on her stories," she tells me, lowering her voice to a whisper. "But I suspect that is merely a bit of fanciful embroidery for the tourists."

She smiles, and I give her a hesitant smile in return.

"I quite think you captured her spirit," she says.

"Whose?" I reply, mystified.

"Miss Annabelle Fairfax's. She's Stinkerbelle, correct? My grand-nephew told me all about your run-ins with her this year. She's a spoiled brat and always has been. Her parents have never been able to say no to her."

I'm not quite sure what to say to this. An answer doesn't seem to be required, however.

"Rupert brought home the school magazine and showed me your story," she continues. "It was very naughty of you to lampoon her in print, but it was also very, very funny. No one but those who know her and her antics will recognize her in the stories, of course, and she will hardly want to draw attention to herself by claiming to be Stinkerbelle in the flesh. So she'll have no choice but to stew in her own juice. Well done, my dear, well done."

She steeples her fingers and regards me thoughtfully. "I realize that my grand-nephew's attentions to you over these past months haven't been all that welcome, but I do appreciate your patience with him," she continues. "He's a bit of an odd duck, but he's a good boy. I've been thinking things over and it occurs to me that perhaps living with an old lady like myself isn't the best situation for him. So I'm sending him off to boarding school this fall. I'm sure it will do him a world of good. And as for your story, I've been thinking about that, too. You know that I used to own a publishing company?"

I nod.

"I'm retired now, but I still have some say in their operations. I've sent your story to a former colleague of mine there. Who knows? Perhaps there's a picture book in it. Your friend Lucy's illustrations are quite clever as well."

I must look shocked, because she laughs. "I can't promise you anything, you understand, but no matter, you have a bright future ahead. I think Miss Austen would have approved of you."

And she leaves the room in a rustle of silk.

I might get a book published? She thinks Jane Austen would have approved of me? I need to sit down. Crossing the room to the alcove, I take a seat by the open window. Below, a breeze plays along the top of the white tent, aglow from the candlelight within. I prop my elbow on the windowsill and rest my chin in my hand, listening to the laughter of the dancers mingling with the strains of the string quartet.

I might get a book published.

All of a sudden I feel a rush of longing for Mrs. Bergson. I wish she were here! I wish I could tell her about all this. I know she'd want to hear every detail, and I know she'd be thrilled for me.

And I know she'd love England, too. I'm really going to miss living here. I'm eager to get back home to my life in Concord—especially now that Stewart and I have smoothed things over—but I've loved living here, too, and I hope I get to come back someday.

I remember a talk Jess and I had once, back in sixth grade, about whether we wanted to know the endings of books or movies ahead of time. Back then, I didn't. I never wanted to have the endings spoiled for me. I always wanted to wait and find out myself.

And now?

I look down at my mother and father, who are standing in the garden talking with Mrs. Wong and Gigi. My mother is holding Chloe, who's fallen asleep on her shoulder. Mrs. Delaney and Mrs. Chadwick and Mrs. Sloane-Kinkaid and Stanley are all lined up out on the dance floor, laughing as they fumble their way through the unfamiliar steps. Megan is laughing too—at something Simon Berkeley just said to her.

Jess, who is looking prettier than I've ever seen her before, is heading for the refreshment table hand in hand with my brother.

Cassidy is racing across the grass with Tristan Berkeley, her red sneakers flashing from beneath her long lavender dress. Has she found her Mr. Darcy? She's certainly changed her first impression of him, just like Elizabeth Bennet. Cassidy swears she's not interested in Tristan, but I think maybe there's a spark there. Of course, there's a spark with Sam Parker, too, and maybe, just maybe, a teeny little one with Zach Norton as well.

Thinking of Zach reminds me of Becca. I'd been feeling a little sorry for her tonight, since she's the only one of us who's here without a partner, but I spot her out on the dance floor with not one but two boys vying for her attention. I guess I don't ever need to worry about Becca Chadwick.

What if I could look ahead, and see how all our stories end? I know all of this might not last forever—we're only in high school, after all, and no doubt there are more sparks of romance to come and more stories still to be written for each of us. Would I want to read them?

I'm not sure. For now, I think it's enough to see everyone enjoying themselves right now, right here, on this beautiful evening.

And would I want to know the ending to my own story?

No.

I want the adventure that comes along with finding out.

A feeling of deep contentment stirs in me as I look out at the party below. The music swells, and it seems to me it carries with it all the

Heather Vogel Frederick

happiness that's singing in the hearts of my family and friends.

Only Annabelle Fairfax looks glum. I would too, if I was stuck on a bench under a tree with Rupert Loomis. I can practically hear his Eeyore drone from here. I grin to myself.

"There you are," says Stewart. "I've been looking all over for you. What are you smiling about?"

"Nothing," I tell him. There's no point dragging Rupert in between the two of us ever again.

My very own Mr. Darcy holds out a gloved hand. "Come on, then. Let's go join the dance."

And we do.

"*Now let us be quite comfortable and snug, and talk and laugh all the way home.*"

—*Pride and Prejudice*

Mother-Daughter Book Club Questions

After reading all four Mother-Daughter Book Club books, do you have a favorite character? Who are you most like?

What did you know about Jane Austen before you read *Pies & Prejudice?* Are you interested in reading her books?

Have you ever lived outside of the United States? Where would you want to live?

With Emma moving away, the book club is worried that they won't be as close. Have you ever had a friend move away? How did you stay in touch?

Emma has some trouble with one of the girls at her new school. Have you ever felt bullied? How did you handle it?

While Emma and her family are in England, Simon and Tristan's family move into the Hawthorne's house in Concord. How would you feel if your family swapped houses with someone else?

Jess tries out for a solo and doesn't get it. Have you ever tried out for something you really wanted? Did you make it?

Megan starts a fashion blog. Do you have a blog? Have you ever thought about starting a blog? What would it be about?

Megan stays anonymous when writing her blog *Fashionista Jane*, and Jane Austen published her novels anonymously. Why do you think Megan made this decision? Do you agree or disagree with it? How do you think Megan's decision to write anonymously is different from what Jane did? Have you ever done something anonymously? If so, why?

Jess rescues a wild fox. Have you ever seen an injured wild animal? Did you do anything to help it? Once the fox heals, Jess has a hard time letting her go. Have you ever had to say goodbye to someone or something that you didn't want to?

The girls decide to start a pie-making business. Do you like to bake? What is the best thing you make?

Moody Tristan is a modern-day Mr. Darcy. Is there anyone in your life who resembles a character from literature?

Mrs. Chadwick believes something in Mr. Hawthorne's book is about her and gets offended. Have you ever upset someone unintentionally? Is there anyone that you think would make a great character in a book?

Pies & Prejudice is a pun on the Jane Austen title *Pride and Prejudice*. Are there any businesses in your town that use puns? Can you think of other clever business names using any of Jane Austen's other books?

The book club visits the town where Jane Austen lived and sees the church where her father preached. Is there any famous person, alive or dead, whose hometown you would like to visit? Why?

Cassidy deals with a very sad loss after Mrs. Bergson dies, but her memorial service is a celebration of her life. Has anyone close to you passed away? How did you get through it?

Mrs. Bergson leaves some generous gifts to Concord and the Mother-Daughter Book Club. If you could give any present to anyone you wanted, what would it be? Why?

Are there any other books you wish the Mother-Daughter Book Club would read?

And so we come at last to Jane.

I've known from the beginning that my fictional book club would eventually be ready to tackle *Pride and Prejudice*. It was a day I awaited eagerly, but also with some trepidation, for Jane Austen is an author I've admired since I first encountered her books in my teens, and I desperately wanted to do her justice. I hope that I have done so, but that is for my readers to decide.

One of the great delights in researching this book was the opportunity I had to travel to England and walk in Jane's footsteps, from her birthplace in pastoral Steventon to the stunningly lovely city of Bath and her home in Chawton. Standing by the modest table there where she wrote half a dozen of the greatest novels in the English language was both memorable and humbling, to say the least.

Many of the locations mentioned in this story really exist, including Ivy Cottage. You won't find it on the outskirts of Bath, however. Its real name is Thatched Roofs, and it sits smack-dab in the middle of Newtown Linford, a tiny village in Leicestershire. My family and I lived there the year I turned twelve, and I have such happy memories of that beautiful cottage that I couldn't resist letting the Hawthornes live there too, so I whisked it a hundred miles to the south for the purposes of my story.

Another place that actually exists is the hotel where the book club stays when they visit Bath. The bedrooms at Tasburgh House really are named for famous authors, and I knew the minute I set foot in the door that it was the perfect spot for my fictional bibliophiles (it was the perfect spot for me, too). It's only a short distance along the canal from there to The George, the lovely old pub mentioned in the story, and to walk from one to the other on a fine evening as the book club and their families do is sheer heaven. I know—I've done it.

Once again, I am indebted to so many people for their help in bringing this book into existence. I couldn't have found livelier travel companions than Lynda Hathaway Sleight and Ali Buxton Miller, who gamely allowed me to drag them all over the British countryside in the name of research, nor could I have been given a warmer welcome in London than the one I received from Patti White and her wonderful family.

Patti and her daughter Frances were enormously helpful in sorting out British school customs and slang, as was Sue Kinsey—I couldn't have muddled through on my own, and I thank you. I'd also like to thank Edith Sisson for generously sharing her expertise in wildlife rehabilitation, Lisa Hoberg for vetting the ice dancing scenes, and the Quigley family for once again providing hockey help (go, Lucinda!). As always, any factual errors that remain are entirely my own doing.

Above all, heartfelt thanks to my own resident Mr. Darcy for love and encouragement, especially on those days when I act less like the charming Elizabeth Bennet and more like her flibbertigibbet of a mother!

Author's Note

What are

The Mother-Daughter Book Club

girls up to next?

Turn the page for a sneak peek!

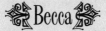

Becca

"When there are boys you have to worry about how you look, and whether they like you, and why they like another girl better, and whether they're going to ask you to something or other. It's a strain."
—Betsy *in Spite of Herself*

"D-E-F-E-N-S-E! DEFENSE, CONCORD, DEFENSE!"

I finish off the cheer with a star jump and a high kick, then fling my maroon-and-white pom-poms skyward, catching them neatly on the way down. As the pep band strikes up "We Will Rock You," I look up in the stands to see if Zach Norton is watching.

He's not.

He's too busy talking to Cassidy Sloane.

Third sees me, though, and waves his trombone from where he's sitting with the rest of the brass section. I wave feebly back.

My friend Ashley swats me with a pom-pom, her dark eyes flashing with mischief. "I didn't know you liked Third," she teases.

Third is actually Cranfield Bartlett III, but nobody ever calls him that, not even his parents.

"Shut up! I do not," I reply, through teeth clenched in a big smile. Ms. O'Donnell, our cheerleading coach, is a stickler for big smiles.

"Eyes on the field, girls," she calls to us.

Ashley and I turn around just in time to see Darcy Hawthorne intercept a pass. There's a roar from the stands behind us—it's almost the end of the fourth quarter, and Concord is down by six. We desperately need another touchdown. Along with everybody else on our side of the field, I scream my head off as Darcy runs the ball back down toward our end zone. He makes it almost as far as the center line before Acton manages to tackle him. Music explodes from the pep band, and Coach O'Donnell gives us the signal to launch into another cheer.

"First and ten, do it again! GO, Concord, GO!" we holler, whipping the crowd into a frenzy.

Turkey Day game is always a big deal for Alcott High. Thanksgiving is when we play our archrivals, and across the field, the visitor stands are a mass of blue and gold. For a split second I find myself wishing I was wearing one of Acton High's cheerleading uniforms. I look so much better in blue than I do in maroon.

On the other hand, we get to wear yoga pants instead of the miniskirts the Acton cheerleaders stupidly chose. Not that I have anything against miniskirts, but it's *freezing* out here. At least they should have opted for fleece leggings under their skirts. Their legs are practically as blue as their uniforms.

I cast a worried glance up at the sky. No sign of snow yet. I really,

really hope the weather forecast is wrong. My grandparents are in town from Cleveland for the holiday weekend, and Gram and Gigi, my best friend Megan Wong's grandmother, have promised to take the two of us shopping tomorrow. I don't want to miss out because of some dumb snowstorm.

Up in the stands, Megan reaches a purple-gloved hand from underneath the blanket she's sharing with Gigi and Gram and waves at me. I wave back at her, and at my grandfather and my brother Stewart and his girlfriend, Emma Hawthorne.

As much as it grosses me out to admit this, Stewart and Emma are kind of cute together. Well, as cute as two total dorks can be, I guess.

My dad blows me a kiss. I blow him one in return, and he stands up and pretends to catch it and tuck it into his pocket. It's silly and kind of embarrassing, but I don't really mind. For one thing, I'm used to it—we've had this little ritual since I was a kid—and for another, my dad can use all the love he can get these days. He lost his job a few weeks ago.

The insurance agency he worked for in Boston has been struggling for a while, and they finally had to lay off some employees. My dad was one of them. He's really sad about it because he worked there a long time, and he liked his job. He's worried, too, I can tell. He and my mother haven't said much to my brother and me, aside from asking us not to say anything about it to our friends for now, but we're not stupid. Stewart's a senior in high school, and I'll be getting my driver's license in a few months. We're practically adults.

As for keeping it quiet, how long is it going to take people to figure out what's going on when they spot my dad driving around town with the

PIRATE PETE'S PIZZA sign on the roof of our SUV? Or when they open the door and there he is with their half-pepperoni, half-veggie combo, wearing an eye patch and a Pirate Pete's skull-and-crossbones baseball cap?

I know he took the job to help out our family and everything, but couldn't he have found something less embarrassing? He says it's perfect because it lets him keep his days free for job hunting, but still. Stewart doesn't care, of course—he's oblivious anyway—but I know my mother finds it just as mortifying as I do. Even she couldn't talk him out of it, though.

"Money is money, Calliope," my father told her. "I'm not in a position to be picky right now."

Last night, after we met my grandparents at the airport, I overheard my mother and Gram talking in the kitchen. Mom told her that the layoff couldn't have come at a worse time, what with her finishing up her master's degree in landscape design, and Stewart knee-deep in college applications. If my dad doesn't find a new job soon—something a heck of a lot better than delivering pizzas—she doesn't know how they're going to manage.

Everybody seems to forget that it's scary for me, too, not to mention inconvenient. I'd really been hoping for a car of my own when I get my license, but fat chance of that happening now.

There's another roar from our fans, and I snap out of my sulk and automatically slap a smile on my face. Out on the field, Darcy dodges a pair of Acton linemen and sprints toward our goalposts. The linemen grab at his jersey, but he wrenches away and surges forward, crossing into the end zone and slamming the ball onto the ground.

Touchdown!

With less than a minute to go in the game, we're tied with Acton! The crowd hardly needs any encouragement from us, but we do our best anyway as both teams get into position for the goal kick.

> Everybody do the Concord rumble,
> Everybody do the Concord rumble,
> Everyyybodyyy rrruuumbbble!

As Darcy's best friend Kyle Anderson, our kicker, takes his spot on the field, you can practically hear all of Concord hold its breath. The ref's whistle blows and Kyle moves forward, keeping his eye on the goalposts. Then he slams his foot against the ball, sending it flying up toward the gray clouds overhead. Up it soars, up and up and—through!

It's a win for Concord!

"Take it home, girls," shouts Coach O'Donnell as our side of the field explodes with excitement. There's nothing forced about the smile on my face now. We treat Acton to the traditional Turkey Day gloat, the very same cheer they fired off at us last year when they won:

> You might be good at baseball,
> You might be good at track,
> But when it comes to football,
> You might as well step back!
> GOBBLE-GOBBLE-GOBBLE-GOBBLE
> Goooooooooooooo, CONCORD!

Fans come pouring down out of the stands, pushing and jostling. Among them I spot Darcy's girlfriend, Jess Delaney. Stuck to her like a tall, skinny barnacle is Kevin Mullins. Kevin just doesn't take a hint. He's had a crush on Jess since we were all at Walden Middle School, and she's just too nice to give him the boot. That's the difference between Jess and me. I don't put up with stuff like that the way she does.

Kevin used to be the smallest kid in the entire school, which was due to the fact that he skipped a bunch of grades. Cassidy calls him the Boy Genius. He shot up this past summer, and now he towers over Jess, who is petite. They probably weigh the same, though. My dad says if Kevin turned sideways and stuck out his tongue, he could pass as a zipper.

"Great job, Becca," Jess tells me. She's wearing a white cable-knit beanie, and only the tail of her thick blond braid is visible. I would kill for hair like Jess's. Mine is blond, too, but it's not thick and wavy like hers.

"Thanks."

She cranes her neck over my shoulder, looking for Darcy. Jess is lucky. Not only is Darcy Hawthorne a great athlete, he's also popular, smart, and a really nice guy. Plus, he still has a trace of the English accent that he and Emma both brought back with them from their year in England. There's nothing more appealing than a cute guy with an accent.

"Gotta go," Jess says, spotting him. "See you tonight!"

"See you!" I reply. She melts into the crowd, with Kevin trailing behind.

"What's tonight?" asks Ashley.

I make a face. "Book club." Not that I don't like book club, but it is Thanksgiving, after all. I was kind of thinking jammies, leftovers, a nap, maybe snuggling up with some holiday classic on TV. My grandmother really, really wanted to attend one of our meetings, though, and tonight was the only night everybody could get together. Cassidy Sloane is in my book club too, and she plays for an elite girls' hockey team. They have some big tournament down in Rhode Island this weekend, and for a while it didn't look like she'd be able to make it to our meeting. Which was fine by me, because the less time I spend around Miss Zach-Stealer Sloane these days, the better. But in the end, it turned out she doesn't have to be there until tomorrow morning.

"Wow, what a fabulous game!" says my father, squeezing through the crowd to reach us. The rest of my family is right behind him.

"No kidding," says Gram, draping a blanket around my shoulders. She gives me a hug. "That was a great halftime dance, sweetie."

"Thanks."

"You girls look half-frozen," says Megan's grandmother. "I think there's still some hot chocolate left in my thermos if you'd like some."

"Thanks, Mrs. Chen," Ashley replies, "but I promised I'd get right home to help my mom." *Call me later,* she mouths to me as she turns to go, pretending to hold a cell phone up to her ear. I nod.

"We should head home and help your mother too," says Gram, linking her arm through mine as we inch our way toward the parking lot. Ahead of us, my brother is acting all mushy-gushy over Emma Hawthorne. He has his arm around her and keeps leaning down to kiss the top of her head. Gak! So gross! I hate PDA when it involves my brother.

I glance over at Megan and scrunch up my nose. She smothers a laugh. Megan knows exactly how I feel about this stuff. That's the good thing about best friends. Most of the time you don't have to say a word, and they still totally understand you.

It's not that I don't like Emma—she's okay. It's just, knowing that she's my brother's girlfriend makes things a little weird sometimes. Plus, we probably never would have been friends if it weren't for the book club. Megan's the only one in it I'm really close to. I have almost nothing in common with the others, and I'm still surprised I like them as much as I do.

Which isn't always all that much. For instance, I'm not wild about Cassidy Sloane these days. Ever since school started this year, she's been hanging out with Zach Norton again.

I look over to where the two of them are standing on the sidelines. Cassidy has her camera out and she's taking his picture. Zach is clowning around and laughing his head off over something she's saying. Watching them, it's easy to tell that he likes her. You can just tell when a guy is interested in a girl, you know? And it's written all over Zach's face that he likes Cassidy.

Last spring, after he asked me to the Spring Formal, I really, really thought maybe he liked me. After all, I didn't have to pester him or drop hints or anything. He picked up the phone all by himself and called. Would he have done that if he didn't like me?

But now he can't take his eyes off Cassidy Sloane, the red-haired giantess from my Mother-Daughter Book Club.

I just don't get it. Back in eighth grade, when Zach surprised Cassidy with a kiss, she was so disgusted she slugged him with her baseball mitt. After that they didn't talk for a whole summer, so I figured that was that and maybe I'd finally have a chance. Even when they patched things up I was still hopeful, mostly because Cassidy made it very clear they were just friends. Plus, she spent most of last year practically glued to Tristan Berkeley, the snotty but incredibly good-looking English guy whose family did the house-swap with the Hawthornes. Tristan needed an ice-dancing partner, and Cassidy fit the bill.

I swear she has all the luck. These days the only guy who's interested in me is Third. Who is fine and everything, but he's, well, Third. Kind of a moose, goofy smile, even goofier sense of humor. He's not exactly Prince Charming.

My mother says I spend way too much time thinking about boys, but I can't help it. Boys are the most interesting thing on the planet.

Most boys, that is. Spotting Third lumbering in our direction with his trombone case, I tug my grandmother through an opening in the crowd. "I can't wait to get home," I tell her. "I'm starving."

"I don't know which I'm looking forward to more," she says, trotting along beside me. "Thanksgiving dinner or the meeting tonight."

Gram was ecstatic when my mother told her she'd get to come to book club. She's hardly stopped talking about it since she got here. My grandmother is the whole reason we're reading what we're reading this fall.

We held our first meeting of the year back in August at Kimball's Farm. Usually, we wait until the end of each year's kick-off meeting to go out for ice cream—it's one of our little rituals—but this year we decided to meet there to celebrate the Hawthornes being home from England. We were just sitting down at a picnic table with our ice cream cones when Jess's mom asked whose turn it was to pick something for us to read.

"I think it's yours," Mrs. Hawthorne told her. Emma's mother is a librarian and super organized, and she's been in charge of the club since the beginning.

"No, Phoebe, I think it's Becca and Calliope's turn," Mrs. Wong said, taking the teeniest lick ever of her strawberry ice cream cone. Megan's mother treats sugar like it's the enemy.

My mother pounced on this the way I pounce on Motor Mouth lip gloss whenever it goes on sale. "That's right! It is. And we've got just the thing."

I looked at her blankly. This was news to me. "We do?"

"Uh-huh," she said, nodding.

"Well?" asked Mrs. Hawthorne.

"The Betsy-Tacy books!"

I let out a groan. This was my mother's idea of "just the thing"? Those books Gram was always going on about? My grandmother gave me the entire set practically the day I was born, and they've been sitting on the bookshelf in my room forever. They were her absolute favorite when she was growing up, which tells you how old they are.

What happened next, though, was probably the high point of my entire three years with the book club.

"What are the Betsy-Tacy books?" asked Emma.

Stunned silence fell over the picnic table. Megan and Jess and Cassidy and I stared at her, our mouths literally dropping open. Emma Hawthorne has read every book in the universe.

"You don't know them?" asked my mother, flicking a glance at Mrs. Hawthorne. "That surprises me, Emma. They're classics, after all."

"Really?" Emma frowned.

"Absolutely. They're about a group of girls growing up in a little town in Minnesota called Deep Valley."

"How many books are there in the series?"

"Ten."

I'll never forget the look on Emma's face as long as I live.

"TEN?" she screeched, whirling around to her mother. "How come you never told me about them?"

"Well," said Mrs. Hawthorne, "it's not that I didn't know about them"—she flicked a glance back at my mother, and I sensed a little tug-of-war going on—"or about the author, Maud Hart Lovelace. I just never got around to reading them."

Beside me, my mother was trying very hard not to gloat. It's almost impossible to one-up Mrs. Hawthorne.

I decided to rub it in. "I've read them," I said, which wasn't exactly true.

My mother read the first few aloud to me when I was little, but I never finished the series. Emma didn't need to know that, though. "Ages ago."

From the expression on Emma's face, you'd have thought I just announced that I was growing a tail. "You *did?* How come you never mentioned them?"

"You never asked," I replied, trying not to look too smug.

Cassidy's mother frowned at me. "Are you sure you want to read them again?"

Across the picnic table, my mother gave me Winona eyes. Gram made up that expression. Winona Root is a character in the books, and this one time Betsy and Tacy and their friend Tib try and hypnotize her into taking them to the theater. It doesn't work, of course, but it's pretty funny the way they all stare at her, trying.

Winona eyes or no Winona eyes, I knew that if I said no, my mother would never let me hear the end of it. There's just no dealing with my mother. "Sure," I replied. "Why not?"

My mother swiftly closed the deal. "Becca's grandmother has offered to buy a complete set for each one of you, if you all agree to read them."

"That's very generous of her," said Mrs. Hawthorne. "She must really love these books."

"She loves Maud Hart Lovelace the way you love Jane Austen, Phoebe," my mother told her. "Mother was born in Minnesota, and she grew up reading the Betsy-Tacy series. She made sure I did too. It's kind of a family tradition."

I shot her a look. Talk about stretching the truth! A family tradition? For her and Gram, maybe, but not for me.

"Can you tell us a bit about the books?" asked Mrs. Delaney. "I'm afraid I'm not familiar with them either."

"Absolutely," my mother replied. "Deep Valley is a small town, very much like Concord only in the Midwest. The stories follow Betsy Ray and her family and friends as they grow up in the late nineteenth and early twentieth centuries—"

Cassidy let out a groan when she heard this, but my mother was ready for her.

"I know, I know, more musty, dusty old books, right? These are different from all the other ones we've read so far, though. They have a very modern sensibility." My mother fished around in her tote bag and pulled out *Betsy-Tacy*. "This is the first book, and it starts when Betsy Ray and Tacy Kelly are five years old—"

"Whoa, dude—I mean, Mrs. Chadwick—are you seriously expecting us to read about a couple of *five-year-olds*?" Cassidy protested. "We're sophomores!"

"Wait, wait, let me finish," my mother hurried to explain. "The books follow the girls all the way through high school and into college and beyond. See?" She reached into her bag again and pulled out another volume, waving it triumphantly. "The last one is called *Betsy's Wedding*."

The picnic table grew quiet as my friends chewed on that.

"You girls are going to feel right at home in Deep Valley, I promise," my mother continued. "Betsy and her friends are fun-loving, and they like pranks and mischief, and above all"—she paused dramatically and lowered her voice—"they like boys."

Cassidy snorted, and her mother elbowed her. "That clinches it for me," said Mrs. Sloane-Kinkaid. "Count me in."

Emma sighed happily. "Ten whole books I haven't read!"

"I don't have time to read ten books," grumbled Cassidy, who looked like she wanted to pop somebody with her ice cream cone. Or better yet, her hockey stick.

"Nonsense," said her mother crisply. "What about all that time you're spending in the car these days?" She reached over and plucked a handful of books from the table in front of my mother. "One hockey tournament in Connecticut and you'd knock these right off."

"On top of all my homework? Mom, get real! I'm already a week behind on *The Grapes of Wrath*." Cassidy crossed her arms and scowled.

"I thought we were going to get to pick the books this year for a change," said Jess softly, looking disappointed. She'd been pushing for some story about a racehorse. Jess still had that stupid horse crush of hers. I got over mine back in fourth grade.

"I thought so too," said Emma. "I want us all to read *Jane Eyre*."

"How about a compromise?" suggested Mrs. Wong. "What if we split the year up this time, and spend the first half—between now and the end of December, say—reading the Betsy-Tacy books, then move on to something else after that?"

"That sounds good," said Mrs. Delaney, and we all nodded.

Cassidy still didn't look convinced. "You mean we're going to read all ten books between now and January?"

Mrs. Hawthorne, who'd been scanning the information on the jacket flaps, pursed her lips. "We could just read the four high school books, I suppose."

"But you have to start at the beginning!" my mother protested. "You'll miss too much!"

"You have a point," said Mrs. Hawthorne. "And Clementine is right, the first four are pretty slim. What if we breeze through them this next month, then dive into *Heaven to Betsy* and *Betsy in Spite of Herself* for November and December? That will take us up through their sophomore year, the same age as you girls."

"But Mom, we can't just ignore half of an author's body of work!" said Emma.

I crossed my eyes at Megan, who squelched a smile. Only Emma Hawthorne would use a term like "body of work."

"Nothing's stopping you or anyone else from reading the rest of them," said her mother. "But this might be a more realistic goal as a group."

Julia and Eliza have always been best friends . . . but everything is about to change.

The Summer Before Boys

Nora Raleigh Baskin

From award-winning author

NORA RALEIGH BASKIN

EBOOK EDITION ALSO AVAILABLE

Simon & Schuster
Books for Young Readers

KIDS.SIMONANDSCHUSTER.COM